DUST &
DECAY

DUST &

ROT &
RUIN

BOOK TWO

DECAY

Jonathan Maberry

SIMON & SCHUSTER BFYR

NEW YORK LONDON TORONTO SYDNEY NEW DELHI

Also by Jonathan Maberry

Rot & Ruin

Flesh & Bone

Dead & Gone (an ebook original)

ACKNOWLEDGMENTS

Special thanks to some real-world people who allowed me to tap them for advice and information, lean on them for support, and in some cases shove them into the middle of the action. My agents, Sara Crowe and Harvey Klinger; my editor, David Gale, and all the good people at Simon & Schuster Books for Young Readers; experts Dr. John Cmar, of Johns Hopkins University Department of Infectious Diseases, and Alan Weisman, author of *The World Without Us* (Thomas Dunne Books); fellow YA authors Nancy Holder, Michael Northrup, Heather Brewer, and Maria V. Snyder; the King of the Zombies George A. Romero; and cadaverine experts Ellery and John Griswold.

SIMON & SCHUSTER BFYR

This one's for Don Lafferty, Arthur Mensch, and Sam West-Mensch.

And—as always—for Sara Jo.

—J. M.

PART ONE
ROAD TRIP

A journey of a thousand miles
must begin with a single step.

—LAO TZU

BENNY IMURA WAS APPALLED TO LEARN THAT THE APOCALYPSE CAME with homework.

"Why do we have to study this stuff?" he demanded. "We already know what happened. People started turning into zoms, the zoms ate just about everyone, everyone who dies becomes a zom, so the moral of this tale is: Try not to die."

Across the kitchen table, his brother, Tom, stared at him with narrowed eyes. "Are you deliberately trying to be an idiot, or is it a natural gift?"

"I'm serious. We know what happened."

"Really? Then how come you spent most of last summer complaining that no one my age tells anyone your age the truth about the living dead?"

"Telling us is one thing. Essays and pop quizzes are a whole different thing."

"Because heaven forbid you should have to remember anything we told you."

Benny raised his eyebrows mysteriously and tapped his temple. "I have it all right here in the vast storehouse of knowledge that is me."

"Okay, boy genius, then what started the plague?"

"Easy one," Benny said. "Nobody knows."

"What are the leading theories?"

Benny jabbed his fork into a big piece of buttered yam, shoved it into his mouth, and chewed noisily as he spoke. It was a move calculated to annoy Tom in three separate ways. Tom hated when he spoke with his mouth full. He hated it when Benny chewed with his mouth open. And it would muffle most of what he said, which meant that Tom had to pay even more attention to the yam-packed mouth from which the muffled words came.

"Radiation, virus, bioweapon, toxic waste, solar flares, act of God."

He rattled it off so there was no break between the words. Also annoying, and worth at least another point on Benny's personal Annoy-O-Meter.

Tom sipped his tea and said nothing, but he gave Benny the *look*.

Benny sighed and swallowed. "Okay," he said, "at first people thought it was radiation from a satellite."

"Space probe," corrected Tom.

"Whatever. But that doesn't make sense, because one satellite—"

"Space probe."

"—wouldn't carry enough radioactive material to spread over the entire world."

"We think."

"Sure," conceded Benny, "but in science class they told us even if one of the old nuclear power plants did a whatchama-callit, there—"

"Meltdown."

"—wouldn't be enough radiation to cover the entire planet even though it has more radioactive materials than a satellite."

Tom sighed. Benny smiled.

"What conclusion can you draw from that?"

"The world wasn't destroyed by radioactive alien space zombies."

"*Probably* wasn't destroyed by radioactive alien space zombies," Tom corrected. "How about a virus?"

Benny cut a piece of chicken and ate it. Tom was a great cook, and this was one of his better meals. Yams, broiled chicken with mushrooms and almonds, and rich green kale. A loaf of steaming bread made from the last of the winter wheat sat near where Benny could plunder it.

"Chong's dad says that a virus needs a living host, and zoms aren't alive. He said that maybe bacteria or a fungus was sustaining the virus."

"Do you know what a bacterium is?"

"Sure . . . it's a bug thingy that makes you sick."

"God, I love it when you display the depth of your knowledge. It makes me proud to be your brother."

"Kiss my—"

"Language."

They grinned at each other.

It had been nearly seven months since Benny's lifelong hatred and distrust of Tom had transformed into affection and respect. That process had started last summer, shortly after Benny's fifteenth birthday. On some level Benny knew that he loved Tom, but since Tom was his brother and this was still the real world, the chances of Benny ever using that *L* word were somewhere between "no way" and "get out of my way I'm going to throw up."

Not that Benny was afraid of the *L* word when it came to someone better suited for it, namely the fiercely red-haired queen of freckles, Nix Riley. Benny would like very much to toss that word up for her to consider, but he had yet to do so. Shortly after the big fight at the bounty hunters' camp, when Benny had tentatively tried to bring up the subject, Nix had threatened bodily harm if he said that word. Benny had zipped his mouth shut, understanding completely why the moment had been so inappropriate. Charlie Pink-eye Matthias and the Motor City Hammer had murdered Nix's mother, and the insane events of the days that followed hadn't allowed Nix to properly react. Or grieve.

Those days had been the weirdest mix of absolute horror, black despair, and soaring happiness. The emotions he'd felt didn't seem to even belong in the same world, let alone the same person.

Benny gave Nix her time for grief, and he grieved too. Mrs. Riley had been a great lady. Sweet, funny, kind, and always a little sad. Like everyone else in Mountainside, Jessie Riley had suffered terrible losses during First Night. Her husband, her two sons.

"Everyone lost someone," Chong often reminded him. Even though they'd been toddlers, Benny and Chong were the only ones among their friends to remember that night. Chong said that it was all a blur of screams and shouts, but Benny remembered it with a peculiar clarity. His mother handing him through a first-floor window to Tom—who was a twenty-year-old cadet at the police academy—and then the pale, shambling thing that had been Dad coming out of the shadows and pulling Mom away. Then Tom running away, his terrified heartbeat hammering like a drum inside the chest to which he held a squirming, screaming Benny.

Until last year Benny had remembered that First Night in a twisted way. All his life he had believed that Tom had simply run away. That he had not tried to help Mom. That he was a coward.

Now Benny knew different. Now he knew what kind of torment Tom had suffered to save him. He also knew that when Mom had handed him through the window to Tom, she had already been bitten. She was already lost. Tom had done the only thing he could have done. He ran, and in running had given value to Mom's sacrifice, and that had saved them both.

Now Benny was fifteen and a half, and First Night was a million years ago.

This world was no longer that world. On First Night the old world had died. As the dead rose, the living perished. Cities were incinerated by the military in a futile attempt to stop the growing armies of the dead. The electromagnetic pulses from the nukes fried all electronics. The machines went silent, and soon, so did the whole country. Now everything east of the small town of Mountainside was the great Rot and Ruin. A few other towns littered the foothills of the Sierra Nevada north and south of Benny's home, but the rest of the old world had been consumed.

Or . . . had it?

During that adventure in the mountains east of town, Benny and Nix had seen something that to them was as inexplicable and potentially world-changing as the zombie plague had been. Flying high, high above them had been a thing Benny had only ever read about in old books.

A jet.

A sleek jumbo jet that flew out of the east, banked in a slow circle around the mountains, and then headed back the way it had come. Now Benny and Nix were counting down the days until they left Mountainside to find where the jet had come from. The calendar pinned to the wall by the back door had black Xs over the first ten days of this month. There were seven unmarked days, and then a big red circle around the following Saturday. April 17, one week from today. The words ROAD TRIP were written in block letters below the date.

Tom thought that the jet was flying in the general direction of Yosemite National Park, which was due east of the town. Benny and Nix had begged Tom for this trip for months, but as the day approached, Benny wasn't so sure he still wanted to go. It was just that Nix was absolutely determined.

"Earth to Benny Imura."

Benny blinked and heard as an after-echo the sound of Tom snapping his fingers.

"Huh?"

"Jeez . . . what planet were you orbiting?"

"Oh . . . just kind of drifted there."

"Nix or the jet?"

"Little of both."

"Must have been more about the jet," Tom said. "There was less drool."

"You are very nearly funny," said Benny. He looked down at his plate and was mildly surprised that it was empty.

"Yes," said Tom, "you were eating on autopilot. It was fascinating to watch."

There was a knock on the door. Benny shot to his feet and crossed the kitchen to the back door. He was smiling as he undid the locks.

"That's got to be Nix," he said as he pulled it open. "Hey, sweetie . . ."

Morgie Mitchell and Lou Chong stood on the back porch.

"Um," said Chong, "hello to you, too, sugar lumps."

BENNY STARTED TO SAY SOMETHING THAT WOULD BE WILDLY CRUDE AND physically improbable, but then a smaller shape pushed her way between the bulky Morgie and the wiry Chong. Even though he saw her every day, seeing her again always made his heart bang around like a crazy monkey.

"Nix," he said, smiling.

"'Sweetie'?" she asked. Not smiling.

It wasn't the sort of thing he ever said to her. Not out loud, and he could kick himself for letting it slip. He fished for a clever comment to save the moment, aware that Tom was watching all this from the table, and Morgie and Chong were grinning like ghouls.

"Well," he said, "I—uhh . . ."

"You're so smooth," Nix said, and pushed past him into the kitchen.

Chong and Morgie mimed kissy faces at him.

"Expect to be murdered," Benny threatened. "Painfully and soon."

"Yes, snookums," said Morgie as he followed Chong into the kitchen.

Benny took a few seconds to gather the fractured pieces

of his wits. Then he turned and closed the door, doing it very carefully even though slamming it would have felt much better.

After her mother died, Nix had first moved in with Benny and Tom, but then Fran Kirsch, wife of the mayor and their next-door neighbor, suggested that a young girl might prefer to live in a house with other females. Benny tried to argue that Nix had her own room—his room—and that he didn't mind sleeping on the living room couch, but Mrs. Kirsch didn't buckle. Nix moved into the Kirschs' spare bedroom.

Nix and the boys crowded onto chairs at the table and were doing a pretty good imitation of vultures with the leftovers. Tom settled back into his chair, and Benny reclaimed his.

"We training this evening?" Morgie asked.

Tom nodded. "Road trip's coming up, remember? Benny and Nix have to be ready, and you two guys need to stay sharp, Morgie. Who knows what you will have to face in the future?"

"You've been working them pretty hard," said Chong.

"Have to. Everything we do from now on will be about getting ready for the trip. It's—"

"—not a vacation," Benny completed. "Yes. You've mentioned that thirty or forty thousand times. I just thought we'd have, y'know, a night off."

"Night off?" echoed Nix. "I wish we were leaving right now."

Benny dodged that subject by asking, "Where's Lilah?"

Lilah was the newest member of their pack. A year older and infinitely stranger, she had grown up out in the Ruin, raised for a few years by a man who had helped to rescue her during First Night, and then living on her own for years afterward. She was more than half feral, moody, almost always silent, and incredibly beautiful. The Lost Girl, they called her on the Zombie Cards. A legend or myth to most people, until Tom and Benny proved that she existed. She wanted to go with Benny, Nix, and Tom into the Ruin to find the jet.

Chong tilted his head toward the back door. "She didn't want to come in."

Chong sighed, and Benny had to control himself not to seize the moment and bust on him. His friend had developed such a helpless and hopeless crush on Lilah that the wrong word could put him into a depression for days. Nobody, including Nix, Benny, and Chong, thought that Lilah had so much as a splinter of interest in Chong. Or maybe she didn't have a splinter of interest in anything that didn't involve blades, guns, and violence.

"What's she doing?" asked Benny, carefully sidestepping the issue.

"Strip-cleaning her pistol," said Nix, her green eyes meeting Benny's and then flicking toward the yard outside.

Lilah treated her handgun like it was her first puppy. Chong said that it was cute, but really everyone thought it was kind of sad bordering on creepy.

Benny refilled his teacup, poured in some honey, and watched Nix pick the last scraps of meat from a chicken breast. He even liked the way she scavenged food. He sighed.

Morgie said, "I'm going to catch the first catfish of the season."

"What are you going to use for bait?" asked Chong.

"Benny's brain?"

"Too small."

It was one of their older routines, and Benny made the appropriate inappropriate response. And Tom gave the expected admonition about language.

Even that ritual, as practiced and stale as it had become, felt good to Benny. Especially with Nix sitting beside him. He fished for something to say that would earn him one of her smiles. Nix's smiles, which had been free and plentiful before her mother's death, had become as rare as precious jewels. Benny would have gladly given everything he owned to change that, but as Chong once said, "You can't unring a bell." At the time—a year ago, when Benny's wild attempt at driving in a home run had smashed through the front window of Lafferty's General Store—he had thought the observation was stupid. Now he knew that it was profound.

So much had happened since last year that he wished could be undone, but it was all written into the past and nothing—not wishing or willpower or nightly prayers—could change it.

Nix's mom was dead.

You can't unring a bell.

"What are you attempting to think about?" asked Morgie with a suspicious squint.

Everyone looked at Benny, and he realized as an afterthought that someone had probably asked him a question, but he'd been so deep in melancholy thoughts that it had sailed right past.

"What? Oh . . . I was just thinking about the jet," Benny lied.

"Ah," said Chong dryly. "The jet."

The jet, and all that it symbolized, was a big silent monster that had followed them around since they'd returned last September. The jet meant leaving, something that Nix and Benny were going to do and Chong and Morgie were not. Tom called it a "trip," suggesting that they would eventually return, but Benny knew that Nix had no intention of ever returning to Mountainside. The same was probably true of Tom, who still grieved for Jessie Riley. Benny, however, did want to come back here. Maybe not forever, but at least to see his friends. Once they left, though, he was pretty sure that their road trip was going to be permanent.

It was a horrible, heartbreaking thought, and none of them liked talking about it; but it was always there, hiding inside every conversation.

"That freaking jet again?" griped Morgie, and gave a sour shake of his head.

"Yeah. I thought that I'd go to the library tomorrow and see if they have any books about jets. Maybe I'll see the one Nix and I saw."

"Why?" Morgie persisted.

"If we know what kind of plane it was," Nix said, "we might have some idea of its range. Maybe it didn't come all the way across the country. Or maybe it came from Hawaii."

Morgie was confused. "I thought you said it came from the east and went back that way."

"They're not air traffic controllers, Morgie," added Chong. "The more they can learn about the jet, the better the chance they'll have to find it. I think."

"What's an air traffic controller?" persisted Morgie.

That allowed Chong to steer the conversation away from

the road trip and into areas of pre–First Night trivia. Benny cut a sly sideways look at Nix, and there it was: just the slightest slice of a smile. She reached under the table and gave his hand a quick squeeze.

Tom, who had been watching this performance, hid a smile behind his teacup as he drained it. Then he set it down with a thump that drew all eyes his way.

"Okay, my young Jedi . . . time to train."

Everyone jumped up, but as they headed outside, Morgie nudged Chong in the ribs.

"What's a Jedi?"

FROM NIX'S JOURNAL

Things We Know About Zombies, Part 1

They are dead human beings who reanimated.

They can't think. (Tom's pretty sure about this.)

They do not need to breathe.

They don't bleed.

They are clumsy and slow.

They can do some things (walk, grab, bite, swallow, moan).

They rarely use tools. (Tom says that some of them pick up stones or sticks to try and break into a house; but he says it's really unusual.)

They aren't very coordinated. (Tom has seen a few turn door handles. They only climb stairs when following prey. No ladders, though.)

**They are really scary!

3

"I AM A COLD-BLOODED, EAGLE-EYED, HEAD CHOPPING, TOTALLY BADASS zombie killing engine of destruction," declared Benny Imura. "And I am so going to—"

Nix Riley batted his sword aside and whacked him on the head.

"Ow!" he yelled.

"Yes, you're truly frightening," she said. "I'm going to fall down and faint."

"Ow," he said louder, to emphasize the point in case anyone missed it.

Chong and Morgie sat on the picnic table. Tom leaned against the big oak in the corner of the yard. Lilah sat with her back to the garden fence. They were all laughing. At him.

"Oh sure, laugh," he growled, shaking his wooden bokken at them. "She hit me when I wasn't looking."

"So . . . look," suggested Chong.

Morgie pretended to cough into his hand but said, "Loser."

"A little focus would be useful," said Tom. "I mean . . . since our road trip's in a week and you are training to save your life. To survive, you have to be warrior smart."

Tom had drilled them so relentlessly in his "warrior smart" program that Benny was considering disowning his brother.

Although it was still early April, it felt like midsummer, and Benny was wearing only a sweat-soaked T-shirt and cut-offs. The months of training had hardened him and packed muscle onto his arms and shoulders. He squared those shoulders and gave Nix a steely stare.

Nix raised her sword and in a loud clear voice announced, "I. Am. Going. To. Swing. My. Sword. Now."

"Hilarious," said Benny through gritted teeth. He brought his sword up, elbows and knees bent at the perfect angles, weight shifted onto the balls of his feet, the tip of the bokken level with his eyes, his body angled for the best use of muscle in attack and the least display of vulnerabilities for defense. He could feel the power in his arms. With a loud, ferocious yell that would have frozen the heart of an enemy on the battlefields of the samurai era, he charged, bringing his sword up and down with perfect precision.

Nix batted his sword aside and whacked him on the head. Again.

Benny said, "Ow."

"That's not how you do it," said Lilah.

Benny rubbed his head and squinted at her. "No, really?" he said. "I'm not supposed to block with my head?"

"No," Lilah said seriously. "That's stupid. You'd die."

Lilah possessed many skills that Benny admired—fighting, stalking, almost unbelievable athletic prowess—but she had no trace of a sense of humor. Until they'd brought her back to Mountainside, Lilah's existence had been an ongoing hell of paranoia, fear, and violence. It wasn't the kind of environment that helped her cultivate social skills.

"Thanks, Lilah," Benny said. "I'll make sure I remember that."

She nodded as if he had made a serious promise. "Then I won't have to quiet you afterward," she said. She had a voice that was soft and rough, her vocal cords having been damaged by screams when she was little.

Benny stared at her for a moment, knowing that Lilah was dead serious. And he knew she would do it, too. If he died and zommed out, Lilah would kill him—quiet him, as everyone in town preferred to say—without a moment's hesitation.

He turned back to Nix. "Want to try it again? I'll block better this time."

"Ah . . . so you're going to try the 'smart' part of 'warrior smart'?" observed Chong. "Very wise."

Nix smiled at Benny. It wasn't one of the heartwarming smiles he'd been longing for. It reminded him of Lilah's face when she was hunting zoms.

Benny did block better, though.

Not that it did him much good.

"Ow!" he yelled three seconds later.

"Warrior smart!" yelled Morgie and Chong in chorus.

Benny glared hot death at them. "How about one of you clowns trying to—"

His comment was cut short by a sharp and sudden scream.

They all froze, looking off toward the center of town. The yell was high and shrill.

There was a moment of silence.

Then another yell cut through the air. It was a man's voice, loud and sharp and filled with pain.

More screams followed it.

And then the sharp, hollow crack of a gunshot.

"STAY HERE!" TOM ORDERED. HE RACED INTO THE HOUSE AND CAME out a moment later, a sword in one hand and his gun belt in the other. This was not a practice sword but the deadly steel *katana* he used in his job as the Ruin's most feared zombie hunter. He slung the strap over his shoulder as he raced past Benny toward the gate. He vaulted it like a hurdler and was running full tilt while he buckled on the gun belt. "Do not move from the yard!"

The last command floated back at them as he vanished over the hill.

Benny looked at Nix, who looked at Lilah, who looked at Chong, who looked at Morgie.

"Tom said to stay here," said Nix.

"Absolutely," said Benny.

And that fast they were off. They grabbed their wooden swords and swarmed through the garden gate, except for Lilah, who jumped it exactly as Tom had done. Then they were running as fast as they could.

5

LILAH OUTRAN THEM ALL. HOWEVER, SINCE LAST SEPTEMBER THEY HAD each put on muscle and built their endurance, so they weren't too far behind. In a loose pack they rounded the corner by the grist mill and then tore along Oak Hill Road.

Benny grinned at Chong, who grinned back. In a weird way, this was fun. They were warriors, the world's last group of samurai trainees. This was what they were training for.

Then, just as they reached the top of the hill and cut left onto Mockingbird Street, they heard a fresh set of screams.

They were the high, piercing screams of children.

That sound slapped the grins from their faces.

Benny looked at Nix.

"God," she gasped, and ran faster.

The screams were continuous. Benny thought they were screams of fear, not of pain. There was a fragment of consolation in that.

They cut right onto Fairview, running abreast, their wooden swords clutched in sweating hands.

Then as one they skidded to a stop.

Three houses stood at the end of a block of stores. The Cohens on the left, the Matthias place on the right, and the

Housers in the center. Townsfolk were clustered in front of the Houser place. Most of them had axes, pitchforks, and long-handled shovels. Benny saw at least four people with guns.

"It's Danny's place!" said Nix in a sharp whisper.

Benny and his friends went to school with Danny Houser; Danny's twin sisters, Hope and Faith, were in the first grade.

They saw Tom on the porch, peering into the open doorway. Then he backed away as something moved toward him from the shadows of the unlit living room.

Benny's breath caught in his throat as he saw the figure emerge from the doorway in a slow, uncertain gait, his legs moving stiffly, his hands out and reaching for Tom. It was Grandpa Houser.

"No!" Benny cried, but Tom was still backing away.

Grandpa Houser's eyes were as dark and empty as holes, and his dentures clacked together as if he was trying to bite the air.

A deep sadness opened in Benny's chest. He liked Danny's grandfather. The old man was always kind, and he told the funniest fishing stories. Now Grandpa Houser was gone, and in his place was a thing that had no conscious thought, no humor or intelligence. No trace of humanity other than the lie of its appearance. It was a zombie, driven by an unconquerable hunger for human flesh. Even from forty feet away Benny could hear the creature's low moan of endless need.

"He must have died in his sleep," Nix breathed.

Chong nodded. "And he didn't lock his bedroom door."

It was a sad and terrible fact of life that everyone who died came back as a zom, so everyone locked themselves in their rooms at night. It was a rare zom who could turn a doorknob, and none of them could work a padlock or turn a key. Someone dying in their sleep and reanimating was one of the constant fears for people in town.

Because this kind of thing could happen.

Benny caught movement to his right and saw Zak Matthias looking at him out of the side window of the adjoining house. Zak had never exactly been a friend, but for the most part he and Benny had been able to get along. They were the same age and had been all through school and the Scouts together. They played on the same baseball team, wrestled in the same weight class, and even sometimes went fishing together if Morgie and Chong were busy. But all that had been before last September.

Zak Matthias was Charlie Pink-eye's nephew. Although they didn't know for sure, Benny and Nix believed that it had been Zak who'd told Charlie what Benny had found in a pack of Zombie Cards: a picture of the Lost Girl.

Lilah.

Charlie had come after Benny and tried to take the card from him. Benny hadn't understood why at the time, but soon learned that Charlie was afraid that Lilah would tell people what was going on out in the Ruin. About the bounty hunters like Charlie who kidnapped kids and took them to fight in the zombie pits at Gameland so evil people like them could gamble on who would win or lose.

Charlie's attempt to erase all knowledge of the Lost Girl and Gameland had led to the murders of Nix's mom and a local erosion artist, Rob Sacchetto—the man who had painted the Lost Girl card.

Zak didn't go to school anymore. His father, Big Zak, kept

him home, and the whole family was mostly shunned by the town. Benny had heard rumors that Zak's dad knocked him around, somehow blaming him for what happened to Charlie.

In a strange way Benny felt sorry for Zak. He looked so lost as he stood there behind the glass and lace curtains, pale from always hiding in the house. Benny wanted to hate him, but he was sure that Zak had had no idea of the terrible things Charlie Pink-eye would do with the little bit of information his nephew had given him.

"Be careful, Tom!" someone cried, and Benny whipped his head back to see that Tom had retreated to the edge of the porch.

"Shoot him, Tom!" yelled the town postman.

"No!" screamed two voices in unison, and Benny looked up to see the Houser twins at the upstairs window. "Grandpa!" they cried, their voices as shrill as frightened birds.

"Shoot him," whispered Morgie under his breath, and Benny turned to look at him. Morgie's face was wet with nervous sweat. "Shoot him."

Tom's gun was still in its holster.

Lilah gave him a single cold shake of her head. "No. It's a waste of a bullet."

Suddenly there was quick movement on the porch as Tom's body seemed to blur. He grabbed the zombie's shoulders and spun him around, then pivoted so that Grandpa Houser flipped over Tom's hip and hit the porch boards. Tom climbed on top of him, grabbing for the pale wrists, bringing them behind the man's back, securing them with cord that he pulled from his pocket. The whole thing was over in the blink of an eye.

"Take him," he barked, and two burly men crept nervously forward to lift the old zom to his feet and drag him away. "Put him in the toolshed. Don't quiet him yet."

When Tom said that, he ticked his head toward the upstairs windows.

One of the other men began climbing the steps, but Tom stopped him. "No . . . we still don't know where Jack, Michelle, and Danny are."

Benny swallowed a lump the size of a hen's egg.

"Should we help?" asked Chong in a voice that clearly showed that he hated his own suggestion.

"Definitely not warrior smart," said Morgie under his breath.

"I'll help," said Lilah in her icy whisper of a voice, and she pushed her way through the crowd. Most of the townsfolk shied back away from her as if she was something wild and dangerous, and Benny realized she was exactly that.

Lilah exchanged a nod with Tom, and they crept cautiously into the house.

"She's definitely warrior smart," observed Chong, "but crazy as a loon."

"Should we go in too?" asked Morgie. "Maybe they could use our help."

"Tom and Lilah? Need our help? Don't be stupid," replied Nix.

Nix, Chong, and Benny turned their heads in unison to face him.

Morgie colored. "Yeah . . . okay," he conceded. "Kinda dumb, huh?"

Chong laid a consoling hand on his arm. "No, Morgie," he said, "not 'kinda.'"

Benny caught movement again at the Matthias place. He saw Zak turn away from the window, but something about Zak's face made Benny stare. Zak's eyes were surrounded by dark rings. As if his whole face looked bruised. Maybe a couple of black eyes. Big Zak?

"Damn," Benny said under his breath.

Nix caught the direction of his stare. "What—?"

"It's Zak," he said quietly. "I think he's hurt. He keeps looking out here."

Nix opened her mouth to say something stinging about Zak, but then she clamped her jaws shut.

Benny looked at the front of the Houser place, and everything was quiet. People were starting to edge carefully up to the porch. He turned back to Zak's house, chewing his lip in indecision.

Then, before he knew he was going to do anything, he was walking toward Zak Matthias's house.

FROM NIX'S JOURNAL

First Night

That's what people call the day the dead rose. According to Tom, it started in the morning in a few places, but by night it had spread all over.

No one knows why it started.

No one knows where it started. Tom says that the first report he heard of was a news story out of Pittsburgh, Pennsylvania.

By dawn of the next day it had spread all over the world. A state of emergency was declared. Tom says that it was too little and too late.

By noon of the following day all communication was lost from over sixty cities in the United States, and more than three hundred worldwide. No one was counting how many towns and villages were overrun.

The radios and TV stations stopped broadcasting on the fifth day. Cell phones were already dead by then.

After that there was no way to know how bad things were.

BENNY WALKED AROUND TO ZAK'S BACK DOOR. HE KNEW THAT WHEN Big Zak got drunk he usually passed out on the living room couch, so the back of the house seemed like the best place to steal a peek inside.

"Benny!" Nix called as she ran to catch up. "What's going on?"

"I—," he began, but he had nowhere to go with it. How could Nix, of all people, understand and accept that Benny wanted to see if Zak Matthias was okay? This house represented everything she'd lost. Benny believed that if their roles were reversed she'd feel the same.

He gave her a meaningless smile—almost a wince—and stepped up onto Zak's back porch. Nix stayed on the grass by the steps. Benny set his bokken down—no way Zak would open the door if Benny was standing there with a big stick—and cupped his hands around his eyes so he could peer in through the kitchen window. There were no lanterns lit.

The kitchen was empty. No sign of Zak.

Benny gave the door a faint *tap-tap*.

Nothing. Benny hesitated. What did he really want to say to Zak? Zak's uncle had murdered Nix's mom. Benny had killed Charlie. Well, probably killed him. He'd hit him with the Motor City Hammer's black iron pipe and watched Charlie fall a hundred feet into darkness.

How would any of that open a doorway into a conversation?

Gee, Zak, anyone get murdered today?

He knocked again anyway.

A figure moved behind the curtain and turned the handle. The door opened, and Benny drew a breath, not sure which words were going to come out of his mouth.

It wasn't Zak.

It was Big Zak.

Not as big as Charlie Pink-eye, but big enough. He wasn't an albino like Charlie, but he had pale skin and pale blond hair. He was every bit as scary as Charlie, though.

Especially now.

The whole front of Big Zak's shirt glistened with bright red blood.

"I—I—," Big Zak croaked, but there wasn't enough left of his throat to manage more. He took a single trembling step out onto the porch and then fell right on top of Benny. The big man's weight crushed Benny to the porch boards, driving all the air from his lungs, banging his head hard enough to fill the world with fireworks.

"Benny!" Nix screamed.

He heard his own voice screaming too.

Benny stared up at Big Zak's face, which was an inch from his. There were scrapes and cuts all over it, and his eyes were wild with pain and terror. Benny struggled to push the crushing weight off of him.

"H-help . . . me . . . ," the man croaked. "P-please . . ."

And then the mad light went out of Big Zak's eyes. All his weight sagged down, empty of tension, of control. Of life.

Benny panicked, wanting that slack, dead weight off him. He desperately shifted his hip under Big Zak and twisted his hips to move the dead man's mass. As he worked the wrestling move, he wondered why Nix wasn't helping. She was right there. . . .

As if on cue, Nix yelled, "Benny! Watch out!"

Big Zak's body slid partially off him, and Benny kicked his way out. "It's a little late for 'watch out'!" he snapped. "I already—"

But Nix was rushing at him with her bokken held high, her face twisted into a mask of mingled hate and fear.

"No!" he yelled. He scrambled backward and collided . . .

. . . into Zak.

Benny whirled and looked into the face of his former friend.

Into the pale, dark-eyed, and blood-smeared face of the thing that been Zak Matthias.

With a snarl of insatiable hunger, Zak lunged for Benny's throat.

EVERYTHING SEEMED TO HAPPEN MUCH TOO FAST.

Zak grabbed the front of Benny's shirt with icy white fingers and pulled. Benny jammed his palms against Zak's chest just in time. Zak's teeth snapped together an inch from Benny's windpipe. Benny shrieked in terror. Zak moaned in hunger and frustration.

"Benny! Down!"

Suddenly there was a flash of brown hardwood and a sound like a watermelon falling off a wagon onto asphalt. Zak and Benny fell in opposite directions. Benny's head hit the floor again, harder. Zak pitched backward away from him, his face gone, replaced by an inhuman mask of blood and damaged tissue.

Benny felt like his own head was shattered. He heard a voice screaming his name.

Nix?

Benny tried to say her name, but the world spun around him and all his internal lights went dark.

"Benny—get up!"

The voice was a million miles away.

"Benny!"

His numb brain gave the voice a name. Nix. And . . . she was yelling at him. Why was she yelling? He tried to ask her, but it came out as a mumble of soft nonsense words.

Then she was pulling at him. Shaking him.

He cranked open one eye. It was like lifting a hundred pounds of bricks.

"Good morning, Nix," he said in a completely reasonable tone of voice. "Would you like some toast?"

Nix slapped him across the face. Hard.

"Hey—OW!"

The slap cleared his battered brain, and he realized that Nix was bending over him, screaming right in his face.

"ZOMS!"

That did it.

His brain snapped back to full awareness. As Nix hauled him upright there was movement to his left, and Benny turned to see Big Zak getting slowly to his feet, blood dripping from rubbery lips and a ruined throat. The zom turned his slack face toward Benny and moaned like a lost soul.

More movement made Benny turn, and there was Danny Houser and his mother shambling across the lawn toward the porch. Both of them were mangled by bites. Both of them were dead. Zoms. Beyond them, inside the Houser place, there were shouts and screams and gunshots.

"Catch!" Nix scooped up Benny's sword and threw it to him. Benny snatched it out of the air as Big Zak took a lumbering step toward him. Nix jumped off the porch and ran to intercept Danny, her sword held high.

Big Zak was too close for a perfect swing, so Benny changed direction and hit him with the heavy handle of the wooden sword. The blow caught Big Zak on the point of his jaw, and the impact sent shocks up through Benny's wrists. Big Zak staggered backward.

Benny cut a look at Nix just in time to see her swing at Mrs. Houser and knock her sideways, but at the same instant Danny rushed forward and grabbed a fistful of Nix's red hair. Benny took a reflexive step toward her, but then Big Zak grabbed his sweatshirt and jerked him off his feet. The zom dragged him forward and up, first to his toes and then completely off the floor. Even dead, Big Zak Matthias was a powerful man. Benny dangled from the zombie's fists and for a moment he stared straight into the unblinking eyes of the dead man.

There was a story kids told one another, that if you looked into a zom's eyes you would see a reflection of what you would look like as one of the living dead. Benny had stopped believing that after that nightmare adventure last September;

but now, staring into the empty eyes of Big Zak, Benny knew exactly how he would look as a zom. Small and washed-out and lost, with all trace of his humanity and personality snuffed out like a match.

"No!" he cried, and as the zom lunged in for a bite, Benny rammed the shaft of the wooden sword into the creature's gaping mouth.

Big Zak bit down with a huge crunch that chopped splinters off the sword and snapped the tips off the zom's incisors.

Then Big Zak flung Benny away as he pawed the bokken out of his mouth. The sword clattered to the floorboards. As the zom turned toward him, Benny pivoted on his hip and kicked out with both feet, slamming his heels into the zom's knees. The impact knocked the zom backward so that Big Zak's heels caught on Zak Junior's fallen body, and the monster fell down with a huge crash. Benny scrambled to his feet, raised the wooden sword, and brought it down with every ounce of strength he had.

CRACK!

The wooden sword snapped in half right where Big Zak had bitten into it, but the blow itself shattered the zom's skull. Big Zak dropped facedown on the boards, moaning and twisting and clutching at nothing. Benny stared at the eighteen inches of jagged hickory in his hands, then reversed it, raised it high in a two-hand grip, and plunged it down at the base of Big Zak's skull. There is a narrow opening where the spine enters the skull. Tom called it the "sweet spot," and it was where the brain stem was most vulnerable. Sever that and the zom was dead forever. Quieted.

He put everything he had into the blow.

And missed. The tip of the spike hit the hard back of the skull and skittered off and finally crushed itself flat on the floorboards beside the zom's ear.

"Oh, crap," Benny said.

Big Zak's twitching fingers scrabbled for Benny's ankles, but there seemed to be no strength left. Benny stepped backward out of reach. The zom moaned softly.

Immediately Benny whirled, looking for Nix. As he leaped off the porch he saw Danny Houser fall, his head tilting on a cracked—but not broken—neck. Nix backed away from him, her chest heaving with fear and exertion.

"Watch out!" Benny yelled as Mrs. Houser rushed at Nix from her blind side. Just as Nix spun, Benny knocked Danny's mother over with a flying tackle that sent them both into a rolling, tumbling sprawl. The zom twisted and hissed like a cat and buried her teeth in his shoulder. He managed to shift as her jaws clamped shut, and all she bit off was a mouthful of soggy sweatshirt.

There was a sudden muffled thump and a shudder went through the zom; then another and another, and Benny realized that Nix was pounding on the monster with her sword, trying to distract or dislodge her.

"Nix!" yelled a voice. "Get back."

The thumping stopped, and a second later the zom's body was lifted off him and Benny looked up to see Tom there. He hooked one powerful arm around the zom's throat, and though the creature thrashed and fought, she was helpless.

A dozen people came running between the houses and into the yard. Chong and Morgie were with them, and when they saw Benny down on the grass covered with blood, they stopped and froze in place. Nix stood apart, her bokken in her hands, winded and terrified but looking unharmed. Everyone looked at her for a second, and then all eyes snapped back to stare at Benny.

Benny started to get up, but suddenly Lilah was there and she had a glittering dagger in her hand. Before Benny could speak Lilah crouched over him and put the edge of the blade beneath his chin. Benny froze.

"Lilah!" growled Tom.

"Look at his shoulder! He's been bitten," she snapped back.

"No . . . ," Benny croaked.

"No!" cried Nix.

Tom handed Mrs. Houser off to Captain Strunk and two other men from the town watch. They gagged and bound her with practiced ease, though their faces were twisted into masks of fear and revulsion. Tom moved to Lilah's side and touched the arm holding the dagger.

"No," he said more gently, looking from her to Benny and back. "If he's bitten, then it's mine to deal with. It's a family thing."

"I didn't get bitten," Benny insisted, but no one seemed to be paying attention to him.

Lilah had eyes the color of honey, but at that moment Benny thought they looked as cold as ice. There was no trace of compassion or humanity on her face. All he could see was the hunter, the loner. The legendary Lost Girl who had killed humans as well as zoms in the Rot and Ruin.

The knife felt like a branding iron against his skin.

Then it was gone, and she stepped back.

"Be sure," she said to Tom. "Or I will."

Benny sagged back against the grass, more exhausted by the last few seconds than by the fight with the zoms.

Nix edged past Lilah, her eyes hooded and angry, and she moved to stand between them. Morgie crept closer until he was shoulder to shoulder with Nix; after a slight hesitation, so did Chong. Their bodies formed a screen. Lilah looked at them with a calculating stare, as if she was sizing them up and deciding how much—or how little—effort it would take to get past them to Benny.

Benny got shakily to his feet.

"I didn't get bit," he yelled. To prove it he pulled off his shirt and flung it on the grass at Lilah's feet. Anger was rising in him now, replacing his terror inch by inch. "See?"

"I see," was all Lilah said. She lowered her knife and turned away. Everyone watched as she walked over to the porch, mounted the steps, and without a pause drove the tip of the blade into the back of Big Zak's skull. Unlike Benny, she did not miss.

"Holy crap," said Morgie.

"Uh-huh," breathed Chong, pale and shaken.

Tom bent and picked up Benny's shirt, examined the bite hole on the shoulder, and handed it back to him. "You sure you're okay?"

Benny looked over to the porch, where Big Zak lay sprawled a few feet from his son. From the thing that had once been a boy the same age as Benny. A friend once. A victim recently.

"I said I wasn't bitten," Benny said, shaking his head slowly as he turned away, "but I'm a billion miles from okay."

FROM NIX'S JOURNAL

Before First Night the United States Census Bureau estimated that there were 6,922,000,000 people alive on planet Earth.

Tom said that news reports claimed that more than two billion people died in the first two days after First Night.

By the time the Internet went down, the estimates of the global death toll were at four billion and climbing.

People in town believe that following First Night more than six billion people died. Most people think the whole rest of the world is dead.

We know that the total population of the nine towns here in central California is 28,261 as of last New Year's census.

THEY ALL SAT ON THE PICNIC TABLE IN BENNY'S YARD, DRINKING COLD TEA and eating enormous slices of apple pie with raisins and walnuts in it. The sun was a golden ball in a flawless blue sky, and birds chattered in the trees. However, this rampant beauty did nothing to lighten the mood of sadness and horror that hovered like fog around them.

Lilah sat apart, cross-legged on the grass. She had not spoken a single word since the confrontation in Zak's yard. No one had, except for some ordinary comments mostly related to the serving and eating of Tom's apple pie. Benny nibbled at his, but he had no appetite. Neither did Nix, though she poked angrily at the dessert until it was a mangled beige lump of goo on her plate. Chong and Morgie ate theirs, though Chong seemed to be eating on autopilot, his eyes focused on Lilah's stern but beautiful profile.

Tom sat on a tree stump, looking angry and unhappy.

"What happened back there?" Benny finally asked. "With Danny and Zak . . . and . . ."

Tom sighed and ran his hands over his face. "It was Grandpa Houser. Looks like he died sitting on the living room couch, reading the *Town Pump*. Michelle probably thought he was asleep. Maybe she tried to shake him awake and he reanimated and bit her. Looks like she ran out of the house to get away. Or maybe to get help. The twins said that they were out with their dad all morning, so maybe Michelle went to get Zak or Big Zak to help her. Not sure what happened next. There's a lot of blood in the kitchen, so it looked like maybe Grandpa attacked them when they came back in. Or maybe Michelle was hurt worse than she thought. Zak must have been bitten there and ran home. I looked inside their house too. There was a lot of blood in the dining room, so Zak must have bled out there, and when he reanimated . . ."

". . . he attacked his dad," Benny said.

Tom nodded.

Benny thought about mentioning his suspicions that Big Zak had been knocking Zak around, but there didn't seem much point to it now. Even so, an ugly thought was forming in his mind. What if Zak had been bitten—by Mrs. Houser or Grandpa Houser—and, knowing that he was infected, had gone home to make sure that was where he'd be when he died and reanimated? Would Zak have done that as a twisted way to pay back the abuse?

Nix reached over and gave his knee a squeeze; and when Benny looked at her he saw a complexity of emotions swirling in her green eyes. She gave him a sad little smile, and he wondered, not for the first time, if she could somehow read his thoughts. Or feel what he felt. What did they call that? Empathy? Benny was pretty sure that was the word.

"This really sucks," said Morgie. "Danny and his folks. Man . . ."

"Zak, too," said Chong.

Morgie gave him a hard look. "We're better off without any of the Matthias family around here anymore. You did us all a favor by bashing Zak's head—"

Nix whirled and grabbed a small fistful of Morgie's shirt. "Shut up!" she said fiercely.

"Hey! What's your problem?" Morgie said, trying to peel her fingers off. "You should be throwing a party. Your mom died because of Zak and his whole loser family. They kidnapped you and you almost died. And I got my skull cracked and I nearly died. What does it take to get you mad enough to—"

"Shut up." Nix's voice was as cold as ice. "Zak didn't know what Charlie would do when he told him about the Lost Girl card."

Morgie sneered. "Yeah? And how do you know that? Did you ask him? Did you ever ask him why he told Charlie at all? How do you know that Charlie didn't tell him exactly what would happen?"

Nix said nothing, but her eyes were green fire.

"How do you know that Zak wasn't a part of all of it?" Morgie continued. "Tom's not the only one training kids our age to be bounty hunters. Maybe Charlie was teaching Zak. Maybe Charlie told Zak all about Gameland and the Z-Games and all of it. You don't know what Zak knew. He could have been as guilty as Charlie and the Hammer."

Everyone looked at Nix, and Benny was expecting her to cry or punch Morgie or do something extreme.

Instead she slowly opened her hand to let go of Morgie's shirt.

"You're right," she said.

Morgie blinked in surprise. "I—"

"I don't know," Nix went on, cutting off whatever Morgie might say. "Neither do you and now neither does anyone. Charlie Matthias and Marion Hammer are dead. We killed them up in the mountains. It's not going to bring my mom back, I know that." A tear broke from the corner of one eye and burned a silver line down her cheek. "But neither will condemning Zak without proof."

Morgie started to reply, thought better of it, and closed his mouth. He looked around for support, but no one would meet his eyes.

Nix wiped the tear with the back of her hand. "Ever since we got back all I've done is hate Zak. And his father, and everyone Zak was ever related to. I wanted them all dead. I wanted them all to pay." Her words were fierce, but her voice was so soft that Benny had to lean in to hear her. She sniffed. "Today . . . when I killed Zak today I actually wanted to. I wasn't just killing the zom that Zak had turned into. I could feel it in my chest. I can still feel it. It's like . . ."

They all waited in silence while she fought to clothe her feelings in words that everyone would understand. Benny put his hand on her knee, just as she'd done to him, but Nix shook her head and gently pushed it away.

"I don't want anyone to cheer about it," she said in voice that was dangerously close to a sob. "And I don't want anyone to make it all right for me, either. I feel like I'm going crazy . . . I feel . . ." She took a deep breath. "I feel polluted."

Nix looked around to see if anyone understood. Tom

nodded first, and Benny understood why. He'd been doing this longer than any of them, and Benny knew for certain that each and every kill Tom made hurt him. Deeply.

Chong nodded as well, and he turned his face away to hide whatever might be showing in his dark eyes. Lilah gave a single, short grunt that could mean anything; but it was not a shake of her head.

Nix turned to Benny, and there was such pain and such hope warring on her face.

"Yeah," Benny said. "You know that I know."

One by one they all turned to Morgie. His eyes were fierce, his jaw set.

He stood up and without a word turned and walked away.

"Morgie!" Nix called, starting to rise, but Tom stopped her with a shake of his head.

"Leave him be," Tom said. "He needs some time."

But Nix didn't leave it. She ran after Morgie and caught him as he slammed the gate behind him. Nix pushed it open again, but Morgie kept walking, almost running. Nix ran to stand in front of him. Benny couldn't hear what she said, or what Morgie said back. At first they were shouting, but their words were muffled by distance. Then Nix was hugging Morgie and for a moment there was no response, then Morgie wrapped his arms around her and they stood there, heads buried on each other's shoulders. Benny could see the hitch of their bodies as they cried.

"Don't go over there, Benny," said Chong softly.

"No," Benny agreed.

They watched for a while, then one by one they turned away.

FROM NIX'S JOURNAL

People in the Rot and Ruin

Bounty Hunters: This is the biggest group of people who go into the Ruin, or sometimes live out there. They do jobs for pay, like clearing zoms out of a town, hunting specific zombies for pay, clearing the trade routes, finding lost people, and other work.

Tom says that most of them are dangerous and not very nice, but that "nicer people generally won't do that kind of work." Mayor Kirsch calls them a "necessary evil."

People in town have been talking about a new bounty hunter moving into the area to take over Charlie Pink-eye's territory. They call him White Bear, but that's all I know about him . . . except that he's supposed to be just as mean and tough as Charlie. Oh . . . great.

Charlie Pink-eye and the Motor City Hammer were bounty hunters, and the people who worked with them were all bad.

Closure experts are a different kind of bounty hunter. They're hired by people to look for family members or friends who have been zommed. This is what Tom Imura does.

Tom finds them if he can (zoms usually don't wander far from where they reanimated), reads them a last letter from the family, and then "quiets" them as humanely as possible.

Other closure experts Tom introduced me to: Old Man Church, Solomon Jones, and Lucy Diamonds.

Bounty hunters Tom trusts: J-Dog, Dr. Skillz, Hector Mexico, Sally Two-Knives, Basher Bashman, Magic Mike, LaDonna Willis and sons, and Fluffy McTeague.

What would my name be if I was a bounty hunter? Reds Riley? Li'l Killer?

I'll have to think about that.

BENNY FELT HORRIBLE AND HELPLESS. MORGIE HAD ALWAYS HAD A CRUSH on Nix and had been on his way to her house to ask her out the night Nix's mom was killed. Morgie had tried to defend Nix and her mom, but the Hammer had struck him on the back of the head with his iron club.

The same club Benny had used to take down Charlie.

Now Morgie and Nix were deep inside the pocket of a shared experience, and the intimacy of it made Benny feel deeply insecure. But when he realized that he was feeling insecure and jealous, Benny wished he could drag his own stupid mind behind the house and kick the crap out of it.

They ate the last of the leftovers from supper and more big slices of pie. They sat in silence, trying not to look at the road. After fifteen minutes Nix and Morgie came back. They each accepted plates of pie and glasses of tea from Tom.

Morgie sat in the empty gap between Tom and Chong, and there were dried tear tracks on his face. Nix sat on the picnic table, but not as close to Benny as she had been before.

As if there had been no interruption, Tom picked up the conversation where his narrative of the events at the Houser place had left off.

". . . and you know the rest," Tom concluded.

"What about Danny's dad?" asked Nix. "And the twins?"

Tom sighed. "The girls told me that they and their dad got home about two hours ago. The girls went upstairs to play, and Jack went into the kitchen. Danny must have come home sometime after Michelle was attacked but before Jack. From the way I read it, Danny, Grandpa, and Michelle attacked Jack when he went into the kitchen. He got away, but he was badly hurt. He got the girls into their room and told them to barricade the door. Then he got his gun."

"He fired that first shot?" asked Benny.

"Probably. Maybe he was planning on quieting Michelle and the others, but he was too badly torn up. I think he realized that he was about to die, and he did what he thought was best to try and protect the girls."

"He shot himself?" asked Nix, horrified.

Tom nodded. "Right at the top of the stairs, so his body would block the others from getting at the girls. Jack must have been too weak to hold the gun right; his bullet missed the motor cortex and the brain stem. All he did was speed up how fast he came back. When we came in, he was just about to break into the girls' bedroom."

Nix sniffed and wiped tears from her eyes.

"All those people," Benny said softly. "And those two little girls."

"More orphans."

It was Lilah who spoke, and everyone turned to her. Her stern expression had softened, and it was clear that she was looking into her own memories. Like Nix, Lilah was an orphan. And like Nix and the little girls, Lilah had lost her sibling as well: Annie, a little sister who was born on First Night and who had died trying to escape the zombie pits at Gameland.

Chong said, "What will happen to them?"

"The girls?" Tom asked. "I think there's an aunt somewhere. In Hillcrest, maybe."

That town was four days' ride to the north, and the route went through some of the worst zombie-infested lands. It was a terrible thing. The girls would go off to another town—and as travel between the few towns left in the Ruin was rare, usually only the bounty hunters and traders risked the journey. Benny knew that people here in Mountainside would never see Faith and Hope again. Probably never even hear about them again, as if they had been erased from the world as so many other people had been erased.

The thought of so much death and loss hit him like a punch to the heart.

Nix, however, was furious, and she pounded her thigh with a small, hard fist. "God! I can't wait to leave this place. I want to get out of here and never come back."

Tom looked at her and then turned his face to the east and gave a slow nod.

"I wish we could leave now," Nix growled, then elbowed Benny. "Right?"

"Absolutely," he said, though he had to force the enthusiasm. At the moment all he wanted to do was go lock himself in his room and sleep until the horror went away.

"I still can't believe you're really going," said Chong softly, but although he spoke to Benny and Nix, his eyes kept darting toward Lilah. "I wish I could go."

"Me too," muttered Nix. "We should all leave. God, I hate

this town. I hate the way people think here. No one talks about First Night. Everyone's afraid to even discuss the possibility of reclaiming the world. They won't even expand the town."

"They're scared," said Morgie.

"So what?" she snapped. "There's always been something to be scared of. Between wild animals, earthquakes, volcanoes, viruses, wars . . . Yet look at what people did! They built cities and countries. They fought off their enemies. They stopped being scared and started being strong!"

"No," said Lilah. "Even the strong are afraid."

Nix turned to her. "Okay, then they learned how to be brave."

"Yes," said Tom. "They also learned how to work together. That mattered then and it'll matter now. None of us could do this alone. I know I couldn't. Not going across the whole country."

"I thought you liked being alone," said Benny, half joking. "The Zen master and all that."

Tom shook his head. "I can handle loneliness, but I don't like it. Every time I was out on a long job I even looked forward to coming home to you. An ugly, smelly, bratty little brother."

"Who will smother you in your sleep," suggested Benny.

"Point taken."

"I want to go," said Lilah abruptly. "Being alone . . . being lonely . . ." She didn't finish and simply shook her head.

Since she'd first come here last year, Lilah had gone back into the forests and up into the mountains dozens of times, and often to the cave where she used to live, bringing back sacks filled with her precious books. Benny, Tom, and Nix had gone with her several times. However, no one commented on her statement. None of them understood loneliness a tenth as well as the Lost Girl.

"I really wish I could go," repeated Chong wistfully, still looking at Lilah while trying not to appear that he was.

"Parents won't cave?" Benny asked.

"Parents won't even talk about it. They think the idea is suicidal."

"They could be right," observed Tom.

"And that's why I don't want you talking to them about it anymore, Mr. Positive Energy," growled Chong. "After the last time you talked about it, Mom wanted to handcuff me to the kitchen chair."

"You could just go," suggested Lilah.

Chong made a face. "Very funny."

"I am serious. It's your life . . . take it."

"You sure that's how you want to phrase that?" murmured Benny.

"You know what I mean," Lilah snapped irritably.

"Yes," said Tom, "and it's a bad suggestion. Chong is a minor, and he has a responsibility to his family."

"First responsibility is to here," she retorted, tapping herself over the heart. "To self."

"Fine, then maybe you should go talk to the Chongs," said Tom.

"Maybe I should."

"But," interjected Benny, "don't bring your weapons."

FROM NIX'S JOURNAL

Things We Don't Know About Zoms

Why they stop decaying after a certain point.

Why they attack people and animals.

Why they don't attack each other.

Whether they can see or hear the way living humans can.

Why they moan.

If they can think (at all).

If they can feel pain.

What they are.

THE REST OF THE DAY WAS QUIET. NIX WENT FOR A LONG WALK WITH LILAH, and Chong trailed along like a sad and silent puppy. Morgie went fishing and Benny slouched around the house, looking at all the familiar things, trying to wrap his brain around the idea that he wasn't going to see any of this stuff anymore. Even the beat-up chest of drawers in his room seemed wonderful and familiar, and he touched it like an old friend.

Say good-bye to this, whispered his inner voice. *Let it all go.*

He took a long, hot bath and listened to a voice speak to him from the shadows in his mind. For months now Benny had heard that inner voice speaking as if it were a separate part of him. It wasn't the same as "hearing voices," like old Brian Collins, who had at least a dozen people chattering in his head all the time. No, this was different. To Benny it felt like the inner voice he heard was his own future self whispering to him. The person he was going to become. A more evolved and mature Benny Imura, confident and wise, who had begun to emerge shortly after the events at Charlie's camp.

The current Benny didn't always agree with the voice, and often wished it would shut up and let him just be fifteen.

After his soak, Benny stood for a while peering into the mirror, wondering who he was.

After seven months of Tom's insane pre-trip fitness regimen, he was no longer the skinny kid he'd been when he had first ventured out into the Rot and Ruin. He actually had muscle definition and even the beginnings of six-pack abs. He made sure that he took his shirt off in front of Nix as often as he could reasonably justify it, usually after hard training sessions. He worked hard to make it look casual, but it was disheartening how often Nix giggled or didn't appear to notice instead of swooning with lust.

Now he looked at his arms and chest, at the muscles earned through all those hours of training with swords and jujitsu and karate; at the tone acquired from endless repetitions with weights, from running five to ten miles five times a week, from climbing ropes and trees and playing combat games. He bent closer, wondering how much of that face belonged to the man he was becoming or to the boy he still believed himself to be. The face seemed to fit more with his inner voice than with Benny's perception of his current self.

That was the problem, and it was at the core of everything. On one hand he wanted to be fifteen and go fishing and play baseball and get in trouble swiping apples from Snotty O'Malley's orchard. On the other hand, he wanted to be a man. He wanted to be as strong as Tom, as powerful as Tom. He wanted people to show him the fear and respect they showed Tom.

Benny knew that once they left Mountainside he would have to become tougher. There would be challenges that would toughen him and strengthen his "legend," just as

Tom's many adventures as the region's most feared zombie hunter had built his legend. No doubt Nix would find him irresistibly sexy the farther from town they got and the tougher he became.

For Nix, everything that mattered was out there.

Benny was more than half sure that if Nix actually loved him, then it was because he had agreed to go with her into the Ruin. Maybe not completely, but in a large part. He would have bet everything he had on it.

So he didn't dare tell her that he wasn't really sure he wanted to go.

Tell her, said the inner voice. *Don't lie to her.*

Benny ignored the suggestion.

The Ruin was dangerous and it was uncertain, and everyone he'd talked to in town said that no one had ever gone past Yosemite Park and come back. Nix wanted to go all the way across the country, if that was what it would take to find the jet. Tom, too; and Lilah.

He stared into his brown eyes and studied the doubt and fear that he saw there.

"Some hero," he said under his breath. "Some legend."

Nix believed that to stay in town was to be stifled and die behind walls, and she wasn't entirely wrong. Nearly everyone in Mountainside feared the Ruin with a dread that was so profound that they almost never mentioned anything beyond the fence line. A few went out, visiting other towns, but even then they traveled in metal-reinforced wagons with the shades pulled down to block out any sight of the Ruin. Only the drivers and their bounty-hunter guards rode outside the wagons. Benny imagined that even in the early spring those wagons had to be sickeningly hot, but the travelers seemed to prefer that discomfort rather than the fresh air that came with looking out the window at the real world. It drove Benny nuts. He wondered what the passengers thought when they were inside the wagon but outside the fence. Did they just shut down their higher reasoning? Did they drug themselves so they slept through the journey? Or was the denial so deep that they somehow regarded entering and exiting the shuttered wagons in the same way they would passing through a doorway? Maybe to them there simply was nothing in between.

It was like a plague, but different from the one that had destroyed the world. This was an emotional pandemic that blinded the eye and deafened the ear and darkened the mind so that there simply was no world other than what existed inside each fenced town.

Most people had long ago stopped talking about First Night; and although no one said it aloud, it was pretty clear that they felt that they were all just waiting for everything else to end. Society had collapsed, the military and government were gone, nearly seven billion people had died, and the zombie plague was still running at full strength. They all knew that their fellow citizens of Mountainside believed that the world had ended and what was left was just the clock winding down to a final and inevitable silence.

It was a horrible thought, and until the big fight at Charlie's camp last year, Benny had been as adamant as Nix in wanting to break free of the town and find someplace where people wanted to be alive. Someplace where people believed that there was a future.

Then there had been that fight. Benny had been forced to kill people.

To kill.

People.

Not just zoms.

How was that going to open the way to a future?

There were so few people left. Barely thirty thousand left in California, and no way to know if there were any more anywhere else. How was killing going to increase that number? It was insane.

Only here, only when he was alone and looking into the eyes of the person he was becoming, could Benny admit the truth to himself.

"I don't want to do this," he said.

His mirror image and his inner voice repeated that truth, word for word. They were all in total agreement.

He got dressed and went downstairs and stood for a long time looking at the map of Mariposa County and Yosemite National Park. He heard voices and went to the back door and listened. Tom was in the yard, talking across the rail fence to Mayor Kirsch and Captain Strunk. Benny cracked the door so he could hear what they were saying.

"It's not just a few people, Tom," said the mayor. "Everyone's talking about it."

"It's not a secret, Randy," Tom said. "People have known I was leaving since Christmas."

"That's my point," replied Captain Strunk. "The scouts and traders are saying that a bunch of rough-looking characters have been moving into the area since Charlie died."

"Everyone in the Ruin is a rough-looking character. Goes with the territory."

"Come on, Tom," Strunk said irritably, "don't pretend you don't know what I'm saying. And don't pretend that you don't know what an influence you've had on things out in the Ruin. There may not be much in the way of law out there, but while you were going out on regular closure jobs, most of the rough trade tended to behave themselves."

Tom laughed. "You're crazy."

"This isn't a joke," said Strunk. "People respect you in town, even if most of them don't say it—"

"Or can't say it," the Mayor interjected.

"—and out in the Ruin you were a force to be reckoned with."

"I'm not the sheriff of these here parts," Tom said in a comical Old West accent.

"Might as well be," said Strunk. "You could have my job anytime you want it."

"No thanks, Keith, you're the law here in town, and you do a great job."

"Again, that's my point," said Strunk. "You know that I won't ever step one foot outside of that fence. No way."

"The bottom line," barked the mayor, "is that we both feel that once you leave, this part of the Ruin is going to turn into a no-man's-land. Traders are going to get hijacked, and if the bounty hunters band together with no one to stop them, then they are going to own this town. Maybe all the towns."

There was a brief silence, and then Benny heard Tom sigh.

"Randy, Keith . . . I appreciate the problem, but it's not my problem. If you'll remember, I proposed a militia for the Ruin.

I made very specific recommendations for a town-sanctioned force that would police this part of the Ruin and all the trade routes. Let's see, how long ago was that? Eight years? And then again a year later. And the following year, and—"

"Okay, okay," growled Mayor Kirsch. "Rubbing our noses in it doesn't help us find an answer."

"I know, Randy, and I don't mean to be a jerk about this . . . but I'm leaving next week. Leaving and not coming back. I can't be the one to solve your problems. Not this time."

Both men harangued Tom, but he cut them off with a curt wave of his hand.

"If you bothered to read my proposal," he said, "you'd have seen that I made several recommendations for how to handle things. Not all the bounty hunters are like Charlie. There are some people you can trust—granted, only a handful, but I trust them completely." He began counting on his fingers as he ran through some names. "Solomon Jones, Sally Two-Knives . . ." He counted off twenty names.

"Oh, please," said Mayor Kirsch, making a face. "Half of them are psychos and loners who refuse to come into town and—"

"They don't need to come into town," cut in Tom. "Meet them at the fence line and talk business. Deputize them. Pay them. And, here's a thought, treat them with a little respect and maybe they'll show some loyalty to you and the town."

"Maybe they behave themselves around you," said Strunk, "but I hear wild tales."

"Really? Well, what wild tales have you been hearing about Gameland? It's back in operation again. Without a militia of any kind, what are you going to do when kids start disappearing? How would you feel about your own kids vanishing off the street and getting dragged off to fight in a zombie pit? Don't pretend that doesn't happen in town. Ask Nix Riley."

There was more, but the three of them began walking toward the garden gate and the road to town. Benny closed the door.

Great, he thought, *just what we need. Another reason to feel bad about leaving.*

The next day was the viewing and funeral for the Houser family. More than two hundred people showed up. Benny and Nix went together. She had been sad and quiet since yesterday, and the day suited her mood. Clouds obscured the sun and turned the air wet and cool, but no rain fell. The trees were filled with crows and warblers and grasshopper sparrows. A grackle—scruffy and dark—landed on the closed coffin of Danny Houser and mocked the sermon like an uncouth heckler, until the grave digger chased him away with a shovel.

Pastor Kellogg wore a black robe and held a heavy and very battered old Bible. There was a rumor around town that the pages of the Bible were stained with blood because the pastor had been forced to use the Good Book to beat the head in of one of his parishioners who had been zommed out and attacked him. It was a lurid story, but Benny believed it was true. There were a lot of stories like that in town. Everyone who had survived First Night had one.

The mayor and his wife were there, dressed in formal clothes, and even Captain Strunk of the Town Watch was in a suit.

Benny did not own a suit, but he wore his best pair of dark

blue jeans and a clean white shirt. Nix wore a pretty dress that Fran Kirsch, the mayor's wife, had sewn for her. The dress was a richer shade of blue than Benny's jeans, and the bodice was embroidered with wildflowers and hummingbirds. The colors made Nix's red hair and green eyes look more intense.

Tom wore a black shirt and jeans and kept his eyes hidden behind a pair of sunglasses he'd recently bought from a trader. He did not say a word the whole time. Chong and his family stood nearby, but Lilah was not with them. Only when Benny looked around during one of the hymns did he see her standing on the far side of the graveyard fence. She wore a dress made from some charcoal-colored cloth embroidered with tiny white flowers. Lilah's snow-white hair danced in the light breeze, and her eyes were in shadow. She looked as cold and beautiful as a ghost.

Benny saw that Chong was staring openly at her.

Morgie Mitchell came to the funeral too, but like Lilah he stood apart from the others.

When the burial was over, only a handful of people walked to the other side of the cemetery for the Matthias service. Nix took Benny's hand as they threaded their way through the tombstones.

"You know what this feels like?" she asked.

He shook his head.

"It's like we're at our own funerals."

Benny almost stopped, but Nix pulled his hand.

"Think about it . . . in a couple of days we'll be gone too. Nobody in town will ever see us again. Someone else will be living in your house, just like somebody else is living in mine now. By Christmas we'll be an anecdote. By next year people will start forgetting our names. I'll be 'the redheaded girl whose mama was murdered.' You'll be 'that bounty hunter's kid brother.'" Her voice was soft, pitched for just him to hear. She trailed her fingers over the curved top of a tombstone. "Ten years from now they won't even remember that we lived here."

"Morgie and Chong will remember."

"Remember what? That we left them behind? That they weren't able to escape with us?"

"Is that what this is? An escape?"

She shrugged. "Maybe it'll be like being born into another world. I don't know."

He glanced at her as they walked down the slope to the Matthias plot, but Nix didn't return his look. Although she was with him, she was wandering somewhere down deep in her thoughts.

Tom and Chong followed behind. Lilah did not.

Zak's family was Catholic, so Father Shannon performed the service. He was an ancient little man with healed-over burns on his face. Like Pastor Kellogg, the little priest carried with him an awful reminder of First Night.

Father Shannon looked at the sparse gathering and then around at the cemetery, as if hoping more people were coming, but no one was. He sighed, shook his head, and launched into another reading of the same prayer for the dead. Nix still held Benny's hand, and her grip tightened to an almost crushing force, grinding his hand bones together. It hurt, but Benny would rather have cut that hand off than take it back at that moment. If it would help Nix through this, he'd give her a pair of pliers and a vise so she could do a proper job.

The priest read the prayers and made the sign of the cross and talked a lot about redemption.

Benny leaned close to Nix and whispered, "He sounds like he thought Zak and his dad were as guilty as Charlie."

"Maybe he's like some other people around here. They seem to think that the whole Charlie Pink-eye craziness finally died out with the last of his family." She shook her head. "People can be so blind."

Benny nodded. He would have given her hand a comforting squeeze, but there was no feeling left in his fingers.

Afterward, Benny, Nix, and Tom walked home together.

At the garden gate, Tom stopped and removed his sunglasses. His eyes were rimmed with red. Had he been crying? For whom? The Housers? Surely not Zak.

"Change of plans," Tom said. "We're leaving tomorrow."

They stared at him openmouthed.

"Really?" asked Nix, a big smile erupting on her face.

"Why?" asked Benny at the same time.

Tom looked up at the moody sky for a moment and leaned his forearms wearily on the crossbar between the fence pickets. "I really can't stand this damn town anymore," he said. "Sometimes it's harder to tell which side of the fence the dead are on."

Nix rubbed his shoulder, and he smiled sadly and patted her hand.

Then he took a breath and turned to give them both a long, appraising stare. "There are conditions. We'll go out for an overnight trip and camp up in the mountains. Not down in the lowlands where all the zoms are, but not in the clearer zones up high. Minimal protection, no luxuries. We'll try some roads we haven't been on together—roads I haven't been on in a couple of years. If you can handle that, then we'll just keep going toward Yosemite and points east."

Tom had planned the trip very carefully, or at least as carefully as a journey through largely unknown territory can be planned. There were a few rest stops along the way, places Tom called "safe houses." The first was Brother David's way station, and the next was an old hotel in Wawona; once they passed that, they'd be on their own.

"If anything weird happens and we get separated," Tom said, "I want you guys to head for the way station or Wawona, depending on where you are."

Wawona was likely to be the safest place along the route. Before First Night, the small town had been home to about 170 permanent residents and a few thousand campers during the tourist seasons. Tom had told them a wild story about the Battle of Wawona, in which a small group of uninfected fought off the rest of the town as the zombie plague swept through the population. The siege of the hotel lasted four months, and when it was over there was a mass grave with more than two hundred living dead in it along with sixteen of the initial uninfected. The only survivors were a grizzled old forest ranger, his two young nephews, and a couple of women scientists visiting from the San Diego Zoo. The ranger still lived up there, and Tom often referred to him by his nickname, the Greenman. The others had gone to live in the towns. Apparently the ranger had become something of a deep-woods mystic.

Nowadays the old Wawona Hotel was a traveler's rest

and temporary storehouse for scavenged goods, and there were always a dozen people at the hotel. Rumor had it that a fire-and-brimstone evangelist named Preacher Jack had taken up residence as well. He was happy to share his version of the word of God with everyone who passed through, and was even reputed to have tried to convert and baptize some zoms.

When Benny asked what Tom thought about Preacher Jack, his brother shrugged. "I haven't met him yet, though I think just about everybody else out there has. A bit eccentric from what I hear, but I guess he's harmless enough. A guy doing what he believes is the right thing. Nothing wrong with that."

Nix sighed, and Tom asked her what was wrong.

"What if we don't find the jet?" she said cautiously.

"We'll keep trying until we get it right." Tom smiled at the looks of alarm on their faces. "Understand me, guys, we are going, let's not kid ourselves about that. The only question is whether you're ready to go now."

Nix nodded. "I'm ready," she said grimly.

Tom gave a noncommittal grunt, which Benny interpreted as *I'll be the judge of that.*

"One more thing," Tom said. "You can ask Chong and Morgie if they want to go with us. Not all the way, just overnight. If so, I can arrange to have Brother David or one of my friends out there take them back to town. J-Dog and Dr. Skillz are always working that part of the Ruin."

"I met them once," Benny said, "at the New Year's party year before last. They're goofy."

Tom shrugged.

"I couldn't understand a lot of what they said," Benny said.

"I can't either." Tom laughed. "They were just break-ing into the professional surfer scene when First Night hit. Surfers have their own lingo, and those two use it like a per-sonal language. I don't think they want people to under-stand them."

"Why not?"

"It's a defense mechanism. Remember that story about Peter Pan and the Lost Boys?"

"Sure, the kids who never grew up."

"They're like that. On one hand they work the bounty trade and they can fight like demons, but on the other they don't really want all this to be real. For them it's like living inside a video game. Remember when I told you about video games?"

"Sure," Benny said, though the concept was incredibly alien to him. "With Dr. Skillz and J-Dog . . . they don't actu-ally think they're at the beach, do they?"

"Hard to say," said Tom. "Everything's a big game to them. They can be ankle deep in blood or fighting a hundred zoms with their backs against the wall and they're cracking jokes in their surfer lingo. It's their way of surviving, and I guess it works for them. Don't ask me how." He paused and smiled. "Lot of people can't stand them. I like them a lot."

"Weird world," said Nix.

"You have no idea, sweetie," said Tom. Benny noticed that he didn't get the ninja death stare for calling Nix sweetie.

Tom gestured to the southeast. "Now . . . the Greenman has a cabin up there. I got word out to him and a bunch of others that we're coming. We'll have friends out there and safe places to rest."

"Chong's mom might go for the overnight thing," Benny said hopefully. "She'd probably think that it would scare the pants off him and get the whole 'go and see the world' thing out of his system." He thought about it. "Probably will work, too. Chong's not big on roughing it."

"And Morgie?" Tom asked.

Nix shook her head. "No, Morgie won't go."

Benny and Tom looked at her. "You seem pretty certain," Tom said.

"I am." But she didn't explain, and they didn't press the issue.

"Okay," said Tom. "If we're going to get out of here, then I have a week's worth of stuff I need to get done today. You two better say your good-byes."

"There's no one I need to say good-bye to," Nix began, but Tom cut her off.

"That's not true and you know it. We're leaving Mountainside, Nix . . . we're not discarding the people who live here. The Kirschs, Captain Strunk, the Chongs . . . they've been kind to you, and they deserve the courtesy and respect of a proper good-bye."

Nix gave a contrite nod, her face flushed with embarrassment.

"And both of you are leaving friends behind. If Morgie and Chong aren't going, then are you planning on walking away from them without saying good-bye? Remember, they think we're going next week. This is going to be hard on them, too."

Benny sighed, and nodded.

"Leaving is never easy," said Tom. "Even when you know you have to go."

FROM NIX'S JOURNAL

People in the Ruin

Traders: They bring all sorts of stuff from town to town in armored wagons pulled by horses covered in carpet and chain mail. You can buy almost anything from a trader, or make a request and he'll get it for you for a price, and traders' goods are always expensive.

Scavengers: These people are nuts. They go into towns and raid houses, stores, warehouses, and other places for all sorts of things: supplies, canned goods, stockpiles of seeds and flour, clothing, weapons, books, and everything else. Sometimes they have bounty hunters go in first and clear out the zoms, but then they have to share their profits with them—so a lot of scavengers prefer to risk going into zombie-infested areas. Tom says that the life expectancy of a solo scavenger is two years, but if they survive, they can make enough money to retire. He says he knows of only three who have retired. He's quieted over two dozen others who weren't as lucky.

Loners: These people scare everyone. They

live alone (or in small groups), and once they've staked out their territory they'll kill anyone who comes close—human or zom. There's a rumor in town that some of them are cannibals.

Tom went back into town to buy some last-minute supplies. Nix and Benny went into the house and upstairs to Benny's room and then out of his window to sit on the porch roof. Benny dragged a couple of big pillows out and placed them side by side.

The gray clouds were dissolving into pale white wisps that looked like wet tissue paper over a blue ceiling. From up there they could see the whole town. To the west, the flat reservoir backed up against the steep wall of mountains and the miles of fence line that framed the town on the north, east, and west. Adjacent to the town, miles upon miles of enclosed farmland vanished over the horizon lines. It had always baffled Benny why the townsfolk had not pushed out the fence line to incrementally reclaim more and more of the Ruin. The traders who plundered warehouses and construction sites in abandoned towns could bring in as much chain link and poles as people wanted, but the town limits hadn't budged in years. There was Town and there was the Ruin, and that was as far as people seemed able to think.

As much as it bothered Benny, it nearly drove Nix crazy. She not only wanted to expand the town, she wanted to go to the coast, take boats, and reclaim some of the big islands just off the California coast: Catalina, San Clemente, or any of the other islands big enough to sustain a few thousand people and fertile enough to farm. Nix had a list of islands in the little leather journal she always carried; and detailed plans for how to remove the zoms. She'd copied reams of notes from books on farming and agriculture.

They lay back on the pillows and looked up at the gulls and vultures soaring high on the thermal winds.

"I'm really going to miss Chong and Morgie," Nix said.

"I know. Me too."

"But I have to go."

"I know," said Benny.

They heard voices down in the yard. Tom and someone else. Nix sat up, but Benny put a finger to his lips and they lay flat on their stomachs and shimmied to the edge of the roof.

Below them, Tom stood talking with a bounty hunter Benny had met a few times at New Year's parties. Sam "Basher" Bashman. He was a slim, dark-haired man who carried two baseball bats. Both were old and battered, but from what Tom had said, Basher had owned them since the days when he played second base for the Philadelphia Phillies in a world that no longer existed.

"So, you're really bent on taking your brother and his girl-friend out there?" asked Basher.

"Absolutely," Tom said.

"Why? No one's seen the jet since that one time. And I've asked everyone about that."

"Still have to look," said Tom.

Basher shook his head. "Ruin's getting weird, man. You

haven't been out there much lately, but people are dying, and it's not zoms. With Charlie gone it's an all-out fight to take over his territory. You think this trip's wise, man?"

"Not really," Tom admitted.

"Then why do it?"

Tom paused, and Benny and Nix shimmied an inch closer to the edge. "If I don't take them out there . . . they'll find a way to go by themselves."

There was more to the conversation, but Tom and Basher were now walking away, heading back to town.

Benny sat up and stared into the middle distance.

Nix turned to look at him, and the afternoon sunlight made her hair even redder. And her eyes greener.

"Benny . . . ? Can I ask you a question and get a real answer?"

Depends on the question, thought Benny. There were some questions he'd rather throw himself off the roof than answer.

"Sure."

"Is he right? If Tom wasn't going to go, if it was just Lilah and me . . . would you go?"

"Without Tom?"

"Yes."

He settled back and looked at the clouds for almost a minute before he answered. It was a good question. The crucial question, and he'd wrestled with it and chewed on it since they'd seen the jet last year. Did he want to go?

Benny weighed his feelings very carefully. The answer was not a thing he could just reach inside and grab. It was buried deep, hidden in the soil of his subconscious and his needs and desires. On some level he knew that he needed to know who he was before he could rationally and accurately answer that question, and since last September he had been constantly trying to explore who he was. Especially in terms of who he was at this moment. If he didn't know who he was now, how could he know who he would be out there in the Ruin? What if he wasn't up to the challenge? What if after being out there he realized that he preferred the comforts of Mountainside? What if he wasn't a crusader for change after all?

Ugly, troublesome questions, and he had no real answers at all.

The ugliest part was that the one thing he was sure of was that he could find those answers only out in the Ruin. For good or ill.

"Yes," he said eventually. "Yes . . . I'd go with you no matter what."

Nix smiled and took his hand. "I believe you." She added, "If you'd answered right away I would have known you were lying. Telling me what I wanted to hear. I'm glad you respect me enough to think it through."

He said nothing, but he squeezed her hand.

"Benny?"

"Yeah?"

"Are you scared?"

"About tomorrow? Yeah," he said, "I'm freaking terrified."

"Me too." After a moment she said, "It's so big, you know?"

"Yeah."

"Leaving everything behind. Everyone we know."

"Yeah."

Five minutes rolled by, and the last of the clouds melted into endless blue. A lone hawk floated high above them.

Nix said, "I want to ask you one more thing."

He tensed, but said, "Okay."

Nix took his face in both of her hands. "Do you love me, Benny?"

Those five words sucked all the air out of planet Earth and left Benny gasping like a trout. His eyes wanted to look left and right to see if there was a way out of this. Maybe he could jump off the roof. Even with everything that had happened since last year, he had never worked up the courage to tell her that he loved her, and she had never even gone within pistol shot of the *L* word. And now she wanted him to come right out and say it. Not in some romantic moment, not while holding hands as they walked through spring flowers, or while snuggled together watching the sunset. Right here, right now, on his porch roof, with all the exits and doorways to a cowardly retreat nailed shut.

Her eyes were filled with green mystery and . . . and what? Challenge? Was this a test that was going to get him fried when he gave the wrong answer? Nix was devious and complicated enough for that sort of thing. Benny had grown up with her; he knew.

That wasn't it, though, and on some level he knew it.

No, when he tried to put a label on what he saw in her eyes, the one that seemed to fit best . . . was hope.

Hope. Suddenly his heart started beating again, or at least beating differently.

God . . . maybe if he jumped off the roof right now he would fly.

Benny licked his dry lips and swallowed a dry throat and in a dry voice said, "Yes."

Nix's eyes searched his, looking for a lie.

Somehow that made Benny feel stronger. He leaned toward her, letting her see everything she could find in his eyes.

He squeezed her hand. "Nix . . . I love you so much."

"You do?" she asked in a voice that was as fragile as a butterfly's wing.

"Yes. I love you. I really do." It felt strange to say aloud. Enormous and good and delicious.

But Nix's brow furrowed. "If you love me, then swear on that."

They were back to the question about leaving. Benny bowed his head for a moment, unable to bear the weight of what she was asking. Nix hooked a finger under his chin and lifted his face toward hers.

"Please, Benny . . ."

"I swear it, Nix. I love you and I swear on that."

Tears rolled down her cheeks, and she kissed him. Then Benny was on his knees, his arms wrapped around her, and both of them were crying, sobbing out loud under the bright blue sky. Even then, even with the terrible shared awareness of what lay behind them and before them, neither Benny nor Nix would ever be able to explain what it was that was breaking their hearts.

Benny thought about what Nix had said in the cemetery. That leaving was like dying.

FROM NIX'S JOURNAL

Questions:

Can zoms experience fear?

Do they know they're dead?

Can they feel any emotions? (Do they hate the living?)

"JUST SO I'M CLEAR ON THIS," SAID CHONG IN HIS CALMEST AND MOST reasonable voice. "You want to take us camping in the Rot and Ruin?"

"Yes," said Tom. "Just an overnight trip."

"Out where the zoms are?"

"Yes."

"Out where there are three hundred million zoms?"

Tom smiled. "I doubt there are that many of them left. I doubt there's more than two hundred million zoms left."

Chong peered at him with the flat stare of a lizard. "That's not as much of a comfort as you might think, Tom."

"Hundred million fewer things that want to eat you," said Benny. "Put it in the win category."

"Hush," said Chong, "there are grown folks talking."

Benny covertly offered a rude gesture.

They were in Benny's yard. Nix sat nearby, wiping down her wooden sword with oil and trying not to smile. Lilah sat cross-legged on the picnic table, strip-cleaning her Sig Sauer automatic pistol. Again.

"Are you going?" Chong asked her.

Lilah snorted. "Better than staying here. This town is worse than the Ruin. If they go," she said, indicating Tom, Benny, and Nix, "why would I want to stay here?"

Benny caught Chong's wince.

Damn, he thought, *that's got to hurt.*

It was clear from the frank look on Lilah's face that she had no idea that her words had just jabbed into Chong's flesh. Benny doubted she had a clue as to Chong's feelings.

"So that's the plan," Benny said brightly, trying to lighten the mood. "A last blast for the Chong-Imura Gang of Badasses."

"Language," said Tom, more out of reflex than anything else.

"'Chong-Imura'?" echoed Nix with a roll of her eyes. "Gang? Oh, please."

"Why camping?" asked Chong gloomily. "Why not just rub us all down with steak sauce and send us running into a herd of zoms?"

"I'm not actually trying to get you killed," said Tom.

"Oh, of course not. Our safely is clearly your first concern."

Tom sipped his iced tea. "We're going to be out there for months. We have to provide for ourselves. Besides, it's a good way to learn woodcraft."

"Woodcraft?" asked Benny. "What, like making chairs and tables and stuff? How's that—"

Chong elbowed him. "No, genius. Woodcraft is the art of living in the wild. Hunting, fishing, setting traps, finding herbs. That sort of stuff."

"How do you know that?"

"Because," Chong said with raised eyebrows, "when you

open those things called 'books,' there are words as well as pictures. Sometimes the words tell you stuff."

"Bite me."

"Not even if I was a starving zom." To Tom he said, "We learned some of that in the Scouts."

"Camping out in McGoran Field is hardly the same as surviving in the Rot and Ruin," chided Tom. "Lilah already knows how to do that. So do I. Benny and Nix learned a little when we were out in the Ruin, but they don't know enough."

"And I don't know any," concluded Chong. He sighed. "And I guess I don't really need any. You know what my parents think about your trip."

"You don't have to come camping with us," said Nix.

Chong sighed again. "No, I guess not."

"The thing is," said Tom, "the stuff Mr. Feeney taught you in the Scouts was all well and good, but it's old world. That's the problem with a lot of what you kids have been taught, and it's the problem with a lot of the books they make you read in school. They're good in themselves, but they aren't part of this world. It's important to know the past, but your survival depends on knowing the present. I mean . . . has Mr. Feeney been outside the gate recently?"

"Not since a few weeks after First Night," said Nix. "He got here around the same time as my mom, and I don't think he ever left again."

Tom nodded. "Right, which means that his knowledge is all based on camping in vacation spots and national parks as they were before the dead rose. He has no idea what it's like out there in the wild."

"The wild," echoed Chong, and looked a little pale. Of

his friends, Chong was the smartest and most well-read, but he was by far the least physical. Benny had to bully him into a game of soccer, and even then Chong preferred to be the goalie.

"When do we start?" Nix asked with enough enthusiasm to make Chong wince.

"First light," said Tom. He narrowed his eyes at Benny. "And that means we are up, washed, dressed, packed, and at the fence by first light . . . not hiding under your pillow pretending that I haven't been calling you to get up for two hours."

Benny made a show of innocence unfairly attacked, but no one bought it.

"Dress for hiking," Tom told them all. He pulled a slip of paper out of his pocket and handed it to Chong. "Here's a list of what you'll need."

Chong's eyes flicked down the list. "There's not a lot of stuff here, Tom."

"You won't want to carry a lot."

"No . . . I mean, there's stuff missing. Like . . . food."

"We'll forage and hunt. Nature provides, if you know how to ask."

"No tents?"

"You'll learn to build a basic shelter. All you need is a sleeping bag. We'll be roughing it."

"No toilet paper?"

Benny grinned. "That's what 'roughing it' means, Chong."

"We'll use bunches of grass or soft leaves," explained Tom.

Chong stared at him. "Please tell me you're joking."

"Early man didn't have toilet paper," said Benny. "I'll bet it even says so in one of your books."

"Early man, perhaps," Chong said icily, "but we did evolve."

Tom laughed. "Go pack."

THE HARDEST PART WAS SAYING GOOD-BYE.

Benny didn't have a lot of close friends in town, but there was Morgie. Nix had already said good-bye to him. Now it was Benny's turn.

He walked, hands in pockets, through the streets of town, looking at the familiar buildings and houses. There was Lafferty's General Store, where Benny and his gang drank sodas and opened packs of Zombie Cards. There were three nine-year-olds sitting on the wooden steps with several packs on their laps, laughing, showing one another cool cards. Heroes of First Night. Bounty Hunters. Famous Zoms. Maybe even one of the ultrarare Chase Cards.

Benny turned onto Morgie's street and saw the Mitchell house at the end of the block, perpetually in the shadow of two massive oaks. Morgie was sitting on the top step, stringing his fishing pole. His tackle box stood open beside him and his dog, Cletus, drowsed in a patch of sunlight.

Morgie looked up from his work as Benny walked up the flagstone path. "Hey," he said.

"Hey."

Morgie bent over the rod and carefully threaded catgut

through the guides. It was an old rod, made before First Night and beautifully tended to by Morgie. It had belonged to his father.

"Guess this is it, huh?" Morgie said in a voice that was flat and dead.

"We might be back," Benny began, but didn't finish because Morgie was already shaking his head.

"Don't lie, Benny."

"Sorry." Benny cleared his throat. "I wish you could come with us."

Morgie looked up, his face pinched and cold. "Really? You'd really want me to come with you—"

"Sure—"

"—and Nix?"

There it was. As quick and sharp as a slap.

"Morgie, c'mon, man. I thought you were over her last year. . . ."

"You've been too busy getting ready for your big adventure . . . how would you know what anyone else was feeling?" Benny started to reply, but Morgie shook his head in disgust. "Just . . . go away, Benny."

Benny stepped forward. "Don't be like that."

Morgie suddenly flung his fishing pole away and shot to his feet. His face was red and filled with fury and hurt. "I HATE YOU!" he yelled. Cletus woke up and barked in alarm, birds leaped in panic from the oak trees.

"Hey, man," said Benny defensively, "what the hell? What's this crap all about?"

"It's about you and her ditching me and going off with her on some great adventure."

Benny stared at him. "You're crazy."

Morgie stormed down the steps and shoved Benny as hard as he could. Morgie was a lot bigger and stronger, and Benny staggered back and fell. Morgie took a threatening step closer, following Benny as he fell, fists balled with rage.

"I frigging hate you, Benny. You pretend you're my friend, but you took Nix and now you're dumping me and going off together. You and that bitch, Nix."

Benny stared in total shock, then he felt his own anger starting to rise. He scrambled to his feet.

"You can say whatever you want to say about me, Morgie," he warned, "but don't ever call Nix names."

"Or what?" Morgie challenged, moving in almost chest to chest.

Benny knew that Morgie could take him in a fight. Morgie was always the toughest of the crowd, the one who never backed down. He had tried to stand up to Charlie and the Hammer at the Riley house, and nearly died for it.

Morgie shoved him again, but this time Benny was expecting it, and all it did was knock him back a few steps. As he staggered, his heel came down on the fishing rod, and there was a sharp *crack!*

They both stared down at it. They had caught a hundred trout with that rod. They had spent thousands of hours sitting on the banks of the stream, talking about everything. Now it lay snapped into two pieces that could never be mended. Benny's heart sank. As symbolic incidents go, it had too much drama and no comfort at all, and he cursed the universe for making a joke like that at a time like this.

Morgie shook his head and turned away. He walked to

the steps, climbed heavily up to the porch, and then stopped. He half turned, and in an ugly growl of a voice he said, "I hope you die out there, Benny. I hope you all die out there."

He went inside and slammed the door.

Benny stood in the yard for a long time, staring at the house, willing Morgie to come outside. He would rather have fought him and gotten his ass kicked than have things end like this. He wanted to scream, to shout, to demand that Morgie come back outside. To take back those words.

But the door remained stubbornly shut.

Slowly, brokenly, Benny turned and walked back home.

FROM NIX'S JOURNAL

Tools of the Zombie Hunter Trade

BOKKEN: A wooden sword developed by the Japanese. The name combines two words, bo ("wood") and ken ("sword"). The bokken is used for training and is usually the same length and shape as the katana, the steel sword carried by samurai. Also called a bokuto.

My bokken is thirty-nine inches long and is made from air-dried hickory. It weighs five pounds.

Benny's bokken is forty-one inches long and made from white oak. (So far he's cracked three of them, and Tom is getting mad at him.)

WHEN THE FIRST PROMISE OF SUNRISE GLIMMERED BEYOND THE TREE LINE of the forest, Tom had them all rigged and ready at the gate.

Over the last few weeks Tom had gotten the mayor's wife to sew each of them a vest made from very tough pre–First Night canvas. The vests had lots of pockets and were extremely durable. Benny filled his pockets with gum, all-weather matches, a compass, spools of wire and twine, and a hand line for fishing. He tried not to think about Morgie as he stuffed this last item into its pocket. Tried and failed.

As they checked their gear, Benny kept looking back toward town.

"He'll be here," Nix said.

But Morgie never came.

Tom bought each of them three small bottles of cadaverine and a pot of mint gel from a vendor at the gate. The cadaverine was a chemical harvested from rotting flesh—and Benny was almost completely sure that it was made from dead animals and not from other sources . . . like maybe dead zoms. Dribbling it on clothes and hair made the living smell like rotting corpses. Zoms did not attack other zoms, so the smell usually kept the wearer safe.

Chong sniffed the cadaverine and winced. "Charming."

Tom handed them the mint gel and said to Chong, "When we use the cadaverine, it's best to rub this on your upper lip. It overwhelms your sense of smell."

Chong began unscrewing the cap, but Tom said, "Not yet. We'll use the cadaverine and the mint as a last resort. We'll conserve it for now."

"Why?" asked Chong. "Why not buy a couple of gallons of it and take a bath in the stuff?"

Benny leaned closed and said under his breath, "Yeah, that'd make Lilah want to crawl all over you."

Without changing expression, Chong murmured, "Feel free to fall over and die."

Benny grinned. He was surprised he still could. He threw one last look back toward town. No Morgie. He closed his eyes and took a deep breath and tried to let it go. The ache, the betrayal, the memory of Morgie's last words. When he breathed, it felt like his lungs were on fire. He kept doing it until something in his mind shifted.

We're leaving, he thought. *It's really happening.*

At the same moment that he thought that, a second thought flitted through his mind. *There's no turning back now.*

The juxtaposition of the two thoughts was deeply disturbing, and he recalled his musings yesterday when Nix asked him if he wanted to go. Part of him answered, *I want to go,* but a different part whispered, *I am going.* They were totally different answers.

Nix, intuitive as ever, caught his eye and with a look asked if he was okay. Without waiting for an answer, she cut a look back to the empty fence, and her shoulders slumped. She looked at Benny and nodded sadly.

Good-bye, Morgie, Benny thought.

"Okay," Tom said, "here's the way we're going to do it. I lead, you follow. When I give instructions, I want you to pay attention. No screwing around."

He was looking at Benny and Chong when he said this last part, and they affected to look like angels falsely accused of grievous sins.

"I'm serious," Tom said. "I know that we're all armed and you've each had some training, but in the Ruin you only get to make one mistake. And then you're dead."

Lilah made a noise low in her throat when Tom said that, and Benny unconsciously touched the point on his throat where she'd pressed her blade on the Matthias lawn after the fight with Big Zak and Zak Junior. Nix must have had the same thought, because she took a half step to stand between Benny and Lilah, and there was no trace of a smile on her face.

Tom adjusted the sling that supported his steel *katana*, then cleared his throat. "Once the fence guards draw the zoms down to the far end, we go out and head straight for the tree line. Single file. I'll lead, then Nix, Benny, Chong, and Lilah. Got it?"

Everyone nodded.

"Keep your weapons slung. Right now speed is more important than anything. The guards will try to keep the zoms distracted until we're clear. After that, we're on our own."

"What if we run into a zom?" asked Chong.

"If we do, I'll see it first. Let me handle it. If it comes at you from the side, Lilah will take care of it." Tom gave them all a hard look. "I don't want any heroics. I'm still pissed at you guys for going up on Zak's porch. You should have called me or Captain Strunk. That's not exactly the way to be warrior smart. I know you think you're hotshots, but you are a long way from being real samurai. A skilled fighter doesn't take needless risks. Do you understand?"

They nodded.

"No," Tom said sternly, "say it."

They said it.

The glimmer of light at the tree line had brightened enough for them to see the zoms wandering in the field or standing like statues. Most zoms only moved to follow prey but would otherwise stop walking and stand still. Benny had seen zoms out in the Ruin with years' worth of creeper vines tangled around their legs. He still wasn't sure if that was sad or terrifying.

Tom finally gave a grudging nod. He stepped up to the gate.

"Get ready," he said quietly, then waved to the sergeant in charge of the night shift. The sergeant whistled, and his men immediately started banging on drums and steel pots as they walked quickly north along the fence line. The zoms in the field stiffened for a moment, drawn through whatever senses they possessed by the noise and movement. One by one they turned, moaning softly, their gray-lipped mouths working as if practicing in anticipation of eating a grisly meal, and began shambling up the field. Benny and his friends watched with awful fascination.

"It's so strange," said Nix quietly. "How can they be dead and do that? React to sound? Follow? Hunt?"

"No one knows," said Tom. "They don't need to eat. They get no benefit from killing. They can go years and years without decaying any more than they already have. No one understands it."

Chong shook his head. "There has to be an answer. Something in science."

"As far as we know, all the scientists are dead," said Tom. "Except for Doc Gurijala, and he was a just a general practitioner."

"Has he ever examined one?" asked Nix.

"No," said Tom quietly, so as not to attract the shuffling zoms. "I suggested it to him a hundred times. I said that it might help us understand what they are and what we're up against. That was not long after First Night, when we still thought there was a way to win. He called me crazy for even suggesting it. I tried him a couple of other times since, but Doc says that science ends at the fence line."

"What does that mean?" asked Nix.

"It means," Tom said, "that Doc Gurijala believes that whatever makes the dead do what they do isn't science. It's something else."

Nix cocked an eyebrow. "Magic?"

Tom shrugged.

Chong said, "Magic is fairy-tale stuff. If this is happening, then there has to be an explanation. Maybe Doc Gurijala doesn't know enough science to understand what's happening. I mean . . . this has to be a specialty."

"Like . . .?" Nix asked.

"I don't know. Physics. Molecular biology. Genetics. Who knows? Just because we don't have anyone here who understands it doesn't mean that we have to jump right into a supernatural answer."

Tom nodded at this.

"What about something else?" asked Nix. "What about something evil? What if it's demons or ghosts or something like that? What if this is something . . . I don't know, biblical?"

"Oh boy," breathed Chong. "What—there was no more room in hell, so the dead started walking the earth?"

She shrugged. "Why not?"

"Impossible."

"Why?" she challenged. "Because you don't believe in anything?"

"I believe in science."

Nix pointed to the creatures in the field. "How does science explain that?"

"I don't know, Nix, but I believe there's an answer." Chong cocked his head to one side. "Are you saying that you don't believe in science? Or are you saying that there has to be a religious answer? And since when did you get religious? You skip church as much as I do."

Benny gave Tom an *Oh boy, here we go* look.

Nix shook her head. "I'm not saying anything has to be anything, Chong. I'm saying that we should keep an open mind. Science may not have all the answers."

"I keep a very open mind, thank you very much . . . but I don't think we're going to get anywhere looking for answers outside of science."

"Why not?"

"Because—"

"Enough!" Lilah's ghostly voice cut through their debate and silenced them. "Talk, talk, talk . . . how does that get anything done?"

"Lilah," began Chong, "we were just—"

"No," she barked. "No talk. Now is the time to run. You want answers? Both of you? Find them out there!"

With that she turned and walked to the gate and stood with her back to them, her spear held loosely in her strong hands.

"Lady has a point," said Tom. "Not really the time for this kind of debate. Let's roll."

He clapped Benny on the shoulder and then walked over to join Lilah. The field in front of the gate was almost clear of zoms now, and the last stragglers were lurching along the field.

Benny gave Nix and Chong a crooked grin. "You two need a referee. Jeez."

Nix smiled a cold little smile and walked briskly away. The two boys lingered a moment longer. Chong said, "So, where do you stand in all this?"

"Where I usually do," said Benny. "Without a freaking clue. And right now that feels like a safe place to stand. C'mon, Mr. Wizard . . . let's go."

The last of the zoms was fifty yards along the fence line now, and Tom nodded to the gateman, who quietly lifted the restraining bar. The hinges were always well-oiled to allow for silence. Tom leaned out and peered through the gloom.

Benny stood beside him, watching the shadowy figures

move away. In a weird way he felt sorry for the monsters; even sorry that they were being so easily tricked. It felt like taking advantage of someone with brain damage or a birth defect. It felt like bullying, even though that wasn't at all what it was.

Tom glanced at him. "What's wrong, kiddo?"

Benny nodded toward the zombies, but he didn't try to explain. If anyone would understand, it would be Tom. His brother placed a hand on his shoulder.

"I know," he said, but added, "But don't let compassion for them trick you into making a mistake."

"I won't," Benny assured him, but his voice lacked conviction, even in his own ears.

Tom gave his shoulder a squeeze, then turned to the others.

"Okay—remember what I said. Keep low, move fast, and don't stop until you're in the trees. Ready? Let's go!"

One by one they slipped out through the gate and ran at full speed to the bank of purple shadows beyond which the morning sun was rising.

Benny turned once more as they ran. The guards had closed the fence, and the town of Mountainside was locked on the other side. Everything he knew, nearly everyone he had ever met was behind that fence. His home, his school. Morgie. All of it was back there. There had been no teary farewells. If Tom had said good-bye to Mayor Kirsch or Captain Strunk or any of the others, Benny hadn't seen him do it, and no one had come to the fence line to see them off.

It was everything that was wrong about Mountainside in a nutshell. Just as the people inside acted as if there was no world beyond the chain-link wall, they would probably write

Tom, Nix, and Benny off as people they once knew. Like the people who died on First Night. The people in town would deliberately forget them; it was easier than imagining what might be happening out here in the Ruin.

In a way, Benny and the others would be dead to the people in town. Would the townsfolk become dead to Benny? Would their memory die in his heart?

He hoped not.

He slowed a little as he ran, searching the span of the fence, willing Morgie to be there. Just to wave good-bye. It would heal everything, fix everything.

The fence line was the fence line, and nobody waved good-bye.

Benny turned away and made himself run faster.

The five of them made no sound, and within a few minutes even the sharpest of the tower guards could not see them. The forest appeared to swallow them whole.

PART TWO

DOWN THE ROAD AND GONE

Life is either a daring adventure or nothing.
To keep our faces toward change and behave like
free spirits in the presence of fate is strength
undefeatable.

—HELEN KELLER

THEY RAN DEEP INTO THE WOODS, FOLLOWING A PATH THAT WAS ALWAYS kept clear for the traders who brought in wagons of goods scavenged from warehouses and small towns throughout that part of Mariposa County—or what had been Mariposa County before First Night had invalidated all the old maps. As the sun rose it was easier for Benny to avoid stepping in the wheel ruts. Chong, who was much less coordinated, tripped several times. Lilah helped him up each time, but instead of it being an act of kind assistance, she growled at him, and each time she shoved him forward a little harder. Nix caught up to run side by side with Benny, and they both grinned back at Chong. He mouthed some words at them that made them laugh and that would have shocked Chong's parents and earned a sharp rebuke from Tom.

After a half mile Tom slowed from a full-out run to a light trot, and a mile later eased down to a walk; and finally stopped for a rest. Benny was winded and walked around with his hands over his head to open his lungs up. He was sweating, but the exertion felt good. Nix's face glowed pink, and her skin gleamed with a fine film of perspiration, but she was smiling.

Chong went over to the side of the road and threw up.

Leaning on her spear, Lilah watched with unconcealed contempt.

It was not that Chong was frail—he had trained as hard as everyone else and his lean body was packed with wiry muscles—but he never reacted well to sustained exertion.

Benny patted Chong on the back, but as he did so he bent down and quietly said, "Dude, you're completely embarrassing our gender here."

Between gasps Chong gave Benny a thorough description of where to go and what to do when he got there.

"Okay," said Benny, "I can see that you need some alone time. Good talk."

He wandered off to stand with Nix, who was taking several small sips from her canteen. Tom came over to join them.

"Chong okay?" Tom asked.

"He'll live," Benny said. "He doesn't like physical exertion."

"No, really?" Tom grinned and gestured to a fork in the road. "Soon as everyone's caught their breath, we'll go that way. It's high ground, so we'll see fewer zoms today. Tomorrow we'll see about going downland to where the dead are."

"Why?" asked Nix. "Wouldn't it be better to avoid them completely?"

"Can't," said Lilah, who had drifted silently up to join them. "Not forever. Dead are everywhere. Even up in the hills."

Benny sighed. "Swell."

"Are we going to hunt them?" asked Nix, her eyes wide.

Tom considered. "Hunt? Yes. Kill? No. I want you to be

able to track them, but I mostly want you to be able to avoid them. We can go over theory from now until the cows come home, but that's not the same as practical experience."

"Sounds wonderful," muttered Chong as he joined them. His color was bad, but better than it had been during the last quarter mile of their run.

"It won't be," Tom said seriously. "It's going to scare the hell out of you, and maybe break your heart."

They looked at him in surprise.

"What?" Tom said slowly. "Did you think this was going to be fun?"

They didn't answer.

"You see, this is one of the reasons I wanted to bring you out here," Tom said. "When everything is theoretical, when it's all discussion rather than action, it's easy to talk about zoms as if they're not real. Like characters in a story."

"They're abstract," Chong suggested, and Tom nodded approval.

"Right. But out here they're real and tangible."

Benny shifted uncomfortably. "And they're people."

Tom nodded. "Yes. That's something we can't ever forget. Every single zom, every man, woman, and child, no matter how decayed or how frightening they are, no matter how dangerous they are—they were all once real people. They had names, and lives, and personalities, and families. They had dreams and goals. They had pasts and they thought they had futures, but something came and took that away from them."

"Which is another one of the mysteries," said Nix under her breath.

"Yeah, yeah, yeah," said Chong, and nudged her with his elbow. She grinned and nudged him back, harder.

Tom said, "We don't know how far we'll have to go to find the jet. If we find it. We saw it fly east, but it could have landed anywhere."

Benny winced. "Ouch."

"No, don't worry about that part. We'll find some clues. Other people will have seen it too, and there are people out here. We'll ask everyone we see . . . but a lot of those folks live in the downlands, and there are large parts of the country that don't have mountains. So it's pretty likely we'll be where the zoms are. No way to avoid it."

"So learn how to be with the dead," added Lilah. It wasn't an eloquent statement, but they all understood her meaning.

Tom clapped Chong on the arm. "You ready to go? The next part is a leisurely walk in the country."

"That's better."

"No, it's not," said Lilah, laying her spear over her shoulder. "Everything out here wants to kill you."

She walked along the path, and Chong stared after her. "Honestly," he said, "I already got the message. That last part? Not necessary."

Nix was laughing as she followed Lilah. Benny laid his bokken across his shoulder, and in a fair imitation of Lilah's whispery voice said, "Everything wants to kill out-of-shape monkey-bangers named Chong. Everything."

He strolled off.

Chong took a deep breath and followed.

FROM NIX'S JOURNAL

Tools of the Zombie Hunter Trade, Part Two

LILAH'S SPEAR. The shaft of the spear is made from a six-foot length of three-quarter-inch black pipe. There are brown doeskin leather bands around both ends and on two places in the middle where she usually holds it. The blade is from a Marine Corps bayonet. The blade is black and eight inches long.

She says this is the fourth spear she's made. She lost one when she was first taken to Gameland (she was eleven, and that spear was five feet long). She lost the second one while running from the Motor City Hammer three years ago. The third one bent while she was breaking into an old library to get books. The fourth one is a year old.

Benny walked alongside Tom for a while. "I overheard you talking with Basher yesterday."

Tom gave him a brief look. "What did you hear?"

"Bunch of stuff. Mostly about trouble out here in the Ruin. About people coming in to take over Charlie Pink-eye's territory."

"Uh-huh."

"So . . . ?"

"What do you mean? So . . . what?"

"Well," Benny said, "aren't we going to do something about it?"

"'We'?"

"Yes, 'we.' You, me, Lilah, Nix . . . I mean, before we leave the area?"

Tom shook his head. "No."

"Why not? These are your woods, man. You spent years out here cleaning them up and stuff."

"No, I spent years out here as a bounty hunter and closure specialist. It was never my job or my intention to 'clean things up.' Not then and definitely not now." He paused and looked back at the others, who were a hundred yards down the road. Nix and Chong were talking together— probably continuing their argument about the mysteries of the zombie plague; Lilah was bringing up the rear, content to keep company with herself. "Look at them, Benny. Lilah's not even seventeen. Nix just turned fifteen. You and Chong will be sixteen in a few months. You're tough, but let's face it . . . you're not an army. I can't even say with total conviction that you're all tough enough to do what we're attempting, and it scares me green to think that I might be leading you to your deaths. I'm not going to make that a certainty by taking you into a pitched battle with fifty or sixty armed bounty hunters."

"But what about Gameland? If they've moved it somewhere closer to town, then they might be grabbing more kids from town. Like they tried to do with Nix. We can't just—"

"I've been trying to get the town to do something for years."

"I know. I also heard you talking to Mayor Kirsch and Captain Strunk."

"What are you, the town snoop?"

"Dude, you were talking in the yard. My window's right there."

"Okay, okay. Point is, the town has to take responsibility for itself. I showed them that it could be done, and I did what I could for a while . . . but it's not one man's job. And it's not the job of children."

"Teenagers, thank you very much."

"Teenagers. Fine. It's not your job either."

Benny looked hard into his brother's eyes. "Are you sure?"

"Yes."

"I'm not. This is our world too. We're going to inherit it. What do you want us to do—wait until it gets worse, maybe totally out of control, before we do something about it? How's that going to help us have a better future?"

Tom stared at him as they walked, and after a dozen steps his frown turned into a small smile. "I keep forgetting how smart you are, kiddo. And how mature."

"Yeah, well, this last year hasn't exactly been about kid stuff."

"No, and I'm sorry about that . . . but in all seriousness, Benny, this is a conversation we should have had before we left."

"So . . . it's too late to make a difference?" Benny challenged.

Tom shook his head. "It's not that . . . it's just that this isn't our town anymore. We're moving on. Others will have to step up to take responsibility for Mountainside." He pointed down the road. "Your future is somewhere out there, and no doubt there will be plenty of opportunities to make a difference, if that's what you want to do."

Benny glanced at him, then back the way they'd come, then up ahead. He sighed.

Tom clapped him on the shoulder, and they kept walking. Eventually Tom pulled ahead, and when Benny looked back, he saw that Nix was now with Lilah and Chong was alone, so he drifted back to walk beside Chong.

As they walked through the tall grass under the burning eye of the sun, Benny kept glancing at Chong. Without turning his head, Chong said, "What? Do I have a booger in my nose?"

"Huh?"

"You keep looking at me. What's up?"

Benny shrugged.

"Quick! Tell me before I lose interest." Chong said it with mock excitement.

Benny took a breath. "Nix."

"What? The fight about science and religion?"

"No . . . it's about us. You know . . . dating and stuff."

"God!" Chong laughed. "The oath!"

When he and Chong were nine, they had sworn a blood oath that they would never date any of the girls they hung with. Since getting back from rescuing Nix last year, they had been together, and Benny had never asked Chong how he felt about it.

"Yeah . . . the oath," Benny said. "I feel kind of bad about breaking it."

Chong stopped and turned to him, his eyes roving over Benny's face. "Wait . . . hold still."

Benny froze. "What? What is it? Do I have something—"

Chong whacked him on the head with his open palm.

"Ow! What was it? Was it a bee?"

"No. I just wanted to see if I could slap some of the stupid out of you."

"Hey!"

"Jeez, Benny, we made that oath when we were nine."

"It was a blood oath."

"We'd cut our fingers baiting fishhooks. That oath was spur of the moment, immature—and dumb. Mind you, we've both had dumber moments. You more than me, of course . . ."

"Hey!"

"But it didn't really matter much then, and it doesn't matter at all now."

They walked about a hundred paces in silence. "We gave our words, Chong," said Benny.

Chong grunted. "You never cease to amaze me," he said. "Though seldom in a good way."

"Yeah, yeah, yeah. So, if you're so wise and insightful, O Mighty Chong, then how come you've never told Lilah that you have a crush on her?"

"Ah. I'm wise and insightful, but not brave."

"Have you tried?"

Chong colored. "I . . . wrote a note."

"What did it say?"

"It . . . um . . . had some poetry. And some other stuff," Chong said evasively.

"Did she read it?"

"I left it where she could find it. Next day I found it in the trash."

"Ouch."

"Maybe she misunderstood. After all, it's not like she's been around the dating scene. All she knows about romance is what she's read in books."

"Maybe, but why not just cowboy up and ask her? Worst she can do is say no."

Chong gave him a withering stare. "Really? That's the worst you think she can do?" He sighed. "Besides, it doesn't much matter anymore. You guys are leaving tomorrow and I'll never see her again."

"Yeah," Benny said softly. "Sorry, man."

They looked covertly over their shoulders to where Lilah

padded along like a fierce hunting cat. She caught them looking at her and growled, "Pay attention to the woods before something bites you!"

They snapped their heads around forward, but Benny was laughing quietly. Chong made a pained face.

"You see what I mean? She lived with us. You should see her before she's had her morning coffee."

"Mmm . . . does that mean that if you two crazy kids had managed to make a go of it, you'd have been the girl in the relationship?"

"How about you go stick a baseball bat up your—"

"Freeze!"

Tom's sharp whisper cut through the air and rooted everyone in place.

Thirty yards up the path Tom stood in a half crouch, his right hand raised to grip the handle of his *katana*. Fifty yards behind them Nix and Lilah were in the middle of the road. Nix had her bokken out; Lilah held her spear ready in a two-handed grip.

"What is it?" Benny whispered, but Tom held up a finger, cautioning him to be silent. On either side of them trees rose in dark columns to form a canopy that obscured most of the sunlight, allowing only stray beams to slant down. At ground level the shrubs and wild plant life clustered so densely around the tree trunks that they formed an impenetrable wall; Benny could see nothing of what might be coming toward them. He and Chong drew their bokkens and shifted to stand with their backs to each other, just as Tom had taught them.

Lilah came running along the path on silent cat feet, with

Nix a few yards behind. The Lost Girl had a fierce light in her eyes as she slowed to a stop beside Tom, making sure to stand well clear of his sword arm.

"What is it?" she hissed. "The dead?"

Tom shook his head but said nothing.

Nix joined Benny and Chong, and the three of them shifted into a three-sided combat formation.

"You see anything?" Nix whispered.

"No," said Chong. "Don't hear anything either."

It was true; the forest was as silent as the grave, an image that did not make Benny feel very good. He sniffed the air. The forest offered up a thousand scents. Flowers and tree bark and rich soil and . . .

And what?

There was a smell on the air. Faint but getting stronger.

"Can you guys smell that?" Benny murmured.

"Uh-huh," said Nix. "Smells weird. Kind of familiar . . . but not really."

Lilah raised her spear and pointed into the woods with the gleaming blade. "There," she said. "It's coming toward us."

"What is it?" Nix asked in a frightened whisper.

Tom drew his *katana*. "Get ready."

"To do what?" demanded Benny. "Fight or run?"

"We're about to find out," said Tom.

"Please," murmured Chong, "don't let it be zoms. Don't let it be zoms."

"No," said Tom, "it's not the dead. Whatever's coming is very much alive."

Benny and the others heard it then. A crunch as something heavy stepped down on fallen twigs, the sound muffled by the nearly decayed carpet of last year's leaves. A moment later there was another sound, different, low and strange. Benny and Nix exchanged a look. She raised her eyebrows.

"Sounds like a bull," she said.

Benny frowned. "Out here?"

"Lots of animals running wild out here," said Tom. "This was farm country before First Night."

The sound came again, deeper and louder.

"Awful big bull," Chong said.

There was more of the twig crunching, and each time the sound was louder and closer.

"Shouldn't we, um . . . run?" suggested Chong.

"Sounds like a plan to me," said Benny.

Lilah hissed at them to be quiet, adding, "Running makes you prey. It's better to fight than be hunted."

Tom opened his mouth to say something, possibly to counter her absolute viewpoint, but then there was a loud snort and grunt as something gigantic crashed through the wall of shrubs and vines. Creeper vines snapped like spiderwebs as it shouldered its way out of the forest and onto the road. It lumbered into the middle of the path not thirty feet from where Benny, Nix, and Chong stood, and it paused, sniffing the air.

It was a monster. Slate gray and black-eyed, standing on four short legs, each with a three-toed foot that was bigger than Benny's head. Immense, with a massive chest and shoulders that were unlike anything Benny had seen in the flesh. In books, sure, but he had thought that creatures like this belonged to a different age of the world.

"Oh my God!" whispered Nix, then immediately clapped

a hand to her mouth as the creature turned its enormous head toward her.

This was easily three times bigger than the largest bull in Mountainside. Benny remembered reading about it. The second largest land mammal in the world after the elephant. The whole thing had to be fourteen feet long and over six feet at the shoulders. Thick humps of muscle stood out on its neck to support the long head with a vast snout, from which sprouted two deadly horns, the longer of which was a thirty-inch spike that could have punched right through Benny's body.

It stood its ground, ears swiveling independently to catch all sound, nostrils huffing to gather the smells of the five people crouched in the road.

Benny stared, eyes goggled wide, mouth open.

"Is that a . . . a . . . a . . . ?" Nix tried to ask.

"Uh-huh," said Chong.

The creature turned its head sharply toward them.

"I'm dreaming this, right?" asked Benny.

"Not a dream," Lilah whispered, but even she looked rattled.

"It's a white rhinoceros," declared Chong, a little too loudly. "But how?"

"Shut up!" warned Tom, but it was too late.

The huge animal suddenly gave a loud, wet snort and took a challenging step toward Chong. The massive rhinoceros grunted, a deep sound that was full of meaning and menace. It pawed the ground and blew out its nostrils.

"Okay," said Tom. "Run."

There was a beat where they all looked at him.

"NOW!"

The rhino tilted its wicked horns toward them, bunched the gigantic muscles of its back and hindquarters . . . and charged.

"Go! Go . . . GO!" bellowed Tom as he grabbed Nix and Benny and Chong and shoved them toward the forest wall. "Into the trees!"

"I'm sorry!" yelled Chong.

"Shut up and run!"

The ground shook as seven thousand pounds of furious muscle rumbled toward them. Despite its size, the animal was incredibly fast. Lilah flung her spear at it, but the blade merely slashed a red groove along its armored shoulder. It did nothing except make the rhino madder.

"Oh," she said softly, and then she was running too.

Tom lingered a split second longer, sighting along the barrel of his gun at the rhino's black eye. Then he whipped the gun away, shoved it into its holster, and ran as fast as his legs could carry him. He caught up with the others and yelled at them to cut left so that they were running almost parallel to the road.

The rhino tried to turn sharply to intercept, but the angle was too sharp. Its huge feet skidded on the dried mud of the road. Then, with a roar, it headed straight into the forest. The rhino's shoulders slammed into a pair of slender pines, snapping them at the base.

"Use the trees," yelled Tom. "Circle around the big ones."

Nix was in the lead, and she shifted her angle to head toward a gnarled old sycamore. She dodged behind it, then spun and pulled Benny and Chong in behind her.

The rhino spotted them and charged. It veered at the last second, so instead of hitting the tree full on, its horns slashed a deep gouge in the wood and shook the old sycamore from roots to leaves. The rhino whirled and rammed the tree again, and Benny threw his arm up to shield his eyes from the spray of splinters the impact blew out of the gouge. The animal tried to chase them around the tree, but they were more agile. It snorted and trotted away, then cut left and rammed again, and this time there was a *crack!* and the sycamore canted sideways and crashed down on the grass with a huge leafy *whumpf!*

"Now what do we do?" whispered Chong in a strangled voice. Benny shot a look at him and saw that his friend's eyes were wide and jumpy with fear that was very quickly going to overwhelm him.

The beast galloped forty feet away and then cut right into a tight circle. This time it didn't attack the tree but instead began angling to come around the trunk and go straight for Chong. The rhino came at them like a thunderbolt.

"HEY!" Nix yelled as she stood up and waved her arms over her head. Instantly the rhino changed the angle of its charge and came straight for her. "Come on!" she cried to Benny, and then she was racing away from the fallen tree.

"What are you doing?" Benny yelled in panic, but as soon

as he said it he understood. Nix tore across ten yards of open field toward a line of massive oaks. The rhino could never hope to knock one of them over.

Benny turned to pull Chong over the trunk so they could follow, but Chong was gone. Benny caught a glimpse of him running away from the oaks, heading toward a cluster of pines.

"Chong, no! Not that way!"

The rhino slowed to a trot and looked from Benny to Nix and then at Chong. Nix was vanishing behind the trunk of a monstrous oak. Benny was still partly covered by the huge bulk of dark roots from the overturned sycamore. Chong had a longer run ahead of him, and the only protection he had was a line of pines. Their bushy branches would hide him, but the soft pines offered no protection at all.

The rhino charged after Chong.

Benny broke from the side of the sycamore and began shouting as Nix had. "Hey! Big and ugly! Over here!"

But if the rhino heard him, it didn't care. Chasing Chong was a straight run and an easy kill. It thundered after Chong, crushing huckleberry bushes and saplings under its ponderous bulk.

Benny made it to Nix's oak and kept running. She was right with him, and they sprinted down the corridor of old oaks, heading for a gap that looked like it might have been either a country lane or a firebreak. Benny pointed as he ran, and Nix nodded. There was a chance they could turn left at the last oak, dash across the break, and enter the grove of pines. Benny figured they could come up behind Chong, pause long enough to beat some sense into him, then grab him and race back to the oaks.

At the break they paused for a moment, looking around for Tom and Lilah. Benny spotted them, but they were on the other side of the rhino. Lilah was climbing into a cottonwood tree. Tom was circling to try and cut the animal's line of approach to the wall of pines.

"Hey!" Tom yelled. "Here!" He jumped up and down, waving his arms. When he got no reaction, he fired a shot into the air. That did it. The rhino skidded to a stop and turned its vicious eye on this new target. Benny was hoping that the animal would be getting tired by now, chasing one thing and then another. No such luck.

"It looks really, really mad," said Nix.

The rhinoceros snorted a challenge, pawed the ground like a bull, tensed, and then launched itself straight for Tom.

"Oh, crap," said Benny, but he wasn't talking about the danger Tom was in. Tom apparently had a plan. Tom always had a plan. No, he caught movement from the pines and saw Chong break cover to watch what Tom and the rhino were doing. The rhino twitched its head as it noticed Chong.

"Oh for the love of—," Benny began, then saved his breath for running.

Chong was smarter than Benny, but in his panic he wasn't using that brain. Rhinos were not like people, cats, dogs, and hunting birds. They weren't predators. Despite the creature's formidable strength and size, it was built for protection. Predators have eyes that look forward. Prey animals have eyes on the sides of their head. Usually that was to allow them to see threats creeping up from all sides. In this case . . .

Once more the rhino wheeled and circled back toward Chong, who screeched, wheeled, and ran back toward the screen of pines.

"Why does it keep going after Chong?" asked Nix as they ran.

"'Cause he keeps heading for those pines," grunted Benny.

"Yeah, but why?"

Tom fired another shot. The rhino ignored him this time and kept charging toward Chong. Tom yelled louder and jumped up and down, but the rhino had its eyes fixed on Chong. "Not that way!"

Chong either couldn't hear or was too scared to pay attention.

Benny and Nix headed into the overgrown firebreak, crashing through the chest-high weeds, heading at a sharp angle to cut into the pines behind Chong so they could lead him out. The edge of the pine screen was fifty yards away. Benny saw that the shrubs and plants around here were already flattened down by the rhino's massive feet, as if it had passed that way a hundred times.

Benny was only a half step behind Nix. Then she screamed and suddenly pitched forward into the grass five feet in front of him. Benny had no way of stopping himself in time, and his foot caught on something and he was falling too. He landed on her legs, the impact punching a yelp of pain out of her.

"Oooof! Sorry!" he said as he rolled quickly to his left.

And looked right into the eyes of a zom.

BENNY SCREAMED.

Nix looked up. She saw the zombie . . . and screamed.

The zom lay in the tall weeds inches from them. It did not scream. It snarled.

Then it lurched forward and tried to bite Benny's face.

Nix grabbed his shoulder and hauled him back, and the creature's teeth bit only empty air where Benny's cheek had been. Benny flung himself backward, pushing Nix and himself away from the rotting teeth of the zom and the reaching white hands, but he wasn't fast enough. One hand closed around his left sneaker, and the teeth chomped down on the rubber toe. Benny howled in agony as his toe was crunched between the zom's jagged teeth.

God! Am I bit? Am I bit? Am I bit? The litany of dread played over and over in his head.

He swung his right foot and kicked the zom in the face, once, twice, again and again. The creature was dressed in farmer's coveralls and had huge hands and shoulders. Even crippled and dead, it was immensely strong. Benny kept kicking, putting all his weight and fear into it, feeling the shock of each impact shoot like hot needles up his shin.

Old bone cracked and rotted teeth snapped and then he was free.

He pushed Nix away from the monster. She got to her feet and started to run, and immediately she screamed and fell. Benny scrabbled backward and turned to see a sight that threatened to tear the soul out of him. A second zom had crawled out of the weeds and attacked Nix. It had once been a huge woman, and it wore the black-and-white rags of a nun's habit. There were two bullet holes in its cheeks, but they were ancient and the bullets had missed spine or brain. The zom had Nix pinned to the ground by the shoulders and was bending to take a bite that would destroy everything good and wonderful in Benny's world.

Nix's face was covered in bright red blood. A black snake of terror reared up inside Benny's chest. But his rage was bigger than his fear.

"NIX!"

He bellowed louder than a bull, louder than the rhino. He screamed a great unintelligible shriek of denial as he launched himself at the zom. His bokken lay forgotten in the weeds. He did not even think of pulling his knife. He crossed his arms over his face and slammed into the zom, hitting it like a thunderbolt.

"Get away from her!"

The impact knocked the zom backward, and they fell together in a hissing, snarling tangle, rolling over and over as Nix's scream filled the air.

The creature was desiccated, however; its arms were strong, but as they rolled Benny felt the dead-weight thump of its torso and legs. The zom's spine must have been shattered below the shoulder blades so that its legs truly were dead.

Its mouth, however, was not.

The zom moaned in desperate hunger as it snapped at him. Their roll ended with Benny on his back and the zom atop him—not at all the way he wanted this moment to end. He shoved a forearm under its chin to keep those teeth from his flesh. He saw movement over the zom's shoulder and there was Nix, her face running with blood and her eyes wild with fear, but she had her bokken in her small, tanned fists.

"Now!" she screeched, and with a grunt of effort, Benny shoved his arms straight up, raising the snapping zom as Nix swung her wooden sword.

CRACK!

The top half of the zom's head seemed to disintegrate, and the creature immediately went limp. With a snarl of disgust Benny threw it to one side.

"Thanks—," he began, but then he felt Nix stiffen beside him.

"Oh my God!"

Benny scrambled to his feet and looked around, and he could feel the blood drain from his face as he beheld a scene out of his darkest nightmares.

The whole field of tall grass in which they stood was filled with zoms. Dozens of them. They lay between the weeds and snarls of wisteria, empty eyes fixed on them, hands reaching, mouths working. Their moans filled the air.

But they were all broken. Shattered legs and hips. Shattered spines. Missing limbs. Huge holes torn through their chests and stomachs. Benny and Nix were surrounded by a legion of crippled zombies. They wriggled forward on broken limbs or grabbed tufts of grass to haul their twisted wrecks of bodies toward the fresh meat.

"What is this?" Nix breathed, horrified.

Benny drew his bokken, and they stood back to back with no clear way out. There had to be two dozen of the monsters. No . . . more than that. Much more. Others were climbing like gray slugs over fallen logs or out of depressions in the ground. Fifty of them. Sixty. More. All those dusty eyes and black mouths and rotted teeth. The dead cried out in rusted voices as they pulled themselves toward the smell of fresh meat and flowing blood. The terrible need, the awful hunger in that moan made Benny's blood turn to ice water in his veins. It was such an ancient sound, old as all the pain and misery in the world.

"We have to get out of here," Benny whispered. He knew that the words were pointless, their meaning obvious, but there was a need in him to hear a human voice amid the dreadful wails of the dead.

A few hundred yards to their left, Benny and Nix could hear the shouts of Tom and Chong and the indignant snort of the huge animal that had chased them all from the road.

And then he understood. "God!" he gasped. "The rhino!"

"What?" Nix asked, and then she got it. "Oh!"

"Let's get out of here."

She dragged her forearm over her face to clear the blood from her eyes. "How?"

Benny licked his lips and took a firmer grip on his sword. "Fast and hard," he said.

He swung his sword and smashed the closest of the zoms,

cracking the hardwood edge of the bokken against its temple. It flopped to one side, and Benny jumped over it. A dozen withered hands grabbed at his sneakers and pants cuffs, but Benny kicked and stamped as if he was being swarmed by cockroaches.

"Come on!" he shouted, but Nix was already running past him. Her sword swished down and cracked and another zombie spun away, its jaw crushed.

They ran and struck and ran. The blood on Nix's face scared Benny so much his heart felt like ice.

Had she been bitten?

His toe hurt terribly.

Are we bitten?

Are we dead?

"Benny!" Nix screamed. "Fight!"

He bit down on his fear and swung the sword. It cracked against a reaching hand and shattered the wrist. He swung again and a zom who looked like he might have been a soldier flopped over on his back, his neck knocked askew. Benny swung and hit; Nix swung and hit; and all the time they screamed and moved and fought.

"That way!" cried Nix, shoving him with her shoulder. Benny pivoted to see a narrow gap in the sea of crawling monsters. He pushed her in front of him.

"Go!"

She went, running and jumping, her sword flashing in a brown blur, the *crack!* against old bone sounding like gunshots.

A pair of zoms—a grocery store clerk and a man in the tattered remains of a business suit—grabbed at him at the same time, each one clamping on to one of his ankles.

Benny staggered and fell. But as he landed he twisted as Tom had shown him, rotating his shins so that the angles of his bones exerted leverage on the thumbs of the grabbing hands. The businessman lost his grip, and Benny pivoted hard to shake loose the clerk, emphasizing his need with a crushing downward blow with the flat end of the sword handle. The zom's skull shattered, and his hand opened with a dying twitch.

Benny scrambled to his feet and ran. Nix was fifty yards ahead of him, but he ran so fast that he'd nearly caught up by the time she reached the narrow gap.

"Go! Go!" he yelled, and together they crashed through the circle of broken zombies and into the trampled area where Chong had run. It felt like escaping from the arms of Death itself.

But the problem was far from over.

There was still the rhinoceros.

Chong was there, dodging in and around a stand of oaks as the rhino lunged between the trunks, trying to gore him with its horns. Only the lucky chance of the trees having grown so close together was keeping Chong alive.

Then they saw Tom standing with his pistol in a two-handed shooter's grip.

"Shoot it in the eye!" Benny yelled as they closed in on where he stood.

Tom ignored him and called out to Chong, "I'm going to fire twice, and then I want you to run behind the trees. Head to your left and go as deep into the forest as you can."

"No!" cried Nix.

Tom cut her a sharp look. "Why not?"

"We just came from there," she panted. "Zoms!"

"Damn."

"Tom! I need to get out of here!" begged Chong as he twisted away from the horn. This time it missed him by inches.

"Benny, Nix . . . head back to the road. Cross it and go into the other side. Find a tree you can climb and wait for me."

"What are you going to do?"

"Just do it!"

Benny and Nix obeyed, but they ran only a dozen yards and then slowed to watch as Tom took a few steps toward the enraged rhino and aimed his gun.

"Sorry about this, old girl," Tom said aloud.

The sound of the shot was strangely hollow. A *pok!* Benny expected it to be louder. The bullet hit the rhino in the shoulder. The creature howled, more in anger than in pain, but a second later it lunged at Chong.

Tom fired again, aiming at the creature's muscular haunch. The rhino shrieked, and this time there was pain in its cry.

It turned with mad fury in its eyes . . . and charged Tom.

"Why doesn't he shoot it in the eye?" demanded Nix, but Benny shook his head.

As the rhino rumbled past where they stood, Benny and Nix waved with silent urgency at Chong. He saw them, hesitated, looked at the retreating back of the rhino, and did nothing.

"Crap!" growled Benny. "He's too scared to move."

Then something pale rose up out of the weeds behind Chong.

"Lilah!" gasped Nix.

"Why didn't you idiots climb a tree?" she demanded. "What was all that running around?"

She didn't wait for an answer, and instead grabbed Chong's shoulder and fairly dragged him along behind her. The four of them ran through the grass and shrubs toward the trees and then out onto the road.

"In here," Lilah commanded, pointing, and the four of them plunged into the woods on the far side of the road. They ran through sticker bushes and hanging vines and leaped a gully and then broke into another clearing. At the far side was a squat and solid tree with a stout limb that dipped low. "Go!"

They raced to it and one by one jumped for the limb. Lilah shoved their butts upward, and when it was her turn she crouched and sprang, caught the limb as nimbly as a monkey, and climbed to safety.

Far away they heard two more hollow gunshots.

And then nothing except the triumphant roar of the rhinoceros.

FROM NIX'S JOURNAL

Tools of the Zombie Hunter Trade, Part Three

Tom Imura's sword is a <u>katana</u>. That kind of sword was developed in ancient Japan by the samurai—the elite warrior class. The <u>katana</u> originated in Japan's Muromachi period (1392–1573). Samurai sometimes wore a second, shorter sword called a <u>wakizashi</u> with it, but that one was used for committing suicide if the samurai felt his honor had been lost.

(When I asked Tom why he doesn't carry the short sword, he said, "I believe in survival, not suicide. Besides, aren't there already enough dead people in the world?")

The <u>katana</u> is known to be the sharpest sword in the world.

His sword is called a <u>kami katana</u>. He says it means "spirit sword" or "demon sword." Kind of cool, but a little freaky, too.

His <u>kami katana</u> has a twenty-nine-inch blade and a ten-and-three-quarters-inch handle. The handle was originally wrapped in black silk, but when that wore down, my mom covered it in silk and leather with some Celtic knots worked into the design.

(Mom really loved Tom.) I miss her. So does Tom.

THEY CROUCHED LIKE FRIGHTENED BIRDS IN THE TREE, WATCHING THE forest and seeing only trees. There was no sign of Tom or the rhinoceros. Benny peered at Nix. Her red hair was pasted to the right side of her face by a film of drying blood. Her cheek was bruised, and she didn't meet Benny's eyes. When he reached out to push her hair from her face, she batted his hand away. "Don't."

"I want to see how bad it is."

"It's not bad. Don't worry about it."

The others went instantly silent. Nix looked at them and then glared at Benny.

"It's not a bite," she said. "I hit my head on something when I fell."

"Show us," demanded Lilah, and when Nix hesitated, she snapped, "Now."

With a trembling hand, Nix touched her forehead, and then slowly pushed the hair back. It wasn't nothing, and it was still bleeding . . . but it wasn't a bite, and Benny breathed a vast sigh of relief. Then his face clouded with concern. There was a jagged cut that ran from Nix's hairline down her cheek almost to her jaw. It wasn't bone deep, but like most head wounds it had bled furiously.

"Oh, man." Benny hastily dug some clean cotton squares from his first aid kit. He tried to apply them, but Nix snatched them from him and pressed them in place.

"I know," she snarled. "It's ugly."

Benny smiled at her. "No," he said, "it's not that. I'm just sorry you got hurt."

Her eyes were hard to read in the shadows under the leaves. She turned away without saying anything.

"We have to go find Tom," whispered Benny.

Nix touched her face. "When he sees this, he's going to make us go back home."

"That doesn't matter, Nix. Right now we have to find him and—"

"He said to stay here," she insisted. "If he's looking for us and we're looking for him, we might never find each other."

"Yes," agreed Chong hastily. He was green with sick fear and sweating badly. He clutched the trunk of the tree as if it was trying to pull away from him. "Staying here is good."

Lilah nodded. "Tom is a good hunter. He'll find us."

"But what if he doesn't?" demanded Benny.

"He will."

"What if he can't?"

"He will."

A voice said, "He has."

Benny whipped his head around so fast that he nearly fell out of the tree. "Tom!"

Tom Imura stood in the waist-high grass at the base of the tree. He was covered with mud and streaked with grass stains.

His black hair hung in sweaty rattails, but he didn't even look out of breath, and he held Lilah's spear in his hands.

"Come on down," he suggested with a grin.

One by one they crawled down to the lowest limb and then dropped. Chong was last, and his legs were visibly trembling.

Benny ran over to Tom. "Don't take this the wrong way," he said, and then gave his brother a quick, fierce hug. He abruptly let Tom go and pushed him back like he was radioactive. "Okay, we're done."

Nix came in for a hug too.

"Heck of a start," Tom said. It was meant as a joke, but Nix's eyes flashed with concern.

"Tom . . . I don't want to go back!"

"I do," said Chong.

She wheeled around, and Benny saw that she was about to fry the flesh from Chong's bones with an acid comment, but then she saw the look of complete despair on his face. Her own expression softened and she left her comment unspoken. Instead she turned back to Tom and reinforced her earlier comment. "I do not want to go back."

"We'll talk about that in a minute," Tom said gently. "Let's catch our breath first."

"The animal?" asked Lilah, accepting her spear back from Tom. There was no blood on it. "Didn't even pierce the skin."

"Yeah, well, for what it's worth, my bullets didn't seem to do her much harm either."

"You could have shot it in the eye," said Benny.

"I would have if I couldn't get Chong and the rest of you out of there. Otherwise it would have been wrong to kill her."

Lilah grunted and then nodded. Nix was less certain. "Will it come after us?"

"It won't. This is her territory. She has a calf hidden back beyond the clearing."

"A calf?" Benny asked. "That thing's a mother rhino?"

"So she was just protecting her baby?" asked Nix.

"Seems so."

"And you never saw it before? I thought you were up in these mountains all the time."

"I haven't been in this particular pass for a while. That calf can't be more than three or four months old. I don't know much about rhinos, but my guess is that Big Mama came looking for a quiet place to have her baby and settled here. Nobody else lives on this side of the mountain."

"Where'd she come from?" asked Benny.

"A zoo, I guess, or a circus. People used to have private collections, too. And animals were used in the film industry. Must be a lot of wild animals out in the Ruin. My friend Solomon Jones saw a dead bear over in Yosemite that looked like it had been mauled by something that had big teeth and claws. And there's that guy lives out at Wawona—Preacher Jack—who swears he's seen tigers. If the zoo animals got out, it could have been anything. Lion or tiger . . ."

"Maybe they'll be cowardly lions," said Lilah under her breath.

Benny laughed. It was the first time he'd ever heard her make any kind of joke.

Tom nodded back the way he'd come. "Before First Night, there were more tigers in America—in zoos, circuses, and private collections—than in all of Asia. As for Big Mama, she was simply doing what any mother does. Protecting her young."

"Not just from us," said Nix.

Tom nodded. "I know. I saw all the zoms. Bottom line . . . don't mess with Big Mama."

Benny nodded and told the others about it. "It was really weird," he concluded. "All those crawling zoms. Scarier than the walking ones."

"No," said Lilah, "it's not. You haven't faced enough of the walkers."

Benny thought back to Zak and Big Zak, and to the zoms he'd faced last year while looking for Nix. "I've had my moments."

Chong cleared his throat. "Zoms couldn't hurt that rhino, could they?"

"Not a chance." Tom laughed. "Maybe the baby, though. I didn't get a good look at it, but if it is still vulnerable, it won't be for long. Those things are like tanks."

He saw the blood on Nix's face and brushed her hair back to examine her. She nodded and pulled her face away from his touch.

"That looks nasty. It needs to be cleaned off."

"It's not that bad."

"That isn't a request, Nix. Out here we don't have Doc Gurijala and we don't have antibiotics. Infection is as much our enemy as the zoms. So, you'll clean that off now, and then I'll take a closer look at it. You might even need stitches. If so, either I'll do it or we'll go back to town. Either way, all wounds will be tended to with the utmost care. End of discussion."

Nix heaved a great sigh, made a big show of pulling out her first aid kit and canteen, and trudged away to sit on a fallen tree and do as she was told.

"I'll help," Benny said, and limped after her, but Tom snaked out a hand and caught his shoulder.

"Whoa, hold on, sport . . . you're limping and there's blood on your shoe. Where are you hurt?"

Benny swallowed, shooting a wary look at Lilah, whose attention had sharpened and was now focused on him. Her fingers tightened on the haft of her spear.

"Hey—don't even think about it," Benny said, pointing a finger at her. "One of the zoms tried to bite through my sneaker, but he—"

"Take your shoe off." Lilah and Tom said it at the same time.

"I—"

"Now," said Tom. His voice was heavy with quiet command. Benny looked at Nix, who had paused in the act of sponging blood from her face. Her eyes flashed with sudden concern.

"Crap," Benny said acidly, and sat down on the grass to pull his shoe off. His sock was soaked with blood.

"Oh no," breathed Chong. "This is all my fault."

Benny made a face. "Oh, please. You didn't bite me."

"The rhino chased us because I startled it. Then I ran the wrong way and made everything worse."

Tom started to say something but Lilah cut in. "Yes. You were stupid."

"She's got your number," said Benny with a grin.

Chong gave him an evil stare. "You're the one whose toe got bitten off by a zom."

Benny muttered under his breath as he pulled his sock off. His big toenail was cracked and bleeding, and the toe was swollen, but there was no bite. Lilah snatched up his shoe to examine it, but Tom took it out of her hands and peered at the toe.

"It's a pressure injury." He blew out his cheeks and handed the shoe back to Benny. "That's twice you dodged the bullet."

"That's a metaphor, right?"

Tom's smile was less reassuring than it could have been.

"Right?" insisted Benny.

"Rinse your sock out," said Tom as he turned away.

"Hey . . . right?"

FROM NIX'S JOURNAL

Some of the traders and bounty hunters claim that the zoms on the other side of the Rocky Mountains are faster than the zoms we have here. There's a girl in my grade—Carmen—who says that her uncle, who is a trader, saw zombies running after people during First Night in Milwaukee, Wisconsin. A couple of other people from back east said the same thing, but most people don't believe them.

I hope this is not true!!!

22

"WELL . . . GO AHEAD AND SAY IT," NIX DEMANDED.

Tom squatted in front of her, gently touching the edges of the long gash on her face. His lips were pursed, and he made a small downbeat grunting noise. "You're going to need stitches."

"I know. Go ahead."

He shook his head. "No . . . I can stitch a wound well enough, but this needs fine work. Otherwise—"

"I'll look like a hag."

"I wouldn't go that far . . . but a deft hand with a needle will reduce the scar to a pencil-thin line. Doc Gara—"

"No!" She brushed his hand away. "I'm not going back to town."

"Nix, c'mon," prodded Benny, who hovered over Tom's shoulder like a worried aunt.

She gave him two seconds of a lethal green stare and then refocused on Tom. "You're not my dad, Tom, and I—"

Tom made a face. "Oh, please, Nix. You're not a petulant little kid, so don't try that act on me. Benny still tries it and it never works."

"It works sometimes," Benny said. They ignored him.

"We can be home in four hours," Tom said. "The doc can stitch you up, we rest up a day or two, and—"

"No."

"Would you rather have a bad scar?"

"If it's a choice between going back and that, then I'll take the scar."

"Why?"

It was Chong who asked the question, and they turned to look at him. He was pale and still looked badly shaken by what had happened. His eyes were dark and filled with guilt.

"Look," Nix said slowly, "if we go back because of this, then what will be the next thing that takes us back? I know how things work with people. If something stops us this soon, then all we'll find out here are reasons to stop and start over."

"No way," said Benny.

"No," agreed Tom.

She picked up the first aid kit and thrust it toward Tom. "You do it."

"Please," whispered Chong. "Don't. This is my fault. I . . . I can't be responsible for you being all messed up."

"Let's not add more drama," said Tom. "I'm not that bad with a needle."

"Nix is beautiful," said Chong. "She should always be beautiful."

Benny held up a hand. "Um . . . going out on a philosophical limb here, but scar or no scar, Nix is always going to be beautiful."

"No doubt," agreed Tom.

Nix flushed, but her expression was still hard.

Chong gave a stubborn shake. "Please. I can't deal with it knowing that it's my—"

"As God is my witness," snarled Nix, "if you say it's your fault one more time, Chong, I will beat you unconscious and leave you for the zoms."

Chong's mouth remained open, the sentence half said but now dead on his tongue.

He turned away and stalked to the edge of the clearing, then squatted down in the grass and laced his fingers over his bowed head.

The first aid kit was still in Nix's hand. Tom hesitated, but then Lilah suddenly leaned in to snatch up the kit.

"She will die of old age before you make up your mind," she said coldly. "I'll do it."

"Whoa," yelped Benny, making a grab for the kit. "Do you even know how?"

Instead of answering, Lilah pulled up her shirt to show her midriff. There were three healed-over scars, one at least nine inches long. The scars were as thin as threads. Benny stared. Lilah had a flat, tanned stomach and the curved lines of superbly toned muscles. She was also holding the shirt a little too high for comfort, and Benny could feel his hair starting to sweat.

Tom, quietly amused, reached up and pushed Lilah's hand down a few inches.

Nix gave Benny another of those deadly green stares and fired one at Lilah, who was oblivious to it. Her understanding of personal modesty was entirely from books and not at all from practical experience.

"You stitched those?" Tom asked.

"Who else?" She dropped the hem of her shirt and turned to show other scars on her legs. Benny hoped that an asteroid would fall on his head at the moment. It wasn't that he wanted to look, but he didn't know how not to look, because he thought that would be even more obvious.

"That's very good work," said Tom. "Better than I can do."

"I know," Lilah said bluntly. She squinted up at the sun. "Better to do it now. Light's good but careful takes time."

Nix turned to Tom. "If she can do it, then can we stay out here?"

Tom sighed and stood. "One step at a time. Let's see how you feel when she's done."

"I feel fine."

"We don't have anesthesia, Nix," Tom murmured. "It's going to hurt. A lot."

"I know." Her eyes were hard.

Benny tried to read her expression and all the unspoken things it conveyed. Over the last year Nix had learned nearly every kind of hurt there was. Or at least every kind of hurt Benny could imagine.

Without saying another word to Tom, Nix turned to Lilah.

"Do it," she said.

23

BENNY COULDN'T BEAR TO WATCH, BUT HE COULDN'T LEAVE NIX ALONE, either. However, she threatened him if he didn't leave, so he slunk away to stand in the shade of a tree with Tom.

"Heck of a start," Tom said softly.

"I'd say 'could be worse,' but I'm kinda thinking that it couldn't. So . . . basically this blows," observed Benny.

"Yes it does," agreed Tom.

They stared out at the endless green of the forest.

"She's strong," said Tom after a while.

"Nix? Yeah."

Minutes passed, and Benny tried to think about anything instead of how it must feel to have a curved needle—like one of Morgie's fishhooks—passed through the skin of your face, followed by the slow pull of surgical thread. The tug at the end to pull the stitch tight. The tremble in the flesh as it waited for the next stitch. And the next.

Benny was pretty sure he was going to go stark raving mad. He kept listening for Nix's scream. And with each second he could not understand why she didn't scream. He would have, and he made no apologies for it. Screaming seemed like a pretty good response to what Nix was going through.

There were no screams.

After what seemed like five hundred years, Tom repeated what he'd said.

"She's strong."

"Yeah," Benny said again.

His fingernails were buried into his palms hard enough to gouge crescent-shaped divots.

"Girls are stronger than boys," Tom said.

"Not a news flash," Benny said.

"I'm just saying."

They watched the forest.

"If this goes on any longer, Tom?"

"Yeah?"

"Shoot me."

Tom smiled.

Benny looked at him and then over to where Chong still sat in the tall grass.

"Is this all really Chong's fault?"

Tom shrugged.

"No, tell me."

"If you really want an honest answer," Tom said quietly, "then . . . yes. Chong didn't listen when he was told to be quiet, and he didn't listen when he was told what to do when the rhino was chasing us."

"He's scared."

"Aren't you?"

"Sure," Benny said grudgingly, "but I've been out here before."

"Don't make excuses for him. You listened to me the first

time we came out here," Tom reminded him. "And that was back when you couldn't stand me."

"I know."

"Not everyone is built to be tough," said Tom. "Sad fact of life. Chong is one of the nicest people I know. His folks, too. If our species is going to make it back from the brink and build something better than what we had, then we need to breed more people like them. It would be a saner, smarter, and far more civilized world."

"But . . . ?"

"But I don't think he's cut out for this."

"I guess."

"It's better that he's not coming with us."

Benny said nothing.

"Do you agree, kiddo?"

"I don't know." Benny sighed. "Chong's my best friend."

"That's why he's here. He only came out here because he's your friend, and because he doesn't quite know how to say good-bye," said Tom. "Saying good-bye is one of the hardest things people ever have to do. Back before First Night, I remember how hard it was just to say good-bye to my friends when I was done with high school. We wrote a lot of promises in each other's yearbooks about how we'd always stay in touch, but even then we knew that for the most part they were lies. Well-intentioned and hopeful lies, but still lies."

"That was different."

"Sure, but things are relative. Just like pain. What Nix is going through is not the worst pain she's ever felt, which is why she can deal with it. For me, saying good-bye to my friends from high school was terrible. We all were going off to colleges in different parts of the country. The old gang I grew up with was falling apart. It felt like dying. It was grief."

Benny thought about the way he had left things with Morgie. He nodded.

"I guess I'm having a hard time adjusting to the fact that leaving is so final."

"It doesn't have to be," said Tom.

"For Nix it does."

Tom nodded.

"What are we going to do about Chong?" asked Benny.

Tom ticked his chin toward the southeast. "There's a back road to Brother David's way station. My friend Sally Two-Knives will be coming through here today or tomorrow. I'm going to wait at the way station until she shows, and then I'll ask her to take Chong back home."

Benny had the Zombie Card for Sally Two-Knives. She was a bounty hunter who worked mostly out of the towns farther north. She was a tall, dark-skinned woman with a Mohawk and a matched pair of army bayonets strapped to her thighs. The text on the back of her Zombie Card read:

> Card No. 239: Sally Two-Knives. This
> former Roller-Derby queen has become one
> of the toughest and most reliable bounty
> hunters and guides in the Ruin. Don't cross
> her or you'll find out just how good she is
> with her two razor-sharp knives!

Like most of the Zombie Cards, it didn't give a lot of information, but Benny always liked the fierce woman's smiling face. She wasn't pretty, but there was humor in her brown eyes.

Brother David, on the other hand, was a way-station monk, one of the Children of God who lived out in the Ruin and did what he could to tend to the living dead. Brother David and the others of his order called the zombies the Children of Lazarus and believed them to be the "meek" who were meant to inherit the earth. Benny couldn't quite grasp the concept, especially after what he and Nix had encountered in the field.

"You and Chong can say your good-byes in the morning."

"Will Chong be safe? I mean . . . will Sally Two-Knives be enough protection for him?"

Tom laughed. "More than enough. She doesn't like killing zoms, so she knows all the routes that are clear and safe."

They were silent for a while, each cutting looks over at Lilah, who was still working on Nix.

When Tom next spoke he deliberately made his tone light. "If we're lucky we'll catch up with Greenman, maybe stay a couple days at his place."

"Greenman, really? Cool! I can't wait to meet him," said Benny. He had the Greenman card too. The image on the card was that of a tall, thin man wearing clothes entirely covered in green leaves, berries, and pinecones. The artist had depicted him wearing a mask made from oak leaves and acorns. The card read:

Card No. 172: The Greenman. Little is
known about this mysterious figure seen
haunting the forests between Magoon
Hill and Yosemite. Is he a myth? A ghost?
Or is he a dangerous madman waiting to
pounce on unwary travelers? Beware the
Greenman!

"Sounds like someone from a story."

"He's real enough," said Tom, "but he is a bit of a character. His real name's Artie Mensch. Used to be a forest ranger
over in Yosemite, but since First Night the Ruin has become a
real home to him. Never comes into town, doesn't talk to too
many people. Prefers to be alone."

"Does he really dress like that?"

"Sometimes. When he has his camouflage on you can
walk right past him and not see him. Fools the zoms, too. And
he's been experimenting with mixtures of herbs to get the
same effect as cadaverine. Not sure if he's worked it out yet."

"The Zombie Card says that he might be crazy," Benny
said.

Tom shrugged. "Most people are a little crazy, especially
since First Night, and doubly so if they live out here. But
Greenman's a good man, and he's a friend to the right kind
of traveler."

"What's the right kind?"

"Let's just say that Greenman wouldn't have invited
Charlie or the Hammer in for tea." Tom stared into the distance as if looking into his own thoughts. "I've spent many a

long night with him. Talking about the old days, and learning what he has to teach."

"You learned from him?"

"Sure. He might be the wisest person left alive. Certainly the wisest I know."

A few minutes later, Benny nodded toward the forest. "How far have you been?"

"Since First Night? All the way to the far side of Yosemite, but I rarely go that deep. Once we pass through the park, it'll be as new to me as it is to you guys."

"And we'll be roughing it all the way?"

"Nah. I dropped off some supplies at Brother David's a few weeks ago. Carpet coats, more cadaverine, some weapons, tents, other stuff. Anything else we need we can get from the traders over in Wawona. Roughing it was just for tonight. For the real trip I want us to be as well supplied as we can be."

Benny looked over and saw that Lilah was applying a bandage. The stitchery was done and Nix still hadn't made a sound.

"Speaking of crazy," Benny murmured.

Tom glanced over. "Nix or Lilah?"

"Take your pick."

Tom snorted. "You ever try to imagine what it's like being inside Nix's head?"

"All the time." Benny shook his head. "I've known her my whole life, and we've talked about everything . . . but then I catch a look in her eye when we're training, or she'll say something odd, and then I wonder if I really know her at all."

"How's that make her crazy?"

"I don't know. I . . . can't quite put it into words. Since last year she's different. She's obsessed about this trip. When we talk about it, most of the time she's really focused and logical, but if I bring up any reservations about it . . . she either bites my head or acts as if I didn't say anything." He looked at Tom. "I know you've seen it too."

"I have," Tom admitted, "but I don't know if it makes her crazy. Her last blood ties are gone, Benny. In a lot of ways she feels that she's all alone."

"She isn't!"

"Sure she is. We're each alone inside our heads, some more so than others. Lilah's been alone inside her head for years, and she may never come completely out."

"So you're saying that Nix is just obsessed and lonely?"

"That's not what I'm saying. I'm agreeing with you that there are forces at work in her life. I don't know if she's truly crazy—as in a danger to herself and others—but I suspect that her sanity is a work in process. Keep your eye on her."

He clapped Benny on the shoulder, and they walked over to see how Nix was doing. She was pale, almost green, and her face—what Benny could see of it under the bandages—ran with sweat. Lilah sat on a tree stump, carefully cleaning the needle with alcohol.

"World's dumbest question," Benny said to Nix, "but how do you feel?"

"Like I was attacked by Mrs. Lafferty's quilting circle." Nix's face was puffy, and she barely moved her lips when she spoke. Her eyes were glassy with pain and the fatigue that comes from enduring pain. "Thanks," she said to Lilah.

"I don't want to go back to that town either," Lilah said, and walked away.

Benny and Nix looked up at Tom.

He sighed, then said, "Okay. We keep going."

THEY RESTED FOR ANOTHER HOUR, AND THEN TOM TOLD EVERYONE TO get ready.

Benny came over to check on Chong, but his friend didn't want to talk. Chong put his pack on, adjusted the straps, and didn't meet anyone's eyes.

"Let's go," said Tom. "I want to make the way station while it's still light. Nix . . . we'll only go as fast as you can manage."

"I'm fine."

"No you're not. You're hurt, and even though it's not as serious as it looks, your body has gone through trauma. Be smart about how you feel. Push too hard and you'll collapse, and then I swear to God I will carry you back to town. Is that clear?"

"Fine."

Tom adjusted the strap that held his sword. "We're going to be going down the mountain, and that means every step brings us deeper into zombie-infested lands. Everyone keep your eyes open, and everyone follow orders." He looked hard at Chong, who gave a single tight nod.

They set out. Tom led the way, and for a few minutes

Benny walked beside him. A mile into the hike, Benny said, "We screwed it up pretty bad in just a few hours."

Tom grunted, but aloud he said, "Despite what I said earlier—and despite a legendary series of screwups—this day could actually have been worse. Not much worse . . . but worse."

"So Lilah keeps reminding me," said Benny quietly. "I think she'd enjoy quieting me."

"I doubt it, but I agree that she can be a bit intense."

"Is 'intense' really a strong enough word?"

"Give her time, kiddo. She's—"

"Lived alone for six years, yeah, I know. I'm not criticizing her for being weird, Tom. It's just a little freaky when someone keeps threatening to kill you."

Tom nodded, but repeated, "Give her time."

Benny let Tom move ahead of him, and he slowed until Nix caught up, but from the stiff set of her bandaged face, Benny knew that she was in no mood for companionship or conversation. He walked with her for a while, but when he noticed that she kept trying to walk faster, he lagged again to let her pull ahead.

He sighed.

He turned and looked back and saw that Lilah was walking side by side with Chong, and they were talking in quiet voices. He grunted in surprise. Lilah was weird at the best of times, and she was usually so unemotional that he wondered what really went on inside her head. When he'd first learned about her from a picture on a Zombie Card, he'd been briefly and intensely infatuated. Now he was just afraid of her.

And maybe sorry for her too . . . though he'd feel much more compassion if she wasn't so damn fast whipping out her knife every time he got a hangnail.

The forest path wound around and began sloping down toward a road that had once been blacktop and was now cracked and torn by the unstoppable roots of trees. Young trees, some of them a dozen years old, stood in the middle of lanes where once cars had driven.

"Careful now," Tom cautioned. "Weapons out, eyes and ears open."

Benny drew his bokken and moved closer to Nix.

They walked through the knee-high weeds, stepping over old bones that might have been human, though Benny didn't want to stop to examine them. Ahead a brown truck lay on its side. Benny could read the letters "UPS" on the rusted back door. The moldering remains of old boxes tumbled out of the back, and what little cardboard remained was bleached white by fourteen years of rain and snow.

Tom held up a clenched fist, the sign to stop. Everyone froze in place.

He gestured for them to stay where they were, then he silently drew his sword and crept toward the truck on the balls of his feet. The woods were alive with birdsong and the buzz of bees. Benny licked his dry lips, waiting for the moment when everything would suddenly go silent. Would there be another animal like the rhino, or would it be zoms?

Tom came up on the truck at an angle that reduced the likelihood of anyone on the far side seeing him. When he wanted to move quietly, he was silent as a shadow. He slid along the top of the overturned truck, took a brief peek around the end, and then vanished behind the vehicle.

Nix drifted to Benny's side. She looked scared, and he realized that with her injury and the bandages she was probably feeling pretty vulnerable.

Benny mouthed the words, "It's okay."

But it wasn't. When Tom stepped out from behind the truck, his sword was held loosely in one hand, the blade angled down toward the weeds. Even from thirty feet away Benny could see that Tom's face was drawn and pale, and his lip was curled in disgust.

Everyone moved forward at once.

"What is it?" Nix asked.

"Was somebody attacked by zoms?" asked Benny.

Tom gave them a bleak stare. "Worse," he said. He looked old and sad, and he turned away to look at the waving treetops down the road.

Nix, Chong, and Benny exchanged frowns of puzzlement, and as a group they walked around to the far side of the truck. The buzzing was louder, and Benny realized that it wasn't bees hunting for nectar in the spring flowers.

It was flies. Black blowflies that swirled in a thick cloud around something on the other side of the overturned truck.

It was a man. Or, it had been a man. He stood straight, arms out to his sides and secured by ropes to the axles of the truck. The man wore only torn jeans and nothing else. Not even skin. Most of him was gone. Torn away. Consumed.

Chong spun away and threw up into the bushes.

Nix was a statue beside Benny, her eyes huge and unblinking, and from where her arm touched his he could feel her skin turn cold as ice.

Benny wasn't sure if he was still standing or sitting. Or dreaming. The world spun drunkenly around him, filling him with sickness, making him want to scream.

This man had not been attacked by zoms.

He had been fed to them.

"Why?"

It was the fourth time Chong had asked the question. Maybe the fifth. Benny couldn't quite remember. Chong kept walking away and coming back and walking away. Each time he came back he demanded an answer. As if there was one that could explain this.

Benny felt totally numb, but he could not make himself look away. Something deep inside demanded that he stand there and look at every inch of the dead man. It made him count the bites. It made him catalog all the things that had been taken from this man.

No. Within his mind a voice that did not feel like his own rebelled at the use of so weak and inaccurate a word as "taken." The cold detachment required honesty in evaluation. *No,* the voice said, *don't lie to yourself. If you hide from the truth behind soft words, then you'll be soft. Then you'll be dead.*

Nothing had been taken. Parts of this man had been consumed. Eaten.

That's the truth of what you are seeing. That's the truth of what zoms do.

As he listened to the voice, he also heard a sound. A sob. He blinked and looked around. Chong had walked away again and now he squatted down by the side of the road, arms crossed over his head, his whole body trembling.

Benny glanced again at the dead man, and then turned to go over to Chong, grateful to have a reason to turn away. It wouldn't feel like cowardice if he was going to help Chong instead of looking at the corpse.

Be strong, whispered his inner voice, then faded into silence.

Benny sat down next to Chong and put his arm around his friend's shoulders. He wanted to say something, but his inner vocabulary did not include any words that would make sense out of this moment.

"I—I'm sorry," murmured Chong. He lifted his head and stared straight ahead. His face was streaked with tears and his nose was running. "I don't—I mean, I can't—"

"No," said a low rasp of a voice, and they both turned to see Lilah standing there. The breeze blew her snow-white hair like streamers of pale smoke. "Tears don't mean you're weak."

Chong sniffed and wiped his nose and said nothing.

Lilah sat down in front of Chong, laying her spear in the dusty weeds. "Benny," she said.

"Yeah?"

"Go away."

Benny started to say something, but he did not. Instead he nodded and got to his feet. He had no idea what Lilah was going to say, or what she could say. Compassion, tenderness, and most other human emotions seemed to be beyond her. Or was he wrong about that?

Benny nodded to himself and walked back to where Nix and Tom stood.

"Tom . . . do you know what happened? Who did this?"

"No," Tom said, but there was something in his tone that made Nix give him a sharp look.

"What?" she asked.

He hesitated.

"Come on, Tom," Benny insisted. "If we're going to be traveling out here, then you can't treat us like this. You can't protect us from stuff."

"It's not that," Tom said slowly. "But . . . tell me something first."

"Okay," said Benny.

"That night last year, when we rescued the kids from the bounty hunters . . . how sure are you that you killed Charlie Pink-eye?"

If Tom had punched Benny straight in the face he could not have stunned him more.

"W-what?" he gasped.

"What are you saying?" demanded Nix.

"I'm not saying anything yet. Answer the question, Benny."

Benny closed his eyes and the memory of that terrible fight was right there. Believing that Tom was dead, Nix, Benny, and Lilah had taken it upon themselves to rescue a group of children who had been kidnapped by Charlie Matthias and his bounty hunter cronies. It had been a foolishly risky plan, with more ways it could have gone wrong than right. The skies had opened and lashed Charlie's mountaintop camp with heavy rains and shocking lightning. At Benny's suggestion, Lilah had freed hundreds of the zoms that Charlie had tied to trees in the Hungry Forest. Using her own living flesh as bait, the ghost-voiced Lost Girl had enticed the legions of dead to follow her up the mountain and into the bounty hunters' camp. Tom had showed up around the same time, having escaped a terrible death by a stroke of luck. During the ensuing battle, all the bounty hunters had died. Lilah had killed the Motor City Hammer—a cold revenge she had ached for since that horrible day years ago when her sister, little Annie, had died trying to escape from Gameland.

Charlie Matthias had slipped away from the slaughter in his camp and had come upon the fleeing children. He'd beaten Lilah and Nix to the ground and was seconds away from killing them all. Benny had managed to recover the length of black pipe that the Hammer had used to bash in Morgie's head—and that Charlie and the Hammer had used to beat Nix's mother to the point of death.

As Charlie went for him, Benny had faked him out and hit him with the pipe. The image, even the feel of the blow, were scorched into his memory. Benny wiped his mouth with the back of his hand.

"He fell all the way down the mountain, Tom."

"But you never saw him land? Or heard him land?"

"No . . . ," Benny said dubiously.

"Damn."

Nix grabbed Tom's sleeve. "Why, Tom?"

Tom sighed. "I've seen two other men killed like this. Years ago, over by Hogan Mountain. Both of them were bounty hunters who tried to cut a slice of this territory." He walked over to the dead man and looked at his bloodless face. "I never knew for sure who did it, but rumor had it that both men had been killed by Charlie Pink-eye."

"THAT'S IMPOSSIBLE!" BENNY AND NIX SAID IT AT THE SAME TIME.

"I hope you're right," said Tom.

"Charlie's dead," insisted Benny. "Unless he broke his neck when he fell, he's a zom. He can't be alive."

Tom said nothing. He drew his knife and began cutting the corpse down.

"Tom," said Nix, "Charlie's dead. I know he is."

"Okay," said Tom. He slashed the ropes that held the man's arms in place and let the body slide to the ground.

"Tom!" snapped Nix. "He's dead."

Tom pulled the man's torso away from the truck and laid him out straight. "I'm not arguing with you, Nix."

"But you believe us, don't you? We saw him fall."

"I believe you."

"Then . . ."

"But you didn't see him land." He folded the man's hands together over his stomach, then straightened and went to peer inside the truck. He rummaged for a moment and came back with a large piece of stained plastic sheeting. Without comment he wrapped the body in it and used rocks to weight down the corners.

"Tom!" barked Benny.

Tom turned angrily. "What do you want me to say, Benny? We didn't stop to examine that side of the mountain. There could have been a slope or a ledge. There might have been enough thick brush to have slowed his fall. Or he could have fallen a hundred feet and been smashed to junk. I don't know. We don't know, and that's the point. I've lived this long without giving in to assumptions."

"But—," Nix began, but Tom cut her off.

"No." He sighed. "Now listen to me, both of you. You want to keep going, right? You don't want to go back to town."

"No!" snapped Nix. Benny, less sure about that, shook his head slowly.

"Okay," said Tom, "then you have to learn to keep an open mind. Assumptions will get you killed. If Charlie is dead, then he's dead. If he's alive, then he's alive. We don't know for sure, but if we don't allow the possibility of it, then we could get blindsided. Would either of you like it if Charlie was alive and got the drop on us? If he was willing to torture people and feed them to zoms just for cutting into his trade routes, try to imagine what he'd be willing to do to us. We killed his best friend, we led a zombie army against his crew, we made him an outlaw all through this part of the Ruin, he can't ever come back to town . . . and you, Benny, beat him in a fight. You really want to wake up and find him grinning at you in the dark? Do you, Nix?"

They said nothing. Neither was able to.

"I've managed to stay alive out here in the Ruin because I'm a realist. I allow the truth to be the truth, no matter how much I might want it to be something else." He waved his hand at the forest. "This might as well be hell itself out here. That line about everything out here wanting to kill you? It's true."

They kept silent. Nix grabbed Benny's hand and was squeezing it harder than she had during Zak's funeral.

"I want you both to learn to think and act—and react—the way I do. I want you to survive. You have to be ready for this to be your world too. You're teenagers now, but out here you're going to grow up fast. That's only going to happen, though, if you're smart and careful and honest with yourself."

Nix said, "Tom . . . do you think there might be other people out here like Charlie?"

"Yes," he said without hesitation. "Or worse."

"Worse?" She shuddered. "God."

Benny nodded. "Then I guess we have to be realistic about that, too."

"I wish I could say otherwise." He looked up at the sun. "We need to move. I don't want to sleep outside tonight. Not after a day like this. Brother David will let us bunk down with him, but we have miles to go and . . ." His words slowed and stopped and for a moment he seemed to stare into the empty air. Then he wheeled around toward the dead man. "Damn! You idiot!"

"What is it?" Nix asked.

Tom didn't answer. Instead he jerked the sheeting back from the dead man and bent close and examined the corpse's neck. He rolled him onto his side and peered close at the skull from all angles. Then he sat back on the ground. "Huh . . . ," he said, looking perplexed.

"What is it?" Nix asked again.

He's been dead for days, whispered Benny's inner voice. "Days," he said aloud.

Tom gave him a sharp look, and then nodded.

Nix still didn't get it.

"His neck isn't broken, is it?" Benny asked.

Tom shook his head.

"No bullet in the head?"

Another shake.

"No sliver?"

Nix caught up with what they were saying, and her eyes were wide. "No one quieted him," she said softly.

"No," murmured Tom.

"So why didn't he . . . come back?"

Tom shook his head slowly. He considered for a moment and then called Lilah to come and examine the body. She stalked over with a pale and silent Chong in her wake.

"Look at this man, Lilah," Tom said. "Tell me how he died."

He didn't explain. Lilah studied Tom's eyes for a moment, then shrugged and knelt by the corpse. Benny noticed that her examination was almost identical, step by step, with Tom's. Her reaction, however, was different. She hissed and whipped out her knife and without a moment's pause drove it into the base of the dead man's skull.

"Yeow!" cried Benny, lurching backward from the flashing blade.

"Whoa now!" said an unfamiliar voice. They all whirled as a stranger stepped out of the woods right behind Lilah.

27

"Little gal's fast with a pigsticker."

The stranger seemed to have stepped out of nowhere and was in the gap between the rear bumper of the truck and a game trail that vanished into the shadowy woods. He was a tall, broad-shouldered but very thin man in a dusty black coat and wide-brimmed black hat. Long white hair hung like strands of spiderweb from under the brim of his hat, and he wore a smile that twitched and writhed on his thin lips like worms on a hot griddle.

Lilah was so startled that out of pure reflex she snatched up her spear and swung the blunt end toward him. The man was at least sixty, and he looked dried up from the hot sun and bitter winters of the Sierras, but he moved like greased lightning. He tilted out of the swing of the spear, snaked out his left hand in a movement that was so fast Benny could not follow, snatched the spear from her hand, and flung it into the woods. Without pausing, the man shoved Lilah on the shoulder with the flat of his palm and sent her crashing into Nix and Chong. Before Benny could even grab the handle of his bokken, Tom was up from where he had been kneeling, and his glittering *katana* was in his hand. But then the man did something Benny would have thought to be completely impossible. Before Tom could complete his cut, the man in the black hat had stepped into the arc of his swing, blocked the elbow of Tom's sword arm, and put the wicked edge of his own knife against the bulge of Tom's Adam's apple.

"My, my, my," said the man softly, his smile never wavering, "ain't we all in a pickle?"

Instantly Tom pivoted, slapped the knife away from his throat, spun like a dancer, and swung the blade in a lightning-fast circle that stopped a hairbreadth from the man's nose.

The man looked cross-eyed at the tip of the blade and gave a comical chuckle. He slowly raised his knife and gave the sword a small tap. The *ping!* of metal against metal lingered in the still air.

"Let's call it one-all and say the rest of the game was rained out," suggested the stranger. Without waiting to see if Tom agreed, the man rolled the handle of his knife through his fingers like a magician and slid the ten-inch blade into a sheath that hung from his belt.

Tom did not lower his sword. He cut his eyes left and right to check the woods, then said to Lilah, "You okay?"

She snarled something low and unintelligible and got to her feet, placing her fist threateningly on the butt of her holstered pistol. Nix helped Chong up, and they looked scared and uncertain. Benny had his sword out now, and he shifted to Tom's right to prepare for a flanking attack.

"Okay," said Tom, still holding his sword out, "who are you?"

"Would you mind lowering your *katana*, brother?" The white-haired man held his hands up and kept smiling. The smile did not quite reach the man's ice-blue eyes. "We're all friends here."

Benny noticed that not only had the man avoided Tom's question, but he knew what a *katana* was. Interesting.

Tom said, "'Friend' is a funny word for someone who attacks a teenage girl."

The man looked—or pretended to look—shocked. "As I recall it, brother, she tried to rearrange my dentures with the butt end of yonder spear. I gave her a little shove by way of increasing our distance and decreasing the likelihood of my having to eat my dinner without teeth henceforth. Then you and t'other youngster here set to drawing swords on me. I drew my knife only to calm things down." His look of shock gradually drained away, and his mouth again wore that twitchy smile. He patted his sheathed knife. "And see . . . I stood down."

Tom did not lower his sword. Not one inch.

"I asked you your name," he said quietly.

"These days people seem to have a bunch of names, don't they?"

Tom said nothing.

"Okay, okay." The man chuckled. "You're being serious here 'cause you're the grown-up and there are kids watching. I respect that. Like a shepherd with his little flock."

"Name," prompted Tom.

"When I came yowling into the world I was called John. Biblical name. Means 'God's grace,' which is a kindly thing to name a babe who ain't yet done a thing worth being remembered for." He removed his black hat and looked at Nix and Lilah. "I'm happy to make your acquaintance, ladies, and at the same time I beg forgiveness for my rudeness and gruff ways. Please accept my apology, which is earnestly and humbly given." He bowed low, almost sweeping the ground with his hat. As he rose, he caught Tom with a grin and a wink. "You look like a traveling man, and that sword of yours marks you as a trade guard or a bounty hunter. So you've probably heard the name I go by."

"Which is?"

The man straightened and opened the flap of his coat to reveal the worn black cover of a Bible tucked halfway into an inner pocket. "Preacher Jack."

Tom's eyes narrowed slightly. "You're Preacher Jack?"

"Yes sir, I am, in both flesh and spirit. You have heard of me, then?"

"We know some of the same people," murmured Tom. "J-Dog, Solomon Jones, Dr. Skillz. Lot of people in my trade pass through Wawona."

A light suddenly seemed to ignite in Preacher Jack's blue eyes, and it seemed to Benny as if the man went pale. The preacher looked at Tom, giving him a thorough up-and-down appraisal, and then turned to look at Benny, Lilah, and Nix. Each time his eyes shifted to another person, Benny thought he could see that strange light flicker in the old man's eyes. All of this happened in the space of a few seconds, but the whole temperature of the day seemed to change. The only thing that stayed the same was the preacher's wriggling smile.

"Well, well, well. What a blessed day, sir, and if you ever put that meat skewer down I'd like to shake your hand, because I do believe I know who you are. Yes, sir. Tough-looking man, early thirties with black hair and black eyes. Japanese sword and Japanese face to go with it. I would bet my last ration dollar that you are none other than Tom Imura. Tom the Swordsman. Tom of the Woods. Fast Tommy. Tom the Killer."

Tom slowly lowered his sword. "I don't use nicknames," he said softly.

"No, not like most folks," said Preacher Jack, pushing a strand of white hair from his face. "After First Night, most of the folks who live out here were more than happy to shed their family names the way a serpent will shed its skin. Gave them a chance to stop being who they were. Gave them a chance to be reborn as different people. Sometimes much better people. Sometimes not, but you'd know all about that, Brother Tom."

Tom merely grunted as he resheathed his sword. Everyone else seemed to let out a breath at the same time, and Benny lowered his bokken. Not that he could have done much. It still amazed and baffled him how this grizzled old man could be as lightning fast as Tom. And besides that, why was a preacher able to handle a knife like a professional fighter?

"Most of those nicknames," Tom said, "were hung on me by people who don't really know me."

Benny caught the careful way his brother was speaking. Tom may have put his sword away, but he was still on guard.

"I'll call you whatever name pleases you, brother," said Preacher Jack, holding out his hand. "I've heard so many interesting and fabulous things about you that I would like to shake you by the hand, yes sir I would."

Tom ignored the hand and used his chin to point to the dead man. "You know anything about this?"

Preacher Jack looked at his own hand as if surprised to find it hanging out there in the air. He gave a rueful shrug and used that hand to adjust his broad-brimmed hat. The preacher walked slowly past Benny and looked down at the corpse. Nix and Lilah stood on the other side of him, giving him guarded glares. Chong had his hands dug into his pockets and was staring at the dirt between his shoes.

"The Children have been at him?" said Preacher Jack.

"Children?" Nix blurted. "We didn't—"

"No," Benny said, "he means the Children of Lazarus. Zoms."

Preacher Jack winced as if Benny had squirted him with lemon juice.

"Ooooh . . . you're right and you're wrong, young sir. Right, in that it was the Children of Lazarus who did for this poor man; but wrong in that 'zom' is an ugly word that decent folk won't use."

"It's just short for zombie," said Benny.

"I know what it's short for, little brother," said Preacher Jack, "but no part of that word should be bandied about. The word comes from Nzambi, the name of a West African snake god. Do you say that you speak that word to worship a pagan animal spirit? Or do you use it as a twist on *sombra*, the Louisiana Creole word for ghost? Because that would be like acknowledging the power of the devil himself here on earth."

Benny was confused. Preacher Jack's voice was as charming as an ice cream seller, but his eyes were as cold as winter frost.

"I—," Benny began, but Nix cut him off.

"My mother taught me that words only mean what we want them to mean, mister." Her voice was cold and precise.

"Oh, that's a nice sentiment, but it's a crooked mile from

the truth. Reality is that words are full of power. The good clean power of the Lord and dark, twisted magic."

"Everybody uses the word 'zom,'" said Benny, though he knew that wasn't true. Brother David never used it and didn't like to hear it, and Benny had no problem editing himself around the monk . . . but now he felt like yelling "Zom-zom-zom!" at the top of his lungs.

Preacher Jack's dark eyes twinkled. "The word is offensive to many, and to the—"

Tom cut him off. "No offense is intended. We can't speak for anyone else, but if offense is taken from what my brother and his friends say, then that burden is on the listener."

"Is it indeed?" Preacher Jack's smile never wavered. "That's a no harm, no foul way of seeing things, Brother Tom, and I respect it. However, it is in the nature of free will that we can agree to disagree."

Tom ignored that, and instead said, "Do you know anything about what happened to this man?"

The preacher knelt beside the dead man. He made some indistinct humming sounds for a moment, then cocked an eye up at Tom. "What in particular do you want to know, Brother Tom? The man has received the ministrations of the Children of Lazarus and has gone to his maker. He's been quieted courtesy of the white-haired young miss's knife. I'm not sure there's more of this story to tell."

"Lilah didn't quiet him," blurted Nix. "He never reanimated."

Preacher Jack swiveled his head like a praying mantis to look at her. "Now is that a fact, girlie-girl?"

"Don't call me that," Nix snapped.

"Oh, I am sorry. Is that phrase offensive to you?"

Oh boy, thought Benny. He wanted to brain this guy with his bokken.

Before Nix could serve up an acid reply, Tom said, "When we found this man, it was clear he'd been dead for at least a day, and he did not reanimate. I'm asking if you know anything about that."

"No, Brother Tom," said Preacher Jack as he stood, "I can't say as I do."

"Any idea who fed him to the dead?"

Benny noted that Tom used "dead" instead of "zoms."

"That is also a mystery to me," said Preacher Jack. "Why on earth would anyone do such a thing?"

"Any idea who he was?" Tom asked. "I hear you're living out at Wawona. Did he come through there?"

"I never laid eyes on this poor sinner before."

Tom almost smiled. "Sinner? If you haven't seen him before, then how do you know he was a sinner?"

"We're all sinners, Brother Tom. Each and every living, breathing resident of this purgatory. Even humble men of the cloth such as my own self. Sinners all. Only the Children of Lazarus are pure of heart and immaculate of soul."

"How's that work?" asked Benny skeptically. "They eat people."

"They are the meek raised up from death to inherit this new Garden of Eden." He opened his arms wide to include the green and overgrown expanse of the Rot and Ruin. "They have been reborn in the blood of the old world, washed clean of their sins, and they now walk in the light of redemption. It is only us, the dwindling few, who cling to old ways of sin and heresy and godlessness."

"Um . . . ," Benny began, but realized that he was no candidate for a religious debate.

Lilah stepped forward. Her eyes looked a bit jumpy, and Benny realized that she was probably unnerved by having her weapon taken away from her so easily. The only other person who had defeated her was Charlie Pink-eye. "You are saying that we are all sinners? That we deserve whatever happens to us?"

"It's not what I am saying, little miss; it's what the Good Book says."

"Being eaten by zoms is in the Bible?" Nix asked, giving him a frank stare; and Benny liked that she leaned on the word "zoms."

"Not in words that crude." He patted the book inside his coat. "But yes . . . the fate of all mankind is laid out in chapter and verse."

"Where?" demanded Lilah. "Where does it say that in the Bible?"

Something shifted in the preacher's eyes. Benny thought it was like a snake looking out through the eyeholes of a mask.

"It's in there for those who read the scriptures," the preacher answered quietly. "But I bet that you've never taken the time to—"

"You'd lose that bet, mister."

Everyone turned. It was Chong who had spoken up. He had retrieved Lilah's spear from the bushes and handed it to her. She accepted it without glancing at him.

Preacher Jack gave Chong an up-and-down evaluation with his eyes and dismissed him with a twitch of his smiling mouth. "I doubt that, son. From what I heard, this young lady's been living hard and wild in these mountains, far from any church or congregation."

"How does that matter? Does a sheepdog stop being a sheepdog if there's no herd or shepherd?" Chong gave his dry lips a nervous lick. "Don't raise theological questions unless you're prepared to debate them."

Preacher Jack's smile still did not dim. "Well, well, well . . . what have you stumbled upon, Jack? A Sunday School class trip all the way out here in the Rot and Ruin?"

"Hardly that," said Tom quietly.

"Then what?"

Chong, Lilah, Nix, and Benny all started to speak, but Tom snapped his fingers, a sound as sharp and urgent as a pistol shot. He gave a hand gesture, a palms-down press as if he was patting the air. It was one of the warrior hand signals he had taught them over the last seven months. *Be silent but be ready.*

"We're out here on personal business," said Tom mildly. "Family business. We don't discuss that business with strangers."

"Is that what we are, Brother Tom?" asked Preacher Jack with a hint of reproach in his voice. "Are we strangers?"

Tom said, "If we'd met in town or at Wawona, or in the sanctuary of one of the way stations, then I suppose I'd feel comfortable enough to swap stories. That's not the case. I find a man tortured and fed to the dead. That's suspicious. Then you step out of nowhere."

"I—"

Tom stopped him with a raised hand. "Let me finish. I offer no hostility and mean no disrespect, but I am not in a position to trust a stranger." He nodded toward Benny and the others. "Manners are going to have to take a backseat to common sense and safety."

"So I see."

"I'm going to ask one more time . . . do you know anything about who this man is, why he was killed, or why he didn't reanimate?"

Preacher Jack hooked his thumbs into his belt, and Benny noted that this put the heel of his right hand on the pommel of his knife. Having seen how fast the man could draw that knife, Benny had no illusions that the gesture was accidental. He carefully tightened his grip on the bokken.

"I don't believe that I have any of the answers you seek," murmured the man in the dusty coat.

"Then I think we're done here."

"Done with me or done with this poor sinner?"

"With both." Tom took a small step back.

Preacher Jack nodded. "Perhaps we'll meet again under more pleasant circumstances, Brother Tom."

"That would be nice, sir, but unlikely. You see, we're heading east."

For the first time Preacher Jack's smile flickered. "What? You're leaving these mountains? When will you be coming back?"

"I don't expect that we will."

That wiped the smile completely from the preacher's face. He looked disappointed and even a little bit angry at this news, and Benny watched Tom as his brother watched the change in Preacher Jack's expression.

"Something wrong?" asked Tom, his own face and voice neutral.

The smile returned, tentatively at first and then with all its twitchy vibrancy. "Wrong? Why, no, except that it would surely have been a blessing to sit down, break bread, and try this whole meeting again in a more civilized way. I fear we got ourselves off on the wrong foot here. Knives and hard words and all."

Now Tom smiled, and it looked genuine, at least to Benny.

"Yeah." Tom laughed. "I guess this wasn't the most genial encounter." He shrugged. "On the other hand, it could have been worse."

"Yes," said Preacher Jack with a glitter in his eyes, "it surely could have."

They stood there, eight feet apart with a dead man lying on the ground between them, and Benny had the impression that there were all sorts of conversations going on at the same time. Words that were not being spoken but that were mutually understood. Except to Benny and, from the look on her face, Nix as well.

Preacher Jack bowed to Nix and Lilah. "If by word or deed I have done anything to offend you fine ladies," he said, removing his hat and bowing low once more, "then I am truly sorry and most humbly beg forgiveness. The Ruin is not a charm school, and in hard times we often forget who we are and where we came from."

Lilah said nothing, but her honey-colored eyes lost some of their intensity. Nix gave a single curt bob of her head.

Preacher Jack turned to Benny. "Peace to you, little brother."

"Um . . . yeah, sure. Back atcha."

Preacher Jack ignored Chong altogether, but he fixed Tom with a knowing smile. "I won't offer my hand again, Brother Tom, for fear that it will once more be left hanging in the wind. So I'll tip my hat and bid you all a farewell. May the Good Lord keep you from snakes and snares and the evil that men do."

With that the preacher replaced his hat, tugged his lapels to adjust the hang of his jacket, and walked back into the woods, where he vanished so quickly into the shadows that the whole encounter might have been a dream. Tom and the others stood where they were for a full five minutes, listening first for Preacher Jack's soft footfalls and then to the forest as the ordinary sounds one by one returned.

Benny let out a chestful of air and turned to Tom. "What was that all about?"

"I really don't know," said Tom.

Benny could see that Tom was troubled. He followed his brother over to the edge of the road, and they both squatted to study the dirt of the game trail along which Preacher Jack had gone. Benny watched as Tom used a twig to measure the man's shoe impressions. "Good-quality hiking shoes," murmured Tom. "Pre–First Night, which means they're either scavenged or purchased for a tidy stack of ration dollars."

Benny nodded and bent low to study the pattern of the shoes, just as Tom had taught him. The tread was pretty well worn, and there was a crescent-shaped nick out of the right heel.

"That nick is pretty distinctive," Benny said, earning him an approving nod from Tom.

"It's as good as a fingerprint. Remember it." Then Tom called the others over to look at it too, pointing out the unique elements of each sole.

"Why bother?" asked Chong. "Is he our enemy?"

"I don't know what he is," admitted Tom, "but out here it's a good idea to observe as many details as you can. You never know what's going to be useful."

"Was that really Preacher Jack?" asked Nix.

Tom rose and squinted down the game trail. "Well . . . he fits the description Dr. Skillz gave me. At least physically."

"Is it okay if I say that he was the single creepiest thing I've ever seen, and I've been face-to-face with decaying zoms?"

Tom nodded. "Yeah, Nix, you can say that and mean it."

"I don't like him," growled Lilah, her fists clenched tightly around the shaft of her spear. "If I see him again . . ." She let the rest hang in the air.

"I think it's a good idea if we all watch our backs," suggested Tom.

"Are you sure he's really a preacher?" asked Chong.

Tom shook his head. "I'm not sure of anything about him. Not one thing."

He looked up at the sky.

Benny started to ask something, but Tom shook his head.

"We're burning daylight," Tom said. "We need to get to the way station, and I need to think while we're doing it. We'll talk then. For now, we'll go at Scout pace. That means we walk two hundred paces, run three hundred, walk two hundred. It'll chew up the miles."

And it'll keep us too busy to ask questions, whispered Benny's inner voice. Smart.

"Nix—this is up to you. Can you handle the pace? No screwing around: yes or no?"

"Yes," she said with real fire. "And I promise to tell you if I can't keep up."

Without another word, Tom turned toward the southeast and set off.

The others followed. Running and walking and running. They didn't have time to ask questions, but about ten thousand of them occurred to Benny, and he knew that the same questions would be occurring to Nix.

Who was Preacher Jack?

Was he connected to the dead man? Who had killed the man? And why? Could Charlie Pink-eye still be alive? Was he out in these same hills? Did he know they were out here?

And, maybe more important than any of those questions: How come the dead man had not reanimated? Since First Night, everyone who died, no matter how they died, came back to life.

Why hadn't he?

What did it mean?

The questions burned in Benny's mind as he ran.

FROM NIX'S JOURNAL

How many people are still alive out there?

Tom says that there's a network of about five hundred bounty hunters, traders, way-station monks, and scavengers in central California. And maybe as many as two hundred loners living in isolated and remote spots. Sounds like a lot, but it's not. Our history teacher said that California used to be the most populous state and that there used to be almost forty million people living here.

28

THEY LEFT THE OLD ROAD AND FOUND WHAT USED TO BE A HIGHWAY, so they turned and followed that. Despite the fact that his toe was hurting like crazy and his clothes were thoroughly soaked with sweat, Benny still mustered the energy to look left and right, left and right, checking every shadow under every tree for some sign of movement that could be either zoms or worse.

Charlie's dead, he told himself, but his inner voice—the less emotional and more rational aspect of his mind—replied, *You don't know that.*

He cut looks at Nix, who was also sweating heavily and yet seemed able to keep going, despite the pain and the injury. It wasn't the first time that her strength amazed and humbled him.

They ran and walked, ran and walked.

During one of the walking times, Benny leaned to Nix. "What the heck was that?"

"Preacher Jack," she said, and shivered. "I feel like I need a bath."

Benny counted on his fingers. "We know—what—seven religious people? I mean people in the business."

"You mean clerics? There's the four in town, Pastor Kellogg, Father Shannon, Rabbi Rosemann, and Imam Murad . . ."

". . . and the monks at the way station: Brother David, Sister Shanti, and Sister Sarah. Seven," finished Benny. "Except for the monks, who are a little, y'know . . ." He tapped his temple and rolled his eyes.

"Touched by God," Nix said. "Isn't that the phrase Tom uses?"

"Right, except for them, everyone else is pretty okay. I mean the monks are okay too, but they're loopy from living out here in the Ruin. But even with different religions, different churches, they're all pretty much the kind of people you want to hang with during a real wrath-of-God moment."

"Not him, though," said Nix, nodding along with where Benny was going with this. "He's scarier than the zoms."

"'Zoms' is a bad word, girlie-girl," Benny said in a fair imitation of Preacher Jack's oily voice.

"Eww . . . don't!" Nix punched him on the arm.

They walked another few paces as the road bent around a hill.

"Weird day," Benny said.

"Weird day," Nix agreed.

Around the bend were dozens of cars and trucks that had been pushed to the side of the main road, which left a clear path down the center. Some of the cars had tumbled into the drainage ditch that ran along one side. Others were smashed together. There were skeletons in a few of them.

"Who pushed the cars out of the way?" asked Chong.

"Probably a tank," said Tom. "Or a bulldozer. Before they

nuked the cities, back when they thought this was a winnable war." He gestured to the line of broken cars, many of them nearly invisible behind clumps of shrubbery. "This is a well-traveled route. Traders and other people out here. All these cars have been checked for zoms a hundred times."

Nix wasn't fooled, and she gave Tom a sly smile. "Which doesn't mean they're safe. We have to check them every time, don't we?"

Tom gave her an approving nod. "That's the kind of thinking—"

"—that's going to keep us alive," finished Benny irritably. "Yeah, we pretty much get that."

To Tom, Nix said, "He's cranky because he didn't think of it first."

"Yes, I did," Benny lied.

They moved on.

As the sun began edging toward the western tree line, they crested a hill and looked down a long dirt side road to where an old gas station sat beneath a weeping willow.

"Take a closer look," suggested Tom, handing Benny a pair of high-power binoculars.

Benny focused the lenses and studied the scene. The surrounding vegetation was dense with overgrowth, but there was a broad concrete pad around the cluster of small buildings. An ancient billboard stood against the wall of trees. It had long ago been whitewashed, and someone had written hundreds of lines of scripture on it. Rain had faded the words so that only a few were readable.

"This is Brother David's place?" asked Chong in a leaden voice. Between the catastrophe with the rhino and finding the dead man, and then the weird encounter with Preacher Jack, Chong seemed to have lost his humor and virtually all trace of emotion. He barely spoke, and when he did his voice lacked inflection. It was like listening to a sleepwalker.

Tom caught the sound and cut a look at Benny, who nodded.

Tom mouthed the words, "Keep your eye on him," and Benny nodded again.

"Yup," said Benny. "He was the first monk I ever met out here. It's him and two girls. Sister Sarah and Sister Shanti."

"And Old Roger," added Nix.

"Who?" Chong asked.

"He's a zom they take care of. Remember I told you?"

Chong nodded but didn't comment.

They descended along a path that ran beside a mammoth line of white boulders dumped there ages ago by a glacier. A thin stream of water trickled between the rocks, but it was so small that it made no sound. Chong lagged behind the rest, and Benny slowed to keep pace with him. When Benny caught a look at Chong's face, he almost missed his step.

There were tears at the corners of Chong's dark eyes.

"Hey, dude. What's—?"

Chong touched Benny's arm. "I'm really sorry, man."

Benny shook his head and started to protest.

"No," Chong interrupted, "I should never have come. You guys are better off without me."

"Don't be an idiot," Benny said, though his voice lacked total conviction. "Besides, this way you get to spend a couple of days with Lilah—"

Chong dismissed that with a derisive snort. "Ever since the rhino thing, I'm less than dog crap to her."

"C'mon, dude, she's like that with everyone. I mean, she's been trying to quiet me for a coupla days now."

Chong merely shook his head. "I spoiled everything."

"No way. Don't even go there."

"I'm sorry I came," Chong insisted, but this time he said it more to himself. Benny was fishing for something encouraging to say when Tom stopped them all with a raised fist.

He scanned the terrain for a moment, then waved everyone over.

"Is everything okay?" Benny asked.

"Let's find out," Tom said guardedly.

Tom headed down the slope and the others followed. For Benny this was the first moment today that wasn't wrapped in tension. He thought Brother David was halfway to being crazy, but he was one of the nicest people Benny had ever met, and the two girls with him were sweet-natured and pretty. All three of them were good cooks, too, and even after everything he'd seen, Benny was sure he could eat a full-size rhinoceros.

They came down onto the concrete pad, on which the single gas pump stood like a great rusted tombstone to a dead culture. Tom knocked loudly on the pump's metal casing. The echoes bounced off the hills and came faintly back to them before melting into silence.

There was no response. Tom narrowed his eyes. "Stay here." He walked carefully to the front door of the station and knocked. Nothing. "Brother David?" he called.

Absolutely nothing.

Scowling, Tom waved the others over and they approached with great caution, their weapons in their hands.

"Be ready," Tom said as he reached for the door handle. It turned easily, and the door swung inward. Tom drew his pistol and moved silently inside. The others crept after him. Lilah broke to Tom's right. Benny slipped in next, with Nix at his back, and they shifted to Tom's left.

However, there was no need of caution.

"Where is everyone?" whispered Nix.

Tom shook his head and took a few tentative steps into the room.

Most of the front part of the station was set up for trading and an attempt at comfort. There were folding chairs, a woodstove, and a table for meals. Benny, Tom, and Nix had stayed here several times and eaten the modest but well-cooked food offered by the Children of God; and Tom always brought some supplies as gifts.

The rest of the way station had been converted into living quarters for the monk and the two female disciples. There were bedrolls and plastic milk crates that served as bureaus and night tables. Sheets were strung on clothesline to provide marginal privacy. Garlands of flowers and herbs were hung from pegs set into the walls.

"Where are they?" Nix asked again.

"Lilah," Tom said, "check the sheds."

She nodded and slipped out the door without a word. It annoyed Benny a bit that Tom never asked him to do something like that, but this wasn't the time to start an argument.

Nix crossed to the stove and looked into the pots, then

held her hand above the burners. "It's cold, but there's food in the pots. Hasn't gone bad yet."

"Teacups on the table, too," said Benny. "And it looks like all their stuff's back there. That's Sister Shanti's traveling bag on her bed. Think they went out for a walk? A day trip or something?"

Tom shook his head. "No . . . looks like they just got up and walked out." He knelt and picked up a pair of reading glasses. One of the lenses was cracked from side to side. "Brother David's." He frowned. "And there's more. I sent a load of supplies here. Carpet coats, tents, cooking gear, extra rations, and some weapons. I don't see any of it here."

The door opened and Lilah came in. "Someone broke the lock on Old Roger's shed. He's gone . . . tracks lead east."

"How long?" asked Tom.

"Late morning."

Tom nodded again. "I think that's when everyone left."

They stood in the dusty sunlight, thinking that through, silently letting the implications shout at them.

"Okay . . . we don't have enough daylight left to get back to town," said Tom, "and I sure as hell don't want to sleep up in the hills tonight. Too many weird things going on."

"I'll second that," mumbled Benny.

"So we have two choices. We hole up here and fortify this place, or we push on to Sunset Hollow. If we run most of the way, we can make it by full dark."

Benny was already shaking his head. Sunset Hollow was where he and Tom had lived before First Night. It was where the zombies of their parents had been kept by Tom for fourteen years; and it was where they were buried now. On one hand it had a high wall and a fence they could lock; on the other hand, Benny was sure that if he went back there he would go totally ape crazy.

"Nix can't do all that running," he said, fishing for a reasonable excuse. "And Chong has to go home tomorrow."

"Don't make this about me," said Nix defiantly. "I'll outrun your narrow butt any day of the week, Benny Imura."

Benny winced.

"Stay here," voted Lilah. "Five of us can hold this place."

"There's no back exit," Tom replied.

Lilah considered that and said nothing. She turned and looked at the others, then frowned. "Where is Chong?"

They all turned to the door, each of them realizing that Chong had not come inside with them.

"Was he outside when you checked around back?"

She nodded but immediately rushed outside. Tom was a half step behind her.

Chong was nowhere in sight.

"THIS DAY CANNOT GET ANY WORSE," TOM SAID UNDER HIS BREATH.

Benny shot him a look. It was the kind of statement that he would never dare make because the universe always seemed to take it as a challenge. He cupped his hands and called Chong's name.

The echoes bounced around and came back empty.

"Oh, come on," growled Tom with mounting frustration. "Somebody that smart can't possibly be this dumb."

"Maybe he went somewhere to go to the bathroom," suggested Benny. "Chong's pretty shy about that stuff . . . so maybe he—"

"Went to the bathroom where? In his damn parents' house? There's an outhouse twenty feet away, and there are bushes everywhere he could squat behind."

"He was pretty upset," said Nix. "Maybe he just wanted to be alone."

Tom turned to her and gave her a long, withering stare. "Alone? In the Rot and bloody Ruin?"

She flushed bright red and immediately started calling Chong's name again. Tom did too. Only Lilah stayed silent. Her damaged larynx made it impossible for her to shout loud enough to do any good; but her honey-colored eyes missed nothing as she turned in a full circle and surveyed the surrounding forest.

Lilah shot Nix an evil look. "Are all boys this stupid?"

"Hey!" said Benny.

Nix didn't answer. She called Chong's name again, shouting it as loud as she could, even though it hurt her injury to do it. If he could hear the shouts, Chong did not answer.

Tom cursed with great vehemence for several seconds. "I am so going to kill him. I'm going to drag him back to town and chain him to his own front porch."

"I'll help," offered Benny, who was as angry as he was scared.

Tom looked from the tree line to the sun and back again. "Damn it." He turned to the others. "Okay, everyone spread out. Find Chong's footprints. He has those wedge-soled boots. Keep your weapons in hand and stay in sight with at least one other person. You find anything, call out. Go!"

The four of them moved away from the front of the station as if they were propelled outward by an explosion.

He's gone, whispered Benny's inner voice. *Be prepared for that.*

Benny didn't want to believe it, but his mind was replaying his last conversation with Chong, and Chong's last words: "I should never have come."

"Come on, you monkey-banger," Benny muttered aloud as he scanned the dusty ground and picked his way through the broken concrete. "Stop screwing around."

Then he found something that froze the blood in his veins. He straightened and yelled as loud as he could.

"HERE!"

Everyone came running. Benny saw the flash of sunlight on Tom's sword as his brother ran up from his left, and the glitter on the wicked edge of Lilah's spear as she closed in from the right. Nix came puffing up behind him. They all stopped and stared. No one said a word. The words had already been said.

They were scraped onto the side of a slab of concrete pushed almost vertical by tree roots. Chong had left them a message. Two words.

I'M SORRY.

Benny looked at what lay beyond the slab of concrete. Miles of white rock left by a glacier. White rock baking in the sunlight. The row of rocks split off into five separate threads that led high into the mountains and vanished into the gloom gathering under the forest canopy.

Benny remembered a basic fact of tracking that Tom had taught him: Rubber-soled shoes don't leave tracks on rock.

There were five possible trails, and there were four of them. The sun was already behind the treetops, and it would be dark in two hours.

With a feeling of sinking horror, Benny realized that Chong, smart as ever, had picked a path away from them that was impossible to follow. In grief and shame, he had run away.

And there was nothing they could do about it.

30

Lou Chong ran as fast as he could over the rocks. His heart pounded, but it also ached. Benny would hate him for this. So would Nix and Tom. Lilah, however . . . well, Chong figured that Lilah would be happy to have him gone. Lilah despised weakness, and Chong felt that "weak" had quickly become his defining characteristic. At least out here in the Ruin.

He felt stupid and ashamed. He should never have agreed to come, and though he briefly thought that Tom was just as much to blame for even suggesting this trip, Chong believed the stuff that had gone wrong was all his own fault. He was fairly certain that Tom was on the verge of turning back, which meant that Chong would be responsible for screwing up what Nix and Benny really wanted. And for denying Lilah the freedom that she craved.

That was the process of logic that had spurred him to run, though now, deep in the woods, he could see that the logic was as thin as tissue paper and filled with holes. He remembered one of his father's countless lessons about logical thinking: "When you add emotion to any equation, you can't trust the results." Shame and guilt were emotions, and the sum at the end of his logical calculations was as untrustworthy as his actions back on the road when the rhino first appeared.

"I'm not cut out for the Ruin," he told himself as he ran. "I'm nobody's idea of Mr. Adventure." His words were pitched to sound funny, but his heart was breaking.

As he ran he made himself remember everything that Mr. Feeney had taught them in the Scouts and what he had read in books about the forests of the Sierra Nevadas. All the tricks about tracking and stalking. And about how to foil pursuit. There was a lot of that in books. The Leatherstocking Tales and old Louis L'Amour novels from long before First Night.

Chong knew about doubling back and leaving false trails. He knew how to circle around and cut his own trail. He knew how to keep from scuffing the rocks. Several times he jumped down from the rocks and ran into the tall grass, then carefully walked backward in his own footprints so that anyone following would think he ran into the field. When he reached the forest, he found a broken branch that still had some leaves on it, and as he ran he whisked the ground behind him to wipe out his trail.

Maybe Tom or Lilah could find him, but he didn't think so. If they were alone and had all the time in the world, sure . . . but they had to watch out for Benny and Nix.

Chong even smiled to himself with how clever he was being. It felt good to do something right, even if the others would hate him for it. Better that than having them hurt again because of him. Especially if Charlie Pink-eye was still alive. It would be better for Benny and the others to keep going east, to get far beyond the reach of that maniac.

Chong knew enough about orienteering to know which way was northwest. And even though he hated physical exertion, he could climb a tree and lash himself to the trunk to wait out the night.

As it grew dark he slowed to a walk. The canopy of leaves was so dense he could catch only glimpses of the sky. Sunset couldn't be more than an hour and a half away. It was time to find shelter.

He saw an upslope and took that, reasoning that high ground would give him a better view to help him pick a likely tree for the night, and allow him to see if he was indeed alone in this section of the forest. Chong was sure he could outrun a zom, but if one came after him, the creature would simply follow him to whatever tree he chose and stand there until the world ended. It could outwait him.

"No thanks," he told himself, and almost jumped at the sound of his own voice. He drew his bokken. He was not as strong a swordsman as Benny, or as fast as Nix, but Chong knew that he was far from helpless, and holding the weapon recharged his confidence.

At the top of the hill he turned in a full circle. Shadows clustered around the base of each tree, and every time the wind blew Chong imagined he could see a ghastly shape lumbering his way. But he saw no zoms.

He spotted a stately cottonwood tree with a couple of branches low enough to grab and many more high up among the leaves. He ran down the hill and began climbing the slope atop of which was the cottonwood. He looked left and right, checking his surroundings, filling his mind with data, being smart and careful.

But he walked right past the two figures standing in the dense shadows beneath a massive old spruce. They, however, saw him.

Tom, Lilah, Nix, and Benny were miles away. Much too far away to hear Lou Chong's screams.

31

BENNY STOPPED AS MOVEMENT CAUGHT HIS EYE FAR TO THE NORTH. A flock of birds leaped out of the distant trees like a cloud of locusts. They swirled and eddied in the air and then gradually settled back down among the dark green leaves.

"What was that?" asked Nix, catching the sudden jerk of Benny's head but missing what he was looking at. She was kneeling among the rocks sixty yards from the way station, trying to determine if a smudge could be one of Chong's footprints.

"Just some birds," he said. Even so, Benny continued to stare.

Lilah climbed up on the rocks from the other side. "Where?"

Benny pointed. The trees were still for a five count, and then the birds jumped up again. As a swarm they moved a hundred yards south and settled in different trees.

"Lilah," Benny asked, "d'you think—?"

Before he could finish, Lilah turned and clapped her hands over her head several times to attract Tom's attention. He was on the far side of the station, but he came at a run.

"What is it?"

Benny described what they'd seen. Tom didn't immediately reply. He looked at the sun again and the long shadows cast by the western line of trees, then he turned and studied the area where Lilah had pointed.

"It's got to be Chong," decided Tom. "Direction's right. Could be heading for the northern trade route."

"Yeah," Benny agreed. Tom had made them study every route and path in the Ruin.

Nix chewed her lip. "Tom, do you think Chong's trying to go back home?"

"Sure. Where else would he go? The question has always been how. There are fifty ways to get to Mountainside from here, and all we know for sure is that he isn't going the way we came."

"Preacher Jack's out there too," said Nix.

Tom didn't reply, but the muscles at the corners of his jaw bunched and flexed.

"C'mon," cried Benny, grabbing at his bokken. "What are we waiting for? Let's go."

"Sorry, kiddo," said Tom, "but you and Nix would slow me down too much. It's going to be dark soon, and I'm a lot faster alone."

It was true, but Benny tried to come up with an argument to get around it.

"I'll go," said Lilah.

Tom shook his head. "No. You're tough, Lilah, but I can't allow it." Lilah stiffened at the word "allow," but Tom didn't back down. "I admit that you're good. You survived out here for years . . . but I'm still better at this. I'm bigger and faster, and I've been hunting these mountains for fourteen years. Besides, the Chongs left their son in my care. This is my fault, and it's mine to make right. I also don't want to argue about this. I want you to stay here with Nix and Benny. You can help them fortify this place. Remember, Sally Two-Knives is due through here tonight, and J-Dog and Dr. Skillz are in the area. Wait for them. Are we agreed?"

Nix, Benny, and Lilah all began yelling at once, telling Tom why they thought the plan was bad, arguing why they should all go, and growling at him for treating them like they were helpless. Tom took about five seconds of it before his face darkened.

"Okay—enough!"

Silence dropped over them like a net.

"This isn't a debate. The three of you will damn well stay here and do as you're told. That means you, too, Lilah."

Three sets of hostile eyes glared raw heat at him. However, what Tom said next changed their looks from hostility to fear.

"If I'm not back in twenty-four hours, Lilah . . . I want you to take Benny and Nix back home."

"What?" demanded Nix.

"Hold on a frickin' minute," snapped Benny.

"Okay," said Lilah.

Benny and Nix whipped their heads around and looked at her liked she'd just betrayed them. Lilah's face was a mask of stone.

Into the silence, Tom said, "Good." He patted his pockets to reassure himself that he had everything he needed, then fished out two of his three bottles of cadaverine and handed them to Benny.

"I don't plan to be gone long enough to need this much," said Tom. "You might."

"Tom, I—," Benny began, but Tom cupped him around the back of the neck and pulled him forward. He kissed Benny on the forehead.

"Stand tough, little brother. You've learned a lot in the last seven months. Use it. Be warrior smart."

Benny nodded. "Warrior smart."

Tom hugged Nix and patted Lilah's cheek. "All of you," he said, "warrior smart."

They nodded.

Tom turned and began running along the line of glacial rocks. He moved with an oiled grace that was deceptively fast. Within seconds he was nearly to the tree line; within minutes he was gone, swallowed up by the darkening forest as the sun tumbled over the edge of the world.

PART THREE
HARD LUCK AND TROUBLE

It is easy to hate and it is difficult to love.
This is how the whole scheme of things works.
All good things are difficult to achieve;
and bad things are very easy to get.

—RENÉ DESCARTES, FRENCH MATHEMATICIAN,
PHILOSOPHER, AND SCIENTIST, 1596–1650

32

AFTER TOM LEFT, LILAH TURNED TO BENNY AND NIX. "IF WE'RE GOING to spend the night here, let's make this place secure."

"Tell us what to do," said Nix.

The first thing they did was find string and lengths of rope and construct a network of lines around the gas station. Lilah set Benny to work gathering cans from the rubbish heap out back and buckets full of small stones. Nix used a hammer and awl from Brother David's tools to punch holes through the cans. Then Lilah strung the cans on the taut lines and filled each one with a few stones. She strung the lines at various heights so that any zom would walk right into them, and the sound of the stones rattling in the cans would be clear and loud. The strings of cans would also hopefully trip up a human sneaking up in the dark. There was some starlight but no moon, and the tripwires were virtually invisible once the sun was down.

They hung towels and sheets over the window to block out any light. Lilah gathered wood for the stove.

There wasn't much else they could do, and so they settled down to wait.

At first it was merely tense. Benny worried about Chong

and worried about Tom. But as time wore on he began to feel irritable and jumpy.

"I wish Tom was here," he complained.

Lilah, who was cleaning her pistol again, shot him a look. "He would be if Chong had not been stupid."

"Okay," Benny snapped, "so Chong made a few mistakes . . . how about laying off him?"

"Why? He has caused every problem since we left town."

"Chong's just scared, okay? You going to tell me you never made any mistakes because you were scared?"

Something seemed to move behind Lilah's eyes, but her voice was cold and steady. "Yes, I made mistakes. But they never put anyone else in danger."

"That's because you never had anyone else," Benny said savagely, and immediately regretted his words as he saw the hurt register in Lilah's eyes. "Oh, crap. Look, Lilah, I didn't mean—"

She gave him a murderous look, flung open the door, and went outside. The sun was a fiery dragon's eye peering through the trees.

Benny stared at the stiffness of her retreating back until Nix came and stood over him, blocking the view. The disapproval on her face was eloquent. Benny closed his eyes.

"What was that all about?" she asked.

"I can't believe I said that to her."

Nix punched him in the chest. Not hard, but hard enough to make her point. She turned and walked away.

Benny's inner voice said, *Smooth.*

"Shut up," he muttered.

It was nearly full dark before Lilah came back into the house. She ignored Benny completely and went to the table and continued with the process of cleaning her gun as if nothing had happened. Nix locked the door and pulled the curtains over the window.

They built a small fire in the stove. They made and ate some food. They drank water from their canteens.

They slowly went crazy from waiting.

Lilah and Nix barely spoke to Benny. At first he felt bad about that, but as the evening wore on he began to resent them for it. An hour crawled by. Outside crickets pulsed in the grass, and a dry wind began to disturb the treetops.

They listened to it as they ate more of the beans and rice. Nix was the cook, and she added some onions, garlic, and spices from Brother David's meager stores. Lilah could cook, but no one alive wanted to eat what she prepared; Benny could cook too, but he had no sense for seasoning. To him spices began and ended with salt and hot sauce.

Another half hour limped by them. Lilah gathered up every knife in the way station and began cleaning them. She placed them in a neat row.

"Are we just going to sit here?" Benny griped as he glared across the table at Lilah.

Nix gave him a cold look and flapped her hand. "There's the door. No one's forcing you to stay here."

"Very funny."

Lilah kicked the table very hard. "Nix is right. You are welcome to leave if you think you can do something useful."

"Maybe I should."

"Maybe you should," Lilah agreed, getting in his face.

"Maybe *you* should," Benny fired back. "We probably wouldn't be in this mess if it wasn't for you."

Lilah looked totally perplexed. "What?"

"Oh, come on. You think this is all Chong's fault, and maybe a lot of it is, but he wouldn't even have come along on this dumb camping trip if it wasn't for how he felt."

Lilah blinked in surprise. "What?"

"You heard me. If you weren't here, then there's no way Chong would have come along. He'd be home safe."

"Benny!" warned Nix, but Lilah cut in.

"Me? Why? What do I have to do with what he does?"

"Because he's head-over-freaking-heels in love with you, Lilah. How can you be so freaking observant and not know—"

"Benny!" Nix jumped to her feet. "Cut it out."

Shut up! snarled his inner voice. Benny ignored both warnings. "It's the truth."

Lilah stared at him with a mixture of confusion and anger. "You should shut up."

He pointed a finger at her. "And you should open your damn eyes, Lilah. He's been mooning over you since you moved in with him. He can't take his eyes off you."

"Shut up!"

"You talked with him back on the road. I'll bet he told you how he feels and you just threw it back in his face."

"Shut up!" Lilah yelled.

"Are you denying it? Didn't he say anything back there?"

"Go away."

"What did you two talk about?"

Lilah glowered. "He asked me if this was all his fault and

I told him the truth. I told him that he was a town boy . . . he isn't strong enough to be out here."

"You told him that? Were you trying to make him run away?"

"No!"

"What did he say to you?"

"It's none of your business, so shut up!" barked Lilah, banging her fist on the table hard enough to make one of the knives roll off and clatter to the floor. In the ensuing silence she bent and picked it up.

Benny knew that he should shut up, that he should leave this alone, but he couldn't keep the words from spilling out. "What happens if I don't shut up? You going to threaten me again? I'll bet you can't wait for the chance to quiet me. And Chong. And maybe Nix, too."

Lilah's face went dead pale. Tears, as small as chips of diamonds, glistened in the corners of her eyes. She opened her mouth to speak, but Nix beat her to it.

"Benny," yelled Nix, "so help me God—"

THUD!

Something hit the front door. They froze, mouths open but silent, eyes staring at the door, ears straining to hear. The wind tossed the treetops. There was no other sound, not even the crickets.

"What was that?" demanded Benny.

Nix held a finger to her lips. Lilah tightened her grip on the knife.

Benny licked his lips. "Oh, crap," he said softly.

Nix picked up both bokkens and handed one of the swords to Benny. They listened to the night. The crickets had stopped. They did that when they were startled, Benny knew. When they were afraid. When there was something there.

They waited, listening for sounds. Hoping to hear Tom call out. Or Chong.

Thud!

Another blow against the door. The sound was both heavy and soft. Muffled. Like a fist wrapped in a towel. Or . . .

Thud! Thud-thud!

Or a hand flung loosely, without purpose or conscious control.

Thud—thud—thud.

Whatever was beating on the door was not Tom. Or Chong. Or anyone alive.

Then they heard the moan.

33

"THERE'S A ZOMBIE OUT THERE," WHISPERED BENNY.

"I know," murmured Lilah is her ghostly voice. She used her free hand to wipe the tears from her eyes. "It must have heard you."

"Heard us," answered Benny, but his defense was weak and he knew it. Lilah snorted.

Thud.

"What's it doing?" Nix asked in a horrified voice. "Is it knocking to get in?"

Lilah shook her head. "Not knocking. Pounding. It wants to get us . . . the door is in the way."

Somehow that chilled Benny more than the thought that the creature was knocking. Even though he couldn't see the zom, the thought of its limp, dead hand striking over and over again, following some impulse that existed in a brain that had otherwise died was intensely creepy. How could science ever explain that? How could anything make sense of it?

The pounding continued. There was no rhythm to it, but each blow carried the same dead-weight force.

"What should we do?" asked Nix.

Lilah's answer was as cold as the flesh of the monster outside, and there was a weird light in her eyes. She looked more than a little crazy. "We kill it."

They gaped at her.

Benny pointed at the door. "You want us to go out there? To open the door and actually go out?"

"If you're afraid," she sneered, "stay here."

Benny suddenly felt like an idiot. "Look . . . about before—"

"Shut up," warned Lilah. "I don't want to talk about it."

Benny felt humiliated, so he tried to stand straighter, and he put what he hoped was a tough-guy, bounty-hunter, zombie-killer glare in his eye.

"What's wrong with your face?" Lilah asked. "Are you going to throw up?"

"No, I—"

Lilah pushed him out of the way. "When you open the door, I'll shove him back. Close the door behind me. When he's quieted I'll knock. Be ready to let me in."

"We will," promised Nix, "but shouldn't you at least put on a carpet coat?"

Lilah sneered at the suggestion. "For one zom?"

Benny cleared his throat. "Look . . . Lilah . . . are you sure you want to do this?"

The Lost Girl gave him a funny look. "What does 'want' have to do with anything? The dead will keep trying to get us. Pounding can be heard."

As if to punctuate her remark, the limp hand struck again. And again.

"Now," she said softly. She held her knife with the easy competence that only came with years of practical experience.

"Now," Lilah said again, and Benny jumped.

"Sorry," he said, and reached for the handle. Lilah gave him a disgusted look.

"Wait!" snapped Nix. She looked at Lilah. "The cans."

Lilah stiffened. "Oh," she said softly.

"Oh, man . . . ," Benny breathed. "How could a zom get through them without . . ." He didn't finish the sentence because there was nowhere to go with it.

"We're in trouble," whispered Nix. "Someone else is out there. Someone alive."

"I know." Lilah stepped back from the door.

Nix closed her eyes for a second. "Brother David and the Sisters didn't just walk away."

"I know," Lilah said again. She slid the knife into its sheath and reached for her spear.

"Wait," said Benny, shifting to block the door. "You're not actually going out there, are you? Not now!"

"Yes."

"Look . . . I'm sorry for what I said, but you don't have to—"

She cut him off by suddenly leaning so close that they were nose to nose. Her golden eyes were fierce and hurt at the same time. "I want to throw you out there."

That shut Benny up.

Thud! Thud!

"Right now, though," Lilah said, turning away from him, "we need to stop the zom from making so much noise. Noise carries at night."

"Lilah," said Nix, "maybe you shouldn't go out there. It could be something a lot more dangerous than a zom."

Lilah's voice was cold. "I'm a lot more dangerous than a zom. Open the door."

"Lilah," whispered Benny, "it could be Charlie Pink-eye out there."

Lilah showed her teeth in a deadly smile. "That would be perfect."

Outside, the zom continued to pound and pound and the endless wind blew like a black ocean. Nix closed the door on the stove and blew out the candles, plunging the room into total darkness except for a faint outline around the door etched by starlight. Benny fumbled for the door handle. He counted down from three and then pulled the door open as he leaped back out of the way.

The zombie was right there, framed by starlight. Tall, thin as a stick, and pale as wax, with black eyes and a gaping mouth. It lurched forward, reaching for Benny, but Lilah suddenly jump-kicked the zom in the chest, driving it backward out of the doorway. She went through the door like a flash of lightning. She caught up with the zom before it could fall, pivoted and slashed at the back of its knee with the bayonet at the end of her spear . It was her signature move, taught to her as a child by George, the man who had raised her after Lilah had been orphaned on First Night. With the tendon cut, the zom immediately dropped to its knees. Lilah kicked it between the shoulder blades, and as it fell face-forward onto the ground, she whirled her spear and bent forward in a powerful two-handed thrust that drove the spear point unerringly into the narrow opening at the base of the skull. The zombie instantly stopped thrashing and twisting and became completely still. Dead . . . for real and forever.

The whole process, from jumping kick to final thrust, had taken less than four seconds.

Benny and Nix crowded the doorway, stunned as always by how fast and efficient Lilah was. And how ruthless. They understood it, but it left them breathless.

"God . . . ," breathed Nix.

"I know," said Benny.

"No," Nix said, rising and pointing. "LOOK!"

Benny squinted to see what she meant. Lilah whirled, bringing her spear up as if expecting a sudden attack. She, too, stared in that direction.

There was plenty of starlight. More than enough to bathe the swaying trees in an eerie blue-white glow. Enough to see the lines of tin cans lying on the ground, the ropes cut and the cans carefully placed upright in neat rows. Somebody else was out here. Somebody smart and careful enough to disable the booby trap. But that was not the worst of it. Not by a long shot. What was truly eerie . . . no, truly terrifying . . . was how that cold moonlight reflected on the pale white faces of the living dead.

On the hundreds of living dead.

"God . . ." Benny's mouth was too numb to say anything more. They were everywhere, an army of lifeless killers that shambled and limped and twitched as they emerged from the utter blackness of the forest. Benny spun and looked left and saw more of them, some walking, a few crawling, all of them moaning louder than the wind. He looked right, going as far as the edge of the station. He could see the long, pale line of tumbled glacial rocks. They were black with the crawling bodies of zombies. The closest of them was a hundred yards away, but they were advancing steadily toward the way station. Benny could not count the dead. They were coming. In minutes they would be here, and there was no way out.

"Please tell me I'm not seeing this," said Benny. "This can't be happening."

"We're dead," whispered Nix. "Oh God . . . oh God . . ."

Lilah turned to them, and in the moonlight Benny and Nix could see that her iron self-confidence had crumbled to reveal a face as bloodless and empty of emotion as the monsters who closed in on all sides. She lowered her spear and it hung from her fingertips, ready to fall.

"We're dead," Nix said again, her voice rising to a hysterical pitch.

"Yes," said the Lost Girl. "We're dead."

34

TOM IMURA WAS AT HOME IN THE ROT AND RUIN. HE LOVED THE WOODS, even as night came cascading down to turn the green world into an almost impenetrable black gloom. Ever since that terrible night fifteen years ago, Tom had spent nearly a third of his life in these woods. Unlike Mountainside, with its stifled boundaries and pervasive fear, the Ruin was a simpler place. You knew where you stood.

Tom reckoned that it was no different than the way the world had been before humans settled the first cities. Back then there had been predators of all kinds, and life was hardscrabble at best. Every day was a fight for survival, but it was that struggle that had inspired humans to become problem solvers. The inventiveness of the human race was one of the most crucial tools of survival, and it was the cornerstone of all civilization. Without it, man would never have turned fire into a tool, or carved a wheel from a piece of wood.

Tom knew that there were zoms out here, but didn't fear them. He respected and accepted them as a physical threat the way he respected and accepted the bears and cougars and wolves that roamed these hills. His philosophy was based on the natural order of things. If a problem came up, he would use every resource to handle it. So far he'd been successful with that strategy, which included saving Benny during First Night, burning the first Gameland to the ground a few years ago, and giving closure to many hundreds of zoms. If, on the other hand, a problem arose that was beyond his mental and physical abilities, and if he died as a result of it, he was at peace with that. It was the way of things. Survival of the fittest, and no one was "the fittest" all the time.

He ran lightly, ducking under branches, leaping small gullies, running no faster than his ability to perceive what the forest had to tell him. Tom had stopped calling out Chong's name. The boy had clearly wanted to run, and calling him might make him hide. In this gloom the best hunter in the world couldn't find someone deliberately hiding. It was getting hard enough to follow Chong's trail. Luckily, the boy had tried that old trick of using a piece of brush to wipe out his footprints. Sure, it wiped out the prints, but it left behind very distinct striations in the dirt and moss. Tom almost smiled when he saw it.

Eventually he reached the point where Chong had stopped trying to cover his trail and his distinctive waffle-soled shoe prints were clear in the fading light.

There were other prints along the path too. Most were animal tracks that were of no concern to Tom. He found some human—or perhaps zom—prints, but most of these were days old, and Chong's tracks overlaid them. One set of tracks made him freeze in place and even touch the butt of his holstered pistol. Old-world hiking boots with worn treads and a crescent-shaped nick out of the right heel.

Tom bent low and studied the prints. Preacher Jack's without doubt, but it was clear that these had been made on his way to the encounter that had happened a few hours ago.

Tom continued his hunt. The forest was growing quiet, and he moved only as fast as he could go silently. It was a tracker's trick: Never make more noise than what you're tracking.

Crack.

There was a sound, soft and close, and within three steps Tom slipped into the shadows between two ancient elms. He listened. Sound was deceptive. Without a second noise it was often difficult to reliably determine from which direction the sound had come. Ahead and to the left? Off the trail?

A rustle. Definitely off to the left. Tom peered through the gloom. The second sound had been like a foot moving through stiff brush. A long pause, and then another crunch.

Tom saw a piece of shadow detach itself and move from left to right through an open patch. It was a quick, furtive movement. Something that walked on two legs. Not a zom, though, he was sure about that.

Preacher Jack? If so, Tom was determined to have a different kind of chat with him than they'd had back on the road.

The figure was coming his way, but from the body language it was clear the person had not seen him. The head was turned more toward the north, looking farther along the game trail.

Judging where Tom should have been if he'd kept moving.

Tom nodded approval. A pretty good tracker, he guessed.

"Tom!" called a voice. A very familiar voice. "Tom Imura. I

know you're up there behind one of those trees. Don't make me have to walk all the way up the slope."

Tom stepped out from behind the tree with his pistol in his hand. The shadowy figure emerged into a slightly brighter spot of light. From the soles of her boots to the top of her orange Mohawk, the woman was tall and solidly built, with knife handles and pistol butts jutting out in all directions like an old-time pirate. In her right fist she carried a huge bowie knife with a wicked eighteen-inch blade.

Something black gleamed on the blade, and though it looked like oil in the bad light, Tom knew that it was blood. The woman's face and clothes seemed to be smeared with it. She tottered into view, and Tom saw that her left arm hung limp and dead at her side.

Tom stepped out from behind the tree. "Sally?"

Sally Two-Knives grinned at him with bloody teeth. "You alone, Tom?"

"Yes."

"Good," she said, and pitched forward onto her face.

35

"BACK . . . BACK!" CRIED NIX IN A FIERCE WHISPER. AS SHE SAID IT she walked backward, herding Lilah and Benny toward the open door. Lilah stumbled along as if her brain had shut itself off. Benny had to push her into the way station. Nix was last in. She tossed down her bokken, grabbed Lilah's pistol, and stood for a moment in the doorway, tracking the barrel left and right, but she did not fire. There was no point. If she had a barrel filled with bullets it would not be enough. Nix lowered the pistol and retreated inside.

"We're dead," Lilah said again, and her voice already sounded dead.

Benny closed and locked the door. "It won't hold for long," he said quietly. "Same with the windows. That glass is old. It might last if a couple of them beat on it . . . but there are hundreds of them out there."

"Thousands," said Nix. "There had to be five hundred of them just coming down over the rocks. It's insane."

It was insane. Last year Benny had seen three thousand of them in the Hungry Forest, but the seething mass of the living dead outside had to number twice that many. It was an army of rotting flesh-eaters. "Where did they come from?" he demanded.

"I don't know," said Nix. "It doesn't make sense. We weren't that loud. And I don't think they could see our cooking fire from outside. Not all the way into the forest and up the mountains."

"Doesn't make sense," said Lilah in a hollow voice.

"What about the cans? Zoms couldn't do that," said Benny.

"I know, Benny," said Nix. She scraped a match and lit the little oil lantern.

"Don't!" gasped Benny.

"Why?" she said softly. The flaring match revealed a crooked smile. "Are you afraid it'll attract zoms?"

Her voice was way too calm. Benny had heard people talk like that right before they went off the deep end. And yet, what could he say? He turned to Lilah for help, but the Lost Girl truly looked lost. She stared at the pistol and knife she still held and then numbly put them into their holsters.

"It doesn't make sense," Lilah said, repeating the phrase in a lost whisper.

Benny shook his head. "No, it doesn't. If this was something normal, Tom would have told us about it. Besides, Brother David's lived here for over a year, and he said there were never more than a few wandering zoms in the area. This is . . . this is insane."

"Insane," echoed Lilah.

Benny did not like what he was seeing in her face any more than he liked what he heard in Nix's voice. Not one little bit. It made him wonder how crazy he looked and sounded.

Crazy or not, they had to do something. Benny looked at the three carpet coats that hung from pegs by the door. He grabbed the coats belonging to Sister Shanti and Sister Sarah and tossed them to the girls. "Put these on!"

Nix immediately slipped into hers, but Lilah let hers drop to the floor. Benny picked it up and pressed it to her.

"Put it on!" he yelled.

Lilah took it but did nothing with it. Finally Nix took it and put it on Lilah the way a mother dresses a child.

"We have to get out of here," Benny said as he belted on Brother David's coat. He lifted the blankets and peered outside. The closest of the zoms was still about fifty feet away. "We can still run."

That made Lilah's face twitch. "Run where?"

Nix said, "She's right, Benny. They're coming from every direction. We're safer here."

"This isn't safety." Benny waved his hands around at the way station. "This is a freaking lunch pail. They're going to close in around us, open this place up, and—"

"Stop!" hissed Lilah, pressing her hands to her ears.

"If we run, at least we have some chance." Benny fished in his pocket and pulled out the bottles of cadaverine. "We have these."

Nix chewed her lip, caught in the terrible trap of indecision.

Then abruptly Lilah's hand darted out fast as a snake and snatched a bottle out of Benny's hand. She opened it and began dribbling the thick liquid onto her sleeves. When Benny and Nix simply stood there staring at her, Lilah growled, "Now!"

It was a freakish moment, as if there had been no disconnect in Lilah, as if she had been strong and in charge all the time. Benny and Nix shared a covert, worried look.

Don't say anything, warned Benny's inner voice. *She's ready to break. Push now and she'll shatter.*

Benny tossed his second bottle to Nix and dug the extras out of his pocket.

"Will it be enough?" Nix asked as she smeared the noxious chemical on her coat.

Benny didn't answer. They each used a full bottle. The inside of the way station reeked as if it was stuffed to the rafters with rotting flesh.

"Weapons and water only," said Benny.

"Good," agreed Lilah.

Nix nodded, but she grabbed her journal off the table and stuffed it into a big pocket inside her vest. Then she belted the carpet coat tightly around her. The coat protected her body and arms and had a high, stiff collar to shield the throat, but it was not a suit of armor. Even the fence guards back home said that enough zoms could eventually chew through one.

Benny slung his canteen over his neck and pulled his bokken from its sheath.

At the door, Lilah paused, took a deep breath, and without turning said, "We go slow. Don't fight unless you have to. Run only if you have to."

"What if we get separated?" asked Nix.

There was only one answer to that question, and Benny's inner voice whispered it to him. *Anyone who gets lost in the dark . . . is dead.* Aloud he said, "We won't."

It was somewhere between a lie and a gamble.

Thump! A dead fist struck the window, rattling it in its frame.

"Me, Nix, Benny," whispered Lilah. "Ready?"

Nix and Benny both lied. They both said they were. Lilah opened the door.

A zombie stood there, arm raised to strike the glass. He was broad-shouldered, his once brown skin bleached to the color of milky tea. Most of his face was gone, and gnawed edges of white bone jutted from the bloodless flesh. The creature took a shambling step forward. It did not sniff the air—Benny had never seen zoms do that—yet through whatever senses it did possess, the creature took the measure of the pale girl with the white hair . . . and then shuffled past her into the room. For the moment it did not judge her as prey. She reeked of the dead, and the dead passed her by.

Benny could see that Lilah's whole body was trembling. This wasn't like that time when she'd freed the zoms in the Hungry Forest. Back then she was on her home turf, and she'd known a thousand paths through those woods. No . . . this was beyond Lilah's experience, and maybe that was what crippled her. She had no plan and lacked either the imagination or optimism to believe that some line of escape would present itself.

Or maybe you screwed her up with what you said about Chong. Benny wished with all his strength that he could step back in time and unsay those cruel and stupid words.

Lilah drew a ragged breath and stepped cautiously outside. Nix went next, turning to squeeze by a lumbering fat man with bullet holes in his stomach. As Benny stepped into the doorway his shoe scuffed the floor, and the fat man turned sharply, gray lips pulling back from green teeth. The zom snarled at Benny, then just as suddenly, the look of hunger and menace dropped away as if a curtain had fallen. Its dusty eyes slid away from Benny, and the monster turned awkwardly and trundled inside, followed by another zom, and another.

Holding his bokken to his chest as if it was a magic charm, Benny slipped outside. Lilah had not waited for him. She was already thirty paces away, walking straight into the sea of shambling corpses. Nix was much closer, her steps slower and uncertain. Nix kept looking back for Benny. Lilah never looked back at all—she kept going. Did she see a way out? Benny wondered. She was moving faster and faster, and soon he couldn't see her at all.

Move or die, growled his inner voice. Benny began walking, moving disjointedly, trying to imitate the artless shamble of the zoms so as not to attract attention.

Don't stop.

He didn't . . . until he reached the edge of the concrete pad by the gas pumps. From that angle he could see almost all the land around the way station. What he saw punched the air out of his lungs and nearly dropped him to his knees. There, in the thick of a seething mass of zoms—an army that numbered uncountable thousands—stood a tall figure with hair even whiter than Lilah's, massive chest and shoulders, gun butts sprouting from holsters at hips and shoulder rigs, and a three-foot length of black pipe clutched in a nearly color-less hand. It was too far away to see his eyes, but Benny was sure—dead certain—that one would be blue and the other as red as flame.

The figure stared right at him. It was smiling.

The zoms shifted and shuffled around the figure. They did not attack him. They surged past him, heading toward the gas station, toward Lilah and Nix. Toward Benny. Then the sea of zoms closed around the figure, obscuring him from Benny's sight.

It didn't matter. Benny had seen it.

Seen him.

"No . . . ," he whispered to himself. "No."

He turned and ran. Not walked, not shuffled like a zom. Benny Imura ran for all he was worth. He ran for his life. As he ran he could feel those eyes upon him, burning like cold fire into his back. God! Where was Tom? Benny thought he heard a sound threaded through the moan of the thousands of walking dead. He thought he heard the deep, rumbling, mocking laughter of the man he was positive he had just seen standing amid an army of the dead.

Charlie Pink-eye.

FROM NIX'S JOURNAL

When I was real little, Mom was having a hard time earning enough ration dollars. Before First Night she'd been a production assistant in Hollywood (a place where they made movies, back before they nuked Los Angeles). She didn't know how to farm or build stuff, and she tried to make a living doing sewing and cleaning people's houses. It was hard, but she never complained and she never let me know how hard she had to work. Then she was sick for a few weeks and fell behind on all the bills.

Then she met Charlie Matthias. He tried to get Mom to go out with him, but she wasn't interested. AT ALL. Then Charlie told her there was a way for her to make a month's worth of ration bucks in one day. It wasn't sex stuff or anything like that. He said all she had to do was quiet a zom.

Of course, he didn't tell her that she would be thrown into a big pit with a zom with only a broom handle as a weapon. It was at a place called Gameland, hidden up in the mountains. People came from all over to bet on what they called Z-Games. Zombie games.

Mom was desperate to earn the money, so she went into the pit.

She never told me about this, and I don't know the details. All I know is that Charlie kept Mom in the pit for a week. I was real little, and Benny's aunt Cathy took care of me.

Then Tom brought Mom home. Tom was all cut up and burned, from what the neighbors told me later. He smelled of smoke and had bloodstains on his clothes. I learned a lot later that Tom had rescued Mom and destroyed Gameland. I think he had to hurt some people to do it. Maybe kill some people. Shame Charlie wasn't one of them.

When Charlie Matthias killed my mom last year, he was going to take me to Gameland. The new Gameland.

God . . . how can people be so cruel?

36

Tom was fast, but Sally Two-Knives was down before he got to her. He knelt beside her and checked her pulse, found a reassuring thump-thump-thump. Then he examined neck and spine before he gently eased her onto her back and brushed dirt and leaves from her face.

"Oh boy, Sally," he said, "you're a bit of a mess here." Her eyelids slowly fluttered open. Even in the bad light Tom could see that her face was taut with great pain. "Where are you hurt?" he asked.

"Everywhere."

"Can you pin it down for me or do I have to go looking?"

Sally snorted. "Since when did you become a prude?" Then she winced and touched her abdomen. "Stomach and arm."

Tom opened the bottom buttons of her shirt, saw what was clearly a knife wound. She wasn't coughing up blood, so he didn't think she had any serious internal injuries. Or he hoped she didn't. He removed a small bottle of antiseptic and some cotton pads from a vest pocket and gently cleaned the wound and applied a clean bandage. He used his knife and cut open her sleeve to reveal a ragged black hole. Tom gently raised her arm and leaned to take a look at the back of it, saw a second, slightly smaller hole.

"A through-and-through," he concluded. "Bullet hit you in the back of the arm and punched out through the biceps. What they'd shoot you with?"

"Don't know," she said through gritted teeth. "Something small. Twenty-two or twenty-five caliber, though it felt pretty darn big going in and coming out."

"Missed the arteries. Didn't break the bone," Tom said. "You always were a lucky one, Sally."

"Lucky my ass. I got shot and stabbed. If that's your idea of good luck, then give me the other kind."

"Don't even joke," he chided as he cleaned the entry and exit wounds, placed sterile pads over them, and began wrapping a white bandage around her arm. "I've seen my share of bad luck already today."

Tom tied the ends of the bandage with neat precision, but inside he was beginning to feel a slight edge of panic. It was now too dark to track Chong. Tom helped Sally sit up and let her drink from his canteen.

"Don't suppose you saw my horse anywhere, did you?" she asked. "I left her tied to a tree, but she must have spooked."

"No," said Tom. "Look, Sal, what happened and who did this?"

"It's complicated," she said. "I ran into a couple of the White Bear crew. You know White Bear?"

He nodded. White Bear had once run with Charlie Pinkeye's gang but had dropped out of sight years ago. "Heard of him but never met him. Big guy from Nevada. Used to be a bouncer at one of the Vegas casinos before First Night, right? Tells everyone that he's the reincarnation of some great Indian medicine men, though from what I heard he doesn't have a drop of Native American blood in him. What's he doing here?"

She hissed in pain as Tom began stitching her stomach wound. He wished Lilah was here.

"OW—damn, son! You using a tree spike to sew that up?" she snarled.

"Don't be a sissy."

She cursed him and his entire lineage going back to the Stone Age. Tom endured it as he worked. Curses were better than screams.

"What about White Bear?" he prompted.

She took a breath. "Since Charlie's gang got chomped by those zoms last year, there's been a lot of talk about who was going to take over his territory. Charlie always had prime real estate. Mountainside, Fairview, couple of other towns, and the trade route all through these mountains. White Bear wants it all. Brought a bunch of his guys with him. Most of them are jokers who don't know which end of a rifle goes bang! But he has a lot of them."

"How many?"

"The two I saw tonight, and maybe twenty more. Maybe twice that number if the rumors are true . . . and he'll probably try to scoop up any of Charlie's guys who are still sucking air."

Tom tied off the last stitch and began applying a fresh dressing. "Why'd they attack you?"

"They didn't. I, um, kind of attacked them." She touched Tom's arm. "Tom . . . I think they have your brother, Benny."

"What?"

"I saw them slapping the crap out of a Japanese-looking kid. Your brother's, what, fifteen, sixteen?"

"Fifteen. What was this kid wearing?"

She thought about it. "Jeans. Dark shirt with red stripes and a vest with a lot of pockets."

Tom exhaled a burning breath. "That's not Benny. That's his friend, Louis Chong. He's Chinese, not Japanese. Besides, Benny's half Irish American."

"What do I know? It's dark, he's a kid, I'm shot for Pete's sake." She squinted at him. "That who you're looking for? The Chinese kid?"

Tom filled her in on what he was doing.

"So . . . you're really going to leave?" she asked.

"That's the plan, but we seem to be off to a bad start."

"So—asking me to meet you at Brother David's . . . that was what? A good-bye?"

He nodded.

"Damn," said Sally. "Things won't be the same around here without our knight in shining armor."

Tom snorted. "I'm a lot of things, Sally, but I'm no one's idea of a shining knight."

Sally didn't laugh. "If that's what you think, Tom, then you're a bigger damn fool than I thought. There's no one in this whole chain of mountains who doesn't know who you are and what you do. And I mean before you served Charlie and the Hammer to the zoms on a silver plate." She paused. "A lot of people look up to you. No . . . they look to you. For how to act. For how to be."

"Come on, Sal, let's not—"

"Listen to me, Tom. You matter to people. During First

Night, and in the years after, a lot of us did some pretty wild things to survive. You don't know. Or . . . maybe you do. Maybe you did some wild things too, but the thing is that since then you've been the kind of guy people can look at and say, 'Oh yeah, that's how people are supposed to act.' There aren't a lot of examples around since the zoms, man, but you . . ." She smiled and shook her head.

Tom cleared his throat. "Listen, Sally, I'm thinking that this is pain and shock talking here, so let's get to the point. Where did they take Chong and how'd you get hurt?"

Sally laughed. "Modest, too. Real shame you're leaving town. Jessie Riley was the luckiest woman in California, and strike me down if that's a lie."

"Chong . . . ," Tom prompted.

"Okay, okay. It was about two hours ago. I was heading to Brother David's when I heard someone yelling. I snuck up and saw this kid trying to fight off a couple of goons. Kid was doing okay at first. Had a wooden version of that sword you carry. The goons were trying to take the sword away from him barehanded, making a game of it. Pretending they were zoms and that sort of stuff. You've seen it before."

"Yes," he said coldly, "I've seen it. What happened?"

"Kid managed to land a good one on one of the guys. Hit him on the shoulder, and I could hear the thwack all the way up the hill. Then the guys stopped playing and laid into the kid with a will. Whipped the sword out of his hands and beat the living crap out of him."

"Damn." Tom thought about the ascetic and intellectual Chong fighting for his life. How brave he must have been, and how terrified.

"By that time I'd had enough, and I'd pretty much figured that the kid must have been your brother. So I came down the hill with a war whoop and sliced myself a piece of those two butt-wipes. Wasn't all girly about it either. Would have just messed them up some and let the pair of them limp out of here, but they tried to get all fancy on me. It didn't end well for 'em, and no loss to the world."

"Wait . . . you said you took them out?"

"Two freaks like them against me? I coulda done that back in my Roller Derby days, and that was before I learned how to ugly-fight."

"No, I mean, if you nailed them, then who—?"

"Must have been a third guy. Never saw him coming. I was about to quiet the two freaks when suddenly something hit my arm from behind and knocked me into a tree. Tried to shake it off, but someone came at me from my blind side, spun me and stabbed me. All I saw was a big man with white hair, and then I blacked out."

"White hair? Sally—could it have been Preacher Jack?"

"The loony-tune from Wawona?" She thought about it. "No, this guy was way bigger. Anyway . . . I passed out, and when I woke up, the kid was gone and so was the big guy."

"What about the other two?"

"Still there. Whoever shot me must have quieted 'em and left 'em for the crows."

Tom sat back and thought about it. "Could the big man have been White Bear?"

She shrugged. "Maybe. This guy was as big as Charlie Pink-eye and his face was all messed up. Burned and all nasty-lookin'."

"Could it have been Charlie?"

Sally narrowed her eyes. "Charlie's dead. You killed him."

"Not exactly," Tom said. He told her about what had happened after Benny hit Charlie with the Motor City Hammer's pipe.

"Well, hell . . . that's not the kind of news a gal wants to hear when she's already feeling poorly. You think Charlie's alive?"

"I don't know. Did the guy who attacked you do it to avenge the men you killed, or was he after the boy?"

"I . . . don't know. But wouldn't Charlie know this kid's not your brother?"

Tom nodded. "He knows Benny and Chong both."

Sally took another swig from the canteen and chewed her lip for a moment. "Before I attacked them, I heard some of what the two punks said to the kid. I heard where they said they were taking him."

Tom knew what she was going to say and he closed his eyes as if he, rather than she, was in physical pain. "Say it."

"Gameland," said Sally Two-Knives. "They were going to try and sell him to the people running that place. Put him in the zombie pits."

"But you don't know if the man who shot you is taking him there?"

"No idea."

"Terrific," Tom said sourly. "They've moved Gameland twice since we took down Charlie's crew. I've been trying to find it . . . and I don't have a damn clue where it is. It could be all the way over in Utah for all I know."

"I don't think so, Tom," she said with a cold smile. "When those boys were taunting the kid, one of them told him that he'd be fighting in the pits by dawn's early light. His words."

Tom looked out at the darkness. "Damn," he said softly.

BENNY RAN RIGHT INTO A ZOM. THE CREATURE TURNED WITH A SNARL, and white fingers scrabbled for his face. He could feel the edges of broken fingernails scratch him, the dry pads of dead fingers slide over his nose and mouth; and then Benny shoved the zom aside with a cry of disgust. It fell against a second zom and they went down. Others tumbled over them in what could have been comedy if the world was not broken and insane. Zoms snarled and bit at him as he ran.

Slow down, warned his inner voice. He tried to slow himself; he ordered his feet to walk instead of run, but they disobeyed. Nix was sixty paces ahead. Fifty.

Lilah was nowhere in sight. Had she run out on them? Had the zoms gotten her? No . . . there would have been screams if they'd attacked her. First her war cries, and then . . . other screams. These thoughts tumbled through his head as he ran. He ducked under white hands, jinked and dodged around zombies who tried to wrap their arms around him. The whole crowd of them was becoming agitated, their awareness drawn to the running meat.

Slow down!

Nix heard him coming and turned to see Benny collide

with another zom and have to bash his way out of its embrace. Other zoms turned at the motion, their moans rising in pitch as their worm-white fingers clawed the air for him.

Slow DOWN!

"Benny!" cried Nix in a fierce whisper. "What are you doing?"

He jerked to a stop by the gas pump. The zoms that had been turning toward him suddenly turned to Nix as she began heading toward Benny. *You're going to get Nix killed.* He didn't need his inner voice to tell him that. The zoms nearest to her were already starting to close in. Nix tensed to run.

"Nix—stop!" Benny hissed. "Just stop. Stand still."

Nix looked absolutely terrified as all around her hungry mouths worked as if already devouring her. "Benny . . ."

"Shhh," he soothed, the sound as soft as a whisper, and then mouthed the words, "Keep perfectly still." If she stopped moving, would the cadaverine do its job? Would the zoms closing in on her lose interest?

It's not going to work. Milling zoms closed around her, the ragged shreds of their clothes brushing her like insect wings in the dark. Nix shivered. The wooden sword in her hands trembled. As the zombies came closer still, she began to raise the sword.

No! Benny almost screamed it aloud, but he clamped his control into place. *It's your fault she's in trouble. Be smart . . . find a way.*

Benny nodded, but in truth he was at the threshold of panic. One wild idea after another flashed through his mind, and he slapped each one away. Brash heroics, a suicidal charge . . . plans that were filled with romantic heroism or tragic sacrifice, but empty of practicality. Consider everything. The place. The time. The light. The breeze.

Benny edged toward Nix, moving with the breeze, swaying, becoming part of the movement of the crowd of dead. *You have everything you need. You have tools. You have resources.*

He wanted to tell the inner voice to shut the hell up and let him think. Charlie Pink-eye was back there somewhere. Maybe aiming a pistol at him right now. Or at Nix. *Don't make assumptions. See only what is there.*

He took one hand off the bokken and slowly, lightly patted his pockets. His fingers touched the remaining bottles of cadaverine. Should he use those? Would more smell help?

No.

He touched a small oblong shape that rattled softly. Use what you have. Benny suddenly had an idea. It was a crazy, insanely dangerous idea. Around him a sea of zoms moaned as they shuffled toward the gas station, toward him, toward Nix.

He shot a look at Nix. She was trembling so badly that her bokken was visibly shaking. A couple of zoms pawed at it. One of them suddenly grabbed it and pulled. Nix began to resist, but Benny shook his head and mouthed, "Let it go." Her eyes flared in horror at the suggestion, but her small hands opened and the zom tore the wooden sword away from her. It took the bokken in both hands, holding it like an ear of corn, and bit down on it. There was a crunch and a crack and the zombie snarled and cast the sword away, one of its teeth still buried in the hardwood.

Moving in ultra slow-motion, Benny slid his free hand into the front pocket of his jeans. The cadaverine bottles clinked, and then he found the oblong box he was looking for. It was made of stiff paper, and it rattled dryly as he removed it.

The zom closest to him turned sharply and peered at him with dust-covered eyes. Benny wondered how it could see with dead eyes. Another mystery that he thought would never be solved. *Don't waste time sightseeing.*

The zom moaned.

Benny moaned back and shuffled a few feet to the left. The zom stood there and watched him go. The dead could not show confusion on their slack faces, but Benny could almost feel the creature's conflict. The impulse to hunt only the living was at war with the stench of decay. It swayed there in indecision as Benny took another shuffling sideways step. The gray eyes never left Benny's face.

Hurry. Moving with infinite slowness, Benny thumbed open the little cardboard box. Twenty-five pale stick matches lay in tight rows. He used his thumbnail to separate one of them. He was about to close the box when his inner voice hissed at him to make a smarter choice.

The zom was still watching him. So were two others. Watching? Or just standing?

The carpet coat was hot, but ice-cold sweat ran in rivulets down the back of Benny's shirt. His heart was pounding so hard he could not understand why it didn't sound like a bass drum. He turned his head slightly and saw that Nix was still there, and he wondered how much time had just passed. Was it three seconds? Ten? An hour? Or no time at all? He couldn't tell. Nothing felt real.

Hurry!

He paused, then placed the first match between his teeth and removed another. He thumbed the box closed and turned it between his fingers, exposing a dark strip on one side. The matches were of the "storm" kind, coated with wax to keep them waterproof, with a chemical mix that would keep them burning in rain or wind.

"God . . . let this work!" He said it aloud, and he said it too loud. The watching zom suddenly lurched forward, its rubbery lips twitching. The abruptness of its movements made the creatures around it twitch and turn and move in Benny's direction. Had they focused on him, or were the others following the first one?

There was no time to sort it out. Benny put the white tip of the match against the strike board and flicked his wrist. The fire was small, but in the darkness of the field it flared like a tiny sun. The snap of ignition and the hiss as the flames consumed the chemicals were shockingly loud.

"No!" Nix cried, and some of the zoms turned toward her.

But many, many more of them were entirely focused on Benny. Holding the match out in front of him, he stared for a moment in nearly brainless shock as the light revealed the full horror of the moment. Hundreds of white faces had turned toward the sound and the flare of light. Their awful moan split the air. The closest zom grabbed his arm, and before Benny could pull away it bit down with savage force on his wrist. Two others closed on him and grabbed at his other arm. Teeth closed around his forearm. The pain was instant and terrible.

Benny bit down on a scream, praying that the carpet coat was protecting him from the disease carried by the bites of the living dead. He kicked out with all his force, catching the closest zom with a flat-footed thrust to the thigh that sent it lurching away. It lost its hold on his wrist, but immediately another zom lumbered past it, reaching for the prize.

Now! NOW!

Benny tore himself free of the other zoms and darted forward as the zom closed on him. He prayed with all his might that the match wouldn't go out. It puffed and flickered in the breeze. He had the stick of the other clamped between his teeth just in case. The zom reached for him, and Benny ducked under the pale hands, thrusting the match into the tattered folds of its clothes. In a flash the dry shreds of tie and suit jacket caught and flames shot up into the night. With a grunt of effort powered by rage and fear, Benny shoved the burning zom into the other creatures who had been closing in. They were all dry as kindling, and fire leaped from one to the other with frightening speed, sparks carried by the night wind.

Within seconds a half-dozen zombies were burning like giant candles. They did not beat at the flames, they did not scream . . . and that was deeply disturbing to Benny. Somehow it was worse that they were so ignorant of pain than if they shrieked and howled, though he could not grasp why. It was unnatural and wrong in more ways that he could count.

He whipped the other match from between his teeth and lit it as another wave of zoms closed in on him from behind. He used his forearm to bash aside the grasping hands and jabbed the match into the lace of a wedding gown, the folds of a loose cardigan, the ripped streamers of a halter top, the coattails of a waiter's jacket. The match burned his fingers, and he dropped it.

"BENNY!" He heard Nix's piercing cry and whirled to see

flames shoot up behind him. It took him a numb second to understand how the fire could have jumped that far, and then he realized. Nix had seen what he was doing, and she—beautiful, brilliant, and brave as he knew she was—had done the same. He almost laughed out loud. She ducked and snatched up her fallen sword and used it to fend off a burning zom.

Then Benny drew his bokken and swung with all the force he possessed, hitting a burning zom on the side of the neck so hard that he felt the shock through his wrist as the creature's neck snapped. The zom fell hard into two others, and they immediately caught fire. A wall of heat slammed into him, and the laugh died in his throat.

"Uh-oh," he said aloud. The sound of his voice didn't matter now. The roar of the fire was immense, the heat like an open furnace.

"BENNY!"

He turned and had to squint through the yellow glare to see Nix moving at a dead run toward the southeast. Something touched his shoulder, and Benny screamed.

The first zom—the one he'd kicked—had just grabbed him with a burning hand. Intense white-hot agony shot through Benny's shoulder as the fiery fingers ignited the fabric of the carpet coat.

Benny shrieked in pain and swung the bokken with all his force. The zom's head exploded into thick flaming pieces and the creature fell away. But its hand still clutched the fabric of Benny's coat. Benny kicked and slapped and hammered at the zom's arm until the blackened fingers fell away. He slapped at the flames on his shoulder. The carpet coat was old but not as sun-dried as the rags the zoms wore, but as he beat out the last dancing fingers of fire, he could feel burns on the skin of his shoulder and upper arm. If it hadn't been for the thick fabric of the coat . . .

Then another hand grabbed him and he whirled, raising the sword to strike, but it was Nix. Her face was black from smoke, and her eyes were wild.

"COME ON!" she screeched, and dragged him away. Heat pounded them like fists on all sides, and the air itself was becoming too hot to breathe.

"Where's Lilah?" he yelled.

"I don't know. God—we have to go!"

They ran. The zoms were drawn to the massive flames, and as they crowded toward the commotion, more and more of them caught fire. The breeze caught pieces of burning cloth and burning flesh and whipped them across the field, setting new blazes here and there and soon . . . everywhere. As they ran it seemed as if the whole world had suddenly caught fire.

FROM NIX'S JOURNAL

(Benny: If you are reading my journal, STOP. This part is private. If I find out that you read this, so help me I'll beat you to death and then when you reanimate I'll beat you to death all over again.)

Dear Future Nix:

I haven't written for a while. I've been too busy collecting zombie information. I tried to talk to Lilah about this, but she doesn't understand boys. At all. Not even a little bit.

Benny keeps wanting me to act like we're a couple. And we ARE a couple, but sometimes I just can't do the lovey-dovey stuff. It feels weird. I never had a boyfriend before, and even though I've liked Benny since—what? Since we were six?—I'm not sure if I want to get totally wrapped up. Not that there's anyone else. We're out in the Ruin and there really is NO ONE ELSE. It's just that ever since last year it feels like there's stuff wrapped around my emotions. Nothing feels really real. Except being scared. That's always real. And being angry. I'm ALWAYS angry. Even when we're all joking, I'm always angry. Benny doesn't know about that. I'm good at hiding it, and boys aren't so good at seeing it.

It's really confusing. Benny and I are never going back home. We may not meet other kids our age. Do I want to be with him because we don't have a choice or because that was our choice?

You're reading this in the future. You know how it all worked out. I don't.

I do like Benny. I probably love him, but it's hard to tell the difference between the crush I've had all these years and real love.

What does that feel like? Will I ever know?

38

When Lou Chong woke up the first time, he thought he was in hell.

When he woke up the second time, he knew he was.

The first thing he was aware of was pain. The bones of his face ached so deeply that his gums hurt. When he tried to move his head, the strained muscles in his neck flared with darts of searing pain that lanced through him. He tried to touch his face, to see how bad he was hurt, but his hands would not move. Which was when he felt the pain in his wrists and ankles.

"W-what?" he asked. Except that he could not speak. A thick and noxious rag was tied around his head, a knot of it shoved between his teeth. All he could do was groan. Like a zom.

He blinked his eyes, trying to clear them. Vision returned very slowly. At first all he saw was dirt and some clumps of crooked grass. At least that helped him orient himself. He was on his side, on the ground.

And he was bound and gagged. Panic was a trembling thing that fluttered inside the walls of his chest. He wanted to scream out, to attract attention, to be able to say, reasonably and calmly, that this was all a mistake. He wanted to apologize for whatever he must have done to have made someone this mad at him. Had Captain Strunk thrown him in jail? Had he and Benny and Morgie broken someone's window? Had they been caught stealing eggs from the Lamba Farm again? Or had one of the town watch caught them throwing the eggs at the old Pettit place?

Pain rolled up and down him like a tide, never pausing, missing nothing. He could not believe that he was capable of hurting in so many places at once.

"Help!" It came out as a weak grunt of meaningless noise.

"Well, well," said a voice. "Look who's awake." A booted foot stepped down inches from Chong's nose. "You was out so long I thought I was going to have to quiet you." The man had a deep voice that was strangely familiar and at the same time alien. Chong's head hurt too much to make logical sense of it.

He tried to crane his neck to look up, but he couldn't move his head far enough. It felt as if the gag was tied in some way to whatever had been used to bind his ankles and wrists.

"Please . . ." It was just noise, but the man chuckled as if he understood.

"You trying to say something, little man?"

There was a flash of silver and then the pressure of cold steel against his cheek . . . and then the ends of the gag dropped away, the tough cloth parting like gossamer as the wicked blade slashed through them.

Free from the pressure, Chong coughed and spat to force the dirty rag out of his mouth. The corners of his mouth felt stretched, his cheeks were raw and abraded. His arms and legs were still firmly tied and he wriggled around, trying to work free of them, but the knots were too tight.

"Don't worry, little man, I'll cut you loose. In my own time, of course."

Chong started to look up, but the man stepped so close that the sour stink of his boot leather filled Chong's eyes and nose.

He tried to speak, but his throat was dry as paste. "W-why?" he croaked. "Who are you?"

The man chuckled again. It was a friendly sound, totally at odds with what was happening. And it was maddeningly familiar. It almost sounded like . . .

But . . . no . . . that was impossible.

The man lifted the booted foot and brought it down on the side of Chong's face. Not a kick . . . no, the man placed the sole on Chong's cheek and slowly applied weight and pressure.

"Shhhh, now. I cut the gag so you could breathe. Wasn't no invitation to ask a bunch of questions you already know the answer to."

Chong frowned and tried to tell him that he was wrong, that Chong didn't know the answers to anything, that this was all some kind of mistake. The force behind the boot increased bit by bit. At first it was only pressure, but soon there was enough weight to make Chong's jaw creak. Then more, and more, and Chong started to cry out. More and more until he thought he would pass out.

"I can keep this up all night," said the man as casually as if he was discussing the weather. "I'll stop when I don't hear any more noise coming out of your mouth. Chew on this thought for a minute, little man. A gag ain't the only way to keep you from talking. I can cut your tongue out too, and nail it to a tree. Don't think for a moment that I'm joking, 'cause I done it before, and to tougher specimens than you."

Chong wanted to scream. Instead he clamped his mouth shut tighter than the gag had been.

The pressure continued. Chong squeezed his eyes shut and tried to find a place inside his head where he could go and hide. He wanted to be home, up in his room, surrounded by the stacks of his beloved books. Back there, if a monster became too terrifying Chong could always close the book. Not here. Not in the dark with the pain and the ropes and the gag.

The pressure stopped increasing as the man listened for sounds from Chong.

"That's the ticket," he said, and removed his foot . . . but not before giving it a last little extra pressure. Somehow that made Chong feel more frightened, that last little bit of pressure. It was unnecessary. The man had already defeated Chong, already proved his power and dominance. That last twist spoke of a deeper, less evolved kind of evil. A sneaky pettiness. Sly and dirty. It made Chong very, very afraid.

For several long minutes there was nothing. No new pain, no sign of the man, no sound of him moving around. Was he standing there, out of sight? Just watching? Chong knew that he was. And that made him even more afraid.

Then the man spoke. "I'll bet your mommy and daddy told you that there are bad people out here in the badlands. People who will do bad things to you. Bad things to stupid little boys running around in the great Rot and Ruin. Bad men doing bad, bad things."

There was a rush of sound and suddenly the man was on his hands and knees, bending low so that his face was inches from Chong's. It was a face out of a nightmare. The skin was a horror show. Every inch of that face was twisted and melted. One eye was completely gone, just a black pit in the lumpy pink and red moonscape. Hair as white as snow framed the man's terrible face. He whispered four words.

"I'm the bad man." Then he laughed and stood up. "You know what we're going to do now?"

Chong did not dare answer. He closed his eyes, not wanting this to be real. Begging the universe to make this a dream.

"I'm going to cut your feet loose so you can walk, and by God you will walk. We got miles and miles to walk, halfway into the night. You're going to walk every inch of it, and you're not going to say anything. Not a word, and by God not a whimper. If you so much as cut a fart I'm going to cut pieces offa you. Nod if you believe me."

Chong nodded. Emphatically.

"Then, oh say round about midnight—the witching hour, as they useta call it back before the zoms—we're going to get somewhere. You know where that is, little man?"

Chong shook his head. Just a tentative little shake. The man knelt again, and his breath was hot and whiskey soaked against Chong's ear.

"I'm taking your skinny ass to Gameland, little man. Now . . . ain't that a world of fun?"

Chong did not dare scream. But oh, how he needed to.

39

THE WORLD SEEMED TO BE MADE OF FLAME AND WHITE FACES AND DEATH. Benny and Nix ran into the night, pursued by inferno heat. They had no clear direction, but there were too many zoms to allow them a straight line of flight.

"How many are there?" Benny gasped. However, it was the last thing he said aloud for a long time, because those four words nearly got him killed. The fire down on the field drew the attention of most of the zoms, but his voice came out unnaturally loud. All the pale death-mask faces around them turned suddenly toward them.

Benny and Nix stopped, shifting to stand back-to-back, swords ready.

I killed us, Benny thought; but immediately his inner voice retorted, *No. Think your way through it. What resources do you still have?*

Benny thought about the matches and almost laughed. If he had, it would have been his last laugh, and it would have been an insane cackle. The fire had saved them in the short term, but if the winds veered, then the blaze would chase them up the mountain—and fire burns upward. There was no lowland path open to them.

Nix took a slow sideways step, and Benny shifted with her. The zoms came closer, but their dark eyes shifted back and forth between them and the blaze. Without more sound to attract them, they were losing interest.

But not quickly enough. Soon some of them would be within grabbing distance. Benny could already smell their dead, dusty, decayed stench. . . .

And that fast he had it. He shifted his bokken to a one-handed grip and slid his hand slowly into his pocket. Not for the matches, though. Instead he pulled out one of his remaining bottles of cadaverine. It was a risk. If they survived this terrible moment, then they would need the chemical to help them get to . . .

To where? Home? Back to the burning way station? Into the endless forest to look for Tom and Chong? East toward Yosemite and wherever the jet went?

Solve one problem at a time, warned his inner voice.

Nix took another step, going slowly so that Benny could keep pace. He didn't dare take the time to look to see if she was merely moving or if she saw a way out. Benny put the cap between his teeth to hold it steady while he unscrewed the bottle. Instantly the sickly sweet stink of rotting meat filled the air. It wasn't until that moment that he realized how much the smoke had blocked the cadaverine smell.

A distant part of him wondered if the zoms would attack one another in the smoke. If they couldn't smell the odor of death, would they attack anything? There was no way to know, and he wasn't about to go back and turn this into a science experiment.

"Benny," murmured Nix in a voice so soft that it was a shadow of a sound.

He didn't answer. Instead he sprinkled some of the cadaverine on his chest and hair. The first of the zoms were within arm's length now, the hands lifting, reaching. And pausing.

Benny jerked the open bottle over his shoulder, splashing Nix's red curls.

"Wait," he whispered. "Give it a sec."

"Benny . . ."

"Shhh."

"No," she insisted. "Look."

He turned the wrong way first, and then faced her and followed the line she indicated with her outstretched bokken.

They were on a slope that led up to a shadowy mass of trees that he could barely see by starlight. There were far fewer zoms up there, the lines of them visibly thinning. However, that was not what Nix was pointing to. A figure stood at the top of the path. Benny had to blink the stinging smoke out of his eyes to make it out. At first it looked like a tall shrubbery, but then it moved to stand more fully in the starlight, and Benny gasped.

From the height, he judged the figure to be a man, but otherwise it was impossible to tell. It seemed like he was wearing a small tree, but then Benny realized that the man wore a long coat onto which leaves and pinecones had been sewn. His face was entirely covered by a round mask made up of oak leaves. Benny knew who it was, even in the dark. He knew him from Tom's description and from his own Zombie Cards.

It was the Greenman. Zoms walked past him, staggering out

of the forest; a few even bumped into him as they stumbled down the grassy path. The Greenman did not move except to raise a slender finger to the "lips" of his mask.

Benny and Nix fell silent and stood as still as statues. Below them the wind was blowing the fire toward the fall of rocks. It was not spreading into the hills, and Benny was grateful for small mercies. He didn't want to cause even more problems for Tom, and he certainly didn't want to start a forest fire.

It took a long time for the zoms to pass. Benny tried to count off the seconds and minutes just to keep from going crazy. He wanted to gather Nix in his arms and hug her hard enough to make them both scream. He wanted noise and peace at the same time. Anything but what was all around them.

Then it was over. The last of the zoms—a sad-faced man wearing the stained rags of a house painter's coveralls— tottered past. He had a butcher knife buried in his chest, but the blade was pitted with rust. The creature turned an empty face toward Benny for a long moment, and despite all the terror that still crouched in his chest, Benny felt sorry for him. He almost said as much. Then the zombie vanished into the smoke and gloom down on the field.

Nix tugged his sleeve, and Benny looked up to see that the Greenman was beckoning them with slow movements of his hand. Then he turned and walked toward the woods without waiting to see if Benny and Nix were following.

"Who is that?" Nix asked. "Is that Lilah? What's she wearing?"

Benny shook his head. "It's the Greenman."

"Why's he dressed like that?"

"Tom says that he found some way to blend into the forest. Even the zoms don't see him." He lowered his sword and reached out his hand. "Come on."

Nix sniffed back tears and took his hand, giving him one of her fierce squeezes. "Where's Lilah?" she asked.

"I don't know. I saw her run . . . but then I lost her."

"Do—do you think she got out?"

"Absolutely," he said carefully. "Lilah's used to taking care of herself." Though as he said it he was remembering the mad, desperate look in her eyes. He wondered about his own sanity. After all, he had just set an enormous fire and was pretty sure he had seen Charlie Pink-eye standing alive but unharmed in the middle of a field of zoms. Benny debated for less than half a millisecond about whether to tell Nix about this now, and realized that it was something best saved for daylight. At the moment they needed safety and time to check for injuries. The burn on Benny's shoulder felt white hot, and he was not 100 percent positive that the carpet coats had saved them from the teeth of the living dead. They could both be infected, and that thought nearly dropped Benny in his tracks.

Nix grabbed his arm and pulled him. "Come on," she said, and they hurried up the hill after the Greenman. However, when they got to the top of the hill and entered the forest path, the strange figure was gone.

FROM NIX'S JOURNAL

Zombies and Fire

When some people tell stories of First Night, they say that they used fire to scare off the zoms. They say that zoms won't cross a line of fire, that they'll retreat from a torch. They say that if a zom catches fire, it will run away. Tom says this is wrong.

He says that a zom will walk through fire. He says that they are attracted to its light and movement. He says that he's seen burning zoms walk as far as a hundred yards before the heat did so much damage to muscles and tendons that they couldn't walk anymore.

And he says that when the army nuked the big cities, waves of radioactive zoms kept coming, and people sometimes died from the intense radioactivity before the zoms could bite them.

What ARE they?

"SOMETHING'S COMING!" WHISPERED SALLY TWO-KNIVES.

Tom Imura got quickly to his feet, his fingers curled around the handle of his sword. They were huddled together under the eaves of an olive tree that grew amid a cluster of tall boulders. As he crept to the edge of the largest boulder, Tom heard the soft hiss of Sally drawing one of her knives. He tuned that out and focused on the darkened woods beyond. Before setting up their temporary camp, Tom had gathered armloads of frail twigs and scattered them along any likely path of approach. The snap of a twig had brought them both to full alertness.

There was a second snap. And a third. Whoever was out there didn't care about making sound. In this world that meant one of two things. Either the person was traveling with a party that was so heavily armed that he had no fear of attracting the attention of the living dead; or they were the living dead. Tom edged farther out and let himself go still, becoming part of the rock, the shadows, and the forest. He had reluctantly accepted some of Sally's cadaverine only because it would have been virtually impossible to get her up into a tree for the night. With one injured arm and a bad stab wound, Sally would be lucky if she could walk. Forget climbing.

A moment later a figure stepped out from behind a bushy rhododendron. It was a boy, a teenager, possibly thirteen when he died. Now immortal in the cruelest sense of the word. His eyes roved across the gap between the boulders and the olive tree but did not linger on Tom. The creature's mouth hung slack, the lips were rubbery. The boy wore a grimy and faded Los Angeles Lakers T-shirt and what looked like swim trunks with a pattern of flaming skulls. The teenager's feet were bare, and the bloodless skin was so badly torn that Tom could see tendons and bones. He wanted to close his eyes or look away, but the boy was still a zom and he was still a threat.

Tom remained still as the dead teenager staggered along the trail and vanished into the gloom. He was about to go back inside the circle of rocks when he paused and straightened. Was the southeastern sky . . . red? The canopy of leaves was too thick to allow more than a glimpse of the sky, but it seemed to Tom that there was a reddish glow. Was it a trick of the light? He couldn't tell.

Tom relaxed and moved back into the protection of the rocks.

"Zom?" asked Sally.

"Zom," agreed Tom.

"You quiet him?"

"No."

She chuckled. "Mr. Softy."

He shrugged. Everyone who knew Tom was aware that he wouldn't kill a zom unless it was part of a closure job or self-defense. This zom had not been aware of him or Sally and was therefore no immediate threat.

Tom settled down and passed her his canteen. She drank and handed it back.

"Been a lot more zoms in these woods lately," she said. "Last week, ten days. Getting so you can't take two steps without tripping over one."

"Really?" Tom said, surprised. "This was always a quiet section. It's why I brought the kids up here. What's drawing the zoms here?"

"Not sure, but there's lots of stuff coming out of the east lately. Weird stuff. I saw a small herd of zebras running along the same game trail as some elk. Bunch of monkeys, too. Haven't seen a monkey since I took my kids to the San Diego Zoo a million years ago, but I've seen a slew of them lately."

"I saw a rhinoceros," Tom said, and told her about the encounter.

"Wow. A lot of these critters are coming out of the denser parts of Yosemite, but even more are coming from farther east. Don't know why. Something out there is scaring wild animals enough to drive them here, and maybe the zoms are following the animals."

Tom chewed his lip for a moment. "Y'know, Sal, I saw something today that really rattled me." He told her about the man who had been tied to the truck and left for the zoms.

"Damn," she said. "That's one of Charlie's old tricks, Tom, but you've seen that before. Maybe somebody's copying Charlie's act. White Bear or—"

"It's worse than that," Tom said, and told her the rest.

Sally gaped at him. "Are you sure about that? He didn't have a broken neck? You're positive no one quieted him?"

"Positive."

"So what the hell does that mean?" she demanded.

"I have no idea," Tom said. "Part of me hopes that it's real, that it's true . . . that maybe whatever this is . . . this plague . . . is finally coming to an end."

"Yeah, and I keep hoping I'll wake up and First Night never happened."

He nodded. "The other part of me is scared by it, Sal."

"You? Scared? Why?"

"Because right now I know how things are. A zom is a zom, and I know the rules of that. But if the game has changed, then nothing I know is certain." He paused. "I've been teaching Benny the way things work . . . but what if everything I'm teaching him is wrong? What if he—"

"Stop," she said, touching her fingers to his lips. "You're talking like a parent now, and that's my territory. Tom . . . the world is always changing. Always. We can't give the next generation a set of guarantees. Best we can do is help them be smart enough and tough enough to deal with whatever comes. You know as well as I do that we're not going to be there forever for them."

"I know, but things are changing just when we're leaving home." Tom gave a moody grunt and sipped from his canteen. "I'm worried about Chong, too. At least Benny's been out here before. Chong hasn't. I have to find him."

"You will," she assured him, then added, "I wish I could go with you. But at least I can get to Brother David's and tell

Benny and the girls how things are. If I see J-Dog and Dr. Skillz, I'll draw them a map so they can find you."

"Why?"

"Backup. They'd like to see Gameland burn down as much as I would."

Tom shook his head. "This is just a rescue mission, Sally. A snatch and grab, and then I'm out of there. I'm not going out there to assault Gameland."

"Again," she said with a wicked grin.

"Again. I burned it down once and Charlie rebuilt it. Now someone else is running it. Maybe White Bear . . . maybe Charlie, if he's still alive. If I burn it down again, they'll simply keep rebuilding it. There are too many corrupt people out here and in the towns to expect a moneymaker like that to stay closed. I can't spend my life burning it down."

"Uh-huh," she said.

"I'm serious. I have kids to protect. Soon as there's enough morning light to see, I have to find Chong and get him home, and then I'm going east with my brother and his friends."

"Whatever you say, Tom."

"You don't believe me?"

"I'm sure you're going to do whatever you think is best."

"That's right, and right now that means getting Chong back from whoever took him."

Sally kept smiling. "And God help anyone who gets in your way."

Tom Imura said nothing.

Nix and Benny were exhausted, scared, hungry, and heartsick. The forest was too vast and too dark for them to mount a search for the Greenman.

Behind them, far below on the field, the fire was burning itself out. They were too far away to see much, though. Had the zoms all burned? Had the fire killed them, or would there be a legion of charred zombies haunting this mountain pass forever? It was a grotesque thought.

Now that the fire was fading, the sky was less intensely red. Benny wondered if Tom had seen the blaze. If so, what would he do? Was he already on his way back to the way station, or was he on the far side of the mountain with the massive forest and tall hills acting as a screen? The wind was blowing to the south, so Tom could not have smelled the smoke. He might not even know.

"Tomorrow," said Benny, loosening the belt of the carpet coat to allow cool air to soothe him, "we're going to have to try and go back. Tom will come back to the way station looking for us."

Nix didn't answer that. Even if Tom returned to the way

station, the ashes of a zom and the ashes of two teenagers would look about the same.

"There's a good tree," said Nix, pointing to a crooked cottonwood. It had very strong lower branches and lots of other stout limbs reaching out in all directions. Benny scrambled up first to test it. Tom had taught him how to pick the right tree. The rule of thumb was that if a branch was as thick as your bicep then it should be able to take your weight. Benny had tested this on dozens of trees and found it to be a reliable guide. Tom had cautioned against some trees, such as sycamores, because they had a nasty tendency to split; and dead trees were to be avoided at all costs.

Benny shimmied up the trunk, letting his legs do the work and saving his arm muscles until he reached the lowest limb. After he tested the limbs and found a couple of good resting spots, he paused to catch his breath and control the impulse to scream. The burn on his shoulder hurt so bad it felt like he was still on fire. But every time he felt that he could not keep the screams inside, he thought of Nix sitting in silence on the tree stump as Lilah stitched her face. He decided that he would die before he dishonored her by caving into his own pain.

Once he had found a measure of self-control, he scrambled down and helped Nix. Though she was a good climber, her injuries had taken a toll on her, and the horror and stress of the past hour had drained her last reserves. It took a lot for her to climb up, and she was totally spent when she finally reached the spot Benny had picked—a nook formed by four limbs growing outward from almost the same point.

Benny crawled down to the lower branch for a last comprehensive observation of the surrounding forest. There were no zoms, which was a huge relief; but also no sign of Lilah or the Greenman.

He removed his carpet coat and threaded his bokken through one of the sleeves and Nix's through the other. The effect was to create a kind of sling that, while probably not strong enough to serve as a hammock, would at least give them some protection if they started to fall. He and Nix positioned it under them, and they settled back against the trunk of the tree. It wasn't exactly comfortable, but it was safe, and that was all that it needed to be to get them through this night.

They drank greedily from their canteens. Benny asked how Nix's face was, and she said that it was okay; however, when he held his wrist to the line of stitches, he thought he could feel some heat. Was it from exertion or the fire? Or was the ugly monster of infection coming to haunt them?

He took his little bottle of antiseptic and a cloth and dabbed at her stitches as gently as he could. He knew that he was clumsy, but Nix endured it. Then he soaked a piece of clean bandage in water and placed it inside his shirt over the burn. It was too dark to see how bad it was, but it hurt worse than anything he could remember. When she asked how it was, he lied and said that it was nothing.

Gradually their panic seeped away. As it left, it was replaced by a wave of deep exhaustion. Nix leaned her head on Benny's good shoulder and said, "How ridiculous is it that after everything that's happened, we can actually say that this wasn't the worst day of our lives?"

Benny knew that she was thinking of those three terrible days last year. The day her mother had been murdered, and the following days when Nix had first been a captive of Charlie and his men, and then had helped Benny, Lilah, and Tom lead an attack on the bounty hunters' camp. Nix and Benny had both killed people that day. Even though there had been no choice at all, those dreadful actions haunted both of them. It had marked them, scarred them inside and out.

"I know," Benny murmured, trying to keep the sadness out of his voice.

Nix found his hand in the dark and laced her fingers through his. "I guess," she said, "that this does qualify as the worst camping trip in history, though."

He laughed. "No question."

They sat and listened to the woods. There was a constant and comforting trill of crickets.

"Lilah's out there," Nix said. "She's somewhere safe. Right?"

"Absolutely," said Benny.

"Tom, too. I'll bet he found Chong and they're in a tree somewhere up the mountains, waiting for dawn."

"Yup." The forest pulsed with the crickets and the soft swish of branches in the breeze. "Look, Nix," Benny said, "I'm sorry about how I acted back at the way station. I guess I was freaking out, you know?"

"No kidding."

"I was being a total jerk."

"Yes you were."

"And a major butt-wipe."

"Uh-huh."

"Jump in any time now and stop agreeing with me."

"Ha!" she snorted. "You ought to have your butt royally kicked."

He sighed. Then Nix nudged him with her shoulder. "You're pretty good in a crisis, Benny," she said, "but you can't take waiting at all, can you?"

"It's not the waiting, Nix . . . it's the not knowing. Drives me buggy."

"Me too."

"Doesn't show," he said. "You and Lilah were doing pretty good until I opened my big fat mouth."

"You're going to need to make it up to Lilah," she said.

Nix was kind. She didn't point out how easy a target Lilah was or how much Benny had probably hurt her. Somehow her kindness made Benny feel even more like a creep.

Sometime later Nix said, "It's not how it's always going to be."

Benny wasn't sure if that was a statement or a question. Either way, his answer was the same. "No."

She squeezed his fingers. He squeezed back. Then her hand relaxed, and Benny realized that Nix had drifted off to sleep. Just like that. Even though he could not see her in the dark, he listened to the slow, deep rhythm of her breathing. He settled back and listened to the night and began to deconstruct the day in order to make a plan for tomorrow, but three seconds later he was asleep too. Above and around them the night spun its web of darkness as the world ground on its axis toward dawn.

42

Lou Chong woke up.

He was still in hell . . . though he was immediately certain that he was now in one of the darkest rings of hell. They had taken his vest and shirt and shoes, leaving him shivering only in jeans. The ground on which he lay was hard-packed dirt. Cold and damp and smelling of decay. Chong sat up and wrapped his arms around his body. He had a lot of wiry muscle but no body fat at all, nothing to keep him warm down here in the clammy darkness.

There was enough light to see, but it was shadowy and gloomy. The walls were also made from dirt that had been pounded smooth. Chong raised his head and saw that the walls rose twenty feet above him, with no ladder, handholds, or rope.

He started to get to his feet but immediately cried out in pain and dropped to his knees. His whole body seemed to be composed of different kinds of aches stitched together into a tapestry of searing pain. The worst hurts were where he had been punched in the jaw, rammed in the stomach with the wooden stock of a shotgun, and kicked in the groin while he lay gasping on the ground. Chong tried not to cry.

Even as he huddled there, fighting the tears and fighting the pain, Chong's mind was working. He knew where he was. Gameland. In a zombie pit.

He had never been here before, nor had he ever seen a zom pit before. It didn't matter. Tom had described them to him and Benny and Morgie many times over the last few months. Tom had used the zom pit scenario as part of their training. One of Tom's many worst-case scenarios. Part of the process of being warrior smart.

"So be warrior smart," he told himself, speaking the words in a fierce whisper through gritted teeth. "What would Tom do? What would Lilah do?"

They wouldn't take whatever was coming on their knees, he was certain of that. He thought about Nix having her face stitched without painkillers and without screams. Nix had to have dug deep to find the strength to deal with that. Just as she, Benny, and Lilah had found the courage to attack Charlie's camp last year, even when they thought Tom was dead.

"Get up," he snarled at himself.

The pain was enormous, and he dropped back onto his knees. A sob broke from his chest. Then another. While he knelt there, his mind did terrible things to him. It conjured images of Lilah standing over him, watching him kneel in sobbing defeat, and laughing.

Laughing at the weak, skinny kid. At the "town boy" who thought he could be a warrior.

At the fool who dared to think that he could ever in a million years win the love of someone as magical and powerful as the legendary Lost Girl. At the loser who had endangered the lives of his friends. At the coward who had run away. The images and the implications were like nails driven into his flesh.

But sometimes shame is a more powerful engine than rage. Like rage, it burns hot; and like rage it tends to consume its own furnace. He bit down on the pain, devouring it, accepting the hurt as something he deserved, and fueled by its energy he planted a foot flat on the ground, pressed the knuckles of his two balled fists into the cold dirt, and pushed himself up off his knees. It took a million years to get all the way to his feet. Straightening his body made it feel like every bruise was being stretched to the ripping point, but the shame would not let him stop until he was up and straight and at his full height.

"Warrior smart," he said, but he loaded the words with scorn.

"Now ain't that just a stirring sight?"

The words were like a bucket of cold water over Chong's head. He jerked backward as if pushed, and he snapped his head upward to see three men looking down at him from the lip of the pit. One was the big one-eyed man with the flowing white hair who had brought him here. The man whose face was a melted ruin. The other two were strangers. They were smiling in ways that leached all the strength from Chong's limbs.

"Who are you?" Chong demanded. It would have sounded better if his voice hadn't cracked.

"'Who are you?'" mocked the big man. His voice made Chong's skin crawl. It almost sounded like Charlie Pink-eye.

Could this be Charlie? When Benny had hit Charlie, had the bounty hunter survived and gone back into the burning camp? Or had the fires from that battle caught up to Charlie as he tried to crawl away? Was this Charlie Matthias? Or had some other monster descended into this already troubled and dying world?

"I'll bet you have a lot of questions, little man," said the Burned Man, as if reading Chong's thoughts. "Well, think on this."

He tossed something down into the pit that struck the dirt between Chong's bare feet. It was a length of black pipe. One end was wrapped with black leather. There was old blood caked on the whole length of the weapon. Chong bent and gingerly picked it up.

"That there used to belong to a friend of mine," said the Burned Man. "He used that there club to kill a thousand zoms. And near half that many folks who wasn't zoms. Yeah . . . that piece of pipe's got some history. It made my buddy famous all across the Ruin and in every town from Freehold to Sanctuary."

The other two men laughed at this, giving each other high fives.

Chong gripped the object that had given the Motor City Hammer his nickname.

"My friend's long since dead," said the Burned Man, "but he'd be right pleased to know that his legend lives on."

"I didn't kill him," said Chong, and then cursed himself for how cowardly and defensive that sounded.

"Maybe not," conceded the Burned Man. "And then again, maybe you did. Or maybe you're friends with those who did. Tiny Hank Wilson was one of the few who survived what happened at the camp last year. He said he saw what happened to the Hammer. Said it was a girl who killed him. That white-haired slut who's been running these hills the last few years. But I don't believe a little girl could take down the Hammer. No sir, I do not believe that. But a strapping kid like you, sneaking up behind him? Maybe clubbing him down when he wasn't looking? That I can believe."

Chong wanted to throw the club at him, but he held on to it. It was all he had.

"So, I think it'd please the Hammer all to hell to know that his favorite little toy wasn't going to be forgotten. That it was still doing some killing." The big man squatted down. "It won't matter to him, or to me, if you live or die, little man. You live and you get to hold on to the hammer. Maybe one day you'll be the Hammer. Wouldn't that be something?"

Chong shook his head but said nothing.

"On t'other hand, if you die . . . well then, we got lots and lots of other kids who'd kill to have something like a nice piece of black pipe for when it comes to be their turn."

Chong finally managed to squeeze three words through his gritted teeth. "Go to hell."

The men all laughed, and the big man hardest of all. "Hell? Boy—ain't you been paying attention? We're already in hell. The whole world's been in hell since First Night."

He stood up and nodded to the other men. They vanished, but almost immediately other faces appeared around the edges of the pit. Men and women. Hard faces with hard eyes and mouths that smiled with icy cruelty. A small rat-faced man and a boy who was clearly his son shoved their way to the edge of the pit and started calling numbers and taking money.

Bets, Chong knew with growing horror. *God . . . they're taking bets.*

The crowd fell into an expectant hush, and every eye turned in the direction where the two companions of the Burned Man had disappeared. When they came back, both of them were wearing carpet coats and football helmets with plastic visors. Between them was a pale figure that snarled and twisted and tried to bite the air.

"Welcome to Gameland," said the Burned Man.

And then they pushed the zom into the pit with Chong.

43

BENNY WAS CHASED OUT OF HIS DREAMS BY MONSTERS.

From the moment he'd fallen asleep, he had gone running through a nightmare landscape where gigantic trees rose on black trunks that towered a thousand feet above him, their leaves burning with intense yellow fire. Benny ran through a field of blackened grass, and with every step a withered white hand would shoot up through the soil to grab him. He dodged and jagged and stumbled as hand after hand burst through the charred topsoil to claw at him.

No zoms emerged . . . just the reaching hands with their broken nails and bloodless skin.

As he ran he called Nix's name, but the hot wind snatched her name away and tore it to soundless fragments. He could not see her anywhere. He ran and ran.

He saw Tom walking slowly away from him among the sea of clutching hands. Benny ran to him and grabbed his arm and spun him around. Tom stared at him with dusty black eyes. Tom's face was the color of old wax, and his teeth were broken stumps. When Tom opened his mouth to speak, all that escaped was the starving moan of a zombie.

"NO!" Benny yelled, and backed away. Pale hands

grabbed his ankles and held him as Tom took one unsteady step toward him, and then another. And another. Benny screamed again and kicked his way free just as Tom's dry fingers brushed his face. Benny ran as ash drifted down from the burning trees.

"NIX!" he cried, but still his voice had no volume. No power.

There was movement and color off to his left, a flash of red, and Benny cut that way. He saw Morgie Mitchell sitting cross-legged on the hood of a burned-out car, his face screwed up with concentration as he tried to repair the broken pieces of his father's fishing rod. Lying slumped against the side of the car was a slender figure covered with bright red blood.

Chong!

Benny hurried to him and knelt down, trying to figure out where his friend was hurt. "Chong! Chong . . . can you hear me? C'mon, talk to me, you skinny monkey-banger."

Chong's eyelids fluttered and slowly opened. There was still life in his eyes, a wet glimmer deep in the brown irises. Chong tried to smile. He began speaking very slowly and softly, and Benny had to bend close to hear.

"Everything out here wants to kill you, Benny," Chong said.

"Chong! Where are you hurt?"

Chong lifted a hand, and with one bloody finger he tapped his temple. "It hurts in here, Benny. Nothing in here works anymore." Then the hand fell limply away, and Chong slumped over sideways, his last breath rattling from his throat.

Benny fell backward, kicking himself away from Chong.

More hands burst through the dirt and clamped around his wrists.

"No!" Benny bellowed, and he twisted and kicked and bit the fingers until they broke apart and became hot ash. He spat out the ashes and scrambled to his feet. Tom was still coming toward him.

"You should have stayed home," Morgie said without looking up from what he was doing. "'Cause you know that you're all gonna die out here."

"Where's Nix?" Benny demanded.

Morgie looked up. Instead of eyes he had two empty black holes in his face.

"She's gonna die too, Benny . . . and it's your fault."

Anger and revulsion warred in Benny's heart, but he backed away. Suddenly hands grabbed him. Not the cold hands of the buried dead, but two small, warm hands. They touched his back, then his shoulders, and finally the sides of his face. Benny turned slowly, gratitude and relief flooding his heart.

"Nix . . . God! Where were you?"

His voice trailed away. Nix Riley was a withered thing. Her red hair hung like limp red strings from a scalp that was patchy and blotched. Her skin was leached of color and there were clear signs of bites on her cheeks and shoulders and arms. Worst of all, her eyes . . . her beautiful green eyes . . . were wrong. They were a diseased confusion of green and gold and black. The effect was dreadful, the eyes of a thing rather than a girl.

"Benny," she said, and then she smiled. Rotting lips peeled back from jagged teeth. "Kiss me."

. . .

Benny screamed himself awake.

He sat up, gasping, heart pounding, his body drenched in sweat. Cold starlight filtered through the leaves, casting the world into a blue-white strangeness, as alien as the dreamscape from which he'd just escaped.

Benny turned to Nix, surprised that his scream hadn't startled her awake. Or had the scream been part of the dream too? He touched her arm to gently shake her.

But her skin was as cold as ice.

"W-what . . . ?" Benny's voice was hollow and brittle.

He turned her over and she moved stiffly, her limbs already freezing into the rigidity of rigor mortis.

"No!" He fumbled at her throat, trying to find her pulse, needing to find at least the thread of it. All he found was slack skin beneath which nothing moved. "NO!"

Benny grabbed her and pulled her to him, a new scream rising like volcanic lava in his chest. How could this be? How was it possible? Was it the cut on her face? No . . . that was just a cut. Had she been bitten? Where? When?

And that fast he knew the answer. On the field. In the dark. As the fire raged and the smoke obscured everything, one of the shambling monsters had bitten her. In their panic and flight, maybe Nix hadn't known. Or maybe she had and didn't dare tell him.

She was like a block of ice in his arms, and Benny cried out her name over and over again. It was impossible. The world could not allow this. It could not be true.

Nix stayed cold and dead in his arms.

Until she moved.

Benny recoiled from her, staring at her, his splintering mind scrabbling for that last bit of hope. *Please . . . let her be okay! Maybe she's just sick. Please . . . please . . . please!*

Nix Riley opened her eyes.

They were the green and gold diseased eyes of a zom.

With a snarl of impossible hunger, she lunged at him.

AND HE WOKE UP.

The forest was as black as death. The crickets pulsed and the night owls hooted. The girl in his arms was a soft, warm reality.

Benny Imura held her. His heart hammered and hammered. Sweat poured down his face, mingling with his tears.

"Nix," he said gently. She moaned softly in her sleep, lost in her own dreams, and snuggled against him. He held her as tightly as he could without waking her. Benny did not sleep again the rest of the night.

He did not dare.

Tom Imura was up long before dawn. He fixed a quick meal for himself and Sally, refilled their canteens from a small stream, and was ready to go by the time there was enough light to be able to distinguish shadows from substance.

It took Sally Two-Knives a little longer to climb out of the well of sleep, but after she'd eaten something and had her fill of water, she looked and sounded much better than she had the night before. "You'll live," Tom said with gentle humor.

"I've actually had worse," she said, carefully probing the knife wound beneath the bandage. "So have you."

He shrugged. "Fact of life."

Sally reached out a hand. "Help me up."

He did. They were both very careful about it, and Sally micromanaged the process with a lot of curses and complaints until she was on her feet and leaning against one of the rocks that formed their shelter. "Well," she said, "that was interesting."

"You shouldn't be up."

"Can't stay here. Besides, my horse is out there somewhere. I find her, I'll be okay."

"Riding a horse with a stab wound is—"

"—going to hurt, no kidding. Better than walking."

"You should try and rest for most of the—"

"Don't even try, Tom. It's kind of you to be nice to a lady—if we can suspend disbelief long enough to use that word for me—but you need to go find that boy, and I need to go find your brother and the girls."

Tom had no argument for that. "Thanks, Sally. Can I do anything for—"

"Get your ass in gear, boy. You're burning daylight."

He smiled. It was only barely bright enough to see the path. Tom nodded and was about to step back when Sally grabbed him by the front of the shirt with her good hand and pulled him in for a whopper of a kiss. When she finally pushed him back, he gasped and blinked like a trout on a riverbank.

"Wow!"

"In case I don't ever see you again, Tom," she said, giving him a wicked little smile. "I don't want you to forget me."

"Um . . . not a chance. Wow." He gave her a last smile, turned, and vanished into the forest.

Sally watched him go. In the brief moment between his smile and his departure, as he turned away, she saw the smile fall away from his handsome face to be replaced by the face of the hunter. She repeated what she'd said the night before.

"God help anyone who gets in your way."

FROM NIX'S JOURNAL

Zom 101

Zom: What just about everyone calls the living dead.

Nom: Nomadic zoms. Ones that walk around but aren't actually following prey. (Most zoms don't move unless they are following something.)

Walker: Another name for a Nom, though some people call all zoms walkers.

Sliver: A thin piece of metal with a sharpened tip used to "quiet" a zom. It's inserted at the base of the skill in order to sever the spinal cord.

Quieting: What people call it when a zom is "killed" permanently.

Benny let Nix sleep until the whole forest was infused with a pink light. He studied the woods, looking for any signs of zoms. Or of Lilah. Or Tom. No sign of the Greenman, either. For the moment it appeared as if they had the forest all to themselves.

Benny touched Nix's face with his thumb, caressing her cheek very gently. He lifted the edge of the bandage and studied the long cut and the delicate stitchery. The wound was a little red and puffy, but it wasn't bad.

Nix made a soft sound and opened her eyes. Green eyes. Not green and gold and black.

"Hey," she said almost shyly, smiling up at him.

"Hey yourself."

"What time is it?"

"Half hour past dawn."

Nix stretched against him and then sat up and yawned so hard her jaws creaked. Then she held her palm up and breathed against it. "Gak! I have monkey breath."

"Mine's closer to one of the great apes," he said.

Their backpacks and gear were back at the way station.

Or in the ashes of it. All they had was what they'd carried in their vests and jeans pockets. Matches, first aid kit, sewing kit, knives, cadaverine. No toothbrushes. Nothing to eat.

Benny handed her his canteen and she rinsed and spat. Then she told him to take off his vest and open his shirt. He was shy about it—not from modesty but because he didn't really want to know how bad the burn was. It hurt less this morning, but his mind conjured images of charred ends of bone sticking out of gangrenous flesh.

The actual wound was almost disappointing. Three lines of blistered skin, each no wider than a pencil and each less than an inch long. The skin around the burns was puffy, but there was no sign of infection.

"You'll live," Nix declared as she finished cleaning the burns with a piece of bandage.

"Doesn't even hurt," he said, but he was sure she didn't believe him.

His stomach suddenly growled as loud as a hungry zom. "We need to find some food."

They removed the bokkens from Benny's carpet coat and climbed carefully down from the tree. It was a slow and painful process; they were both stiff and sore. As they dropped to the grass they both froze.

There was something at the base of the tree. Someone had placed several fist-size stones in a tight circle to act as a base on which was placed a large hand-carved wooden tray. Large, clean leaves covered the tray, and a wonderful aroma drifted out from beneath them. Nix lifted the leaves and gasped. Benny's mouth fell open. The wooden plate was piled high with fat yellow mounds of scrambled eggs, thick fried potatoes, and a mound of fresh strawberries.

"What?" Benny asked, looking around. "Who—?"

"Who cares?" Nix said as she scooped a handful of eggs off the plate. "God . . . there's enough here for ten people."

"We are awake, right?"

Nix laughed and shoved eggs into his mouth. He chewed. It was cold but delicious.

"Does this make any sense?" he asked as scooped up more eggs with his fingers.

Nix shook her head, then shrugged. "Maybe. Possible sense, anyway. Think about it."

It took two mouthfuls of eggs and three potatoes before he caught up with her. "Man, I'm slow!"

"Gee, that's a news flash," she said, her cheeks filled like a squirrel.

"The Greenman!"

"Question is," Nix said, swallowing, "why?"

"He's a friend of Tom's."

She nodded. "Wonder why he didn't hang around to say hi?"

"No idea. Wish I knew where he lived. Tom said it's around here somewhere. Probably pretty well hidden, though. Guy's not supposed to be very social."

They ate for a while, then Nix said, "God . . . there are so many questions. What's happening with Tom and Chong? Where's Lilah? Who took the cans down last night? Why did all those zoms attack us? And what's with that freak Preacher Jack?"

Benny smiled. "Since when did you think I knew what the heck was going on?"

"Always a first time."

"Maybe," he said, "but today isn't that day." He rubbed his hands briskly over his face. "Okay . . . so, what's the plan?"

"Plan?" she replied. "Don't you have one?"

"Um . . . what makes you think the 'no answer' guy is the 'I have a plan' guy?"

"'Cause I don't have a plan either," she said.

"Ah." They looked around, watching the woods as if answers would magically appear. "We could wait here and see if the Greenman comes back."

Benny shook his head. "I don't think he will. He didn't wait for us last night, and he didn't stick around to have breakfast with us this morning."

Nix sighed. "Maybe we should go back and take a look at the field and the way station. From a distance, I mean. See what's what."

"Sure," he said, brightening. "That's very plan-like."

They shared the last of the eggs and potatoes and stuffed their pockets with the strawberries. They wiped the plate clean with leaves and left it at the base of the tree. Benny wrote "Thanks!" in big letters in the dirt.

He turned and caught her watching him, her smile faint and her eyes distant.

"What?" Benny asked.

She blinked, and he thought he saw shutters close behind her eyes. "Nothing."

Back in town Benny would have let that go, but in a lot of ways he felt like he had left behind the version of himself who was afraid to ask these kinds of questions. So he said, "No . . . there was something. The way you were looking at me. What is it?"

Birds sang in trees for almost five seconds before she answered. "Back in town . . . on your roof . . . I asked you if you loved me. Did you mean it?"

Benny's mouth went dry. "Yes."

"You haven't said it since."

A defensive reply leaped to his lips, but instead he said, "Neither have you."

"No," she admitted, her voice small. She squinted into the morning sunlight. "Maybe . . . maybe if leaving town had been easier . . ."

He waited.

". . . it would be easier to say," Nix finished. "But out here . . ."

"I know," he said. "I feel it too."

"Do you understand it?" she pleaded. "I've been trying to, but I can't put it into the right words."

Go for it, whispered the inner voice. *Tell her the truth.*

Benny nodded. "I think so. At least . . . I understand why I haven't said it. Since we left town, we've been in trouble. Our 'road trip' hasn't exactly been a load of fun. Saying 'I love you' out here . . . don't laugh, but it would feel like taking off my carpet coat and walking out into a crowd of zoms. Saying it out loud just makes me feel vulnerable. Is that stupid?"

She shook her head. "No, it's not stupid."

"My turn to ask a question," Benny said, and even though Nix stiffened, he plowed ahead. "Do you wish I hadn't said it? At all, I mean?"

Strange lights flickered in the green depths of her eyes. "When you think the time is right," she said, "try it again and see what happens."

Benny's insecurities wanted to read her comment in all the wrong ways, but his inner voice whispered a different suggestion to him. He said, "Count on it."

She held out her hand. "So . . . want to go for a walk?"

"Well . . . it's that or clean my room, but since my room is a tree . . ."

He took her hand, and they walked under the canopy of cool green leaves. Birds sang in the trees, and the grass beneath their feet glistened with morning dew. The first of the day's bees buzzed softly among the flowers, going about their ancient and important work, collecting nectar and taking pollen from one flower to another. Cyclones of gnats spiraled up from the grass and swirled through the slanting sunlight. The loveliness of the forest was magical and fresh, but it was also immense. Neither of them spoke, unable to phrase their reactions to the rampant beauty and unwilling to trouble the air with the horrors that haunted their hearts.

Despite the warm reality of each other's hands, they felt incredibly alone. Desolate. Even though they knew that Tom and Lilah and Chong were somewhere in this same forest, it was as if everyone else was on a different planet. Mountainside—home—was a million miles away. The jumbo jet could well have been on the far side of the world, or something from an old dream.

The rocky path wound down among trees and shrubs, and most of the way there was no evidence of what had happened last night except the smell of ash on the breeze. Then they rounded a bend, and all that changed.

"God . . . ," Nix said in a hollow whisper.

The field was a massive ruin. Trees had burned to stumps,

bushes had been reduced to ash. The way station was nothing more than a blackened shell.

However, that was not the worst of it. Not by a long shot. Everywhere—on the field, collapsed over the glacial boulders, twisted into bony knots on the concrete slab by the station— were corpses. Last night they had been the living dead; now they were merely dead, the life force burned out of them by the conflagration Benny had set loose with a tiny match.

It was all so still. A blasted expanse of ash and cracked bones. Nix turned away.

Benny lowered his head. "I'm sorry," he said.

Nix touched his arm. "This isn't your fault. You didn't mean—"

"Yes I did, Nix." He turned to her and brushed a strand of curly red hair away from her face. "I started the fire because I didn't know what else to do. I killed all those . . ."

"Zoms, Benny. They're zoms. You can't kill them."

"I know . . . but . . ."

She looked puzzled. "What?"

"They were people once."

"I know."

"What if . . ." He stopped and took a breath, thinking of the terrible heat and of the flames spreading so rapidly on dry skin and old clothes. "What if they could feel it?"

"They can't, Benny," said Nix softly. "They're dead."

"We don't know what they are. The dead are dead, they don't move, they rot and turn to dust. The zoms . . . they move around. Sure, they attack people, but that's the point. Dead people can't do that . . . so what are they really? Why do they moan? Are they trying to communicate somehow? Are they trying to say something? Or . . . does being a zom hurt?"

"Hurt?"

"From what's happened to them, and what's still happening. The wounds that killed them, the decay . . . can they feel it?"

"They're rotting, Benny. Their bodies move around, but there's no intelligence."

He shook his head. "We don't really know that, Nix, and don't pretend we do. Tom's seen them turn door handles and climb steps. He says that some of them pick up stuff to use as weapons. Sticks and stones. The one last night beat on the door. That says something. That says there's something going on inside."

"Benny, a squirrel will pick stuff up. A cat will swat at stuff. It doesn't mean—"

"That's just it!" he cried. "Even if they're only like a squirrel or a cat, or even if they're only as smart as a bug, Nix . . . even bugs feel pain."

She shook her head and looked at the twisted wreckage of zombie corpses lying in the ash. "No," she said. "You're going to drive yourself crazy thinking like that. Tom's quieted thousands of zoms. He never said anything about them feeling pain."

"How would he know?"

"Tom would know," she said firmly. Benny listened to her words, but he also heard something in her voice. A tremor of doubt.

Let it be, whispered his inner voice. *Now's not the time.*

He nodded and Nix looked relieved, thinking that he was agreeing with her. Benny stepped onto the ash and walked slowly over to the way station. The building was a total loss. Only the front wall still stood; the rest lay in heaps. Benny touched a finger to the outside wall. It was almost cool and covered with a thin film of soot. He nodded again, considering things very carefully, and then used his finger to write a message.

T / L / C
WE'RE FINE. HOPE YOU ARE TOO.
HEADING ON. YOU KNOW WHERE TO
LOOK FOR US.
W.S.
B / N

"W.S.?" Nix murmured. "Warrior smart?"

"Yeah. I want him to know we're using what he taught us."

"So . . . we're heading east?"

"I guess," he said. "To Yosemite. It's that or go back to town. I sure don't want to wait around here. I don't know what drove all those zoms down here last night, and I don't want to find out."

He hadn't yet told her about the man he'd seen standing among the zoms. The man he was pretty sure was Charlie Pink-eye. How could he tell Nix that her mother's murderer was still out here, still roaming the world free?

Benny knew he would have to tell her soon. But not here and not now.

Nix touched the wall below the first line. *T* for Tom. *L* for

Lilah. C for Chong. "It's funny, but Mom used those letters to mean 'tender loving care.'" She turned away. "That was a different world."

"Yes, it was," he agreed.

"We don't belong there anymore."

"No."

She narrowed her eyes and surveyed the way ahead. Past the blackened ruins, toward the green expanse of the forest and the mountains in the east. "It's funny," she said. "I actually thought this part—getting started, I mean—would be the easy part. I expected it to get harder later, but I thought that this would be . . . I don't know . . . kind of ordinary. We've been out to Brother David's a million times . . . but we're not even twenty miles from home."

"I don't know if anything's going to be easy, Nix."

She glanced at him, her lip caught between her even white teeth. She said, "Benny . . . if you say, 'Let's go back,' I will. Right now. So help me, God . . . I'll go back."

He looked into her eyes and then turned and stared across the charred field of bones to the path that led up into the northwestern slopes. Then he drew a breath and let it out before he turned back. "You already said it, Nix," he said. "We don't belong there anymore."

Doubt darkened her face. "Do we belong here?"

"I don't know." He knelt and used a handful of withered grass to wipe the soot from his finger. "Maybe we don't belong anywhere. But I got to tell you, Nix, it cost us too much to get this far to go back now. We have to keep going."

"We don't have to prove anything, Benny."

"Yeah," he said, "I kind of think we do." Then he smiled.

The first real smile he'd worn since they left the tree. "Don't ask me what it is, though."

Then he kissed her. First, very lightly on the line of stitches that crossed her brow, and then more firmly on the lips.

She kissed him back, and it wasn't merely reflex. She kissed him like she meant it. Then she stepped back and looked him with green eyes that were filled with a thousand mysteries. For once Benny felt like he understood some of them.

He smiled and held out his hand, and Nix took it. Together they turned away from the charred graveyard of the dead and headed east. The road before them was tangled in weeds, but the sun glimmered like a promise on every blade of grass.

As they walked away they did not see the figure that stepped from behind a stand of fire-blackened pines. It was a tall man. Thin as a scarecrow in a black coat, with white hair that fluttered in the hot wind. He watched the two teenagers as they walked along the road.

The man moved as silently as a shadow as he crossed the field to the way station. He stopped and those cold eyes read the message written in the soot. His lips moved as he read the words, and then he chuckled softly to himself.

He stood for a long time with his lips pursed, considering the words. Then he used the hard, flat palm of his hand to wipe them out. All that remained was a smear of soot. The figure turned and looked at the road. Nix and Benny were tiny dots now, and as he watched they vanished into the far woods.

The man smiled and, quiet as death, followed.

FROM NIX'S JOURNAL

Tom on Quieting Zoms

Tom Imura: "Put a bullet through the brain stem and you switch off your zombie. The same holds for a sword or ax cut, or sufficient blunt force trauma. However, if you inflict minor damage to the brain stem, you may remove some of the zombie's functions . . . he might be unable to bite or unable to maintain balance. The bottom line here is that the real off buttons for a zombie are the brain stem and the motor cortex."

LILAH CROUCHED BENEATH THE SHELTERING ARMS OF A MASSIVE OAK TREE. Cool green darkness wrapped around her. Her white hair was tangled with moss and bits of leaves. There were long rips in her shirt. She had no memory of what had torn the fabric. Sharp branches or broken fingernails. Her pistol was gone. Her knife was gone. She'd left her spear buried in the chest of a zom back at the edge of the burned field. It was hours before she realized that she was no longer carrying it.

She had no memory of most of the night. Her head felt broken. As broken as her heart. When she touched her face she was surprised to find fresh tears, but an hour later the surprise turned to panic when she realized that she was still crying. That she could not stop crying. There were no sobs. Just tears. Cold against the fevered heat of her skin.

From where she crouched she could see Benny and Nix enter the field. She saw what Benny wrote on the wall, and she watched them walk away to the east. She saw the tall man with the snow-white hair follow them. Three times she almost rose to her feet, almost waved. Almost called out their names.

Each time she did not. Each time she felt that her whole body was one lump of useless muscle. Nothing seemed to work, none of the muscle and bone seemed to be connected to her brain. Her body squatted there under the tree, and her mind merely looked out through the prison windows of her eyes.

Tears broke and rolled and fell in a terrible silence.

Lilah had barely known her mother. She had been a toddler on First Night. She remembered screams and pain. She remembered being carried. Sometimes by a woman—probably her mother—and sometimes by other people. She remembered her mother dying as she gave birth to Annie, Lilah's sister. Those memories were a million years ago. Lifetimes ago.

It had not been her mother who raised Lilah and Annie. It had been George Goldman. He wasn't her father. Lilah never knew who her father was. George was another survivor of the zombie plague, the last of the adults to survive out of a group that had fled from Los Angeles. George hadn't known Lilah's mother except for a few desperate hours. They hadn't swapped life stories. Lilah's mother had died, and then she'd come back. As everyone came back. George and the other survivors had done what was necessary.

Lilah remembered that. She'd seen it, and she'd screamed and screamed and screamed until her throat had been torn raw, leaving her with a whisper of a voice.

For years after that George had been the only adult Lilah and Annie knew. He raised them. Taught them to read. Fed them, and protected them, and taught them to fight. Then Charlie Pink-eye and the Motor City Hammer had found them. They beat George and took the girls to Gameland.

Lilah never saw George again. He had looked for the girls. Looked everywhere he could. He went a little crazy, Tom said;

and somewhere out in the Ruin, Charlie or the Hammer had murdered him and made it look like suicide.

In the fighting pits at Gameland, Lilah and Annie had been forced to fight for their survival. Annie was little, but she was tough. Lilah had been older. On one rainy night she had escaped from the locked cabin where they kept her. She stole some weapons and came back to the camp to find Annie, to free her so they could both escape. But Annie had also tried to escape, and the Hammer had chased her. Annie fell, hit her head, and died; and she'd been left there in the mud like trash.

When Lilah found her, little Annie was just coming back from that dark place where the dead go and from which only zoms return. Lilah almost let Annie bite her. Almost.

It had come down to that, to a moment when the only pathway that seemed to lead out of hell was the one where she would become a thing like her sister. It seemed so easy. To simply stop fighting, stop struggling, and give in. Then she looked into Annie's eyes . . . and Annie was not there. Her eyes were not windows into her sister's soul. They were dusty glass through which the only thing that could be seen was the emptiness where Annie had once been.

Lilah had done what she had to do. She had quieted little Annie.

For years she lived alone in the woods. She had no conversations. She spoke to no one. She didn't even speak aloud to herself. She found books and read them. She learned the art of making weapons. She became a hunter and a killer.

Then she met Benny and Nix, and the world changed for her.

Together they destroyed Charlie and the Hammer. Together they saved other children, kids who would not die in the rain like Annie, or be left to grow strange and wild like herself. Nix, Benny, and Tom took her in, took her to their home. The Chongs welcomed her into their family, treating her like one of their own.

Now Chong was gone. Lost and probably dead in the woods. And maybe that was her fault. The thought was like a knife in her own head.

Benny and Nix walked into the east, their bodies seeming to glow with reflected sunlight.

Lilah thought about what Benny had said, and about her own words—to Benny, and to Chong. The tears would not stop.

Time rolled on, losing meaning and dimension to her. Then . . . there was a rustling sound behind her. A day ago she would have turned cat-quick, her senses as sharp as the blades she carried. Now she ignored it—aware but uncaring. If it was a zom, then it was a zom. The most it could do was kill her. Worse had been done to her over the years.

A figure moved from behind her and walked slowly around her.

Not a zom. Not Chong or Benny. Not Charlie.

This figure was dressed all in green. Leaves and sprigs of flowers were stitched onto his clothes. She looked up at him, seeing him indistinctly through the glaze of tears. His face was made of leaves too.

She knew the face and the clothing. She had seen them a dozen times over the years, though always at a distance. Benny had a Zombie Card with his picture on it. The Greenman.

Sunlight glittered on the hard length of something the Greenman held in both hands. Her spear. She said nothing.

The Greenman let it fall to the ground, where it almost vanished amid tall grass and shadows. Then the man removed his mask. It was really a piece of camouflage netting hung from the brim of a green cloth hat. Beneath the mask was a face that was seamed and suntanned. Bald on top and bearded below, the hair as white as Lilah's. Laugh lines were etched around sad eyes.

Lilah stared at the man's face. There were scars, old and new. The Greenman bent and touched the tear tracks on her cheeks. She almost flinched. She could feel it begin inside her muscles, but she didn't. Maybe because she was too tired from lack of sleep, panic, terror and a night of running. Or maybe because this man did not seem to want to do her harm.

He rubbed his fingertips together, feeling her tears, working the moisture into his skin.

"I . . . I'm sorry," she said in a pale whisper.

He smiled at her. "No."

Then he crossed his legs and lowered himself down to the grass. He did not ask her to stop crying. He did not ask her any questions. He sat in front of her, the sunlight making his white beard glow, and he smiled. At her. At the birds in the trees and the first dragonflies of spring. Lilah caved forward onto her knees and crawled toward him. She collapsed a few inches away. The Greenman did not touch her. He did not try to pull her out of what she was feeling.

He allowed, and that was enough.

PART FOUR

HIGHWAY TO HELL

To conquer fear is the beginning of wisdom.

—BERTRAND RUSSELL

48

Lou Chong yelped in fear and backpedaled away as the zombie tumbled into the pit. He pressed his back against the cold dirt wall and threw an arm up to shield his face. The creature struck the ground with a crunch of brittle bones. The crowd above him laughed like they were watching a clown act. People were calling fresh bets based on whether they thought the zom had broken any bones that would prevent him from attacking Chong.

Chong hesitated, looking down at the zom as it moaned and tried to get to its feet.

He wanted to run and hide, but he was in a fifteen-foot-wide pit. Running and hiding were not options. He racked his brain to decide how to survive this. The moment needed action. What was the smart thing to do?

What would Tom do? Before that thought had even finished forming, Chong was moving. He launched himself off the wall, raised the iron pipe over his head, and brought it down with all his force on the back of the zom's head.

Crunch!

The creature dropped to the ground. The crowd above

him went totally silent. A single ration dollar fell downward, seesawing through the humid air.

The zom twitched. One kick of the leg. A tremble of its fingers. Chong growled deep in his throat and hit it again. Harder. This time the crunch was wetter.

The zom stopped moving.

The crowd . . . went wild. Cheers and applause.

Chong lowered the pipe and looked up at the crowd. The Burned Man crouched on the edge of the pit, grinning like a ghoul.

"Well, well . . . I'll be double damned," he said. "Folks, it looks like we got us a bona-fide zombie killer. Yes sir, that's what we have here."

The crowd cheered. Fistfuls of money flashed back and forth. "Give him another!" someone shouted, and instantly the chorus was picked up until everyone was yelling it.

"Okay, okay!" laughed the Burned Man. "Customer's always right. Nestor? Crab? Bring us another gladiator. Let's have something really fresh."

The two assistants wore wicked smiles as they vanished. Betting ramped up until the oddsmaker had to yell at the crowd, "Give me a bloody chance to count, damn you!"

Chong tried not to shiver. In truth he was no longer cold, but he trembled from hair to toes as he waited for the next monster. A shadow obscured the opening, and he looked up sharply to see the long boom of a wooden crane swinging out over the edge. A figure dangled from the pulley, thrashing and twisting. A rope had been looped under its arms, and once it was down, the rope would fall away and the zombie would be free.

The Burned Man leaned over the edge. "We don't want to damage the goods a second time," he said, and the comment drew a fresh wave of harsh laughter.

Nestor and Crab turned the winch, and immediately the thrashing zom began descending into the fighting pit. Chong backed to the wall. This zom was massive. Burly, like a bull wrangler or one of the pit throwers back home. Huge chest and stomach, massive arms, almost no neck, and eyes that blazed with dark fire. His skin showed no signs of putrefaction. He hadn't been dead for very long.

What had Tom told him about the newly risen? They seemed smarter. They were stronger and a little faster. More coordinated. The decay of their motor cortex hadn't yet reduced them to staggering scarecrows.

Chong gripped the pipe and licked his lips again. "Warrior smart," he muttered.

"Let 'er go!" ordered the Burned Man. Crab and Nestor jerked the rope from around the big man's body and whipped it up and through the pulley. The zom dropped the last few inches and landed heavily on its feet.

The creature was immense. Maybe six foot five and at least three hundred pounds, even with no blood left in its veins. Chong was five-eight and weighed 130.

The zom landed facing the opposite side of the pit. Chong had one chance to rush in and bash it with the club. He surged forward, but before his first step touched down he was struck full in the face by a bucketful of icy water. It was so shocking, so surprising, that it stopped him like a punch to the face. Coughing, sputtering, gasping, Chong dropped the pipe and staggered backward, thumping hard into the wall. He pawed water out of his eyes and looked up to see the Burned Man holding an empty bucket.

"Got to make things fair, little man," he said amid shrill laughter and catcalls.

The splash of the water and Chong's own confused sputtering made the zombie turn around. It stared at him with those bottomless black eyes. Pale lips curled back from teeth that were still white and strong.

The pipe lay on the ground five inches from the zombie's feet. Six feet away from Chong.

The zom uttered a moan of hunger that was newly awakened and that could never be satisfied. The monster raised its massive hands and then lunged for Chong.

Sally Two-Knives found her horse drinking from a stream. She clicked her tongue and the big Appaloosa—Posey by name—raised her speckled head and stared. Then she whinnied happily and trotted up the hill to meet Sally.

Sally sheathed her knife, patted the horse's cheek, and kissed her. "You big goof!" she scolded. "You ran off and left Mama out here all alone. What were you thinking?"

"Probably thought you were dead," said a voice from behind her. Sally whirled around, grabbing for her knife. The blade whipped out of its sheath, but the movement tore a cry of pain from Sally.

Despite the pain, she smiled as a man stepped out of the shadows beneath a tall spruce.

He was medium height, built like a wrestler, and bald as an egg, with chocolate-brown skin and a small goatee shot through with streaks of white. He had a pair of machetes slung over his back and a .45 automatic in a Marine Corps web belt strapped to his waist.

"Damn!" said Sally. "As I live and breathe!"

The man grinned. "I thought that crazy horse was yours. I

tried to ride her but she tried to eat me, so we were both let-ting things calm down before we had another go at it."

Sally Two-Knives gave him a charming, coquettish smile. "Solomon Jones . . . why are you trying to steal my horse?"

Solomon opened his arms. "Give us a hug, girl."

Sally did, but gently, hissing a little as Solomon gathered her in his powerful arms. When he heard the hiss he let her go, ranging his eyes up and down and finally taking in the sling and the bandages.

"Whoa, now . . . what's wrong?"

"Well," said Sally, "the old girl ain't what she used to be." She told him everything. Solomon listened with great inter-est. Like Sally, he was an unaffiliated bounty hunter, mostly working the kind of closure jobs that Tom Imura took and doing some occasional cleanups and guard work. He'd come west from Pennsylvania after First Night with his two kids and a ragtag collection of refugees he picked up during the three-thousand-mile trek through what was becoming the Rot and Ruin. Solomon lived in Fairview, where, also like Tom, he had tried and failed for years to get the town to organize a militia to patrol the part of the Ruin that ran along the Sierra Nevada mountain range.

By the time Sally was done telling her story, Solomon was nodding. "This all fits," he said, "but it's worse than you know. White Bear's got more than seventy goons in his crew, and some of them are real gangsters. Actual gangsters from before First Night. There's two I know will be trouble. Heap Garrison and Digger Harris. Digger used to be a leg-breaker for the Mob in Detroit, and wasn't Heap with the Russian Mafia? Or that's what people say."

Sally made a face. "Nice."

"I was looking for Tom," said Solomon. "Ran into Fluffy McTeague over by Coldwater Creek, and he said that Tom was bugging out. Looking for that jet. I thought that wasn't until next week."

"He changed his mind. Wanted to get out of Dodge. Why were you looking for him?" she asked.

"To talk him the heck out of going," said Solomon. "I've been hitting the wall trying to get the militia idea to go anywhere."

"So has Tom."

"So has everyone who's tried to do it alone. I wanted to get Tom to agree to be the spokesman for a committee. Make a case to the towns, one after the other. Campaign for it."

"Might have worked, Sol," she said, "but it's about two days too late. Besides, Tom's got enough to worry about right now."

"With Gameland, you mean? Is he really going to tear it down again?"

"Don't know about tearing it down, but he's going to get that kid back. His brother and the other kids are waiting for him back at Brother David's and—"

"No, they're not," said Solomon firmly. "I just came through there. Somebody torched it. Turned a couple thousand zoms into crispy critters. No trace of Brother David or the girls."

Sally swore. "God . . . you don't think Tom's brother was burned up, do you?"

"Hope not, but I don't think so. There were tracks leading off into the field, off toward Wawona. The kids probably went that way. If I'd known that it was only kids, I'd have gone after them. Bad stuff's happening in the east."

"I know." Sally narrowed her eyes thoughtfully. "You said you saw Fluffy? Anyone else around?"

"With all that's going on? Everybody's around, and I have half a dozen people out looking for Tom."

Sally narrowed her eyes. "How fast could you get them together?"

"Pretty fast. But it'd have to be for a good reason. Why?"

"I'm starting to have a thought here."

"What kind of thought?"

"A dangerous one."

He grinned. "Tell me, girl."

FROM NIX'S JOURNAL

Why do zoms eat only living creatures?

Firsthand accounts of zoms say that they
will attack and eat any living creature.
Humans, animals, birds, insects, and
reptiles. No one knows if they will attack
fish.

It has been speculated that it is warm,
living flesh that attracts the zombies'
appetites, but then how do you explain
zoms who eat insects? Insects don't have
much body heat.

Heat alone can't be what attracts them,
because if that was the case they'd
continue to feed on the recently dead. But
they don't. Once something has died, zoms
lose interest pretty quickly. (It takes hours
for a body to cool to room temperature.)

If zombies are attracted to warm flesh,
then they should logically be compelled
to feast longer on victims in warmer
climates and less so on victims in cooler
climates.

Zoms don't attack people who are wearing
cadaverine. Is it smell that attracts
them? That doesn't make sense, because
a freshly killed person or animal doesn't

smell like decaying flesh, but zoms stop eating it.

THIS DOESN'T MAKE SENSE, AND IT'S DRIVING ME CRAZY!

50

"HOW FAR IS IT TO YOSEMITE?" BENNY ASKED, PEERING AHEAD TO the hazy mass of dark green in the distance.

Nix fanned a cloud of gnats away from her face. "Not sure. How far do you think we've come?"

Benny glanced at the sun. "We've been walking for three hours. With this terrain, figure about three miles an hour. Maybe a little less. Call it two and a half, which means we've come about seven to eight miles since we left the way station."

Nix tugged her journal out of its pocket and flipped open to one of the pages of maps she'd painstakingly copied. There was one map that showed the eastern side of Mariposa County, with the town of Mountainside circled. A strip of cardboard with incremental mile marks measured onto it was clipped to the page. Nix removed it and found another circled spot marked BD/WS. Brother David's way station. "Tom said he wanted to take us to Wawona, over near the Merced River." She did some math in her head and announced, "We could be as close as eight miles to Wawona."

The thought of the big hotel, with its frequent travelers and patrolled woods, was comforting. Maybe if they regrouped there, they could actually make a decent start on the trip to find the jet. "Someone at the hotel might have seen the jet," Benny said. "Tom says that there are travelers through there all the time."

"Like Preacher Jack," Nix reminded him, then added under her breath, "Freak."

Benny nodded and pulled out his canteen for a drink. "We'll be careful. Besides, Tom will know that's where we went."

She took the last of the Greenman's strawberries and gave Benny half of them. "I would love one of Tom's Sunday dinners right about now. A big steak so rare it would moo when I stuck my fork in it. Spinach and sweet corn. And those honey biscuits he makes from my mom's recipes. And one of his apple pies with raisins."

"With raisins and walnuts," corrected Benny. "It's important." They walked, thinking about a feast. "They'll have plenty of food at the hotel."

"If they don't, I'm going to bite your arm off."

The joke conjured an image of her from his dream. "Come on, Nix," he said quickly. "We can be there in a couple of hours."

She looked back the way they'd come. "They will find us, won't they?"

"Sure," he said, and for the first time today he actually meant it. "And we'll be okay until they do."

The fields, valleys, and meadows through which they'd walked had been clear of serious threats. They'd spotted a few zoms, but each time, Benny and Nix circled around them and kept moving. Neither of them felt any desire to attack zoms unless there was no choice. Last year, on his first trip into the

Ruin, Benny and Tom had spied on a trio of bounty hunters who were beating and torturing zombies for fun. The men were laughing and having a good time; however, Benny was instantly sickened by the sight, and the memory was like an open wound in his mind.

"Let's go," Nix said, and they began walking again. Even though it was early April and they were in higher elevations, the sun was hot. Most of the clouds had burned off, and neither of them had a hat.

"Wow," gasped Benny, reaching for his canteen again, "we should sit some of this out and start again when the sun's not four inches from the top of our heads."

"I'm for that," Nix agreed glumly, then brightened and pointed. "Look! Apples."

They left the road and cut through a field to an overgrown orchard. They collected an armload of apples and settled down with their backs to a bullet-pocked stone wall. The stones were cool, and the apples were sweet. There was a burned-out farmhouse nearby, and beyond that was a barn that had once been painted bright red but that fourteen years had faded to a shade of rust resembling dried blood. A line of crows stood along the peaked roof, dozing in the afternoon heat.

Benny and Nix took off their sweltering carpet coats, and both of them were soaked with sweat. Benny was so exhausted that he was almost—almost—too weary to notice how Nix's clothes were pasted to her body. He quietly banged his head on the stone wall. Then he closed his eyes and tried counting to fifty million. Eventually he opened his eyes and busied himself slicing apples for them. After a while, Nix pulled out her journal again and started writing.

"What are you doing?" Benny asked, munching on a slice of apple.

"Making a list."

"Of?"

"Things I don't understand about what's been happening."

"That's going to be a long list. What do you have so far?"

She chewed the end of her pencil. "Okay, I get the rhinoceros. Zoos and circuses and all. That one makes sense . . . but what about the guy we found tied to the truck? Who was he and why was he fed to the zoms? And by whom? And worse . . . why didn't he reanimate?"

Benny glumly shook his head.

"What does it mean?" Nix asked. "What could it mean? Is the plague or radiation or whatever it is wearing off? Or are we just now discovering that some people are immune to it?"

"Wouldn't we know that already?" Benny asked.

"With three hundred million zoms in America? How would anyone know, especially if it was rare?"

"The bounty hunters would know," insisted Benny. "Tom would have known. He's all over the place. He hears all sorts of stuff. If that's been happening, then he knows about it."

"Okay," she said, nodding thoughtfully, "I'll buy that . . . but wouldn't that mean the other idea is more likely?"

"That whatever caused the zoms to rise in the first place might be coming to an end?" Benny thought about it. "That would be pretty amazing."

"If it's true . . . ," Nix said dubiously. "Then there's the big weirdness at the way station. Brother David, Shanti, and Sarah missing. And all the stuff Tom sent for our road trip."

"And the zoms," Benny added. "Tom told me that

sometimes a bunch of zoms would follow something, like a herd of wild horses or a running bear. He called it 'flocking.' Is that what we saw last night?"

"No way," Nix said firmly. "Last night was no accident. It felt like a planned attack. I think someone drove them down out of the mountains like Lilah did with the zoms from the Hungry Forest."

They ate their apples in silence for a while.

"Nix," Benny said tentatively, "there's . . . something I have to tell you. Something I didn't want to say last night."

"Is it about Lilah?" Nix said quickly.

He turned and looked at her.

"Lilah? What about her? Because she ran off?"

Nix colored. "No, never mind. Go ahead . . . what were you going to say?"

He took a breath. "Last night . . . when we were in the field with all those zoms? Before I started the fire? I . . . um . . . saw someone."

"Who?"

Benny cleared his throat. "It was dark. I was scared. There were a million freaking zoms, so I can't be sure and I'm probably wrong, but . . . I think I saw Charlie Pink-eye."

She whipped around and grabbed his sleeve with her small, strong fists. She shook him. "What?"

"Whoa! Ow, you're banging my head against the stones."

Nix abruptly stopped shaking him, but her fists stayed knotted in his sleeve. "You saw him?"

"No, I said I wasn't sure. The dark and the zoms and all—"

"Was he alive or a zom?"

"I . . . don't know."

"Don't lie to me, Benny Imura!"

"I'm not—I don't know. It was just a second. I—I think he might have been alive, but the zoms weren't attacking him."

"He could have had cadaverine on, Benny, just like we did."

"I know. But something wasn't right about it. It might not even have been him."

Nix stared into his eyes for a long time and then let him go with a little push. She suddenly got up and walked a dozen paces away, her arms wrapped tightly around her chest as if she stood in a cold wind. Benny got up more slowly but stayed by the wall.

He watched her as she worked it through. Every angle of her body seemed jagged and sharp, her posture charged with tension. Benny could only imagine what horrors were playing out in Nix's mind. The man who had beaten and murdered her mother and then kidnapped her. The thought that somehow Charlie had orchestrated the zombie assault on the way station was horrible. It also made a queer kind of sense, since a swarm of zombies had been used to destroy Charlie's team. An eye for an eye?

"Nix?"

She ignored him, standing stiff and trembling under the unrelenting sun. Benny waited for her. Three minutes passed. Four. Five. Gradually, by slow and painful degrees, the harsh lines of tension drained from Nix's shoulders and back. When she turned around, Benny could see unshed tears in the corners of her eyes. She looked at him blankly for a moment, and then her eyes snapped wide.

She screamed.

Her warning was a half second too late, as cold hands clamped onto Benny from behind and dragged him backward over the stone wall. Benny twisted wildly around and saw the face of the zom who had him. A tall, thin man dressed in a tunic that looked like it had been made from an old bedsheet.

"No!" Benny cried.

It was Brother David.

FROM NIX'S JOURNAL

Notes from Mrs. Griswold's science lecture on how cadaverine is made:

The cadaverine used in the Rot and Ruin is actually a mixture of cadaverine, putrescine, spermidine, and other vile ptomaines. The pure compounds are caustic, toxic stuff although they can be easily diluted in water or ethanol (but not really diluting the aroma).

Making these compounds is not a project for a home basement chem lab or even a high school lab. The glassware, equipment, and chemicals are usually found in college level or industrial labs, and that equipment has been scavenged and brought to Mountainside.

The original method comes from a German journal dating back to about 1890. This method for reacting dichloropropane with sodium cyanide (a deadly poison) followed by reaction with zinc powder and hydrochloric acid. This gives cadaverine. Yuck.

51

Tom knelt by a cold campfire and studied the ground. This was the second place where he'd found Chong's footprints and signs of violence. The first time had been the spot where Sally Two-Knives had tried to rescue Chong. There were indeed two dead men there, and Tom recognized them. Denny Spurling and Patch Lewis, bounty hunters of the low-life variety who usually ran with a third man named Stosh Lowinski. These were two of the three men Benny had seen torturing and brutalizing zoms on their first trip into the Ruin. Stosh, a beefy man who used a replica Arabian scimitar to kill zoms, was not here. Sally had given them a little taste of their own medicine. Rough justice, but justice of a kind.

Tom knew Sally's history. She'd been a rough, hard-edged Roller-Derby blocker with one of the Rat City Rollergirl teams out of Seattle when First Night changed the world. Sally had been the mother of two little kids, and she'd fought her way across Seattle to her small apartment where her mother was minding April and Toby. By the time Sally got to the apartment building, the lobby was splashed with blood. It took her a couple of years to tell Tom the whole story. It came out in broken fragments, and none of it was pretty. There were no happy endings, and when she reached her tenth-floor apartment, all she found was heartbreak.

Broken and more than half-crazy from loss, Sally headed south in a Humvee she took out of a used car lot. The salesmen at the dealership were long past caring. Sally made it as far as Portland before the electromagnetic pulses released by the nukes killed her car. She raided a sporting goods store for weapons. Previous looters had already taken the guns, so she loaded up with knives, including the two bowie knives that eventually became her trademark and her name.

It was nearly two years before she made it into Mariposa County, where she met Tom and discovered that there were towns filled with survivors. Tom remembered the Sally he'd first met: filthy, wild-eyed, almost feral, and more than half-dead from a bacterial infection she'd picked up from drinking bad water. He had gotten her first to Brother David's and then into town.

Tom knew that Sally felt she owed him a debt, but in his view, if she helped someone else, then a different kind of infection would spread. Generosity could be as contagious as the zombie plague as long as enough people were willing to be carriers.

Tom rose from where he'd been crouching as he studied the scene.

The two men had indeed been quieted and left to rot. Tom wasted no sympathy on them. However, something caught his eye, and he parted some weeds and saw Chong's bokken lying there. He picked it up. It was undamaged. Tom rigged a sling and hung the sword across his chest. As he did so he walked slowly around the clearing, looking at the prints. There were five distinct sets. Chong's waffle-soled shoes. Sally's cross-grained hiking boots. Prints that matched the shoes of the two dead men. And a fifth set that entered the camp from upslope. Tom placed his foot into one of the prints, and it dwarfed his. Tom was not a big man, and he wore a size nine-and-a-half shoe. This print had to be at least a fourteen extra wide, and the impression was ground well into the topsoil. A big man. Tall and heavy.

Like Charlie. Charlie Pink-eye had worn size fourteens.

Tom continued to walk the edges of the clearing until he found an even deeper set of footprints leading away. Same shoes, but clearly a heavier footfall. The answer was there to be read. There were no traces of Chong's waffle soles, which meant that the big man had carried the boy off.

That gave Tom some hope. If Chong was dead, he would have been quieted and left for the crows. If he was alive and being carried, then even a big man could not move at top speed. And it was virtually impossible to cover your tracks while carrying a burden.

Tom was not carrying a burden. He could move very fast, and even a blind man could follow those tracks. He set out, moving quickly. He had the kind of lean and wiry body that was built for running, and he knew how to run. Two hours later he found the remains of a campfire and the clear and distinct marks of Chong's waffle soles. The campfire was almost cold. Dirt had been kicked over the small blaze, and it had cooled more slowly than if it had been doused with water. Tom judged that he was now no more than four hours behind the big man. He was making up the time he'd lost by tending to Sally last night; and the big man had stopped to rest. When they'd started out again, Chong was walking instead of being carried. Good.

"Hold on, Chong," he murmured aloud. "I'm coming for you."

52

CHONG FLUNG HIMSELF TO ONE SIDE AS THE BIG ZOMBIE LUNGED. He hit the ground in a sloppy roll, coming up too fast, slamming into the opposite wall. He'd tried to snatch the pipe as he rolled, but his fingers merely brushed the cold length of it, sending it rolling away from him.

The crowd cheered, though Chong couldn't tell if they were in favor of his attempt or its failure.

The zom turned, much faster than Chong thought it could, and instead of a dead moan, the creature hissed at him. The sound was full of hatred. Chong's mind stalled. Hatred was an emotion. Zoms didn't have any. But he could see the menace and malevolence etched into the snarling face of the living dead thing.

"No . . ."

The crowd must have heard him. They burst into raucous laughter.

"Surprise, surprise, little man!" taunted the Burned Man. "Bet you never seen a freshie like Big Joe."

The zom—Big Joe—took a lumbering step toward Chong. However, its foot came down on the pipe and it rolled under the creature's weight. Chong seized the opportunity and jumped forward, trying to land one of the kicks Tom had taught them. A jumping front thrust, intended to slam the flat of the foot against the opponent's center of mass and knock him backward.

That was the plan.

Chong's foot missed the big zom's stomach and struck him in the left hip. Instead of knocking the zombie backward, it spun his mass, and with his weight already unstable from stepping on the pipe, the creature toppled off balance and fell. The pipe went skipping off the ground and struck the wall with a dull thud. Chong fell hard on his butt, and pain shot from his tailbone all the way up his spine and ignited fireworks in his brain. This new hurt, stacked on top of all his other aches, made Chong feel like he was toppling into a world where nothing but hurt existed.

Even through the pain and disorientation, he knew that if he just sat there, he'd be dead. With sparks still flashing in his eyes, he twisted around onto his hands and knees and fished for the pipe.

The roar of the crowd blocked out the moan of the zombie and the sounds it made getting back to its feet. Just as Chong's fingers closed around the cold iron, the icy hand of Big Joe closed around the back of Chong's neck. The zom plucked him off the ground as if he weighed nothing. Cold spittle splattered on his naked shoulders as he was pulled toward that awful mouth.

Chong shrieked in pain and fear and swung the pipe with both hands up and over his head. It struck the big zom's forehead hard enough to send a jarring vibration down through the metal and into Chong's hands.

The zom did not let go.

"Uh-oh!" jeered the Burned Man, sparking more laughter.

Chong felt the rough edges of the zom's teeth begin to close around his shoulder. He screamed and swung the pipe again and again and again. The teeth pinched him, and the pain was unbelievable. But with the next swing of the club the zom lost its grip on him, and Chong dropped to the floor. He landed hard and instantly scuttled away like a spider, craning his neck to look over his shoulder as the zombie staggered backward, its eyes becoming dull with confusion. The front of its skull had a grooved look where the pipe had hammered it.

But there was bright, fresh blood on its lips!

Chong went crazy. He rushed the monster, swinging the pipe with so much force that he could feel his own muscles pulling and tearing. Spit flew from his mouth; the world seemed to vanish behind a red haze as he brought the Motor City Hammer's black pipe club down over and over again.

The zom fell against the wall and still Chong hammered it. The creature's feet slipped out from under it, and Chong beat on it as it slid down to the dirt floor. Its hands fell limply to the ground, and Chong never let up. Only when the creature slumped and fell sideways, his head a lumpy mass that no longer resembled a skull, did Chong pause, the gory club held high.

Big Joe was dead. The crowd cheered. Chong dropped the pipe and twisted his head to look at his shoulder. The flesh was raw and puckered and torn. Blood poured down his chest and back.

"Oh God," Chong whispered.

He had been bitten.

BENNY THREW HIS WEIGHT FORWARD JUST AS NIX BROUGHT HER BOKKEN down with all her strength. The white fingers shattered under the impact, and Benny was free. He fell onto hands and knees but got to his feet in a heartbeat and ran.

Nix backed away, still holding the wooden sword out in front of her.

"Come on!" yelled Benny, clumsily snatching up their carpet coats.

Brother David was trying to climb over the broken stone wall. Two other zoms shambled around the sides. Sister Shanti and Sister Sarah.

Nix's face went pale with horror and grief. "Oh . . . Benny . . . no."

"We can't help them," cried Benny. "Nix, come on . . . there's nothing we can do."

"We can't just leave them."

"Yes, we can. Come on!"

The zoms were coming toward them, but they were slow and awkward. Nix kept backing up until she stood with Benny near the wall of the old barn, a hundred yards away from the three zoms. Behind them the road unrolled into the distance toward Yosemite. Here . . . there was nothing left but tragedy.

And more questions.

"Nix," Benny said softly. "Please . . ."

She lowered her sword. The zoms were picking their way through tall weeds and stones. The faces of the two young women were empty of all the light and peace that had been there the last time Nix and Benny had seen them. All the vitality and personality and joy that had made these women what they were, that had brought them a measure of contentment even out here in the Rot and Ruin, were gone. Stolen from them.

"Someone did this to them," Nix said, her eyes fierce with hurt and anger.

"I know." He handed over her carpet coat. They quickly put them on, looking at each other, their eyes speaking volumes. So much would have to be left unsaid for now. And if they kept going east, so many things might remain unanswered. Unanswered and unpunished.

Tom had said that the Children of God believed that zoms—the Children of Lazarus—were the meek who had been intended to inherit the earth. Benny did not know if that was true. At that moment he hoped so, because at least it meant that Brother David, Sister Shanti, and Sister Sarah were where and what they had always wanted to be.

That did not make the hurt any less for Benny and Nix. It did not make the rage burn any less hot.

The three zoms continued to lumber toward them. Benny and Nix kept backing up, moving past the rust-colored wall of the barn. Then they froze when they heard the squeal of ancient hinges as the barn door swung outward. Benny whirled, but he was a second too late as a zom lunged at him from the shadows. Waxy lips pulled back to reveal rotting teeth. Benny and the monster crashed to the ground, rolling over and over in the weeds. Two more zoms rushed at Nix. She swung her bokken, catching one across the face; but the second crowded past and grabbed Nix's red hair.

It was all so fast. Even as Benny fought with the zom, a part of his mind was trying to understand what was happening. The zoms weren't slow. They were rotted and decayed, but they weren't slow; and the burly creature trying to tear his throat out was strong. Far stronger than any zom Benny had fought; stronger than any zom he had heard about.

It was impossible.

Gray teeth snapped at the neckline of his carpet coat. Benny drove his knee into the zom's groin, not that he thought he could hurt it, but because Tom had taught him to always try and lift his opponent's mass. The zom's hips bucked up from the impact, and Benny tried to turn, but then he felt cold fingers wrap tightly around his ankle.

Another zom.

More of them were staggering out of the barn. Farmers and women dressed in nurses' uniforms and men in logger's shirts. Kids, too, one of whom still clutched a stuffed bear to her chest. It was horrible and heartbreaking and absolutely terrifying.

"Benny!"

He heard Nix scream his name, but there were three zombies clawing at him now—the big one on top of him, the one holding his ankle, and the little girl with the stuffed bear, who had dropped to her knees and was trying to chew through the sleeve of his carpet coat.

Benny thought, *We're going to die.* His inner voice could offer no argument.

And then a sound split the air.

"WOOOOOOOOOOO-HOOOOOOOOOOOOOOOO!"

It was a huge, barrel-chested war whoop. The kind Morgie let loose when he hit a homer out past the line on McGoran Field. Benny could hardly see past the growling, biting zom, but he caught a flash of movement as something came from his left and slammed into the burly monster. The zom flipped off him. The figure kicked and stomped and then the other two zoms were rolling away and Benny was free. He spun around on the ground, coming up on all fours, the name rising to his mouth.

"Morgie!"

But as soon as he said it, even before he saw who it was, Benny knew that it wasn't Morgie. It couldn't be Morgie. The man who stood over him grinned through the grille of a New Orleans Saints football helmet. He was tall, thin, but wiry, with a carpet coat augmented with metal cut from license plates, each from a different state. He had a spear almost like Lilah's, except that on the end opposite the blade was a round metal ball as big as Benny's fist. He wore a pair of cheap black sunglasses and a good Cheshire cat grin.

Benny knew him from the Zombie Cards. Dr. Skillz.

There was a yell and a grunt, and Benny turned to see another man in similar garb taking the head off a zom with a powerful two-handed stroke of a heavy logging ax. J-Dog.

The two bounty hunters grinned at Benny. They were a little younger than Tom, so Benny figured that they had been teenagers during First Night. Tom had said they'd been surfers and beach bums once upon a time, but Benny had only a vague idea what a "surfer" was, and he'd never seen a beach except in books.

"Far out," said Dr. Skillz. "Benjamin Imura and Phoenix Riley. Wassssabi?"

Dr. Skillz nodded. "Seriously, brah, and Jessie's daughter's gone all aliham."

"Babelini!" agreed J-Dog, though he was smiling, not leering, when he said it. The surfers gave Benny the thumbs-up. "Good call, dude."

"Huh?" asked Benny.

Dr. Skillz nodded. "Where's the big kahuna? And . . . besides that, what are you Menehunes doing out here?"

"Trying not to die," grunted Nix as she swung her bokken at a zom who charged at her from J-Dog's blind side. The zom went flying backward with a shattered jaw.

"Dudette's no Barbie, brah," said J-Dog, and his partner nodded.

"I know, right? Kahuna was on when he said little cat's hyper-fierce gnar gnar."

Nix turned to Benny. "What language are they speaking?"

"Surferese, I think."

She made a face. "Guys?" she warned. "Zoms?"

J-Dog turned, and if he was concerned about the ten zoms circling them, he managed not to show it. In fact, he managed to look bored. "Oh yeah," he said. "Good point." He turned to Dr. Skillz. "Dude?"

"Dude," he agreed, as if his partner had just said something profound. To Benny he said, "You and the crippler chick hang back. We'll jack these land-sharks."

"What?" Benny and Nix asked at the same time.

Dr. Skillz pointed and in plain English said, "Stand over there. Out of the way. Dig?"

Nix pulled Benny to a safe distance.

"Watch out!" warned Benny. "These zoms are different."

"Different how, brah?" asked J-Dog.

Two of the zoms suddenly rushed at him. J-Dog's smile flickered for a moment, but even in the presence of zoms moving with nearly human speed, he wasn't stunned to immobility.

"Whoa," said Dr. Skillz. "That's new."

J-Dog stepped toward the rushing creatures and swung the ax low and wide. The big blade sheared through the knee of the first zom and the calf of the second, and they both went down in a snarling tangle. Dr. Skillz darted past him and with two lightning-fast swings crushed their skulls with the iron ball on the end of his spear.

"Dog," said Dr. Skillz, adjusting his shades, "these land-sharks are seriously truckin'."

"Chyeah," snorted J-Dog. "What's that all about?"

There were eight zoms left.

"Dude—four on the left," said J-Dog. "Go agg."

Dr. Skillz grinned. "Always aggro."

They waded in, ax and spear whirling and striking and smashing and cleaving. Benny and Nix stumbled backward from the carnage as pieces of desiccated flesh and brittle bone pelted them.

"Dude!" called Dr. Skillz, and J-Dog pivoted as one of the zombie children jumped at him, trying to bite his thigh. J-Dog twisted out of the way and quieted the little zom with a stomp of his steel-reinforced boot. And then, suddenly and inexplicably, it was all over. Not one of the zoms was moving, and not one of them was whole. J-Dog and Dr. Skillz stood in the center of a circle of gory detritus. Dr. Skillz looked around, nodding to himself. "Dude," he said.

J-Dog nodded in agreement. "Totally, dude."

They turned to Nix and Benny, pulling off their helmets. Dr. Skillz had long brown hair and a soul patch under his lower lip; J-Dog had long black hair and a goatee. They were both very tan, and when they smiled, their teeth were eye-hurtingly white.

Benny cleared his throat.

"Dude?" he suggested.

FROM NIX'S JOURNAL

My mom said that everyone who survived First Night has PTSD—post-traumatic stress disorder. Chong says it should be called PFNSD, post-First Night stress disorder, which he insists is PTSD plus something called "survivor's guilt."

Some people pretend like everything is okay with them, as if they aren't messed up from what happened. Mom said that this is just a symptom of damage. There has never been a trauma as bad as First Night. Even if you combined all the wars and plagues together, they wouldn't be as bad, so everyone has to be affected.

Other people seem to know that they're supposed to be a little crazy, so they take the craziness and make it work for them. Tom says that's why so many people, especially those who deal with zoms out in the Ruin all the time, took weird nicknames. He says, "It's easier to be like a character in a story than the star of your own tragedy." It took me a long time to understand that.

Tom's friends G-Dog and Dr. Skillz are like that. After I met them, I could see in their eyes how hurt they are. And how scared. But they play a kind of game. The "surfer dude" game, and that insulates them against reality. It's like wearing a carpet coat. A bite will still hurt, but it won't kill you.

It makes me wonder in what way I'm crazy.

54

THE TRAIL OF PRINTS LEFT BY CHONG AND HIS CAPTOR WAS EASY FOR TOM to follow, but the direction was confusing. Instead of heading straight to high ground, where bounty hunters preferred to make their camps, this trail was circling around to head almost due east. That troubled Tom. Could Gameland have been moved to Yosemite? Or was this man taking Chong somewhere else?

Tom heard male voices farther up the path, and he cut quickly behind a line of thick brush and crept toward them in silence. The men spoke with the uncaring loudness of people who were not afraid to be heard. There were three of them, standing in a clearing formed by the crossroads of two well-used trails.

Tom recognized one of them: Stosh—the surviving partner of the two men Sally had killed. His fashioned Arab scimitar was slung from his waist. The others were strangers; big, brutal-looking men. One was a redhead who wore a necklace of finger bones; the other was brown-skinned and wore matched .45 automatics in shoulder holsters. Tom edged closer to listen to their chatter.

"I still don't get why you want to try and sell him to the Bear," said the gunslinger.

"Yeah, why risk it?" agreed the redhead. "Bear don't want to make deals with you, Stosh. He wants to feed you to the zoms and be done."

"Nah, you guys got it wrong," insisted Stosh. "If I bring him Fast Tommy, then it's gonna be forgive and forget. You'll see."

"We'll see the Bear nail your scalp to a tree with you still wearing it," said Gunslinger, and Redhead laughed with him.

"Seriously, man," said Gunslinger, "you ought to cut your losses and head north. Go up to Eden or Fort Snyder. Get outside of Bear's backyard, 'cause even if you managed to bring in Fast Tommy or his puke brother, Bear'd just take them from you and do to you what he did to Bobbie Talltrees. Stake you out and feed you to the swarm. We tried to tell Bobbie the same thing—but did he listen? Nope. Now look what happened."

"I know," said Stosh softly. "That was ugly. Bobbie wasn't a bad guy. And it's not fair for White Bear to blame us for what happened to Charlie. Me and my crew were all the way the heck up Hillcrest when that happened. Nothing we could have done."

"Uh-huh. Bobbie tried to run that by the Bear, and look what it got him," agreed Gunslinger. "The same thing you're gonna get if you don't put a lot of gone between you and the Bear's territory."

"No way," said Stosh stubbornly. He produced a piece of paper from a pocket and shook it at them. "I know how much the Bear wants Tom. You see the prices on this thing? You ever saw bounties like that? No! The Bear wants the whole bunch of them, and he'll kiss my butt if I bring them in. All of 'em. Tommy, that skank Riley chick, the Lost Girl, and Tom's rat-meat brother."

Redhead took the paper and read it, nodding. "Yeah . . . a man could retire off of this."

"If you're lucky," said Tom as he stood up from behind the bush, "it'll cover your funeral expenses."

The three men spun toward him. The black gunslinger made a grab for his twin .45s, but Tom drew and fired in a single smooth move that was too fast for the eye to follow. Gunslinger pitched backward, a neat round hole punched into his forehead above the left eyebrow. It was the kind of kill the bounty hunters called a "one and done." Head shot, no need to quiet the body later.

That left Stosh and Redhead standing on either side of the corpse, both of them gaping in wide-eyed horror. "Holy jeez," whispered Stosh. "Tom!"

Redhead sneered. "I know who it is." He narrowed his eyes to feral slits. "You just shot an innocent man, pardner. You don't know what kind of trouble you're—"

Tom put a bullet in the dirt between the man's feet.

"Save it for someone who cares," he said quietly. "Lose the hardware."

The smoking barrel of the gun offered no option for debate. Weapons clanked as they fell to the ground.

"All of it," warned Tom.

They looked disgusted but began removing knives, two-shot derringers, strangle-wires, and brass knuckles from hidden pockets.

"Kick them away. Good. Now, listen to me," said Tom, his eyes flat and hard. "You guys have one chance to walk out of this alive."

"What are you offering?" demanded Redhead warily.

"Straight exchange. You answer my questions and I let you walk out. If you know anything about me, you'll know that I'm a hard guy to lie to, but you'll also know I keep my word. You walk out and go somewhere else. I don't see you again. You don't work these hills ever again."

Stosh snorted. "What's it to you where we work? Heard you were leaving town."

"Says who?"

"Says everyone. People are talking about it all through the Ruin. Fast Tommy Imura's leaving town for good. Going on some kind of quest to find that jet plane, or at least that's the cover story."

"Way I heard it," said Redhead, "is that you lost your nerve, that you're running from White Bear. White Bear says this whole area is his now. He's bringing in more muscle than you can handle, so you're cutting out to save your butt. The jet thing is just a cover story to save face."

"Anyone really believe that?" Tom asked, amused.

"Doesn't matter. With you gone, the Bear will own the whole Ruin, and folks will believe what he wants them to believe. Bear's like that."

"Everyone needs a hobby," said Tom neutrally.

"What is it you want to know?" asked Stosh. "To let us walk?"

"First, I want that piece of paper," demanded Tom. "It's a bounty sheet, right? Give it to me. Don't get cute about it either. Put it on the ground, weigh it down with a rock. Then step back."

Redhead did as he was told. He backed up until Tom ordered him to stop. Tom stooped and plucked the paper from under the rock and glanced at it. There were four sketches on the sheet. The text read:

> Reward for Four Murderers
>
> Payment on Delivery at G
>
> Nix Riley: ALIVE (one year's ration dollars); DEAD (one month's ration dollars)
>
> Benny Imura: ALIVE (one year's ration dollars); DEAD (one month's ration dollars)
>
> Lilah (aka the Lost Girl): ALIVE (two years' ration dollars); DEAD (one month's ration dollars)
>
> Tom Imura: ALIVE (five years' ration dollars); DEAD (one year's ration dollars)

Tom stuffed it in his pocket. "Who's looking?"

"Everyone's looking," said Redhead. "Whole Ruin's filled with hunters working your trail."

"You're the first I've seen. Except for Stosh's dead friends."

"Then you're looking in the wrong place. Everyone knows the routes you usually take, and we got word from town that you were heading out yesterday. Everybody—and I mean everybody—knows that White Bear's got a stack of cash on this."

Tom considered. He'd taken Benny and the others out on a route he hadn't used in months. His intention had been to keep the kids away from the areas of heaviest zombie infestation, but now it seemed as if that decision had saved all their lives. At least so far.

"Paper says 'payment at G.' G for Gameland?"

"Yeah. This is all off the record, so to speak," said Stosh, grinning at Tom with uneven yellow teeth. "From what I heard, they'll pay double if the young'uns are brought to Gameland with some spunk left in 'em. People say you've been training 'em a bit. That means they'd last a whole week, maybe two in the pits. There's serious money in the Z-Games."

"This is a lot of money. What's White Bear's stake? Especially if I'm leaving?"

Both men looked momentarily confused. "What do you think, man?" asked Stosh, totally perplexed.

"If I knew, I wouldn't ask," said Tom. "And you're wasting my time."

"Oh man," said Redhead, "this is great. This is like those old comedy shows from back in the day. This is fricking hilarious!"

And suddenly Redhead made his move. He kicked a baseball-size rock at Tom and charged forward in a powerful tackle. They must have shared some kind of signal, because Stosh was only a half step behind him. Redhead caught Tom around the chest, and Stosh slammed his shoulders into Tom's thighs. The three of them crashed backward into the bushes in a cloud of torn leaves, dust, grunts, and yells.

And then a single male voice let loose a high-pitched scream.

A death scream.

FROM NIX'S JOURNAL

Information on bites (zombie and human) that I've collected.

I copied some of this from notes Tom put together for us to study before we leave.

Male adult humans bite with more force than adult females.

Adult humans bite with more force than human children.

Zoms do not bite as hard as humans, because their teeth ligaments have decayed.

A "fresh" zombie will be physically stronger in both limb and bite-capability than a weak one, but still less than a human. So the more the zoms decay, the weaker they'll get.

Dr. Gurijala said (after I bugged him about it fifty times), "Teeth are not fused to bone but rather are attached to the bone by a ligament system. As decomposition occurs, this ligament breaks down and releases the teeth. Morphology of the tooth root will sometimes cause them to be retained in skeletal remains, but the cone-shaped roots of the incisors tend to make them more prone to postmortem loss."

The act of biting through skin and actually avulsing or tearing out a piece would require forces at the high range of the human biting force. So zombies aren't likely to tear out large chunks of a person, as people claim in their First Night stories. If they do tear off something, it's probably from a weak and vulnerable piece of anatomy (e.g., an earlobe).

EWWWWWWWWWWWWWW!

55

BENNY, NIX, J-DOG, AND DR. SKILLZ STOOD IN THE ROAD AND WATCHED the three zoms shuffle toward them. Sister Shanti was out in front, with Brother David and Sister Sarah close behind. They were still sixty yards away.

"They're still moving slow," said Benny. "Not like the ones from the barn."

"Totally," agreed J-Dog.

Benny looked at him. "So how come the others were fast? I never heard of fast zoms before. Have you?"

"Tall tales out of the east," said Dr. Skillz. "No one I know's put goggles on 'em, though."

"That's crazy. How can zoms be fast?" demanded Nix.

J-Dog grinned. "Dudette . . . how can they be zoms?"

Dr. Skillz pulled down his sunglasses and peered over the dark lenses at the monk and the sisters. "That's a bummer. Brother David's trippy but totally boglius."

"I can't understand anything you're saying!" grumbled Nix irritably.

"Yeah, okay," Dr. Skillz chuckled, "busted. Let's see if you grok this. The Dog and me are friends with Brother Dave. Between you and me, cutie, I think Dog's sweet on Shanti."

"She's bootylicious—," began J-Dog.

"English," insisted Nix.

"She's fine." Then J-Dog looked down the hill, and his goofy surfer grin drained away to reveal genuine sadness. "She was fine. Sweet, too."

"They were friends of ours," said Dr. Skillz. Benny caught a look in his eyes that was miles from the sun and fun of a beach. In that unguarded moment, he could see the hurt in the hunter's eyes.

"I'm sorry," said Benny. "I liked them too."

The four of them stood and watched the three zoms struggle up the hill. Even though he knew they were beyond feeling anything, it seemed to Benny that each step looked painful. It made his heart hurt.

"Who would do something like that?" demanded Nix.

"A real monster," said Benny.

Dr. Skillz nodded. "For sure. There's killing and then there's murder. Brother Dave and the girls never hurt no one."

"What . . . should we do?"

"Quiet them," said J-Dog. "Put 'em to rest."

"No," said Nix and Dr. Skillz at the same time.

"It's not what they would want," said Benny.

J-Dog sighed, and under his breath muttered, "Son of a bitch must pay."

"Word. But dude, we'd better roll," suggested J-Dog. "Or we won't have a choice."

They turned and hurried away at a light jog, putting a mile of crooked road between them and the zoms. Soon Brother David, Sister Shanti, and Sister Sarah were out of sight. Benny knew that without prey to follow, the zoms would stop pursuing them. He wondered if they would stand in the road for years like so many zoms did.

They slowed and walked under the shade of a line of young white oaks. "Story time," said J-Dog. "The kahuna said—"

"Who?" interrupted Benny.

"Tom, man. Tom's the big kahuna. He's a crusher, he's the legend."

"Okay . . . but can we just call him 'Tom'?"

Dr. Skillz grinned. "You guys are rough."

"We don't speak surfer," said Nix. "We've never even seen the ocean."

"Yeah." Dr. Skillz sighed. "And we ain't seen it since First Night. Sucks."

"Tom," prompted Benny.

"Right . . . Tom said you guys were heading east to find the jet. Said to meet you at the way station, but we just came from there and it's mosty-toasty. Someone had a luau supremo and roasted a lot of zoms."

"That would be us," said Benny uneasily. He and Nix explained what happened.

Dr. Skillz grinned. "Way to think outside the box, duderman."

"We lost Lilah, though," said Nix. "She ran away."

"Spook girl got spooked?" J-Dog shook his head. "Lot of forest to get lost in. Anyway . . . Tom said you'd be hitting Brother Dave's first and then cruising to Wawona, so we caught a wave and here we are."

"Nice timing," said Benny appreciatively. "Thanks."

"Hey, our pleasure," Dr. Skillz said with a grin. "Fast Tommy's saved our butts enough times."

"Totally," said J-Dog. "Wawona's not far from here. Good place to kick back."

"Is that where you were coming from?" asked Benny.

Dr. Skillz removed his shades to clean them. "Nah. We ain't been there in almost three months. Been doing a lot of guard work for the scavenge team way over at Lushmeadows Estates. Got hired to clear out all the zoms and then babysit the scavenger team."

J-Dog gave an enthusiastic nod. "Yeah . . . made some nice green, too. We ran into Tom last week and told him we'd be crashing at Wawona, though. Still some snow high up, so we were gonna rest up, then go high and snowboard. It'll be a powwow for sure. Saaaa-weeeeet!"

"Um. Okay," said Benny uncertainly, not sure what a "snowboard" was.

"We were heading to Wawona," Nix interjected, "but we don't have to. I mean . . . there's four of us now. Shouldn't we go try and find Tom and Chong?"

Dr. Skillz put his shades back on. "No doubt. Kind of surprised Tom isn't already back."

"Wait," yelped Benny, "what are you saying? That Tom's in trouble?"

"I didn't say he was in trouble," said Dr. Skillz. "It's just that a lot of weird stuff's been happening in the last few weeks. We missed most of it 'cause we were over at Lushmeadows. Bunch of animals coming out of the east, and an upsurge in the zom head count."

"And now we got fast zoms," said J-Dog. "Weird times."

"It's weirder than you think," said Benny, and he told them about the man who hadn't reanimated.

"Whoa," said J-Dog. "You sure?"

"Tom was sure," said Nix.

The bounty hunters looked at each other, then turned and looked back the way they had come, as if some kind of answer was painted on the forest.

"For the record, dude, I do not dig this," murmured Dr. Skillz.

The four of them walked in silence for almost five minutes as they considered their next move. Nix asked, "Have you met anyone who saw the jet?"

"Sure," said J-Dog. "Lots of people. Us too. Kinda wild."

Dr. Skillz nodded. "Tom said that's where he was taking you guys. A quest thingy to find whoever has that jet."

"Yes," said Nix firmly. "Whoever fixed and fueled that jet is trying to bring civilization back."

"You sure?" asked Dr. Skillz. "Bad guys and freaks can fly jets too."

Nix either didn't hear him or chose to ignore the remark.

Dr. Skillz abruptly stopped. "Dog," he said, "I think we're making a mistake here."

"Why? Tom wanted us to lifeguard these guys and—"

Dr. Skillz cut him off. "Wawona's only six or seven miles. They can do that without us. But that dead guy bothers the crap out of me. The way he was killed? That's got Charlie's tag on it."

"Totally," said J-Dog. "Charlie or White Bear. They used to run in the same pack; they got a whole lot in common."

"Yeah, and I don't like the idea of the kahuna running those hills." Dr. Skillz glanced at Benny and Nix. "You guys said that Tom took you out on a back road, right? A route he doesn't use much?"

"Yes, he wanted to—"

"I see where you're going, brah," said J-Dog.

"I don't," snapped Nix. "And who's White Bear?"

Dr. Skillz made a face. "White Bear is a very big and very bad hombre. Mucho bad mojo. Even over in Lushmeadows they're talking about him rebuilding the Matthias Empire. Got people all over the place. We saw a dozen of them today, though we steered clear."

"We're peace-lovin' citizens," said J-Dog.

"The Matthias . . .? God . . . ," breathed Nix, putting her hand to her mouth.

"White Bear's no friend to Fast Tommy, and that's for sure," continued Dr. Skillz. "What I'm thinking is that Tom might not know that the Bear's got his goons out. Not if he came out a back way. He'd have missed the traffic. But if he's dogging your boy Chong, then . . ."

"We have to go find him!" declared Benny, taking a decisive step toward the west.

"Whoa! Not a chance, duderino," said J-Dog with a grin. "You two are going to Wawona just like your brother told you to. Skillz and I will find the kahuna."

"No way!" snapped Nix. "You don't expect us to—"

"—stay out of trouble? Yes, we do. If we drag you into a fight with White Bear, Fast Tommy'll fry us for it."

"We can handle ourselves," Nix insisted. "Tom's been training us, and—"

Dr. Skillz gave her a toothy grin. "I'll bet you're fierce as a tiger shark, Reds, but this is about speed, too. We're gonna boogie like banshees. We got tricks for this, and believe me, you don't know 'em."

J-Dog nodded. "We got to catch a monster wave, dig?"

"But—," Benny began, but left the rest unsaid because without a single additional word, J-Dog and Dr. Skillz turned and began running down the road. They ran with the easy grace of athletes. Benny knew that he and Nix could never match their speed.

Nix took a few steps after them, but it was more out of frustration than any hope of catching them. Then she turned to Benny, fists on hips. "Now what do we do?"

Benny sighed and adjusted the sling that held his bokken. "I guess we go to Wawona. At least it'll be safe there." Then he added, "Dudette."

Nix giggled, and that laugh was worth more to Benny than all the homespun comforts in the world. They turned and headed down the road to Wawona.

FROM NIX'S JOURNAL

Tom says that zoms move faster or slower depending on how soon it is after they've reanimated and where they are in the process of decay. He says there are different stages for decay. I checked this with some medical books (and bugged Dr. Gurijala about it, too. I think he thinks I'm really weird).

ALGOR MORTIS (Latin: algor—coolness; mortis—of death): the process a body goes through after death, during which the body cools to ambient temperature. Temperature drops at approximately 1 to 1.5 degrees Fahrenheit per hour.

RIGOR MORTIS (literally "death stiffness"): the stiffening of the limbs following death as muscle cells decay.

VITREOUS HUMOR CHANGES: There is a clear gel that fills the gap between the retina and the lens of the eye. Following death, the potassium level in this gel increases at a measurable and predictable rate, which allows forensics experts to use it to measure time elapsed since death.

ENTOMOLOGY: Insects always appear on a corpse and are crucial to its decomposition.

AUTOLYSIS (literally " self-splitting"): This is the process of postmortem cell disintegration.

PUTREFACTION: the decomposition of proteins by anaerobic microorganisms called putrefying bacteria.

I'm going to go throw up now.

56

It hurt to ride her horse, but Sally managed it. She swallowed her pain and discomfort and kept moving. There were four horses following her up the winding mountain path; other figures moved through the forest to either side of the road. Solomon Jones walked beside Sally's horse.

Sally turned gingerly and looked back at the crew they were assembling.

The barrel-chested man riding a one-eyed Tennessee walking horse was Hector Mexico, and he wore a necklace of wedding bands. He specialized in closure jobs for families. Behind him, Sam "Basher" Bashman was discussing pre–First Night baseball with Fluffy McTeague, a gigantic man in a pink floor-length carpet coat. The three horses behind them bore a little dark-skinned woman—LaDonna Willis—and her twin sons, Gunner and Dieter. The twins were short, but they were nearly as wide as they were tall, and neither of them had ever lost a fight except to each other. There were others, too, bounty hunters and trade guards, and the scavenger-turned-closure-expert Magic Mike.

The crew amused Sally. Except for LaDonna and her sons, they were mostly loners like Sally, people who preferred to live hard and alone in the wild of the Ruin. Often the only connection they had to the towns was through Tom. Maybe a case could be made that few of them were nice people, but all of them were good. They were people Tom trusted, and that counted for a whole lot. None of them were happy that he was leaving. No one had ever claimed that Tom was the leader of this band, or of any group; but it was always understood that what Tom said was the law. At least to the odd assortment of fighters and killers who followed Sally up the hill.

And there was not one of them who liked the idea of White Bear coming in to take over the territory. It had been tough enough under Charlie's reign, because Charlie held contracts from every town, and anyone who wanted work had to go through him. Charlie always took a slice. White Bear was supposed to be worse. Younger, bigger, meaner, and— from what folks who knew both men said—smarter. White Bear was an organizer. The kind of man who inspired others to follow but who ruled with a heavy hand. If he got a solid foothold, then everyone was going to be jumping whenever White Bear yelled "frog."

Plus, there were the rumors about Gameland. Everyone knew that it was back, but some of the rumors said that it had changed. That it was worse.

The men and women who walked or rode up this hill were not fans of Gameland. Not in the least. It was the antithesis of the freedom they treasured. And most of them had kids now, or had lost kids during First Night. Gameland was an abomination, and they all wanted to see it burn.

Sally rode, eating her pain and drawing her plans. All that mattered now was finding Tom in time.

57

TOM CRASHED BACKWARD INTO THE BRUSH WITH BOTH MEN CLAMPED around his body. There had been no chance at all for him to avoid the hit, but as they fell he wrenched his hips and shoulders around so that he wouldn't land first. They hit hard, with Tom on top, Stosh landing on his left side, and Redhead taking the full brunt of his own weight and most of the mass of the others. Redhead's back struck a stone the size of a foot-ball, and the bounty hunter screamed so loud that it chased the birds from the trees. The scream was almost loud enough to mask the sound of his spine shattering. His arms flopped limply away from Tom, and he lay gasping and dying under the weight of the man he had tried to kill.

Tom ignored the man's screams. Without a moment's pause, he twisted sideways and hammered Stosh on the ear with the side of his balled fist. Stosh let go of Tom's legs and tried to block, but Tom twisted around and kicked Stosh in the chest hard enough to spill him five yards down the slope. Tom back-rolled down after him and came out of the roll in a near handspring, driving both of his feet into Stosh's face. The man's head jinked sideways on his neck, and there was a sharp, wet *snap!* Stosh collapsed into a lifeless sprawl.

Tom relaxed. People with broken necks don't reanimate. Another one and done.

Up the slope Redhead was still screaming. With a grunt of anger and disgust, Tom scrambled up the slope. The crippled man saw him coming, and his scream changed to a whimper. He tried to scramble away, but his legs were dead and his arms barely flapped.

Tom squatted down and assessed the man's condition. Then he put a finger to his lips. "Shhhh." The other man fell silent, though he stared with eyes that were huge and filled with terror. "Your back's broken."

Redhead began to cry.

"Listen to me now. You're done. You know that. I can leave you here like this and you can spend your last hours screaming. Lot of zoms in these woods. With your back broken, you might not even feel it when they start tearing chunks out of you. After that . . . well, you'll reanimate, and then you're going to lie here for the rest of time. Crippled and undead and useless."

Redhead was blubbering, mouthing unintelligible words. Tom leaned toward him. "Or . . . you can buy yourself some grace. You square things with me and I can ease you down. You'll never feel it, and you won't come back. It's your call."

The reality of it all hit Redhead, and he stopped mewling. He stared at Tom with eyes that suddenly possessed a dreadful wisdom about the nature of his world. Tom could see the understanding blossom in the man's eyes.

"Okay . . . ," Redhead whispered, then hissed in pain.

Tom nodded. He didn't gloat. That never occurred to him. He removed his canteen and gave the man a sip.

"Who took the boy from Stosh's buddies after they were ambushed?"

"W-White Bear. They were Charlie's guys. White Bear's tearing up everyone from Charlie's crew, 'cause of what happened to Charlie."

"Why? What does White Bear care about what happened to Charlie?"

Redhead almost smiled. "Are you . . . kidding me?"

"Do I look like I'm kidding you? What's the thing between Charlie and White Bear?"

"Jeez, man . . . you can see it when you look at him."

"I never met White Bear."

"Yeah, you did. He was there when you burned down Gameland."

"What? There was no one there like him."

"He . . . wasn't calling himself White Bear then. That was something he came up with after he got hurt."

"You're not making sense," Tom said, "and you're beginning to piss me off."

Redhead looked instantly afraid. "God . . . please don't leave me like this!"

"Shhh, shhh," Tom soothed. "Just tell me about White Bear and Charlie."

"It's all about Gameland," said the man, and Tom noticed that his voice was beginning to fade. Shock was setting in, and the man didn't have long. "When you burned down Gameland, Charlie lost a lot of people, a lot of friends. You know that. But what you don't know is that someone close to him was burned in that fire. Used to go by the name of Big Jim."

Tom grunted. "Big Jim Matthias? Charlie's brother? He was at Gameland that day?"

"Yeah. He got messed up pretty bad, too. Face all burned, lost an eye. Almost died. Charlie sent him way over into Yosemite, to a place he has there. Big Jim got real sick. They say he died for a while, but he didn't come back as a zom. They say that while he was dead he had a vision of some old Indian medicine man, and that when he came back he wasn't Jim Matthias anymore. He was—"

"White Bear," Tom finished, shaking his head. "White Bear is Charlie's brother. I'll be damned. That's why he wants me."

"You . . . and your brother and his friends. He wants you so bad that it's made him even crazier. When he heard you were leaving Mountainside, maybe for good, he put everyone he has out into the Ruin. There's a hundred pair of eyes looking for you, man. You won't make it off this mountain."

Tom didn't comment on that. Instead he asked, "Why's he killing Charlie's men?"

"Not all of them. Just the ones he thinks should have been with Charlie when you hit his camp last year. Blames them, says they should have died protecting Charlie."

"That's crazy."

"White Bear is crazy, man. Plays it cool . . . but he's totally out of his mind. Makes Charlie look like Joe Ordinary Citizen."

"Swell. Okay, now tell me one more thing. Where's Gameland?"

"If I tell you . . . will you do what you promised? Make it easy? Keep me down?"

"I promise."

"Swear it, man. I . . . I used to be Catholic. Swear on the baby Jesus."

Tom sighed and held his hand to heaven. He swore.

The man told Tom where Gameland was. Tom swore again, much louder.

The man tried to smile, but he was fading like a setting sun. "You know, man . . . I almost wish I could see you go up against White Bear and Gameland."

"Yeah, I'll bet you'd like to see me fed to the zoms, too."

Redhead gave him a strange look. "No . . . you . . . don't have to believe me, man, but I'd kind of like to see you kick that crazy son of a bitch's ass. Him and his whole damn family."

A terrible coughing fit hit him, and he hacked and coughed until blood mottled his lips and his face turned the color of sour milk. Then his eyes flared wide and his mouth formed a small "Oh" and he stopped moving. His eyes stared upward into the vast blue forever. The forest was silent except for the buzzing of insects.

Tom's face and body were as still as the dead man's, but inside his heart was hammering with fear. "Gameland," he murmured. "Oh God . . ."

He looked down at the dead man and drew his quieting dagger. Reanimation could take as long as five minutes, but not with traumatic injuries. They were always faster. Redhead's face was slack, his eyes half-closed, and there was no sign at all of the jerks and twitches that signal reanimation. Tom counted out sixty seconds. Then another sixty. The man stayed silent and still. And dead. Inside Tom's head the pounding was getting louder.

He was curious, though. After the man he'd found on the road, he needed to know if that was a total fluke or part of a pattern. It was crucial to understand as much as possible about the living dead.

But Gameland was waiting, and he knew that he had to go, and go now.

Tom counted out another sixty seconds. And another.

Go! Go! Go! screamed his inner voice.

"Damn it," he snarled, and rolled the man over. He drove the blade in to sever the brain stem. He wiped the dagger clean and got to his feet, thinking, *He was going to come back. It was just taking longer for some reason.*

He thought it, but he wasn't sure that he believed it.

With that burning in his mind, he turned in the direction of Gameland. There was no need for tracking now. It was no longer a hunt. It was a trap, and he was heading straight into it. But he had no choice.

He ran.

58

THEY FOUND A ROAD WITH A RUSTED SIGN THAT READ "WAWONA HOTEL, six miles." The sign was pocked with old bullet holes and badly faded, but they could read it, and it filled them with new energy. A line of cumulus clouds swelled out of the west, their bottoms shaved flat by crosswinds and condensation, their tops reaching upward like puffy white mountains.

For a while they walked hand in hand, but as each of them drifted into their own thoughts they let go, content to be in their own space. They topped a rise and paused, watching a spectacle that was both funny and sad. Over the rise, the road wound like a snake through farm fields that had long since grown wild. A horse stood in the middle of the left-hand field, head down to munch the sweet grass, tail swishing at flies. Fifty yards away a lone zombie staggered awkwardly toward it. The zom wore a soiled pair of overalls with one torn shoulder strap. It marched unsteadily yet with clear purpose toward the horse, but when it was within a dozen yards the horse calmly lifted its head to regard the zom, then trotted out of the field and across the road before stopping a hundred yards into the middle of that field. The horse passed almost within grabbing distance of the zom, and the creature flailed at it, but the animal moved in a way that demonstrated an understanding of the danger. Once it was well into the next field—now a total distance of three hundred yards from where it had originally been—it flicked its tail and then lowered its head to continue eating. The zom began walking toward the road and the opposite field, arms reaching, legs carrying it along with the same awkward gait.

"I'll bet that's been happening all day," Benny said to Nix.

She nodded, but her eyes were sad. There was a bit of comedy in the staging of all this: the patient, clever horse and the untiring, mindless zom—the two of them moving back and forth between the fields all day in a freakish pas de deux. A dance for two, probably played out on countless days here in the dust and decay of a broken world.

They did not speak at all for the next few miles. Not until the black peaked roof of the Wawona Hotel rose above the endless trees.

59

THE GREENMAN'S VOICE WAS QUIET, GENTLE. "I KNOW WHO YOU ARE," he said. "Do you know who I am? I think you've seen me a few times. Here and there. People call me the Greenman, or just Greenman. No 'the.' Doesn't matter. You can call me whatever you want. Or not."

They were in the Greenman's cabin, deep in the woods. When Lilah did not respond or even lift her head, he got up and walked into the small kitchen. A moment later there was the aroma of brewing tea.

Lilah sat curled into a large rattan chair, knees drawn up, arms wrapped around her shins. After the Greenman had found her in the woods, he'd sat with her for over two hours, mostly in silence, occasionally singing old songs that Lilah had never heard. Except for one, a song that George used to sing when he was cleaning the small house where he and Lilah and Annie had lived for the early years following First Night.

"California dreamin' . . . on such a winter's day . . ."

Lilah had started to cry, and the Greenman had not said anything to her. He kept quietly singing the song. When it was done, he sang another song. And another.

Now they were in his house. It was filled with plants of

all kinds. They hung in baskets from the ceiling and stood in pots along the walls. Boxes of them hung on both sides of the open windows. Birds sang and chattered in the trees outside, and a squirrel came in and sat eating nuts from the bowl on the table. The Greenman did not chase it away.

He returned from the kitchen with two steaming mugs that he placed on a small table. Then he went and loaded a wooden tray with seedcakes, homemade granola bars, and little pots of jelly and butter. The first time Lilah had ever tasted butter was at the Chongs' house. She stared at the tray and the food and the tea and did nothing.

The Greenman drank his tea, but he didn't say anything about hers. She would drink it or she wouldn't, and he seemed to be content with either outcome. A large cat came in through the kitchen window, cast a wary eye at Lilah, then a longer look at the squirrel, but strolled across the room toward Lilah. For a moment it peered up at her with luminous eyes. Then it hopped up into her chair and rubbed itself against her, its purr louder than the larks in the trees. Lilah unwrapped her arms and the cat stood on its back legs, resting its front paws on her knee, leaning its face toward hers. Lilah cut a quick look at the Greenman, who gave a single small nod; then she gathered the cat up in her arms and held it to her chest as if it was the most precious thing in the world. Or as if it was the one thing that tethered her to the moment.

The cat meowed softly and continued to purr. Lilah bent her head until her forehead touched the cat's cold nose. It gave her a single raspy lick.

Lilah closed her eyes and wept.

60

BENNY AND NIX PASSED THROUGH THE SOUTH ENTRANCE OF YOSEMITE National Park and walked along a road that was virtually weed free—the first clear road they had ever seen out in the Ruin.

They encountered the first fence two miles up the road. It was a heavy chain-link affair similar to the one that surrounded Mountainside, but it was hidden between two rows of thick evergreen hedges that acted as screens.

"Smart," said Nix.

A sign told them that the hotel was two miles along the road.

The road led through a complex network of trenches. There were rows of trip wires, and deadfall pits covered by camouflage screens. Directions for navigating the road safely were written on large wooden signs. Benny appreciated the strategy. Zoms couldn't read. Instead of building defenses that were based on the way people used to protect towns and forts against attacks, these were specifically designed against an unthinking and yet unrelenting enemy. Subterfuge was unnecessary. Benny and Nix peered into some of the trenches and saw heaps of old bones—eloquent proof that the defenses worked.

"The way this is laid out," Benny observed, "ten people could hold off a zillion zoms."

"This is the kind of thing I've been talking about," Nix said excitedly. It was true; since last year she had been making journal notes about how people could take back the zombie-infested lands while at the same time protecting themselves from the dead.

The winding path was lined with hundreds of trees, ancient oaks and many younger trees planted in the last decade or so to reduce visibility. In the distance they could see much larger trees rising up above the forest—monstrous sequoias that towered more than 250 feet into the blue sky. Then the forest opened up and the big Wawona Hotel rose above them like a promise of warm beds, country breakfasts, civil conversation, and stout locks.

"Finally," breathed Nix, exhausted.

The Wawona Hotel had a double row of verandas—one on the ground level at the top of a short flight of steps, and the other built directly above it on the second floor. Whitewashed columns rose to the pitched roof, which was covered in gray shingles that, though weathered, looked to be in good repair. Tall willows blocked most of the view of the upper floor and roof, and these softer trees lent the place a quiet and rustic appearance that was as calming in its way as were the fortifications and weapons. Because of the trees, all they could read of the hotel's name was a large black W painted just below the edge of the roof.

Beside the hotel was a corral filled with horses, most of them standing with heads down as they munched the green spring grass; a few stood by the rails, watching with brown-eyed curiosity. Beyond the corral stood more than two dozen armored trade wagons. In the distance, off behind the big building, were party sounds. Loud voices and laughter.

"If I'd known what this place was like," said Benny, "I'd have tried to get a job here instead of apprenticing with Tom."

"Really?"

"Sure. I'll bet everyone out here talks about the way things are, instead of always going on about how things used to be. You'd have enough stuff to fill up your journal in a week."

She nodded, smiling at the thought. "There seem to be a lot of people here. Maybe we can get together some kind of search party."

They were still sixty yards from the front steps when they heard a sound behind them. A soft footfall, and they turned to see three men standing on the grass verge behind them. Benny realized that he and Nix had been so focused on the hotel that they must have walked right by them. Two of the men were strangers with the hard faces of bounty hunters—one was a brown-skinned brute with a flight of ravens tattooed across his face and down his throat; the other was a hulk of a white man with no neck and mean little pig eyes. They studied Benny and Nix with unsmiling faces. The third man, however, was smiling, and he was known to Benny and Nix.

"Well, well, if this ain't cause to say hallelujah," said the man. He had eyes the color of deep winter ice, cold and blue. As if conjured by the dark magic of the man's smile, a chilly wind whipped past them, rustling the leaves and sending the birds shrieking into the air.

"God!" Nix gasped, and took Benny's hand, squeezing it with her usual bone-crushing intensity.

Preacher Jack's pale eyes sparkled with pleasure, and when his lips writhed into their twitchy smile it revealed teeth stained with chewing tobacco and black coffee. "Now," he said softly, "how is it that I'm blessed with the company of two such fine young people here on my own humble front lawn?"

"What are you talking about? What do you mean your front lawn?"

Preacher Jack chuckled and lifted his chin toward the house. "Funny, you being Tom Imura's brother, and him supposed to be so smart, I'm downright surprised you ain't figured things out yet."

Benny turned to look at the hotel. The chilly wind was blowing through the weeping willows, lifting the leaves to reveal the upper story, and they could now see with terrifying clarity the words that had been painted there. The black W was not the first letter of Wawona Hotel. It was the first letter of "Welcome."

Benny's could feel his insides turn to icy mush. Even Nix's hand lost its crushing force as the two of them read the three words painted across the front of the hotel.

WELCOME TO GAMELAND.

61

CHONG SAT HUDDLED AGAINST THE DIRT WALL. THE TWO ZOMS WERE STILL with him. Silent and still, and yet the horror of what they represented was much worse than if they were still moaning and reaching for him.

Blood still seeped sluggishly from the bite on his shoulder. He had done nothing to dress the wound. He had not done anything at all except to lean his back against the wall and slide down to the floor. Above him the crowd was gone. Even the Burned Man was gone. There had been some rude jokes about him "winning and losing" at the same time; and one of the bettors had told him to "relax." The crowd had left laughing.

If he turned his head, Chong could see the bite. His skin had been caught between the zom's strong teeth, and as the creature had fallen away the pressure had popped the skin, leaving a ragged flap that had bled profusely at first but had now almost stopped.

Chong stared across the pit to the far wall. The hard-packed earth was cold and dark and lifeless. It seemed to present an eloquent window into his own future. The pipe lay on the ground between his bare feet. The weapon of the Motor City Hammer. A killer's tool. Caked with blood, old and new. A weapon to murder humans and quiet zombies.

He picked it up. It was cold and heavy. Could such a weapon be used to kill oneself? he wondered. What would happen if he tried to bash out his own brains, and failed? What would happen if he did nothing? He could not feel any changes inside. He was sick to his stomach, but the nausea had started with the beating he'd gotten yesterday. Would he be able to tell when the infection took hold? What would it feel like? How sick would he get?

The pipe felt very solid in his fist, and Chong thumped the ground with it, wishing that he could get out of the pit and use what time he had left to avenge his own death. To go down fighting.

Would Lilah admire that, at least? A warrior's last stand, taking as many of his enemies with him as possible?

But he knew that the Burned Man would never let him have that chance. Chong knew that he would be left down here until he zommed out or was made to fight one more time. Anger flared in his chest, and he hurled the pipe as hard as he could. It flew across the pit and struck tip-first against the wall, chunking out a lump of dirt half as big as Chong's fist. Dirt and pipe fell to the ground.

So much for being warrior smart, he thought bitterly. He wrapped his arms around his head and tried not to be afraid of dying.

And that lasted for about fifteen seconds. Then he raised his head and looked at the pipe, at the clod of dirt he'd knocked out of the wall. Then at the divot in the wall.

Despite everything, despite a future as dark as that cold wall, he smiled.

BENNY WHEELED AROUND TO GAPE AT PREACHER JACK.

"That's impossible! This place can't be Gameland!" Benny shouted.

"Nothing's impossible in this world of wonders, young Benjamin Imura," said Preacher Jack with a soft chuckle.

"I don't understand! Tom said—"

"Tom ain't been out here for a long time, boy."

"Good thing, too," groused the black man with the raven tattoos. "Used to be a man couldn't piss in these woods without Fast Tommy giving him a ration of crap for it. Your brother's a pain in everyone's butt out here, kid."

"Was," corrected Preacher Jack, holding up a slender finger. "Tom Imura's day is over. None of our fellowship need fear that sinner or his violent ways. A bright new day has dawned out here in the Lord's paradise. Believe it, for it is so."

Nix curled her lip in distaste. "Really? What I believe is that when Tom gets here he's going to kick your ugly—"

Preacher Jack suddenly stepped forward and struck Nix across the face with an open-handed slap that was so shockingly fast and hard that it spun her around and dropped her to her hands and knees.

Benny cried out and tried to catch her while also trying to drag out his bokken. He failed in both attempts. The white man with the pig eyes grabbed Nix by the hair and pulled her away. Benny instantly stopped fumbling with the sword and punched the man in the solar plexus. The man's torso was sheathed in hard muscle, but Tom had taught Benny how to use his whole body to put force into a punch. The little pig eyes bulged, and the man coughed and released his hold. Benny slammed him backward with a two-handed shove that sent the thug crashing into the black man. They both went down amid tangled limbs and vile curses.

Nix struggled to get to her feet, but she was dazed and bleeding. Preacher Jack's blow had opened up some of Lilah's fine stitchery. With a howl of rage, Benny whipped out his bokken and swung it with all his strength at Preacher Jack's grinning mouth.

It never connected.

Preacher Jack was old—in his sixties, with a face as lined as a road map and a body as frail-looking as a stick bug—but he stepped into the blow and caught the wooden sword with one calloused hand. The sudden stop jolted Benny, but the shock of it, the seeming impossibility of it, froze him into the moment. He stared at the hand that gripped his sword and then looked up into Preacher Jack's face. That smile never wavered.

"Surprise, surprise," whispered the preacher. With his free hand he punched Benny full in the face. Benny reeled back, bright blood spurting from his nose and lips. He suddenly fell, and his flailing left arm struck Nix across the temple. They both crashed to the grass.

Worms of flame twisted through the air in front of Benny's eyes, and his whole head seemed to be filled with bursting fireworks. Next to him, Nix groaned softly and rolled onto her side.

The two bounty hunters were on their feet now, and they glared down in fury at Benny. The big white man raised his leg to stomp Benny, but Preacher Jack stopped him with a small click of his tongue. "Digger, Heap—take their toys," said the preacher. The two men seethed for a moment, their hands opening and closing. "Don't make me repeat myself."

They shot frightened looks at the old man and immediately bent to strip Nix and Benny of knives and anything else that could be used as a weapon, including their fishing line and storm matches. The men were rougher than they needed to be, and their searching hands were far more personally intrusive than necessary. Nix yelped in pain and indignation and kicked the pig-eyed man named Heap in the thigh, missing her intended target by inches. Heap snarled at her and stepped back.

Preacher Jack stood over them. "Oh, how strange the world must be to you young people. Strange, and wondrous and full of mysteries," he murmured. Weird shadows swirled in his pale eyes. "I know what questions must be screaming inside your heads right at this very moment, indeed I do."

Benny spat blood out of his mouth. "You don't know anything about us."

"Actually, my young buck, I know more about you than you know about me . . . and that's going to be so unfortunate for you."

"Tom will kill you," said Nix with real heat.

"Oh . . . I pray he tries."

Digger and Heap chuckled.

Nix wiped blood from her eyes. "Tom's going to find us and—"

"Of course he's going to find you, girl. Lord oh Lord but we've made it easy for him to find you. To find me." Preacher Jack stepped closer and squatted down so that he was nearly eye to eye with Benny and Nix. "Mmm . . . didn't expect that answer, did you? Tell me . . . what is it you think is going to happen? Do you think you're going to be rescued by the big bad Fast Tommy? Tom the Swordsman, Tom of the Woods . . . Tom the Killer? Is that what you think?"

"Why are you doing this?" pleaded Nix. "Why can't you people just leave us alone? All we want to do is leave this place."

"Leave? And go where?"

Nix pointed east. "Far away from you and all this stuff. We don't want any part of it."

"You want to go east?" Something moved behind Preacher Jack's eyes, and for a moment he almost looked afraid. Then his eyes hardened. "Oh, my foolish little sinners, you don't want to go east. There's nothing out there for you."

"Yes there is," Nix said. "There's—" She stopped, cutting off her own words.

"What were you going to say? That there's a plane? A big, shiny jet plane?" Preacher Jack shook his head. "I might be doing you a kindness to keep you from that path. Only thing you'd find east of here is horror and heartache."

"As opposed to the good times and bunnies we have here," said Benny. However, despite his snarky comment,

Preacher Jack's words—and that look that had passed behind his eyes—opened an ugly door of doubt deep in Benny's soul. Had Nix caught it too?

"Why?" Nix demanded again. "Why are you doing this?"

Preacher Jack drove the tip of Benny's bokken into the soft ground and leaned on it, laying one cheek against the polished hardwood. "Now that's a wonderful question, little girl. Why indeed? Why did I come out of 'retirement'? Until December of last year I was content to tend to my flock. I was at work in the fields of the Lord, seeing to the Children of Lazarus."

"Zoms," breathed Benny, wanting the word to wipe the smile off Preacher Jack's mouth.

"Ah yes, the tactic of provoking your enemy. Did Tom teach you that? Or is it your own natural sinfulness that leads you to insult a servant of God? No . . . don't answer, boy, because if I hear that word come out of your mouth, I'll cut off your tongue and nail it to your forehead. Don't think I'm joking, little Benjamin, 'cause it wouldn't be the first time I've stilled the offending tongue of a sinner. Ain't that right, boys?"

"Amen to that, padre," they said.

Benny, wisely, said nothing.

Preacher Jack nodded approval. "When word came to me that Tom Imura had murdered Charlie Matthias and Marion Hammer, well . . . I knew that the Lord was calling me to do other work."

"Tom didn't murder anyone!" declared Nix. "Charlie Pinkeye was the murderer! He killed my mother!"

"Shhh, little girl. I believe you'd find it hard to speak lies with your lips sewn shut."

Nix spat at him. Benny tensed, ready to throw himself between Nix and Preacher Jack's retaliation, but the preacher merely laughed and wiped the spittle from the lapels of his dusty black coat. He shook his head, and his smile dimmed a little.

"Oh, child of the dust . . . you are just stacking up sins in the storehouse of the Lord," he said softly. "You speak ill of Charlie, but he was a good man. Trusted by his men, good to his family, and a role model for everyone in these troubled, troubled times. Stupid and sinful people can't see past their own inadequacies to understand the difficult choices a man like Charlie has to make in order to protect what's his." He closed his eyes for a moment. "To know that the man who murdered him still walks this earth is like a splinter in my mind. Tom Imura is an evil man. He's been hounding the Matthias family for years, making spurious claims, interfering with authorized trade, and now he's a bloody-handed murderer."

Benny started to say something, but thought better of it. From the look in this man's eyes, it was clear he wasn't bluffing about his horrible threats. He briefly wondered if there was any value in telling Preacher Jack that Charlie might still alive, that he'd seen him in the field by the way station, but he held his tongue.

"I've seen Tom's type in a hundred places around the world," said the preacher. "Before First Night, before I heard the calling of the Lord that directed me to my sacred purpose,

I was a different man. More like Charlie and White Bear. You see, I was a soldier once. A special operator, though I don't suppose that label means anything to you young'uns. I served my country in black bag operations in Africa and Asia, in the Middle East and South America. We were the righteous ones, the hard ones. Heartbreakers and life takers." He sighed. "Then things got . . . complicated. Too many regulations imposed on the military. So me and a bunch of my brothers in arms went private. We became contractors."

"You mean mercenaries," sneered Nix.

"I'm not ashamed of that word, little girl. Mercs or contractors, it's all the same . . . we served the best interests of the American people. One way or t'other." Preacher Jack laughed again. "Surely you didn't think I learned to handle myself in Bible school, did you? No, and I'm not saying I was a saint because I was loyal to flag and country. Nope, I won't spit that lie into the wind. Truth to tell, I was a sinner back then, I'll admit it and testify my sins, and yet still on the side of the white hats. Still proud to be an American, no matter where I was or on what piece of backwater land I stood." He leaned closer. "Then came First Night. Ah . . . that was the miracle that opened the eyes of this poor sinner. The dead rose to claim the earth. Those who had been left to decay into dust rose instead and claimed dominion over the lands of the living. The Children of Lazarus rose, and in their purity they showed us the errors of our ways. Our sinfulness was revealed. That's when I changed my wicked ways and took to preaching from the Good Book."

Benny found his voice and very quietly asked, "If you're so holy, then explain Gameland. How's that part of God's plan?"

Preacher Jack shrugged. "This world may be paradise for the Children of Lazarus, but to snot-nosed little sinners like you . . . this world is hell. How's that for a cosmic paradox? Heaven and hell coexisting out here in the Rot and Ruin, and the two of 'em forming a brand-new Eden. The towns—why, you might consider them limbo, where souls are just waiting for judgment. As for Gameland . . . now it would be God's own truth to say that Gameland is purgatory. It's where you have a chance to expunge your sins."

"By fighting z—" Benny caught himself before he said the word. "By fighting the dead in pits?"

Preacher Jack nodded. "When a person faces one of the Children, both are being tested for their worthiness. If the Child wins, then it has shown that God's power is alive within it, even though the vessel is dead . . . and the sinner himself gets elevated to a higher being as he joins the Children. If the sinner wins, then by God he's just shown that he is more righteous in the eyes of heaven, and by striking down one of the Children he has removed imperfection from the holy landscape."

What a bunch of crap. Benny's inner voice yelled it, and he almost said it aloud, but he knew that those would be the last words he would speak. He wondered if the old man believed this or if it was some kind of crazy con game. Charlie had tried to justify his actions by saying that he'd earned the right by helping to establish the trade routes that kept the towns alive. Was this more of the same kind of rationalization?

He cut a glance at Nix. The bleeding had slowed, but her eyes were wild with hatred and terror. It made him wonder what lights burned in his own eyes. Aloud Benny said, "What are you going to do with us?"

"I think we all know the answer to that question. Purgatory awaits all sinners." Preacher Jack rose and nodded to his men. "Bring them."

LILAH FELL ASLEEP WITH THE CAT IN HER ARMS AND WOKE TO FIND HERSELF alone. She looked out the window and saw the Greenman working at a picnic table outside. The old man looked up briefly, saw her hesitating in the doorway, smiled, and bent over his work once more. Lilah came tentatively out of the house and stood on the far side of the picnic table, watching him. The table was covered with bowls of herbs and leaves, bunches of flowers, a small flower press, and piles of pine-cones and other items that Lilah did not recognize. There were various tools around. Knives, a cheese grater, carving tools, sewing stuff, wire, and cutters.

"If you need to use the bathroom," said the Greenman without looking up, "there's an outhouse behind that row of pines."

Lilah drifted away and came back in a few minutes. When she did, she found a fresh cup of tea at the far end of the table. The Greenman was shelling nuts into a small wooden bowl. He paused and pushed a bowl of water, a bunch of flowers, and a pair of tweezers to within her reach, always careful not to move quickly or get too close.

"If you want to help," he said, "I'll tell you how."

Lilah looked at the flowers and then at him. She nodded.

"Use the tweezers to remove each petal and place it in the water. Let it float. Be careful not to get your skin oil on the petals. We want them pure. Once you fill the bowl, we'll cover it with cheesecloth and set it out in the sunshine for four hours. We have that much sun left. After that, we'll strain the water through a coffee filter into some jars. I'll add a little brandy, and we'll set it in my root cellar."

"Why?" It was the first word she had spoken in hours.

"We're making flower essences. We'll add walnut and *Mimulus ringens*." He nodded to the thick bunch of large purple flowers with yellow centers. "It's very rare for those to bloom this early. Usually don't see them until June or later, but we needed it now and nature provided. Funny . . . but I didn't know why I picked them yesterday. Now I understand."

"What is it for?"

The Greenman smiled. His face was heavily lined, but when he smiled, all those creases conspired to make him seem much both younger and timeless. "For courage, Lilah," he said.

Lilah tensed. "You know my name?"

"Everyone in these hills knows your name," he said. "Lilah, the Lost Girl. You're famous. The fearsome zombie hunter. The girl who helped bring down Charlie Pink-eye and the Hammer."

She shook her head.

"I know, I know," said the Greenman with a gentle laugh. "No one is really who people think they are. It's unfair. When they give us nicknames and create a story for us, everyone expects us to be that person and to live up to that legend."

He went back to shelling walnuts. "Tom knows something about that. Out here, people see him as either a hero or a villain. Never anything in between, not for Tom. He hates it too. Do you know that? He doesn't want to be anyone's hero any more than he wants to be a villain."

"Tom isn't a villain."

"Not to you or me, no. Not to the people in town. But to a lot of the people out here—people like Charlie and his lot— Tom's the boogeyman."

"That's stupid. They're the villains."

"No doubt." He nodded to the flowers. "Those petals won't jump into the bowl by themselves."

Lilah stared at the purple petals for a moment, then picked up the tweezers and began pulling them off. She tore a few before she got the knack. The Greenman watched, nodded, and picked up another walnut. "Who are you?" she asked. "I mean really."

"Most of the time I'm nobody," said the Greenman. "When you live alone, you don't need a name. I don't need to tell you that." She said nothing, but she gave a tiny nod. "I used to be Arthur Mensch—Ranger Artie to the tourists in Yosemite. That was before First Night."

"When the world changed and everything went bad," she said.

"A lot of folks see it that way," said the Greenman, "but it was death that changed. People are still people. Some good, some bad. Death changed, and we don't know what death really means anymore. Maybe that was the point. Maybe this is an object lesson about the arrogance of our assumptions. Hard to say. But the world? She didn't change. She healed.

We stopped hurting her and she began to heal. You can see it all around. The whole world is a forest now. The air is fresher. More trees, more oxygen. Even in Yosemite the air was never this fresh."

"The dead—," she began.

"Are part of nature," he said.

"How do you know?"

"Because they exist."

She thought about that. "You don't think they're evil?"

"Do you?"

She shook her head. "People are evil."

"Some are," he admitted. He set the walnut shells aside and began shaving the walnut meat with the cheese grater. "People are all sorts of things. Some people are evil and good at the same time. At least according to their own view of the world."

"How can people be good and bad?"

His dark eyes sought hers. "In the same way that people can be very brave and very, very afraid. They can be heroes and cowards from one breath to the next. And heroes again."

Her eyes slid away. "I did something bad," she said in a tiny voice. "I ran away."

"I know." It was acceptance of information but in no way a judgment.

"I—I haven't been afraid of . . ." Lilah swallowed. "I haven't been afraid of the dead for years. Not since I was little. They just . . . are. Do you understand?"

"Sure."

"Last night, though . . . there were so many."

"Was that it? Was it just that there were a lot of them?

From what Tom told me, you used to play in the Hungry Forest. What was different about last night?"

The cat came out of the woods, jumped up on the table, and settled down with its legs tucked under its fur. Lilah began plucking more petals. "I left Benny and Nix behind at the way station. I just . . . ran."

"Were you running from the dead? Because there were so many?"

"I—I don't know."

"Yeah," he said gently. "You do."

Lilah looked at the purple flower petal caught between the iron jaws of the tweezers. "This stuff gives courage?"

"Not really." The Greenman smiled. "It helps you find where you left the courage you had. Courage is tricky, oily. Easy to drop, easy to misplace."

"I thought that if you had courage you always had it."

The Greenman laughed out loud. The cat, who had been dozing, opened one eye and glared at him for a moment, then went back to sleep. "Lilah, nothing is always there. Not courage, not joy, not hate or hope or anything else. We find courage, lose it, sometimes misplace it for years, and sometimes live in its grace for a while."

She digested this as she worked. "What about love? Is that elusive too?"

"I have two answers for that," he said, "though there are probably more. One answer is the big answer. Love is always there. It lives in us. In all of us. Even Charlie Pink-eye, bad as he was, loved something. He loved his friend Marion Hammer. He had a family. He had a wife, once. Before First Night. Everyone loves. But that's not what you meant and I know it. The other answer, the smaller answer, is that when we love something we don't always love it. It comes and goes. Like breath in the lungs."

"I don't understand love."

"Sure you do," said the Greenman. "Tom told me about Annie, and about George. I met George once, a long time ago, when he was out looking for you. He was a good man. A genuine person, do you understand what I mean?"

"Yes." Tears glistened in the corners of her eyes.

"He loved you, and I believe—I know—that you loved him. Just as you loved Annie. No, you understand love just fine, Lilah."

She said nothing.

"Or do you mean another kind of love?" he asked, arching one eyebrow. "Boy-girl love? Is there someone you love? Is there someone who loves you?"

She shook her head, then shrugged. "There is a boy named Lou Chong."

"Benny Imura's friend? Tom told me about him, too. A smart boy."

"He can be stupid, too!" Her words were quick, and she stopped and shook her head again. "In town . . . Chong is smart. He knows science and books and stars and history. I can talk to him. We talked on his porch, at nights. Every night since I lived there. Seven months. We talked about everything."

"He sounds nice."

"He is . . . but out here . . . he isn't smart." She threw down the tweezers. The cat gave a disgusted grunt, stood up, turned around, and lay back down.

"Tell me," said the Greenman as he reached over, picked up the tweezers, and handed them to her. After a long pause, she took them.

Lilah told him everything that had happened since Tom led them out of town. By the time she was done, all the flower petals had been plucked and were floating in water.

"If Chong loves you," said the Greenman, "do you love him?"

"I don't know!" she snapped, then, more softly, "I don't know how to."

The Greenman chuckled. "You wouldn't be the first to feel that, but maybe the first to admit it. So . . . what does this have to do with running away from Benny and Nix? Take a breath. Think about it. Answer when it feels right."

She took the breath. "Benny kept saying that Chong ran away because of me. That I made him because of what I said."

"What did you say?"

"Back on the road . . . I told Chong that . . ." She wiped her eyes. "I told him that he was a stupid town boy and he shouldn't be out here. I wanted him to go home. I told him to go home. Then, when Benny told me it was my fault . . . I . . . it made me forget how to use my spear. Or my gun. My hands wouldn't think anymore." She shook her head. "I'm not making sense."

"Yes," said the Greenman, "you are."

"I made Chong run away."

The Greenman leaned on his forearms and regarded her with a kindly smile. "A wise man once said that we can't make anyone feel or do anything. We can throw things into the wind, but it's up to each person to decide how they want to react, where they want to stand when things fall. Do you understand?"

She shook her head.

"It's about responsibility. Chong felt responsible for what happened. Your words didn't force him to run away."

"I wish I could . . . un-say them."

"Yep. I'm sure. But it's still on Chong; it was his choice to run. He could have stayed, no matter what you said. Just as you could have stayed after what Benny said. It doesn't make it right that hard words were said, but it doesn't make you or Benny wrong for saying them. That's yours to settle with yourself. Chong chose his path. Benny chose his when he spoke. You chose yours when you ran."

"But it was the wrong choice!" she cried.

"That's your call, honey," he said. "Do you know why you ran away?"

She shrugged. "Before . . . I met Benny and the others . . . I knew the world. How it was. Zoms and bounty hunters and me. My cave, the way of hunting. Quieting zoms. Fighting men. Traps and hunting and all of that. It was just me and everything else. Me. I knew me. I knew what wasn't me. But after I met them, things became . . . complicated. I had people. I had to care about them."

"And that scared you because the last time you cared about someone was with Annie and George? No, don't look surprised, Lilah. I lost people too. Everyone did. After you lost them, you stepped away from humanity. Not by choice, but out of a need to survive. You became used to being alone and not caring for or about anyone. Then you met Benny and Nix and you started to care."

"It hurts to care!" she yelled as loud as her damaged voice would allow. Then, more quietly, she added, "It's scary, and I never used to be afraid. If I lived, I lived. If I died, who would know? Who would care? Annie and George were gone. Without them it was like I had . . . armor. I don't understand it."

"You probably do on some level."

"Benny said that Chong only came along because he loved me." She shook her head in amazement at the thought. "I don't understand that. I mean . . . I read books about love and romance, but it's not the same."

"No," he conceded. "It surely is not. How does that make you feel, though? To have someone love you?"

She shook her head again. "Annie loved me. George loved me."

"And you loved them . . . but now they're dead," said the Greenman softly. "And you probably feel guilty about that." Lilah gave him a sharp look, but he continued. "I'm guessing here, but you probably feel guilty because you had already escaped from Gameland and you didn't get back in time to save Annie. And George died while he was out looking for you. Are you afraid that if Chong loves you, and if you fall in love with him, that he'll die too?"

"He's . . . already gone." Her face screwed up, but she forced herself not to sob. "Nothing makes sense anymore. Last night we went outside, and the trip wires were down. All those zoms were there. Too many of them. I—I looked into all those dead eyes. I saw Chong. In my mind . . . dead. Tom, too. Benny and Nix. I saw them all dead. Everyone I care about. Dead. I felt like I was dead too."

"Ah," said the Greenman gently. "That's called terror. It's confusion and a little paranoia and a nice big dose of panic. Everyone has those moments. Everyone. Even heroes like Tom."

"But I ran away. I can't take that back. I ran away and left Benny and Nix there. I didn't help them, and I didn't go looking for Chong. He left because of me. Because of how I treated him. Because of what I said to him. Benny said so."

"Benny's just a boy," the Greenman said, "and I'll bet he's just as confused and scared as you. Sometimes people say terrible things when they're scared. They don't mean to, but they can't help it. They lash out because if they can see that their words hurt someone else, it makes them feel as if they aren't completely powerless."

"That's stupid!"

"No, it's unfair, but for the most part it's unintentional. If Benny's anything like Tom, he's probably kicking himself for what he said. He'd probably give a lot to roll the clock back to yesterday and make it right to you."

"He can't! He said it."

"That's true. He said it, and it hurt you, and with everything else that's going on, all of you are probably in the same place. Confused, scared, and doing things you wish you could undo."

Lilah wiped her eyes again. "I'm sorry for what I said to Chong. I do wish I could take it back."

The Greenman stopped working for a moment. "Let me tell you a truth, little sister. No matter what choice you make, it doesn't define you. Not forever. People can make bad choices and change their minds and hearts and do good things later;

just as people can make good choices and then turn around and walk a bad path. No choice we make lasts our whole life. If there's ever a choice you've made that you no longer agree with, you can make another choice."

"I can't undo it, though."

"That's not what I said. I'm pretty sure undoing it would involve time travel, and I don't happen to have a time machine."

She almost smiled at that.

"Everyone's been there," said the Greenman. "First Night wasn't the only crisis. We've all had our moments of weakness and failure. All of us. We've all suffered through dark nights of the soul."

"So is that it? Will I have to live the rest of my life like this? Not doing the right thing? Not saying the right words?"

"That's your choice. You can't change the past. Ah, but the future . . . you own the future." The Greenman smiled. "So, you tell me . . . what choice do you want to make now?"

Digger and Heap herded Benny and Nix into the hotel, guiding them with slaps and kicks. Preacher Jack walked behind them, humming to himself. Benny was sure it wasn't a hymn.

They entered the main lobby, which was piled high with crates of goods scavenged from local towns. Sturdy shelves had been erected on every inch of wall space, and these were crammed with canned goods, sacks of grain, jars of spices, and bottles of everything from extra-virgin olive oil to Kentucky whiskey. One wall had a rack of guns running from floor to ceiling: shotguns, rifles, automatic weapons, rocket launchers, and every kind of handgun. Most of these Benny had seen only in books. And there were barrels filled with bayonets, machetes, swords, spears, axes, and clubs. Against one wall were six crates labeled c4. Benny had never heard of it, but on each case, in big red letters, three words were stenciled: DANGER: HIGH EXPLOSIVES. He swallowed.

There were enough weapons to start a war . . . or to reclaim the wastelands from the living dead. Benny saw Nix staring longingly at the collection.

Digger noticed and slapped the back of her head. "Don't even think about it."

"Wouldn't dream of it," Nix said under her breath.

Benny ground his teeth and swore on the graves of his parents that he would make these men pay for touching Nix.

They pushed Benny and Nix through the hotel and up several sets of stairs until they stood in the doorway of a dusty attic. The room was empty except for cobwebs.

"Make yourselves comfy," said Heap as he shoved them into the room. "Call room service if you want anything." The men were laughing as they slammed the door shut and locked it.

Benny pressed his ear to the door and listened until he couldn't hear their footfalls on the steps anymore. Then he tried the door handle. It jiggled, but the lock was tough and the door was too solid to kick open. With a sigh of resignation he turned to Nix.

"We'll get out of this," he promised.

She looked dazed and small in the dusty light. "How? Benny—they're going to put us in the zombie pits! They did that to my mom!"

"I know . . . but she survived, Nix . . . and she wasn't a fighter. We are. Warrior smart, remember?"

Nix sniffed. "I don't feel like a warrior right now."

Benny forced a grin. "Then we'll have to concentrate on being smart. Remember what Tom said. 'When you're in a dangerous situation'—"

"—'immediately assess your resources.'"

They looked around. The room was completely empty. Bare floor, bare walls with cracked plaster that had crumbled in places to reveal the thin wooden bones of the walls, a light fixture that hadn't worked in fifteen years hanging from the ceiling, and a cracked window that looked out into the horse corral.

"Okay," Benny said, "so . . . we're not big on supplies." But when he looked at Nix, she was smiling. "What?"

She told him. Then he was smiling too.

TOM IMURA STOOD JUST INSIDE THE SPILL OF SHADOWS CAST BY THE TALL willows that bordered the old hotel. Anyone standing three feet away would not have seen him. He might have been a ghost, or a layer of the deepening twilight shadows. Only his mind was in motion, and that was a howling firestorm of rage and frustration and self-hatred. Despite all logic to the contrary, his mind kept shrieking out that he was responsible for this. For all of this. For Chong. For Benny and Nix. For Gameland. All of it.

This is my fault. I should have seen this coming.

No, that wasn't quite right. He had seen this coming. He had been warned. By Basher and Sally, by Captain Strunk and Mayor Kirsch. Warned that he could not just walk away, that perhaps it was his destiny to stop Gameland once and for all.

He was sure that Benny and Nix were being held inside. After he'd left the dead bounty hunters, he had gone racing back to the way station, found it in ashes, then saw footprints leading toward Wawona. Benny and Nix's shoes, no doubt about it. And Preacher Jack's following them. Tom had raced along the path and only paused a moment when he saw that

Preacher Jack's prints veered away from a straight pursuit and took a shortcut toward the hotel.

Tom had found the scene of slaughter by the barn, had read the tale in the scuff marks and knew that J-Dog and Dr. Skillz had been with Benny and Nix for a time. But he also saw that the two surfers had turned and gone back into the hills. Their path must have missed Tom's by no more than half a mile.

Now Tom was at Gameland, and now he knew the full horror of things. White Bear had taken over the old hotel and transformed it into a killing ground. There were single zombie pits all around the building, and a cluster of larger ones out back in an enclosure made from a line of trade wagons and a circus tent. There were dozens of guards and hundreds of people—traders and others—so Tom had backed away and now stood watching from the edge of the woods.

Preacher Jack was here. The footprints had led right to a spot where they had encountered Benny and Nix again. There were clear signs of a struggle and drops of blood. Tom's mind ground on itself, lashing him for not seeing this sooner. For not acting preemptively instead of going off on this road trip.

Any innocent blood that falls is on me, he told himself.

The Matthias clan was moving in because of Charlie's death and because Tom was leaving. It was a double power vacuum, and White Bear was making his bid to fill it. Tom didn't yet know how Preacher Jack fit into this, but he and White Bear would make a formidable team. The people of Mountainside were not going to do anything to stop it. That was obvious, but who else was there? Sally? J-Dog and Dr. Skillz? Basher? Solomon Jones? There were plenty of fighters who could make a serious stand against White Bear, but only if they were a unified front, and that was a million miles from likely.

Rage was building in his chest, and he could feel his body start to tremble. He wanted to scream. He needed to give a war cry, draw his sword, and go charging into the hotel and kill White Bear, Preacher Jack, and as many of their people as he could. That would feel good. It would feel right. It would also be suicide . . . and it probably wouldn't save Benny, Nix, or Chong. Rage was sometimes a useful ally in the heat of a fight, but it was a trickster. It made everything seem possible.

He needed to go in there cold. So he closed his eyes and murmured the words he had drilled into his brother and the others. "Warrior smart." He breathed in and out slowly, letting the rhythm vent the darker emotions from him. Guilt and rage, hatred and fear were pathways to weakness and clumsy choices. With each inhalation he made himself think of happier times, of things that had filled his heart with peace and hope and optimism. Benny and his future. That day last year when Tom realized that Benny no longer hated him, that maybe his brother understood him. Rescuing Nix. Finding Lilah. Training the teenagers. Laughing with them in the sunlight. Eating apple pie in the cool of the evening.

They were simple memories, but their simplicity was the source of their power. As Tom remembered smiles and laughter and Benny's goofy jokes, the rage began to falter within him. As he recalled watching from afar as Benny and Nix fell in love, the reckless anger cracked and fell apart. And as he remembered the promise he'd made to Jessie Riley as she lay dying in his arms—that he would protect Nix—his resolve rose up in his mind like a tower of steel.

He stood in the shadows and found himself again. He found the Tom Imura that he wanted and needed to be. He took another breath and held it for a long moment, then let it out slowly. He opened his eyes. Then he made himself a promise. "I do this one thing and then I'm done. I do this and then I take Benny and the others and we go east."

Tom adjusted his sword and checked his knives and his pistol. If there had been anyone there to see his face, they would have seen a man at peace with himself and the world. And if they were wise, they would know that such a man was the most dangerous of all opponents—one who fights to preserve love rather than perpetuate hatred.

When he moved, he seemed to melt into the darkness.

66

Lou Chong heard a scream. Not a warrior's cry. It had been high and wet and filled with pain; and it had ended abruptly. Laughter and shouts rose up immediately and washed the scream away. Chong knew what it meant. Someone else had been fighting a zom, and had lost.

The thought threatened to take the strength out of his arms, but he set his jaw and held on. Literally held on. For the last two hours he had been using the Motor City Hammer's black pipe club to chop divots out of the packed earth walls of the pit. It was grueling work, and to do it he had to gouge divots deep enough for his feet so he could stand in them and reach high to chop fresh holes. His muscles ached. Sweat poured down his body. His toes were numb with cold from standing in the holes, and his arm trembled between each strike.

He never stopped, though. Every time pain or exhaustion or fear tried to coax him down the wall and away from what he was doing, he held a picture in his mind. It wasn't a picture of himself fighting another zom. It wasn't even a picture of running free from this place. Chong knew that he had been bitten. He knew that he was going to die.

No, the picture he held in his mind was that of a girl with honey-colored eyes and snow-white hair and a voice like a whisper. A crazy girl. A fierce and violent girl. A lost girl who didn't even like him.

Lilah.

If he was going to die, then he was going to die as a warrior. If Lilah didn't—or couldn't—love the weak and intellectual Chong, then perhaps she would have a softer heart when remembering the warrior Chong who fought his way out of Gameland. As Lilah herself had fought her way out years ago.

And maybe . . . just maybe . . . he could save some of the other kids trapped here in Gameland. Like Benny and Nix and Lilah had done last year. If he couldn't go with them on their journey, if he was to die sometime in the next few hours or days, then he wanted his life to mean something. He wanted to matter.

He reached and slid his fingers into the hole he'd just chopped, and pulled. His muscles screamed at him, but his mind screamed back at them. The rim of the pit was only three feet above him now.

One more hole to go.

THE DOOR TO THE DUSTY ROOM OPENED, AND DIGGER AND HEAP CAME in. The two thugs looked at the wires that had been torn down from the ceiling fixture and at the hole in the wall, which was bigger than it had been and revealed broken laths. Piles of torn plaster and broken lath littered the floor by the wainscoting. Benny and Nix were covered with plaster dust. The two men cracked up laughing.

"What'd you two morons try to do?" asked Digger between brays of laughter. "You try to chew your way outta here?"

"Yeah," said Benny with a sneer. "We were hungry."

Heap laughed, but Digger hit Benny across the face with a backhand blow. Benny saw it coming and turned with it, a move Tom had taught him to shake off some of the power of a hit. It made it look like Benny took the blow and shook it off.

Digger and Heap exchanged a look. "Tougher than you look, boy," murmured Digger, getting up in Benny's face. "You make it out of the pits with a whole skin, you and I might have to go out behind the barn and dance a bit. Bet you ain't nearly as tough as you think you are."

"Save it for later," warned Heap, and they all turned as Preacher Jack entered the room, followed by a stranger who was taller than the old man and more massive than Charlie Pink-eye had been. The man's face was a ruin of melted flesh. One eye was a black pit, and the other as blue as lake water. He wore heavy cloak of white bearskin. Even though Benny had never seen him before, he knew at once who this had to be. White Bear.

"So this is Tom Imura's kid brother and Jessie Riley's daughter," said White Bear with a grin. "Well, I'll be a dancing duck if they ain't cute as puppies, the both of 'em."

Heap and Digger chortled, and Preacher Jack smiled his ugly smile. "Figured you'd want to have a word with them before we get started," murmured the preacher.

"Oh yes indeed," said the big man, and he entered the room. Beneath the cloak of bear fur he wore hand-stitched leather pants and moccasins. His bare chest was marked with large burned patches too. He wore at least a dozen necklaces of oyster shells, beads, and feathers, and he had silver rings on every finger. He stood in the center of the room and exuded so much personal power that he appeared to fill the place, dwarfing the others. Only Preacher Jack seemed undiminished. The big man grinned at Benny and Nix. "You two know who I am?"

"White Bear," said Nix.

"That's right," said the big man, obviously pleased. "But do you know who I am?"

They shook their heads.

"I am the spirit of the Rot and Ruin. I'm the old medicine reborn to save the world from itself. I'm the immortal White Bear, born in fire and born of fire." He glared at them for a long moment, and then he cracked up laughing. The other men joined him, and the four of them howled at a joke neither Benny nor Nix understood. Finally White Bear dabbed at a tear at the corner of his remaining eye. "Okay, okay . . . so that's the public relations line. That's what we tell the rubes to get them all excited. Works pretty well, too. Misinformation and disinformation make the world go round."

"What are you talking about?" demanded Nix.

"Call it a campaign strategy," replied White Bear. "You always need a good campaign strategy if you're running for office."

Benny narrowed his eyes. "Running for what office?"

"Chief badass of the whole damn Rot and Ruin," supplied Digger.

"In so many words," agreed White Bear. "Y'see, when we heard that your brother Tom was clearing out of the area, we figured it was a ripe moment to come in and make some changes. Time to stop screwing around with the silly rules they got in nowhere places like Mountainside and Haven and suchlike. Charlie was getting ready to do that too, but he was . . . um . . . reluctant to make his move with Tom in the mix."

"That's because he was afraid of Tom!" snapped Benny.

The smile flickered on White Bear's face. "Boy, you don't need teeth or both eyes to go into a zom pit. Say another word about Charlie and I'll do you ugly before I feed you to—"

"Bear," said Preacher Jack quietly. It was all he said, but it stopped White Bear for a moment. The big man nodded and took a breath.

"Yeah, okay," he said, but he fixed his wicked eye on Benny. "Charlie wasn't afraid of nobody on God's green earth, you little snot. He was a man of honor, and he showed respect to your brother. Not fear . . . respect."

Benny didn't want to make things worse, so he said, "Okay. I understand that."

White Bear gave a single, curt nod. "Tom Imura may be a pain in my butt, but he's a warrior, and I won't put the lie to it and say he isn't." Heap and Digger grunted agreement, and even Preacher Jack nodded. "But Tom's leaving, and he's as much as said that this area ain't his concern no more. That means it's fair game, and what was Charlie's is mine by right, and so I'm moving in and taking over. I got big plans for this area. Big plans. Good plans, and you want to know the funny part? The real knee-slapper of a joke?"

"Um . . . sure," said Benny.

"I'll bet your brother would even approve of what I got in mind."

Nix made a sound low in her throat, but White Bear didn't hear it.

Benny said, "What do you mean?"

"It's long past time for people to stop being afraid of the dead," said White Bear. "The, um, Children of Lazarus." He shot a sideways look at Preacher Jack, and Benny caught a flicker of disapproval on the older man's face. "We have to share a world with them, but there's room for everyone to have what they want."

"How?"

"We're going to reclaim the Ruin, kids. As much of it as we can. We're moving the dead out of here. We'll herd them all—"

"'Guide' them," corrected Preacher Jack.

"Okay, guide them out of these hills. We'll put people to work building new fence lines, but we'll do it at rivers and gorges and natural barriers. We'll take back farmable lands, we'll run cattle again. Not just a few hundred head like they got in town—we'll run tens of thousands of heads. We'll plant a million acres of food. And we'll figure out how to start the machines again. Mills and factories, tractors and combines. Maybe some tanks, too, to keep everything working smooth."

"Who's going to do all that labor?" asked Nix dubiously.

White Bear grinned. "There's a lot of lazy people sitting behind the fences. Me and my crew have been working all these years, taking all the risks. Now it's time that other people broke a sweat and got their hands dirty."

"You're talking slave labor," said Nix.

"It's not slave labor," protested White Bear, trying to look innocent, "it's cooperative labor. No different from the ration dollar system we got now. They want to eat, then they'll work. They work, and we'll protect 'em."

Benny turned to Preacher Jack. "What about the Children of Lazarus? I thought you said that this world was theirs now?"

The preacher's lips twitched. "Don't confuse philosophy with practicality, child."

"What's that mean?"

"It means that the dead don't need farmland and clean water," said White Bear. "They's already been raised up to the Lord, so to speak. All they need is to be. So . . . we'll just herd—I mean guide—them to areas where they can be without chowing down on us. Hell, nobody's using Utah and Arizona and New Mexico. Who needs fricking deserts? We'll keep 'em there, and they won't know or care."

"Such is the will of God," agreed Preacher Jack, and the two thugs with him murmured, "Amen."

"How are you going to guide millions of—" Benny almost said "zoms" but caught himself. "How are you going to guide all those dead?"

"It was the dead who gave us the idea," said White Bear. "'Bout a year ago they started moving in packs. Swarming, you might say."

Nix frowned. "Flocking?"

"We call it swarming, but yes," said the preacher. "It's one of God's mysteries."

White Bear nodded. "It started down in Mexico and in some of the Nevada towns. Masses of the dead who had been standing around doing nothing for years just up and moved. Scared the stuffing out of some people. Bunch of settlements were completely overrun. Every week it gets worse. Or better, depending on how you see it. Something causes a couple of the dead to start walking, and soon all the others in the area do the same thing, hundreds—sometimes thousands of them— all shuffling in the same direction. Weird." He chuckled. "The thing that's going to make this work, kids, is that we figured out how to steer the swarms."

Benny stiffened. "You led a swarm to Brother David's last night!"

"I did that," admitted Preacher Jack. "White Bear's scouts said that Tom was heading there, so I sent some of my lay-preachers out to gather some swarms. It was wonderful, wasn't it? I counted seven thousand of them." His smiling face turned dark. "And then you burned them."

Uh-oh, said Benny's inner voice. "You, um, saw that, huh?" he asked, trying on a smile that didn't fit.

"I saw everything." Preacher Jack's eyes were filled with dangerous light.

"I didn't see you."

"That's because you did not look up."

"Huh?"

"Until the fire reached me I was sitting very comfortably on a folding chair on top of the way station. A grand view to watch the Children of Lazarus come down the mountain slopes. It would have been a grand view to watch them drag you and this slut and the white-haired witch out of the station. I wanted to see them feast on your bones."

"You really blame me for defending myself?" Benny said, standing straight. "You claim to respect Tom for being a warrior, and you blame me for defending myself when you attack me? I mean . . . what did we ever do to you?"

White Bear smiled at him with burned lips. "See this face? Tom did this when he set fire to Gameland. Nearly killed me."

"Tom was—"

"Hush, boy," snapped Preacher Jack. His smile had not returned, and the unsmiling version of him was even more frightening. "White Bear's face is his face. Warriors have scars, and his scars are between him and Tom. That's not the reason you owe us a blood debt. No . . . the reason you two and Tom and that witch Lilah are going to pay, indeed must pay, is because you tricked the Children of Lazarus—God's own sacred swarm—into attacking Charlie and his men. That alone is crime enough to flay the flesh from your bones."

"But he—"

White Bear suddenly stepped forward and grabbed a fistful of Benny's vest and with a flex of his huge biceps lifted him completely off the floorboards. He breathed right into Benny's face. "You killed Charlie. I don't understand it, because Charlie was a powerful man and a great warrior, but somehow you blindsided him and you killed him. You!" He spat full in Benny's face. "You killed my brother."

Benny stared in absolute shock. "I—I—"

White Bear swung around and slammed Benny against the wall. Nix screamed and rushed the big man, tried to claw his face, but Heap and Digger each grabbed an arm and pulled her back.

"And then two days ago we get news from town," said White Bear in a deadly whisper, "that my other brother, Zak, and his boy are dead . . . and guess who was involved in that?" He pulled Benny off the wall and slammed him into it again. The thin laths cracked as Benny's shoulders and head crunched through the plaster. "Both of my brothers are dead because of you and your puke brother and your puke friends. My only nephew is dead! Zak Junior is dead. Killed by you and this redheaded daughter of Judas!"

With that he flung Benny across the room so that he crashed into the far wall and slid down into a heap. Nix tore free of the bounty hunters and ran to him. Benny coughed and moaned softly. Blood trickled from his hairline and left ear.

White Bear stood above them, his chest heaving, his face alight with hatred. Worse still was the look on Preacher Jack's face. It was as if his features were lit from within; his eyes burned with fire and an absolute madness that was more frightening than anything Benny had ever seen. He and Nix huddled together and stared up at the preacher as he stalked across the room and bent over them.

"You killed Charlie Matthias and you killed Zachary Matthias," whispered Preacher Jack. And then the man whispered four words that made the whole world spin into red lunacy.

"You killed my sons."

The words hit Benny harder than the battering White Bear had given him.

"W-what . . . ?" he stammered.

"How would justice survive in the world if I let you go unpunished?" said Preacher Jack icily. "How would that make the world right again?"

Benny tried to say something, anything that would make those words untrue; but then Preacher Jack straightened and turned away.

"Enough," he said. "Take them to the pits."

PART FIVE

FUN AND GAMES

Understand death? Sure.

That was when the monsters got you.

—STEPHEN KING, 'SALEM'S LOT

68

CHONG REACHED UP FOR THE EDGE OF THE PIT. HIS LEGS TREMBLED AND threatened to collapse, his knees were like rubber, his muscle like jelly. People roared and applauded somewhere else, but he knew that it was only a matter of time before someone came back here. He was never a lucky person, so he had long ago learned to use what fragments of luck came his way.

He reached and reached, his fingers clawing at the edges of the pit, but the dirt there was looser, the edges scalloped from shovel blades and weakened by the weight of people leaning over to look at the pit fights. He dug his fingernails into the dirt, scrabbling, sending showers of soil down onto his face. He sputtered and coughed and spit it out; he shook his head like a dog to get the dirt out of his eyes.

Then something closed around his wrist. It was sudden, immediate, and as hard as iron. And abruptly he was being pulled out of the pit.

He opened his mouth to cry out, but a second hand clamped down over his mouth.

Chong was caught!

69

LILAH CROUCHED ON THE LIMB OF A TREE AND STARED AT THE STARLIT facade of Gameland. For two hours now she had watched people arriving on horseback and in armored trade wagons. Townsfolk and people who lived rough out in the Ruin. Coming for the Z-Games. Coming to wager on the lives and deaths of children in the zombie pits. She ached to run wild among them with her spear, to show them what it felt like to be hunted. All the way here she had hoped to come upon Benny and Nix, but all she'd found were their footprints . . . and later signs of a scuffle near the front of the hotel. She was sure they had been taken.

It hurt Lilah to know that this place had been taken over by bad people. Tom had been sure that it was a safe place for them to rest. To prepare for the road trip.

What would Tom do when he found out? Where was he? And . . . Chong.

Back in the forest the Greenman had given her a map and pointed out the fastest way and led her to the edge of the field that ran along the road to Wawona, but he refused to go with her.

"There's going to be a fight," Lilah said. "Won't you come with me?"

He smiled at her with eyes that seemed ancient and sad. "No. I'm done with fighting. It tore away too much of who I was. It took me a long time to find myself again. I made a choice never to fight again."

"But—I need you."

"No, honey, you need you. You were lost, but now I think you've found you again. If it's your choice to go and help your friends, then that is your choice. Not mine."

Then he had kissed her on the head and vanished into the woods. Lilah stood watching the trembling leaves, wondering if he was even real or if her visit with him had been part of some fantasy that she had pulled from one of her books. Then she'd turned and began hunting along the trail to Gameland. She evaded a dozen guards and slipped past ditches and over fences and finally found the tree that overlooked the hotel. This was a different Gameland from the one where she and Annie had been forced to fight. Different, but still the same.

For several painful minutes she thought about what she could do, weighing it against what the Greenman had told her, and what she had confessed to him. His words echoed in her head, not louder than the words of the madmen in the arena, but in gentle ways that she could hear with greater clarity and understanding.

Let me tell you a truth, little sister, the Greenman had said. *No matter what choice you make, it doesn't define you. . . . what choice do you want to make now?*

As she crouched there, Lilah looked into her own future.

Without Benny and Nix, Chong and Tom, there was nothing. She could return to her cave and exist, but she now knew that such a life was no life at all. It was empty, and the thought of returning to that loneliness was beyond unbearable.

Somewhere down there were her friends.

"Friends" was such a strange word to her. She knew it on an intellectual level from a thousand books, but since Annie and George died, she had never experienced it. Then Benny had come looking for her. As had Tom. Benny and Nix accepted her, welcomed her into their lives. They had brought her to their home, their town. They had included her in everything. They had introduced her to Chong, and he had fallen in love with her. Fallen in love. With her.

Lilah brushed away a tear. How had she repaid such kindness, such generosity? With harsh words and threats. With bitterness and dismissal. And with inaction when she saw Preacher Jack follow Benny and Nix into the east. A word . . . a single word from her would have prevented this moment. A single action, a stroke of her spear, would have canceled out even the possibility of what was happening below. She had chosen to pull away, and now she saw the cost of that choice.

So, you tell me . . . what choice do you want to make now?

Lilah had thought about that for hours. The choice, her new choice, burned in her mind. She smiled . . . and climbed down from the tree and continued her hunt.

70

THE THUGS WALKED BENNY AND NIX OUTSIDE, AND AS THEY EXITED the hotel it was like stepping into a weird modern version of the ancient Roman circus. There had to be more than two hundred people gathered in the field behind the hotel. Bleachers made from planks and pipes had been erected, and these were completely packed by a laughing, yelling, jeering crowd. The scene was lit by dozens of torches set atop tall poles, and their light cast the whole scene into a fiery unreality, where every pair of eyes reflected flickering flames. The whole area was fenced in by three walls made of armored wagons that had been parked tightly together, and the front was the entire back wall of the Hotel Wawona. On the right-hand side, between sets of bleachers, was a huge circus tent whose flaps were closed. Guards stood in a long row in front of the flaps, and on the top of the tent, painted in huge red letters, was the word BELIEVE.

Benny saw that the amphitheater surrounded seven large pits dug into the bare earth. The crowd cheered and yelled and laughed and made obscene jokes as Benny and Nix were led to the edge of the first pit. The dozens of guards were armed with knives and swords and spears. No guns, Benny noticed, and he thought about that. Were they afraid of wild shots in so densely packed an area? Or was there some other concern?

"Where are all these people from?" whispered Nix as she bent close to him. "Who are they?"

Benny shook his head. "I don't know. Other towns, maybe. Or settlements. Families of bounty hunters . . ." His voice trailed off as he realized that he knew a few of the faces in the crowd. Not bounty hunters, but people from Mountainside! Not forty feet in front of him was Mr. Tesh, who owned a stable near the reservoir; and over by the circus tent was Barbara Sultan and her husband. They were corn farmers. He saw his high school gym teacher making a bet with an oddsmaker; and a few yards away from him was the woman who owned the feed and grain store on Main Street. He pointed this out to Nix, and she gasped.

"That's Mrs. Rosenbaum!"

When the woman saw them looking at her, the smile on her painted mouth flickered for a second; then the man next to her made a joke, and they both burst out laughing. It was madness. These weren't just strangers, these were people they knew. People they saw every day. He wondered how they managed to come here. What excuses and lies had they told to hide the ugliness of their appetites?

"I hate them all!" snarled Nix with incredible viciousness. Ever since they had learned that they were in the power of Charlie Pink-eye's brother and father, she seemed ready to explode. Her eyes were filled with a glaring brightness, and her hands were shaking badly.

Don't go away from me now, he begged silently, but when

he tried to take her hand, she snatched it angrily away and stared at him as if he were an alien from Mars.

The buzz of the crowd suddenly changed as Preacher Jack and White Bear walked with their heads up, proud as kings, into the center of the amphitheater. The audience erupted into thunderous applause. White Bear encouraged the applause with upward waves of his big arms.

Nix leaned close again. "Want to hear something funny?"

"Um . . . sure, Nix," he said carefully. "Seems like a great time for a joke."

Her eyes glittered like glass as she nodded toward White Bear. "I actually like his plan."

Benny almost smiled. "Sure. Except for the slavery part." He nodded toward the crowd. "I wonder how loud they'll be cheering when White Bear's goons are putting them to work herding zoms and building fences."

"Shaddup!" growled Digger, cuffing them again.

Preacher Jack raised his arms, and the crowd instantly fell silent. It was so quiet that Benny could hear the crackling of the torches and the popping of the canvas on the circus tent.

"My brothers and sisters," Preacher Jack began in a voice that was deep and strong, "thank you for coming here to share in this auspicious event on this glorious day. A day we will all remember for as long as God grants us breath. As they did in biblical times, we hold these games in celebration of an important event. We are about to begin writing a new chapter in the storied history of mankind. We will begin a new holy book chronicling the foundation and consecration of a new Eden."

The crowd exchanged looks, surprised at what appeared

to be a sermon and uncertain where it was going.

"I wanted to share this day, not only with my family and friends"—and here he gestured to White Bear and then to the audience—"but with my congregation as well."

A ripple of hushed conversation whisked through the crowd.

"I asked my congregants to join us in celebrating a new era of peace and fellowship as we poor sinners prove ourselves worthy to share in this paradise. Join me in welcoming the members of the First Church of the New Eden!"

The crowd began to applaud, and the guards by the tent turned and began pulling back the canvas flaps. When the crowd saw that there were hundreds of people sitting in tightly packed rows of folding chairs, they applauded with greater enthusiasm, welcoming more folks to this party. Then one by one the people in the audience stopped applauding until there was only one person—a silly drunk in the far corner—clapping; and then he, too, stopped. There was a long pause in which silence reigned over the entire amphitheater, and Benny could feel Nix stiffen beside him. His own heart was hammering.

Suddenly a woman screamed, and the crowd surged to its feet. There was instant turmoil as people fought to move away from the congregation. The guards waded into the packed mass, shoving people, clubbing some, yelling at them. Preacher Jack still stood with his arms raised, a smile of great joy on his face.

Benny stared in total horror. There had to be five hundred folding chairs set in rows in the tent. Each chair was filled, but each congregant was lashed to the chair by strips of white cloth that were wrapped around their legs and chests. They all writhed and struggled against the bonds. Not just to escape . . . but to attack.

The entire congregation was zombies.

"Oh my God!" gasped Nix, and shrank back, but Digger grabbed her shoulder and kept her in place. Benny had been unable to move and stood stock-still.

White Bear reached under his cloak of bearskin and brought out a pump shotgun that hung concealed on a sling. He pointed it at the sky and pulled the trigger. There was a huge *BOOM!*

Everyone froze.

"Sit down!" he roared, and racked the slide on the shotgun. There was another moment of silent indecision, and then the crowd obeyed. In the stillness of that moment they could see that the zoms were unable to rise or attack. A few people crept back to their seats, then more, and within minutes the entire crowd was back in their places. Nobody was smiling except for Preacher Jack.

And Nix. "Did you see the looks on their faces?" She giggled. And that was when Benny realized that Nix had crossed over into some other place.

Preacher Jack raised his hands. "Be at peace! The Children of Lazarus are all bound . . . we are all safe from one another, and that is the way that harmony can grow."

The audience buzzed with troubled chatter, but gradually they all stopped talking to one another and looked at him.

"This is still a night of sport and celebration. This is what you came for!" The preacher half turned and pointed one hand down at the pits and the other at Benny and Nix.

The crowd stared for a moment longer, and then they roared with cheers and applause.

"Ah, crap," said Benny.

White Bear goosed the applause for a full minute and then gradually quieted everyone with downward waves of his hand. "In ancient times," he said in a voice every bit as loud and booming as his father's, "those who had committed terrible crimes would suffer public execution."

A ripple of applause.

"Or public humiliation."

Bigger applause.

"But we are a civilized people!"

Applause and expectant smiles. Everyone knew what was coming now; everyone was in on the joke.

"My father is a holy man, and he says that the world is both heaven and hell and Gameland is purgatory."

Someone in the back of the crowd actually yelled, "Hallelujah!"

Benny felt outrage bubbling in his chest. He was not the most devout churchgoer, but even he knew that this was no kind of religion. Preacher Jack might be crazy enough to believe some of this, but for White Bear it was all about manipulation.

White Bear roared, "So here in purgatory sinners get a chance at redemption. They get a chance to earn the right to be part of New Eden."

Someone—Benny thought it was a guard—began a chant of "New Eden!" and soon the whole crowd was shouting it out as if it was something they believed in already. *Sheep*, Benny thought. *Just sheep*.

Nix laughed aloud, but only Benny heard her. It scared him as much as what White Bear was saying.

"So, tonight my father and I are going to set an example. We are making a new law, and we will be the first to abide by it!"

"Tell us, White Bear!" someone shouted, and everyone clamored the same.

White Bear pointed to Benny and Nix. "We got two sinners here. Two murderers. They led an attack on the camp of Charlie Matthias. You all knew Charlie, and you knew him as a good and decent man." If the applause was not as enthusiastic, Benny saw, it was at least very loud. "They murdered my brother. And a few days ago they participated in the murder of my other brother, Zak, and his son. The blood of my family is on their hands!"

The crowd booed and called for blood to pay for blood.

Here it comes, Benny thought, and braced himself.

White Bear quieted the crowd once more. "But hear me—these are no longer zombie pits. It is forbidden to call them that ever again. These are the Pits of Judgment. Sinners go in there to face their crimes. Heaven itself decides the truth. If the accused is innocent, or if there is true repentance in his heart, then he will emerge unharmed from the pit. And if not . . ."

The crowd waited for it.

". . . then the Children of Lazarus will make a sacrament of their flesh!"

The crowd went wild. Benny stared. Maybe some of them had started to believe this nonsense, or maybe it was all just a new game to them. Either way, they were totally sold on it.

White Bear, as grand a showman as his father, held one hand aloft so that the audience held their breath, and with the other he pointed at Benny and Nix. "It is time!" he proclaimed. "Cast them into the Pit of Judgment."

Benny's last thought before Digger and Heap pushed him over the edge was, *Oh, brother.*

Then he and Nix were falling into darkness.

71

CHONG TRIED TO FIGHT THE HANDS THAT PULLED HIM FROM THE PIT, BUT his attacker bent close and in a fierce whisper said, "Chong— it's me."

Chong stopped struggling. The figure let go of him and moved into a patch of starlight.

"Tom!" Chong began to cry out, but Tom clamped a hand over his mouth.

"Shhhh!"

Chong nodded. "How'd you find me?" he whispered.

Tom quickly explained how he'd left Benny, Nix, and Lilah back at the way station, and about his encounter with Sally Two-Knives.

"I—I'm . . . Tom, I'm so sorry—"

"Save it. This is a lot more my fault than yours, kiddo. Even so," Tom said, tapping him hard in the chest, "do not let it happen again. From here on out you follow orders exactly as given, understand?"

"Absolutely loud and clear."

The sounds of laughter and applause, the screams and jeers, were much louder. The noise was coming from behind the place, past the line of close-parked wagons. There were a few small zombie pits out here, but Tom suspected the real attraction was over there.

"Benny and Nix are here somewhere," Tom said, "and I have a bad feeling about where they are."

As if to counterpoint his comment, the crowd erupted into furious applause.

"What are we going to do?"

"First things first," said Tom. "You look pretty banged up. Are you all right?"

When Chong took too long to answer Tom pulled him into a patch of light that was screened by hedges.

"Tell me," he ordered.

Chong turned and showed him his shoulder. "I was bitten."

Tom closed his eyes for a moment and sagged back against the edge of the porch. "Ah . . . kid . . . damn it . . ."

"In the pit. They made me fight. I won . . . both times, but I got bit."

"How long ago was this?"

"I don't know. Five, six hours. I can't really tell."

Tom gave him a puzzled frown. "How are you feeling? Have you been vomiting? Any double vision? Pain in your joints?"

"Just a little dizzy and nauseous."

Tom looked at the bite again. "You should be showing symptoms by now."

"H-how long do you think I have?"

"I don't know," said Tom. "It's different for everyone."

Chong knew that was true. Some people got sick right away; others took as long as a day before they felt it. In the end it was going to be the same. The plague had a 100 percent infection rate. No one ever survived it.

From behind the building they could hear Preacher Jack making a speech.

"Have you seen other prisoners?" asked Tom.

Chong shook his head. "No, but I heard people talking about them. There's supposed to be a bunch of other kids here. In the hotel, I think."

"Then that's where Benny and Nix will be. Preacher Jack took them."

Chong touched Tom's arm. "There are things you need to know. While I was still in the pit, I heard White Bear talking to someone. I'm pretty sure it was Preacher Jack. White Bear is Charlie's brother and he . . . he called Preacher Jack 'Dad.'"

Tom grabbed Chong's wrist. "Preacher Jack is Charlie Pink-eye's father?"

"I know . . . it's scary, but it makes sense."

"Only to madmen, kiddo."

Chong looked away to the west. "Tom, where's Lilah?"

Tom shook his head. "I . . . don't know where she is. She could be with Benny and Nix, or she could be out there somewhere."

"Out there" was a vast and featureless black nothing.

Chong licked his lips. "What . . . what do we do now?"

Tom handed him a knife. "We go find Benny and Nix," he said.

BENNY AND NIX FELL INTO DARKNESS. NEITHER OF THEM SCREAMED. Benny was too furious, and Nix . . . well, Benny didn't know what Nix was feeling. He thought he heard her laugh as the darkness of the pit swallowed them. Benny waited for the crushing impact at the bottom of a long fall, but his feet struck something soft and yielded. He hit and bounced and spun, and only then did he crash to the dirt. Behind him he heard Nix rebound and then thud down.

There was enough light to see, and as Benny sat up painfully he saw that just below the hole was a sloppy stack of old mattresses, positioned to catch their fall and keep them from shattering their legs.

"Very considerate of them," Nix muttered.

"I don't think they care much about us."

"No, really?" replied Nix sarcastically.

"I mean," said Benny, "that it's probably not as much fun to watch cripples fighting zoms."

"Again . . . really?"

They got to their feet and looked around. No zoms and not much light. The pit wasn't circular, and they could make out tunnels leading off in six separate directions.

White Bear squatted on the edge of the pit, grinning in

a way that made his burned face look like a monster out of a nightmare. "Here are the rules," he growled. "If you're paying attention, you might already have guessed that this ain't a straight pit-fight. There are tunnels and side passages and a few surprises cut every which way. Some of them are dead ends, and I do mean 'dead.'"

"Ha, ha," said Benny.

"You might also have guessed that you ain't alone down there."

Benny expected Nix to say "No, really?" again, but she held her tongue, so Benny supplied the sarcasm. "Well, we figured that . . . these being zom pits and all."

"Watch your mouth, boy," snapped White Bear.

"Really?" he said, and liked how it sounded. "What are you going to do? Beat us up and throw us in a pit full of the living dead?"

White Bear seemed to chew on that and apparently decided that Benny had a point.

"You were starting to tell us about rules," prompted Nix.

"Yes indeed, little cutie. My dad placed a church bell down there. It ain't easy to find, but it's there. Find it and ring it and you get a free ticket out of there."

"Until when?" demanded Nix. "Until tomorrow's games? And then the next day and the next until we're dead?"

"Nope. This is a real deal, straight up and hand to God. You ring that bell and we pull you out of there and put you on the road. No weapons or rations or none of that stuff, but you walk free."

That seemed to catch Nix off guard, and she turned sharply to Benny. "Is he telling the truth?"

"I . . . think so," Benny said quietly. "What's he got to lose? If we die, then Preacher Jack proves to the crowd that we're sinners. If we make it out and they let us go, Preacher Jack and White Bear prove that their word is good. Either way they win."

Nix chewed her lip. He stepped closer and touched her cheek.

"Hey . . . are you okay? No, wait—that is the stupidest question ever asked. What I mean is—"

Nix blinked and smiled, and for a moment she was back. The old Nix. Strong and smart and sane. She grabbed Benny and gave him a fierce hug, and in a tiny whisper filled with enormous emotion said, "I don't want to die down here, Benny."

"Hey!" yelled White Bear. "When you two lovebirds are done making out, can we get a move on? Lot of people paid good money for this."

Benny and Nix made the same obscene gesture at exactly the same moment. White Bear laughed out loud, and the audience applauded.

Before Benny released Nix he whispered, "We can do this. Find the bell, get out."

"Warrior smart," she said.

"Warrior smart," he agreed.

"Hey!" yelled Nix. "Aren't we supposed to have weapons or something?"

Preacher Jack leaned out over the edge. "The Children of Lazarus carry no weapons, and yet they strike with the power of the righteous. How would it be fair to arm you against them?"

"Okay," said Benny, "then are we going to face two zom—I mean two Children—who are the same size and weight and age as us?"

The smile on Preacher Jack's face was truly vile. It was filled with everything polluted and corrupt and unnatural that could show through smiling lips and twinkling blue eyes.

"Prayer and true repentance are your true weapons," he said.

He stepped back, and other faces began filling the edge of the pit. Torches were placed in stands mounted on the rim, and their light turned the maze into a dim eternity of dirty yellow shadows.

Nix suddenly grabbed Benny's arm, and he turned to see that the shadows were not empty. Things moved down the twisted tunnels. Stiff figures shuffled toward them through the gloom, and then they heard the low, hungry moan of the living dead.

CHONG STOOD IN THE SHADOWS AND WATCHED TOM IMURA WALK UP onto the hotel porch. There were two guards there, both of them armed with shotguns. They stiffened as Tom mounted the steps. One guard gestured for him to stop on the top step.

"If you're here for the games," he began, "you need to go around—"

Those were his last words. Chong never saw Tom's hand move. All he saw was a flash of bright steel that seemed to whip one way and then the other, and suddenly both men were falling away from Tom. Blood painted the wall and door of the old hotel.

It was the fastest thing Chong had ever witnessed, and on a deep gut level he knew that it was necessary, but it was also wrong. These men were part of Gameland, they were forcing kids to fight in zombie pits, and yet their lives had ended in the blink of an eye. They were discarded. Tom used *chiburi*—a *kenjutsu* wrist-flick technique that whipped all the blood off his sword blade. The sword gleamed as if it had not just been used to take two human lives.

Tom turned as Chong crept up the porch steps. He looked sad. "Sorry you had to see this, Chong."

"Me too," said Chong sadly. "Guess we had no choice."

"Not if we want to save Benny and Nix."

"This is war," said Chong. "And these people are monsters."

Tom put his hand on Chong's uninjured shoulder. "Listen to me. There are good people too. No matter how bad this gets, kiddo, never forget that. There are more good people than bad."

Chong said nothing. He absently touched the bite on his other shoulder. "Aren't you going to quiet them?" he asked.

"No. We need all the help we can get. Let them wander around and confuse things. I'll take care of them later if there's time. Right now we have to find Benny, Nix, and Lilah."

Chong said, "I hope she's okay." He was aware that he'd said "she" rather than "them," but Tom didn't seem to mind.

"Sorry things didn't work out with you two," Tom said. "For what's it worth . . . she couldn't do any better."

Chong didn't reply.

Tom quietly opened the front door and stepped inside. And stopped dead. His eyes went wide, and when Chong followed him in, he also stared. On one side of the room, weapons, ammunition, and explosives were stacked from floor to ceiling; on the other were hundreds of smaller, more well-used guns and rifles, each of them hanging on a nail driven into the wall. Small paper tags hung from each trigger guard.

"What is all this?" asked Chong in a hushed voice.

Tom listened for sounds of other people, heard nothing. Then he touched the barrel of one of the new rifles. "Probably scavenged a military base."

Chong pointed to the older weapons. "And these?"

"They probably collect firearms from everyone who comes to Gameland. They did that before. Keeps people from shooting each other over bets." He bent and read several of the small tags. "Damn."

"What's wrong?"

Tom held out one of the pistols. "Read the tag."

"Lucille Flax." Chong looked up, confused. "I don't understand. Mrs. Flax is my—"

"—math teacher. I know. There's a shotgun here with Adrian Flax's name on it. That's her husband."

"Wait," said Chong, "are you trying to say that they're here? That my math teacher and her husband come to Gameland?"

"How else would you read it?"

"It doesn't make sense! They're regular people. . . . Mrs. Flax doesn't come to places like this. She can't!"

"Why not? Chong . . . no matter how often you see someone, you can't ever say that you really know them. Everyone has secrets, everyone has parts of themselves that they hide from the world."

"But . . . Mrs. Flax? She's so . . . ordinary."

"Well, kiddo, it's not like people walk around with signs saying, 'Hey, I'm actually a creep!'"

Chong kept shaking his head. "And I was running home to people like that?"

"Remember what I said. There are more good people than bad. Even so . . . you always have to pay attention."

Chong sighed. "I guess this shouldn't hit me so hard. After all Benny, Morgie, and I used to hang around Charlie and the Hammer all the time. We thought they were—"

"—cool. Yep, I know."

"Still. My math teacher? Jeez . . . so much for civilized behavior."

"Walls, towns, rules, and day-to-day life doesn't make us civilized, Chong. That's organization and ritual. Civilization lives in our hearts and heads or it doesn't exist at all."

Then Chong spotted something that made him yelp. He ran across the room to a big urn in which long-handled weapons stood like a bouquet of militant flowers. He slid two items from the urn: a pair of wooden swords.

Tom took the bokkens from him. "Son of a—"

They both froze as they heard a sound from somewhere else in the hotel. A sharp cry. A child's yelp of pain.

Tom turned and looked at the broad staircase.

"That's not Benny or Nix. Too young," gasped Chong in a horrified voice.

"I know," Tom said bitterly, and headed up the stairs. "Stay behind me and let me handle things."

They moved up the stairs as quickly as they could, but the building was old and the stairs creaked. Luckily, the laughter from outside was so loud that most of the noise was hidden. However, when they were near the top step, one board creaked louder than all the others. The hallway was empty and poorly lit by lanterns set on shelves along the walls, with doors leading to rooms on both sides. One door stood ajar, and from that there was a sharp call.

"I'll be right back," said a man as he stepped into the hall. Chong estimated that he was at least twenty feet from where Tom crouched on the top step. It seemed like a mile. The man looked up and down the hall and was starting to turn back to the room when he saw the figures crouched in the shadows of the stairway.

"Hey," he said, his voice rising an octave in alarm. It was the last thing he said. Tom surged forward, racing at full speed toward the man. His rush was so sudden that the twenty feet melted into nothing. Steel flashed and red sprayed and then the man was falling. Without a second's pause, Tom kicked open the door and leaped into the room.

Chong was running now.

There were screams and the rasp of knives being drawn, then a single muffled gunshot. The bullet punched through the plaster wall a foot behind Chong, making him jump. He crouched low and peered inside the room. The sight was one that he knew he would never forget.

It was a big room, a suite. Along the far wall was an old iron radiator, and through its metal structure the guards had run three lines of chains. The chains were connected to iron rings that were bolted and locked around the necks of at least forty children. The oldest was Chong's age, an Indian girl with one eye puffed shut and a split lip. The youngest was no older than six. All of the kids were bruised, and each one looked absolutely terrified. A smoking pistol lay on the floor with a man's severed hand still attached to it.

The rest of the room was a slaughterhouse. Five men lay on the floor, or sprawled over furniture, or in a heap on the bed. Three men were still on their feet. Tom was one; the other two were guards. One of the guards was wandering away from the fight, hands clamped to a ruined throat, eyes already fading into emptiness. The remaining guard held a machete in his hands but he, too, was backing away from this man, this thing that had burst into the room in a storm of death. The machete dropped to the floor as he brought his hands up in total surrender.

The entire fight was over already.

Chong stared at Tom. Benny's brother looked as cold and calm as if he was watering his rosebushes or cutting a slice of pie, even though his face was splashed with fresh blood.

"Is the hallway clear?" Tom asked in a disturbingly serene voice.

Chong stammered an affirmative.

Tom nodded. He extended his sword toward the remaining guard. "Are there any other guards on this floor?"

"N-n-no! Two on the porch and us . . . I mean me. God . . . don't kill me, please . . . I got kids of my own."

Tom stepped forward and touched the bloody sword tip to the guard's cheek. "Do your kids have to fight in the pits?" The curl of his lip was the only clue to the emotion he was keeping in check behind his bland face.

The man flicked a guilty look at the children huddled by the wall.

"These kids . . . I mean . . . hey, man, I was just doing what I was told. White Bear and his old man call the shots around here."

Tom flicked the blood off his sword, careful not to let a single drop go anywhere near the kids, all of whom were locked into a moment of traumatized silence. He resheathed his sword.

"Keys," he said. The man very carefully dug into his pocket and then gingerly held out a ring of keys. Tom snatched them from him and tossed the ring to Chong. "Get them into the hall."

While Chong rushed to free the captives, Tom walked forward, making the guard stumble backward until the man's back hit the wall. Tom stopped, his face an inch from the terrified guard's. "You know who I am?"

"Yes . . . oh God . . . please don't . . . I know who you are . . . don't . . ."

Tom bared his teeth. "Where's my brother?"

BENNY PRESSED NIX BACK AGAINST THE WALL AS THE FIRST OF THE DARK shapes moved toward them. The pit they were in was thirty feet across, with large blank sections of wall interspersed with side tunnels. The torches were too high to reach.

"Mattress!" Nix blurted, and they rushed over to the stack of rotten old mattresses and began dragging them toward the tunnel with the zoms.

Benny squatted and upended one and used it to block them from view. "Might not stop them," he warned. "And my cadaverine's worn off."

"Better than nothing," she grunted as she dragged another one over and pulled it upright. There were only three mattresses, but they nicely blocked half the tunnels. "Maybe it'll confuse them, slow them down."

Benny jerked his head toward one of the open tunnels. There was no movement in that one, but torchlight spilled down from another opening around the far bend. Benny pulled Nix inside, and they peered up to see if White Bear or the crowd could see them. The crowd booed and yelled for the dead to go fetch their dinner.

"I think we're good," whispered Nix. Immediately she

pulled out the tails of her shirt and reached inside her clothes. Benny did the same, and they knelt down and placed several hidden items on the ground. When the guards had locked them in the empty hotel room, they had thought that the two teenagers were helpless; but Tom had spent the last seven months teaching them to never be helpless. He said that in ancient times a samurai warrior was never unarmed, even if he had no sword, knives, or spear.

"All weapons are made," he once told them. "They're fabricated from the things we find: wood, metal, rope, leather, stone. Nature always provides, but only a smart warrior can look at what circumstance offers and see the potential."

While waiting for White Bear to come and take them to the pits, Benny and Nix had looked at what the room had to offer: an old light fixture, crumbling plaster walls, dry laths, a window. Now on the ground in front of them they examined what circumstance had provided. They had several lengths of broken lath—thin, narrow strips of some straight-grained wood; several yards of copper-cored electrical wire; and long pieces of jagged window glass wrapped in torn strips from their shirts—strips whose absence was hidden by their vests. All their pockets were filled with plaster dust.

There was a loud moan from around the bend. One of the zoms had reached the end of the first tunnel. The crowd began cheering. Benny hoped the wall of mattresses would confuse the zoms. Every second mattered to Benny and Nix.

"Hurry," breathed Nix.

They worked as fast as they could. They placed layers of jagged glass between strips of lath and used the wire to bind it in place. Benny wrapped the wire around and around as tightly as he could. While he did that, Nix used another piece of glass to slash strips from their pant legs and then poured the white plaster powder into pouches made from those strips. When she was done, she and Benny swapped jobs. She took the make-shift glass-bladed hatchets and used more strips of their jeans to bind the laths from end to end, wrapping them the way an ancient weapons maker would wrap the haft of a war ax. Benny took the pouches and tied loose knots in them and began stuffing them in his pockets.

There was a soft thud as one of the mattresses fell into the main pit. A second later a white hand grabbed the corner of the mattress wall, and then a lifeless face moved into view. Black eyed and black mouthed, it moved past the temporary obstruction, then turned toward them and moaned. The sound was answered by other moans behind it.

Benny and Nix snatched up their weapons and began backing away. There was another chorus of moans. This time the sounds were behind them, coming from another tunnel. Benny turned sharply and saw three zombies stagger around the far bend, their dead faces painted yellow by torchlight.

Far above the crowd howled, and a commentator began calling out what was happening to those members of the crowd who couldn't see. "Looks like we're coming up on round one, folks," he yelled in a fast-paced, high-pitched voice. "And oh! Here's a twist: Somehow our two competitors have managed to sneak in some weapons."

There were eight zoms shuffling through the main pit now, and more coming out of the side tunnel; but still only three in front of them blocking their easiest line of flight.

"Benny," Nix whispered, "we have to try."

"Okay," he said, but his throat was dry. "Let's go!"

Hatchets in hand, they raced forward, screaming at the top of their lungs. There were two men and a woman in the first pack. The closest one was a wild-looking man wearing the bullet-pocked remains of a carpet coat. He bared his teeth and lunged at Benny, but just as the white hands were about to close on him, Benny jagged right, parrying the grab with his left hand; then he pivoted and chopped down on the back of the zom's head with the hatchet. The layered chunks of glass bit deep into the weak area at the base of the monster's skull. It was a good hit, a solid hit, and for once Benny's aim was right on the money. The zombie pitched forward.

At the same time, Nix broke left from behind Benny and threw herself into a tight shoulder roll right under the reaching arms of the second zom. She came straight up out of the roll, pivoted on the balls of her feet, and slashed her hatchet across the back of the zom's knee. It was one of Lilah's favorite combat tricks. The withered tendon parted like bad string, and the zom started to fall. Nix rammed it with her shoulder, and the creature crashed sideways into the third zom so that the two of them fell.

"Go!" Benny yelled, grabbing the shoulder of her vest and pulling her. One zom was down for good, one was crippled, and one would be able to get back up; but the most important thing was that for a moment the three of them sprawled in the middle of the tunnel, creating a temporary roadblock.

Above them the commentator was fumbling to explain this to the crowd, and his words were met by a mixed chorus of boos and applause.

"Freaks!" snarled Nix.

Benny saved his breath for running. They rounded the bend and skidded to a halt as two more zoms lumbered toward them. A side tunnel broke right, and Nix started to go that way, but Benny didn't like it. There was no light at all down there.

The closest zom was an enormous fat man in the shreds of a blue hospital gown. He had almost no face left. Nix tried to dodge and kick, hoping to break the man's knee, but her aim was off and her foot rebounded from the monster's fat thigh. It swiped at her and she had to leap backward to keep from being caught. Benny tried the same kick attack and hit the knee, but the fat man's leg wouldn't break. As it wheeled on this new attacker, the second zom—a prissy-looking woman with gray hair in a bun and her intestines hanging out—threw herself on Nix.

Nix screamed and brought her feet up just in time, catching the zom on the chest and in the gooey mass of its entrails. The zombie scrabbled at Nix's vest with white fingers and kept darting forward to try to bite.

Benny was too busy to help. The fat zom shambled toward him, its bulk blocking the narrow tunnel. It pawed at him as Benny chopped at it with the hatchet, knocking bloodless chunks of flesh from its face and chest.

With a final scream of wild rage, Nix swung her hatchet and buried the long glass spike in the zombie's eye socket. The monster reeled back, shuddered, and then fell, tearing the handle out of Nix's hand.

Benny stopped trying to get away and instead put one foot on the wall and used it to launch himself at the zom, hitting it high on the chest and driving it backward with both hands. The monster's heels hit the other zom and he toppled backward, with Benny holding onto its shirt all the way to the massive *thump!* The zombie never stopped grabbing for him, and the creature was immune to the shock of the impact beyond a shudder that rippled through its layers of dead fat. The creature bit down on Benny's ragged shirtsleeve and began shaking it the way a terrier shakes a rat. Benny hammered at it with the hatchet until he tore through the remaining tendons of the zom's face and the lower jaw simply fell off.

Benny gaped at the monster for a moment, then threw his weight sideways and went into a sloppy roll that nonetheless brought him to his feet. As he turned he saw Nix working her hatchet back and forth to free it from the dead zom's eye socket. It came free with a dry *glup* sound, and then the two of them were running again.

Nix threw him a single, crazy smile of triumph as they ran.

Is she . . . enjoying this? The impossible thought banged around inside Benny's head.

The crowd was going crazy up there, but mostly applauding now. People threw stuff down at them—unshelled peanuts, cigarette butts, balled-up betting slips. White Bear was laughing with a deep-chested rumble, thoroughly enjoying the show. As they ran past another opening, Benny shot a quick look up and saw Preacher Jack. He did not know the man well enough to be able to read the subtleties of his expressions, but what Benny saw at that moment required no interpretation. It was a look of pure, malicious joy.

Why? Benny wondered. *We're winning.*

When they rounded the next bend, that question was

answered in the most horrible possible way. The next corridor was a dead end that ran twenty feet into a blank wall.

There were at least a dozen zoms in there. But that wasn't what made Benny slam to a halt and stare in abject terror. It wasn't what pulled a scream from the deepest pit of Nix's soul.

The thing that plunged the world into absolute nightmare was the huge creature that rose up before them in the dark. A great and terrible zombie. Bigger than any they had faced. It was massive, corded with muscle and covered with scars from countless battles as a human. It wore a leather vest from which the tips of hundreds of sharp steel nails jutted out like a terrible cactus. Iron bands studded with steel points circled its neck and wrists, and a skullcap of gleaming steel covered its head and tapered down the neck to prevent any injury to the brain stem. When its lips curled back, Benny and Nix could see that someone—some madman—had filed its teeth to razor spikes.

Even all that, from its size to its fearsome armament, was not the worst thing about it. It was Nix who spoke the word that made it all beyond horrifying.

She spoke its name.

"Charlie . . ."

75

Outside the hotel . . .

Lilah found a shed filled with old sporting equipment. Deflated balls, old fishing rods, Frisbees. She stared at the junk . . . and smiled.

Yes, she thought, *this is perfect.*

Inside the hotel . . .

"Tom!" Chong called from the hallway. He had just come back from escorting all the captive children into another room.

"I told you to stay with the kids," barked Tom.

"Um . . . the kids are fine. Really." Chong wore a quirky and bemused smile. "But . . . there's something else. You'd better come."

Tom turned from the guard. The man had collapsed into a weeping, cringing pile, and looking at him disgusted Tom. He jabbed the guard with a toe. "Stay!"

The man nodded and held his hands up, palms out.

Tom crossed to the door and stepped out into the hall. His hand flashed toward his sword, and a war cry almost tore itself from his throat. Then he froze in total shock.

The hall was full of people. All of them were heavily armed. Tom's mouth hung open. One of the people reached out a hand and gently pushed on Tom's chin to close his mouth.

"You're going to catch flies with that," said Sally Two-Knives with a wicked grin.

Tom looked around, seeing faces that could not be here. "I don't—I mean—"

"You owe me two ration dollars," said Fluffy McTeague to Basher. "I told you he wouldn't know what to say."

Farther down the hall, J-Dog and Dr. Skillz were removing the dog collars from the kids. They looked up and grinned.

"Kahuna!" said J-Dog.

"Yo, brah!" said Dr. Skillz.

"How are you here?" exclaimed Tom.

Sally and Solomon filled him in on the discussion they'd had in the woods. "We started gathering everyone up," said Solomon, shaking Tom's hand. "You're a popular guy, brother. Everybody's either looking to warn you or looking to trade you to White Bear for serious cash money."

"I saw the bounty sheet. Not just me . . . they want my brother and his friends. Dead or alive."

"Worth more alive," said Hector Mexico. "Dead? Eh, not so much."

"We don't want you to leave, boss. End of an era," said Basher. "No way we were going to let White Bear write the last chapter of Fast Tommy's story."

Tom frowned. "So . . . this is a rescue party?"

"Par-teeee!" chanted J-Dog and Dr. Skillz.

"But this isn't even your fight."

Solomon Jones answered that. "It's always been our fight,

Tom. And with you gone—dead or gone east—then it's going to be our war."

Tom shook his head.

"Son," Solomon said with a smile, "don't you know when the universe cuts you a break?"

"Not lately, no."

"Well, get used to it, 'cause the cavalry has arrived."

"Only downside," said Sally, "is that there are twenty of us and about four hundred of them. And I'm not going to be much good in a fight once I run out of bullets."

Now it was Tom's turn to smile. "Are you kidding? Didn't you guys see what was in the front room?"

Basher shook his head. "No, we climbed in through a ground-floor guest bedroom all ninja-like. Snuck up the back stairs."

"Then you may be the cavalry," said Tom, "but I'm Santa Claus. Let's go downstairs and open some presents."

76

CHARLIE PINK-EYE LOOMED IN FRONT OF BENNY AND NIX. SIX FEET SIX inches of him. One eye was a milky pink, the other one—once as blue as his father's—was black and dead. His skin, once the creamy white of an albino, had turned the color of a mushroom: gray-white and blotched with fungus and decay. Flies buzzed around him, and maggots wriggled through flaps of his dead flesh. He snarled and took a lumbering step forward. And now Benny understood what he had seen out in the field by the way station. It hadn't been Charlie leading an attack of zoms . . . Charlie had been a zom himself, part of a swarm led there by Preacher Jack. Led there . . . and led away before the fire could consume him. When Benny had seen Charlie smile, it wasn't a smile at all but the snarl of a hungry zombie.

It was grotesque. It was bad enough that Charlie had not fallen a thousand feet to smash himself to ruin at the base of the mountain. It was worse still that he had become one of the monsters that he and the Motor City Hammer used to hunt. What was far, far worse was that Charlie's own father and brother had kept him alive as a zom, armored him like a gladiator, and put him down here in the shadows to be their pet monster. Their Angel of Death for a new and corrupt

Eden. Even though Benny understood few of the mysteries of any religion, he knew with perfect clarity that this was a sin that could never be forgiven. This was blasphemy.

"Nix," Benny whispered, "*run!*"

But Nix did not run. She couldn't. She was rooted to the spot, staring with horror at a nightmare monster version of the thing that had murdered her mother.

"Charlie," Nix murmured again. Benny looked at her, and his heart sank to see that the madness that had swirled in her eyes now owned her. This was what she had feared. Charlie, the monster who had murdered her mother. Charlie, alive or undead, but still moving through her world. Still hunting her. On some level Nix had come to believe that this would happen. This very thing.

When Benny had struck Charlie on the ridge and sent him tumbling into the darkness, Nix had not been a part of it. Charlie had overpowered her and Lilah; and it was a combination of dumb luck and warrior rage that had guided Benny's hand as he swung the Motor City Hammer's iron club. Charlie had fallen, but they hadn't found his body. He was never quieted. For Nix, there was no closure. In some twisted way Charlie had escaped. And that had broken something inside Nix's head. Maybe in her soul, as well. And with a flash of insight Benny realized that Nix's desire to leave Mountainside was as much about running away from the possibility of facing Charlie, alive or dead, as it was about finding a new life.

Charlie Pink-eye took a lumbering step toward them. Benny snarled and pushed Nix back.

"God . . ." Nix's voice was small and fragile.

Benny let out a bellow of fury and swung his hatchet,

trying for a killing shot through the eye socket. Instead the glass blade dug into the front of Charlie's cheek, punching through the sinus. The zoms in the dead-end tunnel moaned with raw hunger and shuffled forward, but Charlie's massive body blocked the way. With a feral growl Charlie lashed out and knocked Benny sideways into the wall. The glass blade of the hatchet snapped, and the handle fell from Benny's fingers. The blow was so fast and strong that for an insane moment Benny wondered if Charlie was somehow still alive. It was impossible, though. No . . . no, this thing was dead. Still . . . it was fast. Too fast. And so powerful!

Benny slid to the floor. Charlie bent down, grabbed Benny's vest, and pulled him off the floor. Razor teeth gleamed like daggers in the torchlight. As Charlie pulled him close, Benny could see the gleaming tips of the nails that covered the monster's body like a porcupine. Benny raised a knee and managed to get the flat of his shoe against the zom's lower stomach—the only area not covered by the nail vest. He kicked out, trying to squirm out of the grip with leverage, aiming blows to dislocate the jaw or break the neck. He tried every trick of combat and physics Tom had taught him. The nail heads scratched him, and soon Benny was bleeding from a dozen shallow cuts. Then two dozen. Blood flew from the injuries, and though none of them were serious, the smell of fresh blood in the air seemed to drive Charlie and the other zombies wild. They snarled and moaned and bit the air.

Charlie's big head darted forward, and his razor teeth bit down with devastating force—but not on Benny's flesh.

Suddenly Nix was there, squeezing in between Benny and the monster, and she rammed her hatchet up into its mouth.

The rows of filed teeth chomped down on the weapon and crunched on glass and wood. Nail tips pressed into Nix's vest. The canvas was sturdy, but it wasn't designed for this kind of protection. Not even a carpet coat would work if she didn't get out of there soon.

Charlie flung Benny away and grabbed Nix instead. Benny crashed to the ground again. Pain exploded in his shoulder, numbing him all the way to his fingertips. The other zoms tried to reach past Charlie to get to Nix. Wax-white hands poked through the crooks of Charlie's elbows and reached over his shoulders and around his sides, clawing at Nix's vest and hair. In their attempts to grab her, they were also pulling her into the nail vest.

Benny hauled himself to his feet, saw his broken hatchet, dove for it, and came up with the splintered wood in his right hand. Nix still had her hatchet buried in Charlie's mouth, and he was actually trying to chew his way through it to get to her. Benny rushed to Nix and looped his bad left arm around her waist while he chopped and pounded at the white hands with the hatchet handle. He broke fingers and wrists and some of the white hands flopped away, useless to their owners. One creature had a solid handful of Nix's hair, and Benny could not shatter its wrist, so he did the only other thing he could do: He used the remaining bits of glass still tied to the hatchet and sawed through her hair. She sagged forward, but Charlie still had her.

Benny rammed the sharp end of his hatchet handle up under Charlie's chin. He drove it with such force that it punched through into the zom's mouth and pinned his jaws shut. At least for the moment. Immediately, Nix brought her knees up and aimed her feet just below the nail vest, then kicked out with all her force as Benny pulled with all of his. They burst free from Charlie's grasp and fell backward; Benny hit the ground first, and Nix landed hard on top of him, driving most of the air from his lungs.

For the moment Charlie ignored them and clawed at the wooden spike that sealed his jaws shut. The other zoms pushed forward to get past him.

"Dust!" Benny croaked, and Nix tore a pouch of plaster dust from her vest and flung it at them. The dust exploded into a white cloud that swirled thickly around the zoms.

Benny didn't know if the powder would do anything more than distract them for a moment. They had thought to use it against Digger and Heap, but for now it gave them a slender doorway of time. Nix grabbed Benny's wrists and hauled him to his feet, slapped his shoulders to spin him, and then shoved him forward, keeping her hands on his back as he stumbled away from the zoms.

"Nix—are you okay?"

She gave him a wild-eyed stare. "I need to kill him," she answered in a fierce whisper.

"I know," he said, though they both knew that it was virtually impossible, and it was suicide to try. "Come on, let's go."

During this brief but awful fight they had been only dimly aware of the shouts and laughter from above. There were plenty of boos now. Defeating Charlie, however briefly, seemed to have turned the crowd against them. That or maybe the sheep were too afraid of Preacher Jack and White Bear to show any other reaction.

White Bear bent down into one of the pit openings,

grinning like a ghoul. "Run as fast as you want, but there's no way out."

Nix pivoted and flung one of the pouches at him. White Bear got his hand up to block it, but the pouch flapped open and he was showered with white plaster dust. He reeled back, coughing and gagging and cursing. There was a quick ripple of surprised laughter, but it died down immediately as White Bear wheeled on Benny and Nix with a murderous glare.

They ran from under the pit opening, vanishing into the shadows. They heard zoms ahead of them, and they realized they were running back toward the main pit. They scrambled into a turn. Behind them Charlie Pink-eye was shambling toward them, the spike of wood no longer pinning his jaws shut.

That left the dark side tunnel. "No lights," Benny said.

Nix chewed her lip, looking up and down the corridor. The front of her vest was dotted with drops of blood from where the tips of the nails had cut through her clothes and into her skin. Pain twisted her mouth as she said, "No choice."

They ran into the darkness. Above them the crowd became suddenly silent.

"God!" panted Nix. "What now?"

PREACHER JACK STOOD NEXT TO WHITE BEAR, BOTH OF THEM SCOWLING down into the pits. "This is taking too long," said the old man.

"Kids are pretty good," replied White Bear. "I'm actually starting to enjoy this."

Preacher Jack snarled, "They should be dead by now."

"Lighten up, Dad . . . Charlie's got their number. Those kids are Happy Meals, you'll see."

Preacher Jack leaned closer still. "You listen to me, boy, if they find that bell and we have to let them go, then—"

White Bear laughed deep in his chest. "Dad, for a man of faith you could use some more for your own kin. I got everything under control, and . . ."

His words trickled down and stopped as he realized that the crowd had suddenly fallen silent. The people weren't looking into the Pits of Judgment. They were staring in shock at the back of the hotel. Preacher Jack and White Bear whipped their heads around to see a figure standing on the porch. He had a pistol in a belt holster and a long Japanese sword slung over his back.

"Imura," murmured Preacher Jack; then he threw back his

head and bellowed the name. It echoed all around the arena. "Imura!"

Beside him, White Bear grinned like a happy ghoul. He stepped forward and pitched his voice for all to hear. "Well, ain't this just a treat? Come to watch the fun and games, Tom?" He laughed, but only the guards laughed with him. The people in the bleachers shifted in shocked and uncomfortable silence. Preacher Jack held up his hand, and every face turned toward him.

"Why am I here?" answered Tom with a faint smile. He spoke loud enough for the crowd to hear him. He held out a copy of the bounty sheet and showed it to everyone. "It's pretty clear that you wanted me here."

"That's true enough," answered Preacher Jack. "You and your little pack of sinners and murderers."

"By that you mean my brother, Benny? And Nix Riley, Louis Chong, and Lilah?"

"Sinners all." Preacher Jack nodded.

"Where are they, Matthias?" Tom demanded.

"Oh," said Preacher Jack, not looking at the pits, "they're waiting for their chance at redemption."

Tom crumpled up the bounty sheet and dropped it off the porch into the dust. "This is between you and me. Leave the kids out of it."

The preacher spat on the ground. "This is between your family and mine. You killed two of my sons and my grandson. Don't pretend you don't understand that, Tom Imura. It was you who made it about families. You owe me a blood debt."

Tom ignored the jeering catcalls of the guards and the nervous buzz of the crowd. He locked eyes with Preacher

Jack. "Charlie dealt the cards, Matthias, don't you pretend he didn't. He ran these hills like they were his personal kingdom, and he didn't care who got hurt as long as he got what he wanted. He was a parasite, a thief, a murderer, and an abuser of children."

"You don't dare—," began White Bear, but his father touched his arm.

"Let the man have his say. Then we'll see what justice wants from this moment."

As he said it, he let his eyes flick toward the pits.

Down below, completely hidden in the shadows, Benny and Nix stared upward as if they could see what was happening. The voices were muffled. Benny's heart beat like a drum, and in the dark Nix grabbed his hand to give it a powerful squeeze.

"Nix," Benny breathed, "is that Tom?"

Tom walked to the edge of the porch so everyone could see him. "Years ago Charlie and his thugs tried to raid Sunset Hollow. That was my home, my family's home. I marked the place as off-limits. Everyone respected that except Charlie. He never respected anything . . . but things didn't work out so well for him. I gave him and his men a chance to walk away. They didn't take it. Later, when it was just Charlie kneeling in the dirt begging for his life, I let him live because he swore to me—swore to God above—that he'd change his ways, that he wouldn't do this sort of thing again. That he wouldn't hurt people again. I let him live, Matthias. I showed him mercy, but as soon as he slunk away he started back up worse than ever."

"I've heard that story before," said Preacher Jack. "It was a lie then and it's a lie now. No one ever beat Charlie in a fair fight."

Tom ignored that. "Last year Charlie opened a new Gameland, and he went hunting for the one person who might tell me where it was. Lilah. The Lost Girl. To find her he broke into Jessie Riley's house. He beat that good woman to death and kidnapped her daughter, Nix. You know what happened then."

"Yes, I know. You laid false charges on Charlie, then you and yours went out and ambushed him in the woods and killed him when he wasn't looking."

"False charges? I was there, Matthias. I held Jessie Riley in my arms when she died. I know what happened. Charlie asked for what he got, and my only regret is that it wasn't from my own hand."

"Yes . . . that hell-spawn brother of yours, that devil's imp, managed some trickster ambush and killed my firstborn son."

The crowd buzz intensified. There were dozens of versions of the battle at Charlie's camp, and small arguments broke out as facts and suppositions were thrown out.

White Bear spun around and roared, "SHUT UP!" His bellow echoed off the walls of the Wawona Hotel. The crowd cowered into silence.

Preacher Jack took a threatening step toward Tom. "You had your say, such as it was. Now hear me on this, Tom Imura. Your time is over. Your reign of corruption, bullying, terrorism, and murder is done. I call a blood debt on you and yours, and like a farmer who burns a whole field to kill an encroaching blight, I will burn the name of Imura from this world. Your sins against my family are uncountable, and so I curse you and yours for all generations." As he spoke he turned in a slow circle to likewise address the shocked and silent crowd. "Anyone who stands with you falls with you. So say I and so say mine."

Silence owned the moment except for the constant low moans of the dead strapped to the chairs under the circus tent.

Down in the Pits of Judgment, Benny whispered, "What's happening?"

"I don't know," said Nix. "We have to let Tom know we're here!"

Behind them the shadows were filled with hungry moans.

"Don't make a sound," Benny whispered. Calling out to Tom was a good plan, but not at the moment. Not unless Tom was right there with a ladder ready to let them climb out, and from what Benny heard, that wasn't the case. If they called to him now, it might be a fatal distraction for Tom.

Benny and Nix felt their way along the walls of the tunnel. It was absolutely pitch black. Even the torchlight from the main corridor faded and died within a few yards. They fought to keep their breathing as silent as possible, listening for the scuff of a shuffling dead foot or the soft moan of hunger. Except for the powder, they had no weapons left, and Charlie was still out there along with at least fifteen zombies. Maybe more. Time was running out.

Tom Imura sighed. "I tried," he said, shaking his head. He reached over his shoulder and slowly drew his sword. All around the arena the guards, already alert, raised their weapons, edged forward, and pointed guns at Tom's heart. He ignored them as he straightened his arm and pointed the tip of his sword at Preacher Jack and White Bear. Firelight gleamed along the smooth steel and sparkled on the wicked edge. "Hear me on this," Tom said, his voice clear and strong. "You've spoken your piece and you've laid your curse, Matthias. Now hear mine. Not a curse . . . but a promise. I speak to everyone here, so listen to what I have to say." He paused and surveyed the crowd. "Walk away," he said. "Lay down your weapons, throw away your betting slips, and walk away. Gameland is closed. Walk away."

White Bear stared at him. "Says who?"

"Says the law."

"This is the Ruin! There is no law."

Tom's sword pointed at him, the tip as unwavering as if Tom was a statue made of steel. His eyes were fixed on White Bear. "There is now."

Preacher Jack snorted. "You have no right. You have no power. The Matthias clan is the only power in the Ruin . . . now and forever."

"Walk away," Tom said again, turning now to the crowd. "Last chance. Everyone here gets a pass if you walk away. Everyone except Preacher Jack and White Bear. To use their words: If you stand with them, you fall with them. Walk away."

"You're a fool and a madman," declared White Bear. "You come here alone and make some kind of brainless grandstand play." He gestured to one of his guards, a beefy man who had been a running back for the Oilers before First Night. "Take that stupid sword away from him and drag his ass over here."

The guard racked the slide on his pump shotgun and grinned. "Absolutely, boss."

Tom lowered his sword and raised his empty left hand, pointing his index finger like a gun at the approaching guard. He raised his thumb as if it was a pistol's hammer.

"Last chance," he said to the man.

"You're freaking crazy, Imura," said the guard. "You always were."

"Your call." Tom dropped his thumb and said, "Bang."

There was a sharp *crack* and the guard was plucked off the ground and flung backward. He landed on his back, gasping, eyes wide, blood pumping from a dime-size hole in the center of his chest. Tom blew across the tip of his finger as if he had really shot the man. The crowd sat stunned, unsure how to even react. Even Preacher Jack and White Bear were frozen in place.

"I warned you," Tom said, his smile gone now, his voice suddenly harsh and bitter. "You should have listened."

And then the killing began.

"BENNY!" CALLED NIX SUDDENLY. SHE SPOKE IN A WHISPER, BUT IT seemed dangerously loud. "I think I found something."

"What is it?" he said, fumbling blindly in the dark to try and cross to her side of the tunnel. Then he heard her cry out in revulsion at the same moment that he caught the smell. The stink of rotting flesh. They had worn cadaverine so long that they had become used to it, but their cadaverine was gone and this stink had not come from a bottle. "Nix . . . ?"

She pulled him down to where she knelt and pressed something hard and round into his hand. Benny knew at once what it was. A bone. He felt around and discovered other bones. Bones that had been completely cleaned of flesh, and some that the zoms had not finished stripping.

"God!" Benny said, and almost dropped it.

"Benny," Nix whispered, her lips right against his ear. "It's heavy. . . ."

He grunted as he got her meaning, but it still disgusted him. He felt the shape and length of the bone. A heavy thigh bone. About eighteen inches long, with bulbed heads at both ends; one end much bigger where it hinged into the hip. He weighed it in his hand.

There was an awful sound behind them. They had made too much noise. The zoms were coming.

"Hurry!" Benny said, and they clattered among the bones and found another thigh bone for him and a pair of stout shinbones for Nix. The darkness was filled with moans and the shuffle of slow feet. Time was up.

"At least we'll go out fighting," Benny said.

Nix jabbed him sharply with the bone. "Don't give me a hero speech, Benny Imura. I want to get out of this."

Even though she couldn't see it, Benny grinned in the dark. Crazy, brave, unpredictable, wonderful Nix Riley. He loved her so much that he wanted to shout. So he did shout. He gave a huge, wild war whoop as he raised his grisly weapons and charged down the tunnel to meet the living dead. Nix gave a weird, high, ululating cry and followed him.

The arena guards bellowed in fury and raced toward Tom.

"NOW!" bellowed Tom, and gunfire erupted from four windows in the hotel, and the front rank of guards went down in a bloody tangle. Hector Mexico leaned out of a second-floor window and lobbed a pair of fragmentation grenades into the stands. The crowd started to scatter, but some were too slow. The explosions were enormous. Then there was a chorus of screams from the guards over by the tent, and immediately the screams were drowned out by the moans of the living dead as dozens of zoms swarmed over them. The crowd did not immediately understand what was happening even as the dead shambled out into the arena; then they saw the two men in carpet coats and football helmets hacking and slashing at the cloth strips that held the zoms in their chairs. The men were laughing as they worked.

Then the back doors of the hotel burst open, and Solomon Jones led the team of free and unaffiliated bounty hunters out into the fray. Magic Mike, LaDonna Willis and her twin sons, Vegas Pete, the hulking Fluffy McTeague in his pink carpet coat, Basher with his baseball bats, and all the rest.

Tom leaped from the porch and slammed into the stalled and shocked guards, his sword mirror-bright for a moment longer—and then it was laced with red.

Lilah stared in shock from the top of the left-hand bleachers.

Tom!

She couldn't believe what she was seeing. Tom Imura, against all odds, leading a charge of armed fighters against Preacher Jack and the crowds at Gameland. It was insane. It was impossible. And yet it was real.

She stared past the panicked spectators. She had all the items she had taken from the sports shed, along with a bucket of pitch and a lantern. Wasting no time, Lilah used a fishing hook on a line to snag a deflated soccer ball, dipped it in the pitch bucket, set it ablaze with the lantern, and hurled it far over the crowd. It splatted against the back of one of the guards, who was immediately wreathed in yellow and orange flames. The man's shrieks rose into the air louder than any other sound. Immediately the row of spectators in front of Lilah spun around, their faces showing a mixture of fear, shock, and anger.

Lilah gave them a wicked smile as she pelted them with burning balls. The screams of the spectators drowned out those coming from below, and now the entire set of bleachers was in full panic. Was Chong here too? She looked around but could not see him. Lilah bared her teeth in a feral grin, lit another ball, and threw it.

Sally Two-Knives was in no condition for hand-to-hand combat, but she could pull a trigger. She stared down the barrel of an army sniper rifle, laid the crosshairs on one of the Gameland guards, squeezed the trigger, and grinned like a harpy.

Crack! The kick of the gun hurt her, but she took that pain and turned it to bitter ice inside her heart. Sally had lost her children to the zoms during First Night. It was the worst thing that had ever happened to her, and every night she dreamed about what it must have been like for April and Toby as the monsters came for them. The people here made the horrors of the zombie plague into a game. They forced children to fight for their lives. Children.

She squeezed the trigger again. *Crack!* There was no trace of remorse in her eyes. Not so much as a flicker. The heavy kick of the gun hurt, but she used that pain to fuel her rage. Sally found another target and fired. *Crack.* And another.

Benny and Nix crashed into the first of the zoms. It was too small to be Charlie Pink-eye, which meant that it didn't have a nail vest or an armored skullcap. Benny rebounded from it and swung first one thigh bone and then the other at his own head height. There was a light crack as the first club hit something—an outstretched hand, perhaps—and then a much heavier CRACK as the second one slammed into something too solid to be a head. A shoulder? Benny raised both clubs and brought them down above the shoulder level, and there was a wet crunch. Then the zom was falling, brushing past Benny as it collapsed.

"On your left," Nix said from that side, and he heard the *whoosh* and crunch of her clubs. Bone-club met lifeless skin and shattered the undead bones beneath it. Fighting wild and blind, they pushed forward, taking turns to smash one-two, one-two, breaking arms and wrists and fingers in order to reach skulls and necks. Benny's arms ached, particularly his bruised left arm, but he kept going, kept swinging. Nix was growling like a hunting cat, grunting with each hit.

Then there was light! Not the reflected glow of the torches at the edges of the pit, but huge yellow light. A ball of fire came bounding into the tunnel. Literally a ball of fire. Benny saw that it was some old sports ball, a cricket ball or a softball, that burned with intense flames as it rolled. Benny could smell smoke and the stink of pitch.

The flames illuminated the T juncture of the tunnels, and Benny's heart sank as he saw that there were zombies in every direction. At least twenty of them, and five rows back on his left was the towering form of Charlie Pink-eye.

A second flaming ball dropped through the ceiling twenty yards down, and it landed on the back of a zombie in a business suit. The creature caught fire almost at once.

Benny shot Nix a quick look. Was this some new twist on the game? Did Preacher Jack want to burn them or kill them with smoke if the zoms couldn't do the trick? Or was Tom trying to help in some way they didn't understand? Either way it didn't matter; there was no way to fight past all the dead who clogged the tunnels.

White Bear shoved his father out of the way as Magic Mike charged at him, firing shot after shot from a nine-millimeter pistol. A round plucked at the bearskin cloak, and White Bear grabbed a mortally wounded spectator and shoved him in the direction of the shooter. Magic Mike tried to dodge, but the startled spectator slammed into him and then both went down.

White Bear leaped over the dying man and landed hard atop Magic Mike. He grabbed the bounty hunter's hair and chin and snapped his neck with a vicious twist. He was grinning as he heard the bones break.

Chong crouched inside the hotel, safe behind the bricks of the rear entrance foyer. He wanted to see Nix, Benny, and Lilah emerge safe from the pits or wherever they were, but he had no desire at all to join this fight. He wanted to be back in Mountainside, safe in his room with his stacks of books. Or maybe fishing in the creek with Morgie.

Lilah.

You're a town boy, she had said back on the road. *You're useless out here.*

There was a flash, and Chong watched as fireballs suddenly arced over the field and dropped into the sea of battle on the field. At first he was alarmed, thinking that this was another trick of White Bear; but then he saw the figure that rose above the row of burning corpses at the top of the bleachers. A magical figure out of some ancient myth. Gorgeous, long-limbed, incredibly lovely, and totally alien.

Lilah!

There was a sudden ripple of gunfire—the harsh chatter of an automatic rifle and the single pops of handguns—and then Chong saw the Lost Girl spin away, the last flaming ball dropping from her hands as she plummeted limply away into the darkness.

Chong screamed her name. "Lilah!"

"No . . . ," he whispered a moment later. They had just shot her. He had just watched her die. Chong grabbed his bokken and ran screaming into the madness.

Tom began cutting his way through the crowd toward White Bear. He wanted that man. And his psychotic father. Tom wanted to destroy the Matthias plague for good. His sword was like a living thing in his hand, moving without conscious thought. A man rushed at him with an ax, and suddenly the man was falling, his face gone. Another man raised a pistol, but hand and pistol suddenly flew away amid a piercing shriek. Three zoms came at him—two shambling slowly and one moving with unnatural speed. Then they were gone, falling in pieces. The sword sculpted a crooked path through the melee and nothing, alive or dead, could stand before him.

Four guards rushed up to shield Preacher Jack with their own bodies, and in a tight knot they ran from the center of the arena to the protection of a far corner. There was a *crack*, and one of the guards fell, half his face shot away. "Go . . . GO!" growled Preacher Jack, and the others did not hesitate or falter. They ran. *Crack* and another went down, his thigh pumping blood. Then they were in a cleft formed by the edge of the bleachers and a wagon. There was no angle for gunfire from the hotel.

Preacher Jack breathed in and out through his nose like a furious dragon. He was seeing everything he and his sons had built being torn down—again. By Tom Imura—again!

He wanted Tom dead so badly it was like acid in his throat. Preacher Jack grabbed the shoulder of his closest guard and spun him toward the aluminum siding that covered the wagon.

"Tear this off," he ordered. The guards set to work to open a doorway out of the kill zone.

It was madness. Zombies staggered out from the circus tent. They had no mind, no loyalties, no ability to discern Preacher Jack's enemies from his allies. They attacked everyone. J-Dog and Dr. Skillz, both of them drenched in the last of their personal stock of cadaverine, cut the dead free—all of them, Preacher Jack's entire congregation.

As the zoms shambled out into the arena, J-Dog wiped sweat out of his eyes. "Dude, that old preacher's gonna be piiiiiiiiiiiiiiiiissed."

"Totally, brah," agreed Dr. Skillz. He bent and picked up two objects Tom had given him. A pair of bokkens. "Let's boogie!"

They ran toward the pits.

As he ran, Chong smashed and struck and bashed and broke, and even big guards fell to his assault. Before that moment, before Lilah fell, Chong had never hurt another person or raised his hand in anger to anyone but a zom. Now he saw faces break as he swung his sword; he felt arms shatter.

He knew that they would kill him. There was no way out of this except through death's doorway, but he didn't care. He was already bitten. But he had seen Lilah die . . . he had nothing left to lose. So Chong ran forward into his last moment, accepting death because it had already accepted him, wanting to follow Lilah down into the darkness so that she would never again be lost and alone.

On the other side of the hotel, Carrie Singleton and Foxhound Jeffries, respectively the youngest and the oldest of the bounty hunters who had come with Sally and Solomon, led a string of children into the woods at a fast run. Carrie had a crossbow and picked out a path that made maximum use of the trees and hedges to hide their escape. Foxhound had cross-belts of throwing knives. Once upon a time he had been a circus performer, a knife thrower who could put a blade through a playing card tossed into the air. Twice guards tried to stop them; each time they learned the error of that choice.

"What's going on up there?" Benny demanded. Everything above them was a single wave of confused noise: shrieks and gunfire and the clash of steel on steel. "How could Tom be doing all this?"

Before Nix could say anything there was a different cry—a weird whoop of what sounded like pure joy—and then a figure dropped down through the pit opening. Tall, thin, wearing a football helmet and a carpet coat covered in pieces of license plates. He landed feetfirst on the shoulders of a zom, and the impact snapped the creature almost in two. He clutched three items in his hands: a spear that was almost identical to Lilah's, and two curved wooden swords. The man pivoted and grinned at Benny.

"Hey! Little samurai dudes!" shouted Dr. Skillz.

"How . . . ?" demanded Nix.

"Where . . . ," began Benny.

Dr. Skillz tossed one of the swords to him. He dropped the thighbone and caught it. Nix dropped her shinbone and caught the other.

"Surf's up!" yelled the bounty hunter as he swung his broad-bladed spear over their heads. He spun in place like a dancer, and suddenly two zoms were falling sideways while their heads fell in the opposite direction.

A thousand questions burned on Benny's tongue, but more zoms closed in and there was no time to do anything but fight.

Two of Solomon's friends, Vegas Pete and Little Bigg, trade guards from Haven, saw Preacher Jack and his men go running for cover behind the corner of the bleachers.

"Let's get that son of a hound," grumbled Bigg.

"Go for it," agreed Pete, and they ran a zigzag across the field, smashing zoms out of the way and shoving panicked spectators into the open pits. Pete fired a Winchester rifle from the hip, and Little swung an old-fashioned cavalry saber he'd long ago scavenged from a museum. Guards and spectators fell before them. Preacher Jack's two remaining guards rushed them. Vegas Pete missed with his last shot and broke the rifle over one guard's head. The second guard snatched up a pitchfork and ran at Little Bigg, but Little parried the thrust and ran the man through.

That left Preacher Jack stuck in the corner with the two trade guards grinning at him.

"Now ain't this a pickle?" asked Preacher Jack mildly. He should have been cowering. He should have been looking desperately for a way out. He was fifteen years older than these men, and where they were packed with muscle, he was a stick figure.

"Call off your goons, old man," said Vegas Pete, "and you might walk out of this with a whole skin."

"Well," said Little Bigg as he pulled his saber free, "I wouldn't say a whole skin."

Preacher Jack's lips twitched and writhed.

"Glad you think this is funny," said Pete, "'cause we're gonna—"

Preacher Jack kicked Pete under the kneecap and simultaneously chopped him across the throat with the stiffened edge of his hand. There was a sound like an eggshell cracking and Pete was backpedaling, fingers clawing at his throat as he tried to drag in air. His face turned red and then purple and he fell.

Little Bigg wasted no time gaping. He slashed a killing blow at Preacher Jack, but the old man leaped forward inside the swing. He head-butted Little, punched him in the chest and bicep, and snatched the saber out of his hand. There was a flash of silver and then Little Bigg was falling, his eyes wide with total incomprehension. It was all over in three seconds.

"Amateurs," sneered Preacher Jack. He laid the saber

within easy reach on the bleachers and set to work pulling at the aluminum siding.

Chong reached the bleachers where he had seen Lilah fall. He swore to himself that he would defend her body until this was over, and then—*Oh God,* he thought, *then what?*

He would have to quiet her. But . . . could he do it? The thought of it made him crazier still. He slashed at the legs of a man who stood on the bleachers trying to reload a pistol. The man fell, and Chong thrust the blunt point of the sword into a guard's groin. The guard screamed and doubled over, and Chong knocked him flying into a line of five zoms. The creatures were already covered with blood, and two of them had been spectators themselves less than three minutes ago.

Chong kept swinging and swinging. At one point he found himself fighting almost side by side with Solomon Jones. The bounty hunter had a machete in each hand, and they whirled like windmill blades. Zoms and humans fell around him like harvested wheat.

"Get to cover, kid!" yelled Solomon, but Chong ignored him, and then a surge of battle swept him and Solomon apart.

"Lilah," Chong said, mouthing her name like a battle chant. "Lilah!"

Benny and Nix fought back-to-back, swinging their swords at legs and necks and heads. Dr. Skillz worked the other tunnel, and despite the young bounty hunter's laid-back persona, he fought with the speed and precision of an experienced killer. He shattered bone with the reinforced butt of the spear and cut off hands and heads with the blade.

The burning zombie had crumpled to the ground, but not before two others bumped into it and caught fire. Heat and smoke were becoming a real problem.

"We have to get out of here!" Benny yelled, then broke into a fit of coughing.

"Waiting for a ride," Dr. Skillz shouted back.

"What?"

As if in answer, a length of knotted rope flopped over the edge of the pit, and J-Dog poked his head in. "Um . . . dudes? Stop screwing around. It's getting gnarly out here." Then he was gone; a second later someone screamed, and one of White Bear's guards dropped bonelessly into the pit.

"You climb," Dr. Skillz yelled. "I'll hold 'em off!"

Benny backed away from the press of zoms. There were four of them between him and Charlie. "Nix, c'mon!"

She half turned to look at the rope, but then she shook her head. With renewed fury she wheeled back and kept hammering at the zoms.

"What are you doing?" Benny demanded, but then he understood. He had been defending himself against the zoms, but Nix had been attacking them, chopping at them to fight her way toward Charlie. "God! Nix—don't!"

Nix rammed a zom in the throat and knocked it down with a foot-sweep.

"Hey! Kids!" growled Dr. Skillz. "The rope . . . not a freakin' request here!"

Benny took and grabbed the dangling rope, but Nix was still cutting her way toward Charlie. Four zoms stood in her way now, and Charlie was clawing at them to get to her.

"I'm going to regret this," muttered Benny, and he flung the rope toward Dr. Skillz.

"What the hell?" the bounty hunter demanded, but then two zoms rushed him and he had no time for anything except fighting.

Benny jumped over a fallen zom to where Nix fought. As she cut down another zombie, one of them lunged for her blind side. Benny swung his bokken like a baseball bat inches above Nix's head and hit the zom across the face. The blow snapped its head back, and the creature fell against Charlie with such force that its head and back struck the vest of nails and drove Charlie back a full step.

Nix finished another zom with the same ruthless precision. Her face was flushed with exertion and panic and rage, and her freckles stood out like a brown constellation on her skin. Charlie lumbered forward, his white hands barely two yards from Nix.

The remaining zom was nearly as tall as Charlie but only half as wide. He had a face like a quiet schoolteacher, but when he snarled, his jagged yellow teeth said all that needed to be said about the dreadful gulf between what he had been in life and what he had become in death.

Benny mouthed the word "Sorry" as he swung his sword. The blade hit the man on the crown of the head, and the zom instantly collapsed to its knees. Benny raised his arms to swing again, but the zom fell limply against him, and they both toppled back.

In the few seconds before Benny could crawl out from beneath the corpse, he witnessed something that was as awe-inspiring and magnificent as it was heartbreaking and terrifying. Nix Riley stood in front of Charlie Pink-eye. He was six and a half feet tall; she was barely five feet. He weighed three hundred pounds; she was less than a third of that. He was covered in spikes and armor, and he wore an invulnerability to pain that was a dark gift of the zombie plague; Nix wore a vest and shirt and jeans and did not even have a carpet coat to protect her.

Benny struggled against the zom's limp body, but his own leg was folded under him, and there were bodies heaped everywhere. "NIX!" he screamed.

Nix Riley looked at him for a brief second. The crazy look burned in her eyes and a weird, terrible smile played on her lips. Then she turned back just as Charlie reached for her.

It was all over so fast. . . .

Her bokken snapped out and slammed Charlie's hands aside. Finger bones cracked and twisted out of joint. Without pausing, Nix shifted and swung the sword around and down and cracked it across Charlie's left knee, and the impact knocked sweat from her face and arms. Plaster powder erupted from her pockets and filled the corridor with a pall like a grave-yard mist. Charlie charged toward her, but his knee buckled and his leg crumpled sideways and crashed down onto the shattered knee. Nix's sword swept through the cloud of pow-der, a ghostly image that was strangely beautiful. The tapered hardwood blade caught Charlie across the side of the mouth so hard that broken fragments of teeth struck the wall and stuck there, buried to half their length. Nix reversed her angle and struck the other side of Charlie's mouth, destroying his jaw and shattering the last of his razor-toothed grin.

Still the zombie reached for her. Crippled and with shattered bones, it could still drag her down and kill her.

Nix stepped backward with the delicate grace of a dancer so that Charlie's reaching hand lunged too far and the monster fell forward onto its face. Nix kicked at the steel helmet, once, twice, and then it went skittering off into the dark.

"This is for my mother, you son of a bitch!" she whispered, and she brought the bokken up and down with every ounce of strength and hatred and love that she owned. The blade struck the base of Charlie's skull—and both blade and bone shattered. The big man, the monster of all their nightmares, collapsed down and lay utterly still.

Benny finally tore his leg from under the corpse. He struggled to his feet, then paused, staring at the damage. Staring at Nix.

She looked down at what she had done, and at what it meant . . . then suddenly her face screwed up and she began to cry. Benny rushed to her, grabbed her, and held her, and she clung to him. Her tears were like boiling water on the side of Benny's neck. The fires of madness that had burned in her eyes for so long . . . flickered once more and went out, and her face wrinkled into a mask of bottomless pain and release.

"I k-ki-killed him!" she wailed.

"Yes, you did," he murmured into the foamy red tangles of her hair. "You killed the monster."

Benny looked over to see what was happening with Dr. Skillz, but just as he looked up he saw J-Dog leaning into the pit again. "Dudes? If you're done goofing off down there, we could use a little help up here."

Dr. Skillz held the zoms off as Nix and Benny climbed out of the pit. Dr. Skillz came up after them. Benny and Nix stared around them at the absolute carnage. Scores of people lay dead, and some were already starting to reanimate. Hundreds of zoms filled the arena, and hundreds of people fought them and fought one another. There didn't seem to be any sense to it. No battle lines.

"Where's Tom?" yelled Nix.

Benny shook his head. "I don't know."

Then Benny saw something that twisted his mind into a weird new shape. He suddenly recognized some of the fighters. Not the ones attacking him, but the people fighting White Bear's men. These were faces he knew from Zombie Cards. It was a surreal moment.

"S-S-Solomon Jones?" Benny stammered. Nix whipped around to see where Benny was pointing, and sure enough, the legendary bounty hunter with the twin machetes was carving a path along the bleachers. A dozen yards away Hector Mexico stood on the top step of one set of bleachers, firing blast after blast from his shotgun into anyone who came at him. He was surrounded by heaps of the dead. Across the arena Basher Bashman had a baseball bat in each hand and was using them to block people from entering the hotel—which was the only exit, unless people wanted to jump from the top of the bleachers, and that was a forty-foot drop. J-Dog now guarded the other door, and his double-bladed ax was painted bright red with blood. Others from the Zombie Cards were peppered throughout the battle.

"I don't understand," said Benny, but Nix just shook her head.

White Bear's guards, the ones who still had guns, kept trying to shoot their way into the hotel, but there were sharp *cracks* from one of the upper hotel windows, and one by one the armed guards pitched backward, dead before they hit the ground. Benny craned his neck to see who was firing and had a brief glimpse of the Mohawk and intense face of Sally Two-Knives peering along the barrel of a high-powered sniper rifle.

"Where's Tom?" asked Nix again. Then she grabbed Benny's arm and pointed. "There!"

"TOM!" Benny whirled and yelled, but if Tom heard him, he had no time to respond. A wave of guards and bounty hunters were closing in on him. They were armed with spears and swords and knives and pitchforks. Benny saw Tom smile.

Benny had seen his brother fight before, back in Charlie's camp seven months ago, but even that battle was tiny compared to this. At least a dozen men closed in on Tom, and he smiled. Then his body became a blur of movement. As a man with a reaper's scythe came at him, Tom lunged in and down and his blade whipped a silver line across the man's midsection. Without even watching to see the effect, Tom rose and parried a pitchfork thrust and cut the man through arms and throat in a single move. A burly bounty hunter ran at him with two yard-long blades, but Tom darted forward between the weapons, and his blade rose through chest and chin and skull. The cuts were fast and elegant, worlds away from the awkward hacks and slashes of Benny's moves with the bokken, but Benny knew the cuts. He practiced them every day. Benny was very good, but Tom was a master.

Tom moved like a dancer, seeming to skim along the surface of the ground, turning gracefully to evade, using each turn to put incredible power into his cuts. It was ugly and beautiful at the same time, a ballet of destruction that pitted Tom's lifetime of dedication to swordplay against brute strength and seemingly overwhelming odds. Yet with each flickering second of time the odds became less and less, as it seemed that Tom was building around himself a castle of corpses.

Then a shout tore Benny away from the scene. He turned to see Heap charging toward him, but then a monstrous pink shape stepped into his path. Benny almost laughed at the sight of Fluffy McTeague in a pink carpet coat with a multicolored ruff and dangling diamond earrings. He looked silly, but he grabbed Heap by the throat and belt and heaved him all the way over his head, and with a bull roar threw him into a knot of the living dead. The big thug was instantly swamped by white hands and yellow teeth, and Benny could find no splinter of sympathy in his heart.

"Saves me the trouble," Benny said to himself.

Fluffy caught him watching and gave Benny and Nix a charming smile and a comical wink. Then he reached inside his voluminous coat and produced two sets of brass knuckles. He was still smiling as he plowed into the melee.

"This is nuts," Benny said. Nix simply shook her head and then looked past him and screamed. Benny whirled and saw Preacher Jack pulling off aluminum siding on one of the wagons. He was seconds away from escaping. Without even thinking what they were doing, Benny and Nix launched themselves that way. Nix held Benny's sword; Benny had the jagged stump of hers. Would that be enough against one old man?

It was one of the living dead who changed everything.

Had Preacher Jack's own men not reanimated, he might never have seen Benny and Nix, and everything would have ended there. But just as the preacher tore off the last piece of siding, a hand clamped around his ankle. The old man looked down in mild surprise and irritation. He jerked his foot free, turned to reach for his saber, and saw the two teenagers running straight at him. He picked up the saber and quieted his guards with two quick thrusts. Vegas Pete began to twitch a moment later, and Preacher Jack finished him. Little Bigg, however, sprawled there in the dust and did not move. Preacher Jack grunted. It was not the first time he had seen this. He shrugged, turned, and strode forward to slaughter Tom's brother and the Riley girl.

Chong got to the top of the bleachers by leaping over the people who had been burned by Lilah's attack. He stepped through the screen of smoke. And Lilah's body was not there. He looked over the edge to see where she had fallen. But she was nowhere.

Then something hit him on the side of the head with such shocking force that he sagged to his knees and tumbled onto the burning bodies. He screamed and twisted away from the flames and went rolling onto the next bleacher with a jarring thump.

Chong felt warmth on his face, and when he touched the side of his head, his fingers came away red with blood. He lifted his aching head to see a massive form come lumbering toward him. It wasn't a zom or a guard.

It was White Bear.

"Well, well, little man," grumbled the man with the melted face. "If it ain't dead man walking." White Bear was splashed with blood, though Chong didn't think that any of it was his, and he carried two improbable weapons: a heavy wrench in his left hand and a crowbar in his right. Behind him was a trail of destruction—crushed and broken bodies, human and zom. "Get up, boy . . . at least have the stones to die on your feet."

Chong tried to rise, but the blow he'd taken to the head made the whole world spin sickeningly. His knees buckled. Blood ran down his face and into his mouth.

"Then take it on your knees, boy," seethed White Bear. "I'm going to wear your skull on a chain around my neck so everyone will know you don't mess with White Bear."

Chong fumbled for his fallen bokken. "Tom will kill you," he said with a bloody smile.

"Not a chance."

Chong shook his head. "No . . . Tom will kill you. You're going to die out here tonight, and the best you can hope for is to come back as a zom. You and your fruitcake of a father."

"Watch your mouth, little man."

Chong spat blood on White Bear's shoes. "Or what? You'll kill me?" He turned to show his injured shoulder. "I'm already dead, remember? I got bitten in the pit. You killed me, and if I can't kill you, then Tom will. Or Solomon Jones or Sally. You and your father are vermin . . . and your time is over."

"Go to hell," growled White Bear as he raised his crowbar high over his head. Chong raised his bokken, but they both knew how this moment was going to end.

"Lilah," Chong said, and he wanted it to be the last word he ever spoke.

As White Bear's arm reached the top of its lift there was a loud, wet *whack!* White Bear paused, crowbar still held high, but now his eyes were open too wide, as if his eyelids were glued to his forehead. He suddenly coughed, and dark blood bubbled over his lips and down his chin.

"What?" said Chong.

But White Bear had no answer. He shuddered and abruptly dropped to one knee, the crowbar falling harmlessly to the dirt. Then a slender figure rose up behind him. The figure was wild-eyed and covered with soot and blood and sweat. She had hair as white as snow and eyes the color of honey, and in her strong brown hands she held a spear made from black pipe, the blade buried to the hilt between White Bear's shoulders.

Lilah placed her foot on White Bear's back, and with a snarl of disgust she kicked him face-forward into the dirt and tore her blade free. Chong, who had spoken her name a hundred times in the last few minutes, could not make a single sound.

* * *

Tom Imura saw White Bear fall, and a tiny smile touched his mouth. He would rather have handled that maniac himself, but there was justice in what had just happened.

The fight was going both well and badly. The good news was that Gameland was disintegrating around him. At least half of White Bear's men were down, and an equal number of spectators. The bad news was that when he'd told J-Dog and Dr. Skillz to let a few zoms loose to liven things up and provide a distraction, he had meant just that: a few. Not all of them. The zoms were like a tidal surge that was gradually pushing the living across the arena. People were falling into the pits, and so were zoms, and at this point Tom didn't think anyone was coming back out of those holes alive. At this rate the zoms were going to turn this whole place into an all-you-can-eat buffet, and that was definitely not part of Tom's plan.

A pair of guards rushed at him, both armed with woodsmen's axes. Tom parried one ax swing and slashed high, ducked under another and cut low, and the two men were down. Behind them were six zoms, and Tom realized that he was caught with an open pit to one side and the dead on the other. He'd have to fight. He did. But this kind of slaughter burned layers off his soul. He knew that. Why hadn't the people here in the arena taken his offer and walked away? Not one of them had gone. Why?

He cut at the arms and legs of the zoms, and kicked the limbless torsos into the pit. This was blunt butchery, nothing more.

In a moment's respite he turned and waved at Sally. When she spotted him, Sally gave a thumbs-up and abruptly vanished from the window. Tom whirled. Now he had to find

Benny and Nix, and then get everyone out of the place while there was still a chance.

Across the field, Preacher Jack strode forward with his stolen saber in his bloody hand. He slashed left and right, cutting down anyone who stood between his fury and the two teenagers who had just escaped from his Pits of Judgment. A hard-faced young man with a Chinese broadsword suddenly appeared and used his free hand to push Benny and Nix back. Benny recognized him as Dieter Willis, one of the twin sons of the famous LaDonna Willis who had been a hero of First Night. Dieter was wiry and strong and was known to be one of the best swordsmen in the Ruin.

"Get back," he growled. "I got this."

Dieter rushed at Preacher Jack, feinting high and then attacking low in a blinding assault. Preacher Jack caught the blow on the edge of his sword and riposted with a counterattack that was too fast to follow. Dieter staggered back and brought his sword up again, but then faltered, his eyes registering total surprise. The broadsword tumbled from his fist, and he clamped his hands to his throat, but it was too little and too late to staunch the spray of blood that erupted from the savage wound. The preacher didn't even bother to watch him fall. He stepped aside to avoid the spray of blood and kept walking toward Benny and Nix. He had barely broken stride to cut down one of the Ruin's most feared fighters.

There was a scream, and LaDonna herself came charging out of the crowd, a heavy cleaver in each hand. Preacher Jack turned to her and let her come to him. Then he parried her cleavers one-two and whipped his sword across her throat.

She fell without a word onto the limp body of her son. Nix howled in fury, and Preacher Jack turned to her and smiled.

"Come and get yours, girl," he taunted.

"No!" Benny yelled, and snaked out a hand to grab her. He caught the hem of her vest and yanked her backward just as Preacher Jack lunged forward to try and drive his sword into her chest. The tip of the blade missed Nix by an inch, and Benny hauled her over him as he did a desperate back-roll. He heard the *whoosh* of the sword and felt the thud of the blade as Preacher Jack tried to chop them as they rolled. Two zoms rushed at the preacher from his right.

From the tangled heap where he and Nix landed, Benny saw Preacher Jack's moment of indecision as he was faced with the choice: Cut down the zoms in front of everyone and prove that his so-called "religion" was nothing more than a sham and a con game in which he had no genuine belief; or let the Children of Lazarus use his flesh as a sacrament. Benny had no doubt how Brother David would have handled this same challenge.

Preacher Jack was no Brother David, and Benny doubted that the "preacher" was even from the same species as the gentle way-station monk. With a growl of annoyance, Preacher Jack stepped into the rushing zoms—and cut them down.

"Hypocrite," jeered Nix, yelling the word as loud as she could. Even through the din of the battle, Preacher Jack heard her. He wheeled on them, his face almost purple with wrath.

"I'm going to enjoy strapping you down and letting the Children feast on—"

Nix threw a pouch of powder in his face. The old man tried to slash it out of the air, but his blade merely cut it open, and that made it worse. A cloud of plaster powder enveloped Preacher Jack. He spun away, coughing and gagging, and that fast Benny was up and running. He drove his shoulder into Preacher Jack's side and sent the man sprawling.

Right into one of the zombie pits. Into the Pits of Judgment.

Benny saw the white faces and white hands reaching up for the man as he pinwheeled down toward them, his sword slashing uselessly at empty air.

"I saw you get shot!" Chong exclaimed. "I saw you fall."

Lilah held up the spear. A big chunk of the blade was missing, and the remaining portion was twisted at a weird angle.

"They shot this. It knocked me down."

"Thank God!" Chong said. He wanted to grab her and hug her, but instead Lilah grabbed him, and for a delicious moment he thought she was going to kiss him. Instead she slapped him across the face. Hard.

"Ow!" he cried, staggering back. "What was that for?"

Her face was an almost inhuman mask of fury. "I heard what you said," she yelled as loud as she could with her raspy voice. "I heard! You were bitten?"

Chong turned his shoulder away and put his hand over the bite, not wanting her to see it. "It's okay. Don't worry about it."

"Okay?" she demanded. "How is it okay?"

Chong wanted to run and hide, but he held his ground. "I . . . it's my fault."

"Did you let yourself get bitten?"

"No . . . I mean—everything. All of it, since we left town.

It's my fault. You were right. I'm a town boy. I have no business being out here." He sighed and let his hand fall away from the bite. "And I guess this is proof. I'm no good out here."

Lilah threw down her spear and grabbed his shoulder, using both hands to squeeze the edges of his bite until drops of blood popped up. "How long ago?" she yelled, and when he didn't answer right away, she screeched at him. "How long ago?"

"Ten hours ago. Maybe twelve."

"Are you sure?"

"No," he said. "It could have been longer. . . ."

Lilah let go of his arm and jammed her fingers under his jaw to feel his glands, then pressed her hand to his forehead. There was a moan behind her as a zombie lumbered out of the smoke; and with a grunt of irritation at being disturbed, Lilah whirled, grabbed the creature by chin and hair, and snapped its neck with a vicious sideways twist. Then she turned back to Chong, grabbed his hair, and pulled him close so she could examine his eyes.

"Tell me what happened," she screamed. "Exactly what happened."

"What—now? There's a big freaking fight going on and—"

"Now!"

Chong shook his head and told her in quick terms how the big zom had clamped teeth on his skin just as Chong hit him with a pipe. Lilah made him repeat that part.

Then she slapped him again. Harder than the first time. It rocked his head sideways, and he almost fell.

"OW! What the hell?" Chong demanded, reeling.

"You stupid town boy," she said harshly. "You're not dying."

"Wait . . . what?"

"The zom had your skin pinched between his teeth but you fell away from him. It tore a flap of skin off. That's all . . . the infection is in the zom's mouth, not in its teeth . . . you did not get bitten!"

Chong stared at her.

"You aren't allowed to die!" she growled, and her eyes seemed to radiate real heat.

Chong's mouth opened and shut several times without sound. "I—I—" And then he suddenly dropped onto his knees. Lilah knelt in front of him and there were tears in her eyes, sparkling like diamonds in the firelight.

"I—," Chong said. "God . . . I thought I was . . ."

She took his face in both her hands and stared at him with almost lethal intensity. "You are not allowed to die!" she said fiercely, growling the words with her graveyard voice. "Not now! Not ever! Promise me or I'll kill you."

Chong almost smiled. "I promise," he said.

Then, despite fire and gunplay and screams and the living dead, Lilah did what she had never once done in her entire life. She kissed a boy.

"We have to get out here," barked Tom as he raced to intercept Benny and Nix. "Right now!"

"How?" asked Benny, looking around. The zoms were everywhere. Before Tom could reply there was a huge explosion, and they turned to see several of the wagons that formed one of the walls of the arena disintegrate into a fireball that knocked down at least a third of the surviving people in the place. Zoms were flung halfway across the gaming floor, and a dozen spectators and guards fell screaming into the open pits.

"That's our cue," said Tom. "This whole place is about to blow itself into orbit. We have to go now!"

"But we can't go! Chong . . ."

"Here," came a painful reply, and they turned to see a bloody, limping Chong running alongside Lilah—who looked strangely distracted despite the carnage. Nix ran to embrace Chong and Lilah, but Benny looked from Tom to the burning wagons to the hotel.

Chong asked, "Did I hear something about this place blowing up?"

"All to hell and gone," said Tom, grabbing them and shoving them toward the smoking hole in the wall of wagons. "There's five hundred pounds of C4 in the hotel lobby, and I rigged it. MOVE!"

And they were running. As they raced Benny cut a last look around. Many of the bounty hunters were down; the rest were already leaping over flaming wreckage.

Tom yelled, "Go . . . GO!" They ran into the smoke and through flaming wreckage and out into the cool darkness of the big field. Behind them the last of the guards and spectators were still fighting the zoms. Benny wondered if they were all crazy. Did they think they could win? Or were they so locked into the moment that violence was the only response they were capable of? He hated them and pitied them and ran from them.

Benny ran with his arm wrapped around Nix. Lilah dragged Chong with her. Fluffy McTeague ran with Sally Two-Knives in his arms like a baby doll. J-Dog and Dr. Skillz were racing each other and laughing; and a whole phalanx of the surviving bounty hunters followed them off to the left, into the woods. Tom was heading right, straight for the hedge-rows and the road.

Benny opened his mouth to shout at Tom, to ask him if he was sure that he knew how to rig an explosion, when the world seemed to detonate around them and the entire Wawona Hotel leaped high into the night sky. A massive glowing fireball punched hundreds of feet into the air, ignit-ing the surrounding trees, vaporizing the water in the ponds, and flinging the armored wagons far out into the fields. Benny and Nix zigged and zagged as flaming debris crashed down all around them with the force of a meteor shower. The grass caught fire and superheated winds pursued them like a host of demons.

Benny heard Tom cry out in pain and saw him stumble, but his brother picked himself up and staggered on. Debris struck the ground all around them.

"Go!" Tom growled through bared teeth.

They ran all the way to the gates and beyond, and down the road into darkness. Debris continued to fall for a full five minutes, as if the ghosts of Gameland were hurling artillery at them. They ran and ran until they could not run any more. They were all spread out across a mile of firelit landscape, Benny and his friends in the field, the bounty hunters deep in the forest.

Tom slowed to a walk and then a shaky stagger and finally stopped, waving at the rest to stop. Chong and Lilah stumbled and collapsed to their knees, shocked that they were alive. Tom bent forward and rested his hands on his thighs. He looked totally spent. Benny sank to his knees and hugged Nix, and she clung to him. She smelled of smoke and blood. He kissed her face and hair and the tears on her cheeks.

Then Benny heard a sound and saw Tom walking slowly toward them.

"We made it!" said Benny, fighting a crazy laugh that threatened to break from his chest.

"Yes," said Tom in a whisper of a voice. "We made it."

"Benny . . . ," Nix said softly, and he turned as Chong and Lilah came walking toward him. They both looked like they'd been through a war, and Benny figured that was a pretty fair assessment. There was an awkward moment when the four of them stood and stared at one another. Everything that had happened since they'd left town—could it really only be two days ago?—floated like embers in the air between them.

Benny smiled first and punched Chong lightly in the chest. "You stupid monkey-banger!"

Chong grinned, and despite the dirt and blood on his

face, it made him glow. He arched his eyebrows in best "wise sage" style and observed, "As usual, you opt for an erudite and insightful comment that is entirely appropriate to the moment."

"Bite me."

"Not even if I was a zom."

They burst out laughing, and Benny grabbed his best friend and gave him a hug so fierce that it made them both yelp with pain, which made them laugh harder. Then Benny stopped and cut a look at Lilah. The moment stalled. His inner voice was trying to feed him clever lines, but he mentally told it to shut up. Aloud he said, "I'm an idiot, and I'm sorry."

Lilah glared at him. Nix shifted to stand next to her, and took her hand.

"Yeah," Benny said, "that's cool. If you guys want to team up and beat the crap out of me, go for it. I deserve it after what I said."

"Why? What did you say?" asked Chong, but no one answered him.

"It's okay, Benny," Lilah said in her icy whisper. "I'll kill you later."

Benny's throat went dry. "Hey, wait. . . . I—I—"

Then Nix and Lilah burst out laughing. Chong, who had no idea what was going on, laughed anyway.

"God!" cried Nix. "Did you see the look on his face?"

"Wait," Benny said again, "did you . . . just make a joke?" That made the others laugh harder.

"I can make jokes," said Lilah, and then playfully punched him in the chest the same way Benny had to Chong. Except her playful punch was about fifty times harder.

"Ow!" he yelped. The others kept laughing, at him, at everything, at the realization that they had all survived. Rubbing the fiery bruise in his chest, Benny laughed too.

They turned to Tom, beckoning him over, wanting him to laugh, needing to see the grim sadness washed off his face. Benny hugged his brother. "We did it, man! Now can we finally get the heck out of this place. Ready for a road trip?"

Tom didn't laugh. His eyes were fixed on the burning hotel. "Yes," he said again, his voice even quieter. "I guess it's time to leave. . . ."

"God, yes," agreed Nix. "I think we just saw the last of our bad luck go up in smoke."

Tom sighed, and then he suddenly dropped to his knees. The others stared at him in surprise.

"Tom?" asked Lilah.

Tom gingerly opened the flaps of his vest. "Damn," he murmured.

Nix screamed.

Benny saw it then. Blood. So much blood. He screamed too.

Tom coughed and slumped forward. Nix and Benny caught him and lowered him carefully to the ground. Benny ripped open Tom's shirt. What they saw tore a sharper cry from Benny and another scream from Nix. When Tom had stumbled during the flight from the hotel, Benny thought he had been hit by a piece of flaming debris. But that wasn't it . . . it was a thousand times worse than that.

Tom had been shot.

"We have to stop the bleeding!" Nix cried. She no longer

had her first aid kit, so she dug through Tom's vest pockets and grabbed rolls of bandages to uses as compresses.

"What happened?" demanded Chong.

"Benny," Nix said urgently as she worked, "this is bad. I can't stop the bleeding."

"Let me help," said Lilah as she pulled the first aid kit from Tom's vest and removed several cotton squares.

"IMURA!"

The voice that roared out of the darkness seemed to belong to a monster, a demon from out of hell itself. They all turned to see a tall figure emerge from the smoke, with fires burning the world behind him.

Preacher Jack.

He held an old-fashioned six-shot pistol in one hand and the curved cavalry saber in the other. His black coat was streaked with soot and blood and his face was pale madness in the starlight. "Imura!" he shouted. "Did I kill you? Did I kill the son of a bitch who murdered my sons?"

"Benny, Nix . . . ," wheezed Tom, grabbing Benny's sleeve. "Run!"

Benny peeled Tom's hand away. "No," he said fiercely. "We have to stop him."

"You can't stop him," gasped Tom. "He's too fast . . . too strong. He'll kill us all."

As he spoke, Tom tried to get to his feet, but a furious wave of pain crashed him back down onto his knees. Nix tried to help him up, but her hands slipped on the blood.

"Keep the compresses in place," warned Lilah.

Benny got to his feet and watched Preacher Jack stalk

toward him. He knew that Tom was right. None of them were a match for this madman, old as he was. Preacher Jack had been a soldier and killer his whole life, and the hard years since First Night had only made him tougher. There was no way Benny could beat him, but maybe he could stall the old mercenary long enough for Lilah or Chong to wound him. Or kill him. Even if it meant sacrificing himself to make that possible. Benny looked at Tom, injured and helpless. And at Nix. And Lilah and Chong. He would die for any one of them. He might have to die for all of them.

Benny turned back to the preacher and raised the jagged stump of Nix's bokken. It was the only weapon he had left. It was broken, but the end was sharp. Maybe that would be enough.

Or would it? Preacher Jack stopped ten paces away and raised the pistol.

Damn, Benny thought. *So much for heroic last stands.*

Then he felt something move behind him and there was Chong, coming up to stand at his side, his bokken in his hands. He smiled at Benny and took another step forward, putting himself between Benny and the pistol.

"What are you doing?" Benny whispered, but Chong ignored him.

Preacher Jack sneered. "Out of the way, rat meat."

"Bite me," said Chong, and his voice quavered only a little. "You want Tom, you'll have to shoot me first."

Preacher Jack grinned, and his teeth were bloody. "Hell, boy . . . I'm going to shoot all of you."

"You won't have time. One of us will get you," Benny said, not sure if it was true. Preacher Jack also had the sword.

Lilah snatched up her spear and stood on Chong's other side. She pointed the broken blade at the preacher. "You're mine, old man."

"No!" cried Tom weakly. "No . . . all of you—run!"

"Not going to happen," said Chong firmly. "I'll die before I let him win."

"This ain't about winning, boy," Preacher Jack said with a laugh. "This is about justice. You killed my sons! You killed my whole family. Don't you understand the full weight of your sin? You did what First Night and three hundred million dead could not do! You killed the House of Matthias!"

"Your sons were trash," said Benny, his voice heavy with contempt. "Your whole family is nothing but trash. You're everything that was wrong with the old world, and you want to rebuild that world and make it in your image. You want the world to be about pain and suffering and hurt. How can you pretend to be a preacher, a man of God, and do the things you do?"

Preacher Jack eyed him with burning hatred. "You don't speak to me like that, boy. You don't dare."

And he pulled the trigger.

Click!

The hammer fell on a spent cartridge. Preacher Jack pulled the trigger again and again and then, with a snarl, he threw the empty pistol at Benny.

Benny ducked.

Suddenly Lilah was running at Preacher Jack, driving her spear toward his chest and screaming like a banshee. The blade was an inch away when he suddenly pivoted and let it slice through his lapels; he kept turning in a circle and drove his elbow into the back of her head as she passed. Lilah pitched forward onto the ground. Preacher Jack pivoted toward her, raising his foot for a kick that would have shattered her face— but Chong was up and moving faster than Benny had ever seen his friend move. He dove at Preacher Jack and tried to tackle him.

The attack made the kick miss, but it did not take the preacher down. Preacher Jack caught Chong as he flew at him, and with a snap of his hip sent his attacker pitching off into the grass. Chong landed hard. Preacher Jack stamped down, but Chong rolled desperately away.

Benny was up now, clutching the broken bokken as he closed in on Preacher Jack's blind side. He jumped forward, stabbing at the man's unprotected back, but the man shifted as quick as lightning and flashed out with a backward kick that caught Benny in the chest. Benny flew backward, landing in a heap.

Lilah climbed to her feet and rushed the preacher, faking high and low, and aimed a vicious cut at the man's knee, but Preacher Jack blocked the cut with his sword. Lilah rebounded from the cut and slashed again and again and again, and for a moment her attack was so ferocious that the preacher gave ground, backing away and parrying the blows as fast as he could, his sword flashing in the moonlight. For a few golden seconds Benny thought that Lilah was going to do it, that she was going to kill the man; but then he side-slipped the spear and caught the shaft with his free hand. He instantly chopped down with the sword, and Lilah was forced to let go to save her hands. He kicked her and sent her tumbling to the ground, then flung her spear out into the smoke and shadows.

Benny and Chong climbed painfully to their feet and spread out to flank Preacher Jack. The old man smiled at the tactic, shaking his head in amusement. "Children's games," he said. "If that's the way it has to be, then let the lesson begin."

They rushed him, but Preacher Jack was too fast. He stepped into Chong's sword thrust, parried it, and whipped his blade across Chong's body. Blood exploded out from Chong's bare chest and he was suddenly staggering back, his sword dropping to the grass, his hands clamped to his body to staunch the bleeding.

That left Benny on his feet.

"Now you, boy," said Preacher Jack. "I'll cut you some and then let you watch what I do to the others. When you beg me for death, I'll show you how merciful I can be."

Benny had no quip, no smart retort. He knew that he was doomed. He had twenty inches of burned and broken wooden sword to try and stop a man who had killed untold numbers of people. A soldier. A warrior. A killer, and a man who was the architect of all the pain in Benny's world.

With all that, Benny still had to ask the question that had been burning in him since they had first met this man.

"Mr. Matthias," Benny said, "do you . . . do you even believe in God?"

Preacher Jack's smile flickered and then intensified, the original secretive grin replaced by a goblin's leer. "There is no God," whispered the old man. "There's just the devil and me and the Rot and Ruin."

The sword glittered as Preacher Jack suddenly faked a few cuts at him, taunting and playing with him. The tip of the sword was a silver blur, and Benny felt a burn on his cheek and knew that he had just been cut too fast to even see.

"Drop the weapon, boy," demanded the preacher. "Put it down and I really will show you mercy. I'll let you and these other pukes walk out of here. But I want Tom. I want his head and by God I'll have it."

"Never!" declared Nix, clutching Tom to her.

"Don't . . . ," Tom said weakly as he fought to get to his knees. His eyes were burning and his sweating face was bright with fever.

"Why don't you just give up?" snapped Benny as he backed away. "Your crew is dead. Gameland is destroyed. Why are you still—"

"I am Gameland, boy! Don't you get that? While I'm alive, it's alive, and I'm going to build it back, bigger and better than ever. I'll build it in the center of Mountainside if I have to . . . and there won't be anyone left to stop me. Not you and not your brother. Look at him! He's halfway to dead already. He just needs a little push."

Benny saw the future. It was as if the whole world had become bright and clear, and in that clarity he saw how this was going to play out. With sinking horror and grief he knew that there was only one path to walk, and that path was a red one. Preacher Jack began to raise his sword for the final cut. It was all spiraling down.

Benny had backed away as far as he could. Tom was beside him, on his knees, blood spilling down his stomach and thighs. With painful slowness Tom reached over his shoulder to grasp the handle of his sword.

"Gameland is closed," he whispered. "That is the law."

"There is no law," snarled Preacher Jack as he lunged forward. Benny turned away from the cut, his hand moving toward Tom. Tom began to pull his sword, but there was not enough strength left in him. He knew it. Preacher Jack knew it. Benny and Nix knew it. The sword came only partway out of the sheath, and Tom's hand began to open as his strength failed.

Then Benny's hand closed around the handle, just below Tom's. It was a sloppy grip, awkwardly placed, but it had power in it, and Benny turned and the sword ripped itself free from the scabbard as Benny turned and Preacher Jack's sword whistled through the air and Benny turned . . . and turned. . . .

And the moment froze.

Preacher Jack stood there, tall and triumphant, his lips curled into his crooked smile.

Tom Imura knelt, head bowed, hands empty.

Benny stood between Tom and Preacher Jack, his right hand extended all the way out to one side, the sword—Tom's *kami katana*, the demon blade—extended far into the night. All along the silvery edge of the blade there were threads that glistened like black oil.

Preacher Jack spoke first.

He said, "No."

Quietly. Wetly.

Then his sword dropped from his hand, and with infinite slowness he leaned backward and fell onto the grass. There was a line of black wetness stretched across his throat from side to side.

Nix looked up at Benny and saw that his arm was starting to tremble. Then his mouth. She got quickly to her feet and pulled him to her, pushing his arm down. The demon sword fell, and drops of blood flew from it.

Chong staggered to his feet and put a toe under Preacher Jack's shoulder and rolled him over. He bent and slid a knife from the old man's belt, placed the tip at the sweet spot, and shoved. Tears gleamed like molten silver on his cheeks, but his eyes were as hard as pebbles.

He turned to look at Benny, who gave a single distant nod of approval. Lilah staggered to her feet, and the four of them closed in around Tom. Tears rolled down their faces as they worked, pressing bandages in place, propping Tom's head in Benny's lap. From the forest the bounty hunters came running. Solomon Jones and Sally were first. J-Dog and the others followed. They lit torches and sorted through their medical kits.

"Oh God," cried Sally as she studied the wound in Tom's chest. "Get me a needle and thread!"

Tom smiled and shook his head. A small movement. "No," he said. "No . . ."

Nix looked around at the bounty hunters, panic and fury in her face. "We have to do something!"

Sally Two-Knives pulled Nix to her, and despite the pain it must have caused her, she held Nix to her bosom.

Solomon knelt and touched Tom's arm. "We'll take care of them, Tom," he promised. "We'll get them all back home—"

"No, Solomon," Tom whispered. "No . . . that's up to . . . them. It's their lives . . . their choice."

Solomon nodded and sat down, his eyes filled with sadness and tears.

"Benny," Tom said, so softly that only his brother heard him. Benny bent close.

"I'm here, Tom."

"Benny . . . I . . . I want you to give me your word."

"Anything, Tom . . . just please . . . tell me what to do."

Tom's other hand lifted a couple of inches, and he pointed to the east, where the false dawn was teasing the edges of morning. "Keep going," he whispered. "Keep going until you find what you're looking for. You and Nix. Lilah, too."

"I will," Benny promised him. "I'll find somewhere we can be safe."

"No," said Tom firmly. "No . . . find somewhere you can be free. Alive . . . and free."

Nix began to cry. She picked up Tom's hand and held it to her cheek.

"Be strong," Tom whispered. "I . . . wish that I could go with you. To see you grow up. To see who you'll become." He smiled. "But I guess I have . . . and I'm so proud of you. Of all of you."

Benny caved in over his hurt until his forehead rested on Tom's. Benny's tears fell like rain.

Tom raised a finger and wiped away one tear. "Funny . . . all I wanted to do . . . was get out of . . . that damn town."

He closed his eyes for a moment, and his breath was very shallow. Lilah and Chong huddled close to Nix. They were all crying, broken sobs that drove jagged cracks in their chests. Lilah took Tom's other hand and held it to her chest as if the beating of her heart could encourage his to keep going. Tom opened his eyes again, and it seemed as if he was looking at something far away, over the horizon, far beyond what any of them could see.

"Benny . . ."

"Yes," said Benny, his voice nearly shattering on that single word.

"I . . . I'm going to try not to come back."

Then Tom Imura closed his eyes.

A terrible sob broke from Benny's chest. Nix leaned toward him and held him, and Lilah and Chong crawled over too. They held one another as dawn tore open the morning.

EPILOGUE

I'M GOING TO TRY NOT TO COME BACK.

That was what Tom said. The last thing he said. He would try. It wasn't a promise, and Benny knew it. People couldn't make those kinds of promises. Maybe in another age of the world, before the horror, before First Night, a dying brother might have said it differently. He might have said, "I'll try and reach you. No matter how far I go, I'll try and reach you. Just so you know it's okay over there. On the other side."

That was before. The plague had changed everything.

J-Dog and Dr. Skillz wasted no time. They made a stretcher out of spears and coats, and they, along with Benny, Nix, Lilah, and Chong, quickly carried Tom into the empty shed where Lilah had gotten the deflated sports equipment she'd used for fireballs during the fight. It stood apart from the hotel, the only building left intact after the blast. The other bounty hunters followed. No one spoke. They laid Tom down on the floor. Dr. Skillz set something on the floor beside the stretcher. When Benny saw what it was, he shook his head. The bounty hunter nodded and left without comment, but he left the object behind.

"I can stay in here," offered Lilah. "And . . ."

Benny shook his head. "No," he said. "No . . . this is mine to do."

Lilah nodded, and even she looked grateful to be spared that horrible task. Chong wrapped his arm around her and they left the shed, both of them weeping quietly.

Nix was the last to leave.

"He said he was going to try and not come back," said Benny.

"I know," she said, her eyes still streaming with tears. "Benny . . ."

"Please, Nix . . . I need to be with him. Just Tom and me. Now . . . please, Nix, time's running out. It'll happen soon."

Nix squeezed her eyes shut in pain, but she nodded. Benny kissed her on the forehead and held the door while she left. Benny sat on the floor and watched Tom. He could almost feel the others outside. Nix would do this for him, Benny knew that. So would Lilah. So would Chong. Chong would do anything for Benny. After everything that had happened, Chong would die for him. Benny knew that.

Should he hate Chong? Should he blame him?

He searched inside his heart for hatred, but it simply was not there. Chong had never wanted this. All he had wanted was to go home and to stop being a problem for everyone. Only that. Not this. Benny still loved Chong. There would be wreckage, there would be scar tissue, but Chong was Chong and Benny was Benny. There would always be the two of them, carrying on, moving forward. Growing up.

The sheet that covered Tom's body was still. There was no breeze; the fabric did not flutter.

"Please," whispered Benny.

I'll try not to come back. Benny reached down and picked up the thing Dr. Skillz had left for him. A sliver. It was polished and cool. One end was blunt for pushing, the other sharp for piercing. A pretty thing, well made. An ugly thing, dreadfully intended.

He held it in his hand while he stood and waited. Seconds fell around him like leaves from a dying tree. Inside his chest he felt something change. His heart dropped from where it had always been, falling to a lower place. A darker place. And there, he knew, it would remain.

The world itself had become darker.

I'll try not to come back.

Benny pressed the cold, flat blade of the sliver against his forehead and closed his eyes.

"God," he whispered, "please . . ." Others who had died recently had stayed dead. Most had come back, but not all of them. Not all.

Outside he could hear the first birds of morning. The world was waking up, unheeding of what had happened. Benny stared at the closed windows and wondered how nature could be so stupid, so cruel. How could the day just go on as if nothing had happened? So much was broken now. Time should be broken. Tom was gone. There had been a stopping of him. The world should have stopped then too. And yet it ground on.

Tears burned in Benny's eyes.

I'll try not to come back.

I'll try.

The sheet lay undisturbed. Slowly, slowly Benny sank to his knees. Holding the sliver in his right hand, he reached out with his left and took the edge of the sheet between his fingers. His tears burned like ice on his cheeks.

"I'm sorry," he said in a voice that was almost not there.

He pulled back the sheet. Tom Imura's face was slack, his eyelids closed, lips slightly parted. Benny swallowed and tightened his grip on the sliver. Any second now.

He'll come back, Benny thought. *The world is the world and the plague is never going to end.* He knew that what he had to do was going to end him. Not Tom . . . it would end Benny. He looked into the future and saw that horrible moment and knew that only darkness waited for him afterward.

"I'm sorry," Benny said again, and he bent and kissed Tom's forehead. "I love you, Tom. I wish I'd said that more."

Benny turned Tom onto his side to expose the soft spot at the base of the skull. The sweet spot, Tom called it. He cradled Tom's head in his lap.

I'll try not to come back.

Benny knelt there, holding his brother, holding the sliver. Waiting for horror.

-2-

FIVE MINUTES LATER BENNY IMURA UNBARRED THE DOOR AND STEPPED out into the morning sunlight. He still held the sliver in his hand. Nix took a step toward him and stopped. Benny was so pale, his eyes rimmed with dark, his mouth slack.

"Benny . . . ?"

Chong stepped forward, but Lilah stopped him. Not by grabbing his arm, but by taking his hand.

"Benny?" Nix whispered.

Benny raised his eyes to hers. They were wet and haunted.

"Benny?" she asked again.

Benny licked his dry lips. "Tom said that he would try not to come back."

Nix came closer, touched his face. "I know, but . . ."

He shook his head, and Nix fell silent.

Chong went quickly past him, pulling Lilah with him. They entered the shed and were in there for almost a full minute. Then they came back out into the sunlight, both of them wearing frowns of confusion.

"Benny," said Chong softly, "what does it mean?"

"What happened?" asked Nix.

Lilah had her knife in her hand, and she slowly slid it into its sheath. "Tom . . . he . . ."

Benny looked up at the clean sunlight and slowly lifted the hand that held the sliver. The others looked at it, mouths open, eyes wide. Benny opened his fingers and let it fall. The sliver struck the flagstones with a musical clang. Nix stared down at it. The metal gleamed in the bright light, the blade smooth and polished.

And totally unmarked.

"My brother kept his word," Benny said.

-3-

Morgie Mitchell walked through the sun-dappled streets of Mountainside, hands deep in his pockets, shoulders slumped, head down. He barely noticed the other people. He was sunburned from hours spent at the fishing hole, but beneath the red there was a paleness that made him seem ghostly and insubstantial to the people who passed him on the street. He seldom met their eyes, and when he did his gaze was wet and dark and filled with shadows.

"How you doing there, Morgie?" asked Captain Strunk, but Morgie walked past him without comment. He headed out of the main part of town and down a country lane to a small cottage surrounded by a rail fence and lush bushes. Morgie stopped at the garden gate and looked into the yard. The grass was worn down to the dirt in places where Tom Imura had led them through hundreds of hours of drills with wooden swords and practice knives. He leaned on the fence rail and closed his eyes. The memories of wood clacking on wood and grunts of effort were as clear as if he could hear them right now.

Morgie sighed.

He opened the gate and walked up the garden path and around to the front porch. He sighed, mounted the front steps, and stopped at the door. Morgie knew that if he knocked there would be no one home. There couldn't be. Benny and Tom, Lilah and Chong . . . and Nix . . . they were all gone. Far away, and with every second they were going farther. Gone forever.

Knocking on the door was stupid. It was a futile act, and he knew it.

He knocked anyway.

The house was small, but he could hear the three knuckle raps echo off the wooden walls.

No one answered.

Morgie turned around and leaned his back against the door. He slowly slid down to the floor. Larks sang in the trees and dragonflies chased each other through the grass. Morgie Mitchell bent forward as if caving in over physical pain. He laced his fingers over the back of his head and sat there as the world turned and turned. His lips moved, saying two words over and over. They might have been *I'm sorry*, but there was no one there to hear him.

-4-

They buried Tom in the field and built a cairn of rocks over him. No one read a service. They were no preachers among them. Most of them prayed, some of them just wept. Benny endured it all, and Nix was at his side.

When it was over, Sally Two-Knives came over with Tom's sword in her hands.

"This is yours now."

Benny took the weapon. With it Tom had killed zoms and evil men. And with it Benny had ended the reign of terror that was the Matthias clan. He held it out with both hands and bowed to it in the old samurai fashion; then he slung it the way he had seen Tom do a thousand times.

Seeing this made Sally cry, and she kissed Benny and turned away.

Benny walked over to the wall of the building where he had sat with Tom. He took off his sword and laid it on the grass and went inside. He emerged a minute later with a can of black paint and a brush. He used his knife to pry open the lid.

"What's that for?" asked Chong.

Benny dipped his brush into the paint. "I want to leave something behind." He used the brush to write on the wall.

GAMELAND IS CLOSED.

THAT IS THE LAW.

—T. IMURA

He considered what he had done, and then added his own name below Tom's.

Dr. Skillz took the brush from him, dipped it in the can, and wrote his name below that. Then J-Dog, Chong, Lilah, Solomon Jones, and everyone else did the same. When they were done, they looked at the wall.

"Someone else might try it again," said Lilah. "Somewhere else."

"No," said Sally, "not when we tell what happened here."

"Will it make a difference in Mountainside?" asked Nix.

"Yeah," said Solomon, "it will. After this . . . I think it'll make a difference everywhere this story is told. Tom just became a legend. That's the only thing more powerful than a hero."

"He never wanted to be a hero," said Benny softly.

"It's not a matter of what he wanted, little dude," said Dr. Skillz, "it's a matter of how it is. The big kahuna is riding a permanent wave."

Benny nodded. He understood that.

At noon the bounty hunters began preparing to leave.

They tried to get Benny and the others to come with them back to Mountainside, but that was a fight they were never going to win.

"What about you?" asked Sally as she stroked Chong's scarred and bruised face. "This wasn't even your journey."

"It's my journey now," Chong said, glancing at Lilah, who looked confused. The Lost Girl blushed and turned away, but she was smiling as she did so.

"What am I supposed to tell your folks?"

As he thought about that, Chong touched the line of stitches Sally had sewn across his chest. "Tell them that I love them . . . and tell them that I'm alive."

"They won't understand. They'll be devastated."

"I know . . . but this is something I have to do."

Sally sighed and nodded and limped away to find her horse. The other bounty hunters made their good-byes. Before they left, each of them gave some supplies to Benny and his friends. Weapons, food, tools, and advice to help them on their journey. Nix thanked them. Benny said nothing. He stood facing the east.

When the others were gone, Nix came and took Benny in her arms. She hugged him and kissed him. "I love you, Benny."

Benny gently touched her lips with his fingertips. "I love you."

It was only the second time she had said those words to Benny. Hearing them, and saying them back, made Benny feel truly alive. It made him feel powerful.

He bent and picked up Tom's sword. Tom had used that weapon to save them both on First Night. He felt Nix watching him. "Tom told me that samurai believed these swords carried their souls. I don't know if that's true . . . but I think for Tom it was. He didn't leave us, Nix. He's always going to be with us." He cut a look at her. "Sounds corny, I know, but . . ."

"No," she said honestly. "It's beautiful. And I think it's true."

Benny nodded and slipped the sling over his head and tied the sword in place the way he had seen Tom do every time he prepared for a journey into the Ruin.

He turned to Nix, Lilah, and Chong. "Tom kept his word," he said in a strong, quiet voice. "I'm going to keep mine."

Each of them nodded.

"Warrior smart," said Chong, meaning it.

"Warrior smart," agreed Lilah.

Nix sniffed back the last of her tears. Her red hair was tied back in a ponytail, and her freckles were like bright fireworks on her face. Her eyes, though, were older than Benny remembered. "Warrior smart," she said.

Benny looked into the east, and Preacher Jack's words came floating back to him. *I might be doing you a kindness to keep you from that path. Only thing you'd find east of here is horror and heartache.*

Then he looked back at the cairn. Could anything out there be more horrible or heartbreaking than this? He could almost hear Tom's voice. *Keep your eyes and mind open. Always be ready.*

"Warrior smart, Tom," he promised aloud.

They set out together, walking abreast down an over-grown road under the bright morning sunlight. Not even Tom knew what was on the other side of the forest. No one did. Maybe the jet and maybe not. Maybe something else. Whatever it was, it wouldn't be this place. Not Mountainside with its fear and fences. Not these mountains with blood and pain soaked into every acre of dirt.

Despite everything, they walked with their heads up, tall and proud. Warriors who had come through fire and pain. The last samurai of the old world. Or perhaps the first of the new.

Benny paused only once at the top of the next rise. He looked back and saw the thin column of smoke that still rose from the ruins of Gameland. He believed that it was closed for good now. Tom would be happy. And thinking that, he smiled again, and faced the east. He and Nix, Lilah and Chong walked over the crest of the ridge, heading toward the unknown, leaving only their footprints behind in the dust and decay.

LONERS

№
172

THE GREENMAN

Little is known about this mysterious figure seen haunting the forests between Magoon Hill and Yosemite. Is he a myth? A ghost? Or is he a dangerous madman waiting to pounce on unwary travelers? Beware the Greenman!

THE BOUNTY HUNTERS

No. 239

SALLY TWO-KNIVES

This former Roller-Derby queen has become one of the toughest and most reliable bounty hunters and guides in the Ruin. Don't cross her or you'll find out just how good she is with her two razor-sharp knives!

HEROES OF FIRST NIGHT

No. 281

BIG MIKE SWEENEY

Legend says that even the hungriest of the living dead would not attack this mysterious young man. Nothing has been heard of him since he rallied a group of survivors from Bucks County, Pennsylvania, and led them deep into the haunted woodlands of the state forest.

J-DOG AND DR. SKILLZ

THE BOUNTY HUNTERS

№ 44

These ex-surfer dudes are unaffiliated bounty hunters working the Ruin. Some say they're crazy and reckless; others believe that's just a front for a pair of deadly hunters. Either way, J-Dog and Dr. Skillz are lightning fast with spear and ax!

WILD CARD

№ 191

WHITE BEAR

Once a bouncer and mob enforcer in Las Vegas, White Bear has returned to the Ruin to claim the bounty-hunting empire once ruled by Charlie Pink-eye and the Motor City Hammer.

Don't miss the next exciting chapter in the world after First Night!

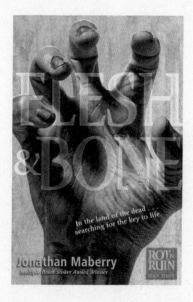

Reeling from the tragic events of *Dust & Decay*, Benny, Nix, Lilah, and Chong journey through a fierce wilderness that was once America, searching for the jet they saw in the skies months ago. If that jet exists, then humanity itself must have survived . . . somewhere. Finding it is their best hope for having a future and a life worth living.

But the Ruin is far more dangerous than any of them can imagine. Something strange is happening to the zombies: Swarms of faster, smarter zoms are coming from the east, devouring everything in their paths. Has the zombie plague mutated, or is there something far more sinister behind this new invasion of the living dead?

BENNY IMURA THOUGHT, *I'M GOING TO DIE.*

The hundred zombies chasing him all seemed to agree.

Fifteen minutes ago nothing and nobody was trying to kill Benny Imura.

Benny had been sitting on a flat rock, sharpening a sword and brooding. He was aware that he was brooding. He even had a brooding face for when other people were around. Now, though, he was alone, and he let the mask fall away. When he was alone, the melancholy musings were deeper, more useful, but also less fun. When you're alone, you can't crack a joke to make the moment feel better.

There were very few moments that felt good to Benny. Not anymore. Not since leaving home.

He was a mile from where he and his friends had camped in a forest of desert trees deep in southern Nevada. Every time Benny took another step on the road to finding the airplane he and Nix had seen, every single inch forward, he was farther from home than he had ever been.

He used to hate the idea of leaving home. Home was Mountainside, high in the Sierra Nevada Mountains of central California. Home was bed and running water and hot apple pie on the porch. But that had been home with his brother, Tom. It had been a whole hometown, with Nix and her mother.

Now Nix's mom was dead, and Tom was dead.

Home wasn't home anymore.

As the road had unrolled itself in front of Benny, Nix, Chong, and Lilah, and melted into memory behind, the vast world out here had stopped being something ugly, something to fear. Now this was becoming home.

Benny wasn't sure he liked it, but he felt in some strange way that it was what he needed, and maybe even what he deserved. No comforts. No safe haven. The world was a hard place, and this desert was brutal, and Benny knew that if he was going to survive in the world, then he would have to become much tougher than he was.

Tougher even than Tom, because Tom had fallen.

He brooded on this as he sat on his rock and carefully sharpened the long sword, the *kami katana* that had once belonged to Tom.

Sharpening a sword was an appropriate task while brooding. The blade had to be cared for and that required focus, and a focused mind was more agile when climbing through the obstacle course of thoughts and memories. Even though Benny was sad—deep into the core of who he was—he found some measure of satisfaction in the hardships of the road and the skill required to hone this deadly blade.

As he worked, he occasionally glanced around. Benny had never seen a desert before, and he appreciated its simplicity. It was vast and empty and incredibly beautiful. So many trees and birds that he had only read about in books. And . . . no people.

That was good and bad. The bad part was that there was no one they could ask about the plane. The good was that no one had tried to shoot them, torture them, kidnap them, or eat them in almost a month. Benny put that solidly in the "win" category.

This morning he'd left the camp to go alone into the woods, partly to practice the many skills Tom had taught him. Tracking, stealth, observation. And partly to be alone with his thoughts.

Benny was not happy with what was going on inside his head. Accepting Tom's death should have been easy. Well, if not easy, then natural. After all, in Benny's lifetime the whole world had died. More than seven billion people had fallen since First Night. Some to the zombies, the dead who rose to attack and feed on the living. Some to the mad panic and wild savagery into which mankind had descended during the collapse of governments and the military and society. Some were killed in the battles, blown to radioactive dust as nuclear bombs were dropped in a desperate attempt to stop the legions of walking dead. And many more died in the days after, succumbing to ordinary infections, injuries, starvation, and the wildfire spread of diseases that sprang from the death and rot that was everywhere. Cholera, staph and influenza, tuberculosis, HIV, and so many others—and all of them running unchecked, with no infrastructure, no hospitals, no way to stop them.

Given all that, given that everyone Benny had ever met had been touched by death in one way or another, he should have been able to accept Tom's death.

Should have.

But . . .

Although Tom had fallen during the battle of Gameland, he had not risen as one of the living dead. That was incredibly strange. It should have been wonderful, a blessing that Benny knew he should be grateful for . . . but he wasn't. He was confused by it. And frightened, because he had no idea what it meant.

It made no sense. Not according to everything Benny had learned in his nearly sixteen years. Since First Night everyone who died, no matter how they died, reanimated as a zom. Everyone. No exceptions. It was the way things were.

Until it wasn't.

Tom had not returned from death to that horrible mockery of life people called "living death." Neither had a murdered man they'd found in the woods the day they left town. Same thing with some of the bounty hunters killed in the battle of Gameland. Benny didn't know why. No one knew why. It was a mystery that was both frightening and hopeful. The world, already strange and terrible, had become stranger still.

Movement jolted Benny out of his musings, and he saw a figure step out of the woods at the top of the slope eighty feet away. He remained stock-still, watching to see if the zom would notice him.

Except that this was not a zom.

The figure was slender, tall, definitely female, and almost certainly still alive. She was dressed in black clothes—a loose long-sleeved shirt and pants—and there were dozens of pieces of thin red cloth tied around her. Ankles, legs, torso, arms, throat. The streamers were bright red, and they fluttered in the breeze so that for a weird moment it seemed as if she was badly cut and blood was being whipped off her in ragged lines. But as she stepped from shadow into sunlight, Benny saw that the streamers were only cloth.

She had something embroidered on the front of her shirt in white thread, but Benny could not make out the design.

He and his friends had not met a living person in weeks, and out here in the badlands they were more likely to meet a violently hostile loner than a friendly stranger. He waited to see if the woman had spotted him.

She walked a few paces into the field and stared down the slope toward a line of tall bristlecone pines. Even from this distance Benny could tell that the woman was beautiful. Regal, like pictures of queens he had seen in old books. Olive-skinned, with masses of gleaming black hair that fluttered in the same breeze that stirred the crimson streamers.

Sunlight struck silver fire from an object she raised from where it hung on a chain around her neck. Benny was too far away to tell what it was, though he thought it looked like a whistle. However, when the woman put it to her lips and blew, there was no sound at all, but suddenly the birds and monkeys in the trees began twittering with great agitation.

Then something else happened, and it sent a thrill of fear through Benny and drove all other thoughts out of his mind. Three men stepped out of the woods behind the woman. Their clothes also fluttered in the wind, but for them it was because the things they wore had been ripped to rags by violence, by weather, and by the inexorable claws of time.

Zoms.

Benny got to his feet very slowly. Quick movements attracted the dead. The zoms were a dozen feet behind the woman and lumbering toward her. She seemed totally unaware of their presence as she continued to try to make sounds from her whistle.

Several more figures stepped out of the shadows under the trees. More of the dead. They kept emerging into the light as if conjured from nightmares by his growing fear. There was no choice. He had to warn her. The dead were almost upon her.

"Lady!" he yelled. "Run!"

The woman's head jerked up, and she stared across the swaying grass to where he stood. For a moment all the zoms froze in place as they searched for the source of the yelling voice.

"Run!" yelled Benny again.

The woman turned away from him and looked at the zoms. There were at least forty of them, and more were materializing from the darkness under the trees. The zoms moved with the jerky awkwardness that Benny always found so awful. Like badly manipulated puppets. Their hands rose as they reached out for fresh meat.

However, the woman turned slowly away from them and faced Benny once more. The zoms reached her.

"No . . . ," Benny gasped, unable to bear the sight of another death.

And the zombies lumbered past her. She stood there as a tide of them parted to move around her. They did not grab her, did not try to bite her. They ignored her except to angle their line of approach to avoid her and continue walking down the slope.

Toward Benny.

Not one of them touched the woman or even looked in her direction.

Confusion rooted Benny to the spot, and the sword hung almost forgotten in his hand.

Was he wrong about her? Was she one of the dead and not a living person at all? Was she wearing cadaverine? Or was there something else about her that made the dead forgo the feast at hand for the one that stood gaping at them down the slope?

Run!

The word exploded inside his mind, and for a crazy moment Benny thought that it was Tom's voice shouting at him.

He staggered as if punched, and then he wheeled around and ran.

HE RAN LIKE HELL.

This was no time to contemplate mysteries. He pounded down the slope faster than a jackrabbit as the mass of the dead growled out a moan of hunger and followed.

A zom rose up out of the tall grass directly in his path. There was no way to avoid the thing, not with all the momentum of the downward run, so he tucked his head and drove his shoulder into it like he was trying to bust through a line of offensive backs on the school football field. The zom went flying backward, and Benny leaped over the thrashing creature.

More zoms came at him, rising up out of the weeds and staggering out from behind tumbled boulders. Benny still held Tom's sword, but he hated using it on zoms. Not unless he had no choice. These creatures were not evil, they were dead. Mindless. Unless he could completely quiet one of them, chopping at them seemed . . . wrong. He knew they couldn't feel pain and wouldn't care, but Benny felt like some kind of malicious bully.

On the other hand, there was that whole survival thing. As three zoms closed in on him in a line he could not bull his way through, the hand holding the sword moved almost without conscious thought. The blade swept upward through one set of reaching arms, and the hands flew high above, grasping nothing but air. With a deft twist of his shoulder, he flicked the blade sideways and a zom's head went flying into the bushes. Another cut left the third zom toppling to one side with one leg suddenly missing from mid-thigh.

"Sorry!" Benny yelled as he burst through the now disintegrating line of three zoms.

But there were more.

So many more, coming at him from all directions. Cold fingers fumbled at his face and tried to grab his hair, but Benny jagged and dodged and dove through them toward open ground.

His foot hit a rock and he sprawled forward; the sword flew from his hand and clattered thirty feet down the slope.

"No!" he cried as the sword vanished in the tall, dry grass.

  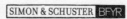

Benny Imura couldn't hold a job,
so he took to killing.

This book is full of heart.
Hearts that just don't beat anymore.

ROT &
RUIN

Jonathan Maberry
Author of *Patient Zero*

DUST &

Zombies were
people, too.

DECAY

Jonathan Maberry
Author of *Rot & Ruin*

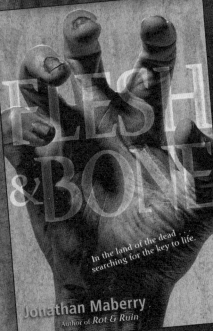

FLESH
&
BONE

In the land of the dead . . .
searching for the key to life.

Jonathan Maberry
Author of *Rot & Ruin*

EBOOK EDITIONS ALSO AVAILABLE

SIMON & SCHUSTER BFYR
TEEN.SimonandSchuster.com

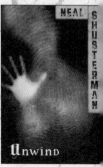

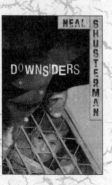